THE STONE CARVERS

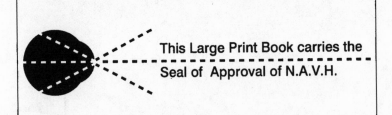

This Large Print Book carries the
Seal of Approval of N.A.V.H.

THE STONE CARVERS

JANE URQUHART

Thorndike Press • Waterville, Maine

LP

Copyright © Jane Urquhart, 2001

Published in 2003 by arrangement with Viking Penguin, a member of Penguin Group (USA) Inc.

Thorndike Press® Large Print Women's Fiction Series.

The tree indicium is a trademark of Thorndike Press.

The text of this Large Print edition is unabridged. Other aspects of the book may vary from the original edition.

Set in 16 pt. Plantin by Liana M. Walker.

Printed in the United States on permanent paper.

Library of Congress Cataloging-in-Publication Data

Urquhart, Jane.
    The stone carvers / Jane Urquhart.
        p. cm.
    ISBN 0-7862-5205-7 (lg. print : hc : alk. paper)
    1. World War, 1914–1918 — Ontario — Fiction.
2. Brothers and sisters — Fiction. 3. Germans — Canada — Fiction. 4. War memorials — Fiction. 5. Stone carvers — Fiction. 6. Single women — Fiction. 7. Ontario — Fiction. 8. Clergy — Fiction. 9. Large type books. I. Title.
PR9199.3.U7S76 2003
    813′.54—dc21   2003040661

For G.P.
and in memory of Sandra Gwyn

"I have been eating and sleeping stone for so long it has become an obsession with me. And, incidentally, a nightmare."

— Walter Allward

In June of 1934, two men stand talking in the shadow of the great unfinished monument. Behind them rises a massive marble base flanked by classically sculpted groups of figures and surmounted by an enormous stone woman who is hooded and draped in the manner of a medieval mourner. At her back, a shedlike building occupies the space between twin obelisk-shaped pylons, each with their own wooden rooms attached to it at a great height.

The taller man wears a dark overcoat and hat and carries a pole, about the size of a walking stick, that he swings out in front of him now and then as if to make a point. The other man, less formally clad in an oilskin jacket buttoned tightly over his round belly, appears to be more involved in the conversation, looking intently at his companion and rising on his toes and opening his arms while he is speaking. All around them, all around the monument is a sea of men and mud, except in the far distance where the dark mountains of the coal fields of Lens can be seen to the northeast, and the white slabs of grave-

7

yards, some only partially sodded, can be seen to the south and to the west.

Despite the fact that the ground the men stand on is French, and the month is June, it is not a warm day; there is no sun, and the wind howls across the coal fields toward the monument in increasingly strong gusts so that the taller man is forced to place a hand on his hat. At one point both men stop talking and look up at a large wooden shed that stands on a forest of scaffolding and is secured by thick ropes to the larger of the two pylons. They listen to the strange noise these ropes make as they rub together, a noise the taller man knows to be remarkably similar to the sound of two pines scraping against each other in a wind-filled Canadian forest. Along with the wind and the sound of the ropes there is the staccato noise of several stonecutters' tools as men in overalls carve words onto the extensive stone wall. The taller man walks across broken marble and rutted mud to see how this work is going. He says a few words to one of the stone carvers, then returns to his companion.

It begins to rain.

I

THE NEEDLE AND THE CHISEL

There was a story, a true if slightly embellished story, about how the Ontario village was given its name, its church, its brewery, its tavern, its gardens, its grottoes, its splendid indoor and outdoor altars. How it acquired its hotel, its blacksmith's shop, its streets and roads, its tannery, its cemetery, its general store. This was a legend that appealed to fewer and fewer people in the depression of the early 1930s. Times being what they were, not many villagers had the energy for the present, never mind the past — the tattered rail fences and sagging porches of the previous century seemed to them to be just two more things in need of repair. The tannery and blacksmith's shop had disappeared years ago, and though the general store was still a fixture, its counter was so warped and scarred it looked as if it might have once served as a butcher's block.

It was difficult to believe, in those days, with the older parts of the village in a state of decay usually associated with the decline of a complete civilization and the newer sections consisting of sloppy, half-finished attempts at twentieth-century industry, that one hundred years ago there was no sign of western European culture in the region. Difficult also to believe that it took only one hundred years for this culture to break down under the weight of economic failure.

Still the tale continued to be dear to one thirty-eight-year-old spinster who lived half a mile away from the village at a spot known as Becker's Corners and all of the good Sisters at the small Convent of the Immaculate Conception near the top of the village's only hill. These women believed the story connected them, through ancestry, through work and worship, and through vocation to the village's inception. They believed it also connected them to the great church, under whose shadow, in the seldom-visited cemetery, their forebears slept beneath iron crosses that leaned at odd angles to one another, as if trying to establish contact after a long season of isolation and neglect.

The nuns and the one spinster clung to the story, as if by telling the tale they became witnesses, perhaps even participants in the awkward fabrication of matter, the difficult architecture of a new world.

12

* * *

In the middle of the nineteenth century, in the small village of Inzell, Bavaria, the wonderfully named Pater Archangel Gstir had no opinions about difficult architecture. In fact, Father Gstir was such a contented young man, a young man filled with such happy certainties, that beyond his faith and his fierce desire for a suitable bell to adorn the Romanesque belfry of the little parish church of St. Michael where he was pastor, he had few strong feelings about anything at all. He was troubled by neither women, nor fashion, nor financial insecurities — the usual afflictions of young men. In his church he was surrounded by a devout and devoted flock of parishioners, and once he stepped outside he was presented with a view of some of the finest mountain scenery in Bavaria, a region not now, and certainly not then, impoverished when it came to ravishing landscape. He spent his weekdays after morning mass cheerfully encouraging German-speaking boys in the study of classical languages, history, natural science, and liturgy. He ate well, enjoying Bavarian beer and his choice of European wines with his meals, and after these meals he took long walks along the edges of the gorgeously scenic Knappensteig, where he was able to admire the peaks of the Watzmann, the Hochkalter, the Hocheisspitze, and the Reiter Alpe. It was his habit on these promenades to pray to the Creator of all this beauty at the charming outdoor shrines and crosses scattered liberally across the hills and mountains. During one of these periods of reflection, just as he was beginning to be distracted by a rare wildflower — blue with black markings, quite unlike anything he had pressed in his album so far — he was startled by an announcement from God Himself with whom he often carried on conversations in his mind. "Go to Canada," He told him now. "There is much work for you to do there."

Father Gstir was astonished. As far as he knew he had not, until that very moment, even *thought* about Canada. Snow, he mused vaguely, and savages. "The English," he whispered aloud, "and, I believe, some French." He plucked the wildflower from the grass, placed it inside his breviary, and tucked the small book firmly under his elbow. "There must be some mistake," he said to the Creator and continued along the mountain path, forgetting about Canada altogether.

The spinster was particularly fond of this moment in the story because it always brought to mind an increased awareness of the serendipitous quality of one's presence here on earth. Where would she be had Father Gstir resolutely decided to ignore God's call? Indeed, where would anyone be had the slightest incident not occurred in the chaos of details that led to their birth. The past need do no more than shrug its shoulders or lift its eyebrows for us to cease to exist. But the wonderful thing about saints, the spinster had been known to remark to the nuns — for she was confident that Father Gstir, recognized or not, was a saint — is that saints have no choice.

God forgot neither Father Gstir nor Canada and was moved to remind the Bavarian priest of His wishes in a direct and ultimately fateful way. In the middle of a spring week, while Father Gstir was removing his vestments after morning mass and silently preparing his Sunday sermon in which he would compare each of the virtues to a mountain wildflower, the postmaster knocked at the door of the vestry.

Father Gstir pulled back the bolt and invited the man in. "You were not here

15

at mass, Johann," he said.

This was a joke between them. Johann Heipel, postmaster of Inzell and a very devout man, could never attend weekday morning mass because of his letter-carrying duties. He felt this very deeply and often confessed it — much to Father Gstir's amusement.

But on this day, the postmaster did not respond with the customary explanation. Instead he reported excitedly that there was a letter from the bishop.

Father Gstir had never received a letter from the bishop, despite his writing regularly to this venerable person petitioning for funds to replace the bell and, in his braver moments, for a limewood altar for a side chapel in the church. A wonderful ringing was in his mind as he tore open the envelope.

The message, which made mention of neither bell nor altar-piece but which nevertheless made quite clear that the bishop had received Father Gstir's petitions, read as follows:

May 30, 1866

Our esteemed King Ludwig, benefactor of the Ludwig Missions, has lately interested himself in a small group of our people who have established themselves in the wilds of Canada where they have no priest to minister to them or to instruct their children in the ways of the Blessed Church of Rome. I have noted from your many letters that you reside in an alpine district where the air is necessarily much colder and fresher and therefore more like the air of Canada. Because of this, and because of your rumoured great good humour, you have therefore been chosen by me to complete this Holy Task & etc. . . .

The Sisters at the Convent of the Immaculate Conception knew the contents of this letter by heart, as did the spinster, who had memorized it in her youth. They also knew that Father Gstir would have been moved by the letter to recall his inner conversation on the Knappensteig and at the same time the authority of his holy vows. Some of the nuns wondered why the spinster had not taken holy vows herself, since she had no husband, and it was unlikely at this late date that one would appear. But most of the Sisters suspected that the spinster was completely unsuited for convent life, and were content to appreciate the way she dusted and polished the church pews, washed and sewed the altar cloths and linens, and decorated the altar with flowers in the summer.

They were also very grateful for the small Madonnas she carved for their rooms, and the complete crèche she had made, down to the last animal in the manger, to be assembled outside the church in the Christmas season, though all of them believed that carving was men's work. They knew the spinster was unsuitable for convent life because of her fondness for men's work — carving, farming, tailoring — her fondness, and her skill.

Like every other man, woman, and child in Bavaria, Father Gstir was well aware that King Ludwig was mad, and he knew that an interest in Canada was precisely the kind of course the King's mad mind was likely to take. Was the bishop mad as well? Were the alleged Bavarian settlers also suffering from diseases of the brain? Instead of being ministered to in that wild place, should they not instead be encouraged to return to civilization? He put the last of these questions as delicately as possible to the bishop in an eloquent letter that also included a list of reasons why he,

Pater Archangel, was a completely inappropriate candidate for the task, ending with a hopeful reminder regarding the bell. The bell, he told his superior, would ring out from the beautiful Romanesque belfry, the last vestige of the original parish church that had been founded in 1190 by Archbishop Albrecht II of Salzburg and that had unfortunately burned in 1724. Did the bishop not agree that the fact that the belfry and its splendid onion dome were spared in the conflagration was surely a kind of miracle, one that should be celebrated by a perfect bell, with a perfect pitch, rather than one filled with cracks that therefore emitted a disturbing sound that put the pastor in mind of a choirboy singing a Bach chorale just slightly off-key.

The bishop did not reply but sent instead the necessary documents for the journey.

Until Pater Archangel Gstir came to Canada, he had been able to walk along the edges of life in much the way he had walked along the edges of the beautiful Knappensteig. He had been an observer, albeit an appreciator. The mountain tracks he trod were lined with wildflowers; the views were gorgeous and distant. He loved climbing up to heights, but even more he loved gazing into depths. He turned from prayer at an outdoor shrine and looked down into deep green valleys. He stood in the altar and smiled upon his parishioners. Occasionally he climbed the miraculous belfry to inspect the faulty bell, and then he was able to look down on the whole village as it went about its business. All this would change when he came to Canada. He would become, as a result of geological, geographical, and meteorological necessity, a participator.

A year almost to the day after he had received the bishop's letter — a year that had included a six-month-long hellish journey over water and land to the place then called Upper Canada — Father Gstir found himself in a pinewood forest trudging over an uncompromisingly flat terrain with a cloud of the Devil's own insects, called blackflies by the English, buzzing over his head and the head of his horse. His territory — his parish — covered approximately two thousand square miles of practically unpopulated backwoods, an area filled with all manner of birds, beasts, and insects of prey. His task

20

was to travel from one squalid cabin to another, avoiding those dwellings occupied by Protestants, known in these parts as Orangemen, bringing joy, comfort, and spiritual guidance to the German Catholics who had squatted on the land. Most of these settlers were so busy removing trees — and in a most unattractive fashion — that they hadn't thought about the Blessed Virgin since they were children, if they had thought about her at all. The women had been glad to see him because his appearance suggested there might be someone — anyone — to administer last rites when they died in childbirth, as they so often did. The older men were respectful, though few had the reading skills or the time to study the catechism. The young men were difficult, sometimes almost surly, for it was they who ruled this domain, where physical strength was the key to survival. Still, it was one of them who had suggested that the good Father travel ten miles farther north, where a number of Alsatians and a few Bavarians were settled around the establishment of a sawmill.

"Don't bother with us," said one of two young and alarmingly large backwoods brothers to Father Gstir as he tried to intercept them in the muddy yard of their cabin. "Leave us alone, old man, we've no time for redemption."

Father Gstir deeply resented being called an old man, for he was far from old, in fact not much older than the brothers themselves.

"Go to the settlement ten miles to the north," they told him. "Storekeepers and millers there have lives soft enough for religion."

The priest decided to forgo the correction he had been planning in regard to his age. "I'll not give up on *your* souls," he said. "But what then is the name of this village?"

"Doesn't have a name," said one of the brothers. "Ten miles north, sawmill, gristmill."

Father Gstir set off in the direction the two brothers had indicated, the black cloud of flies accompanying him. When he had imagined Canada and his posting there, it had been the cold, the endless wastes of snow that he had dreaded. Now he longed for winter, prayed for it, for at least in winter there were no flies and the swamps and rivers would freeze, making his progress easier and the way shorter. But as he rode mile after mile in the heat and humidity of that early summer afternoon, he became aware that the swampy areas were becoming less frequent, that the ground was hardening underfoot, and that there was a slight rise in the level of the earth. He was enchanted by the appearance now and then of perfectly round ponds of water, a geological oddity he would soon learn were called "kettles" by the locals, though no one could explain why. It was shortly after he had skirted the edge of one of these that he emerged from the forest at a cleared area on the brow of a hill.

What lay before him was a view of his first deep Canadian valley, one with signs of settlement near a shining stream, and he fell in love at once. He had to admit, however, even in the midst of his sudden infatuation, that the place was a cluttered mess, all vegetation having been recently torn up or chopped down, leaving behind acres of mud littered with uprooted and rotting tree stumps. Any attempts at architectural construction — even the sawmill and gristmill — looked temporary, haphazard, and dangerously frail, the boards from which the structures were built pale and raw in the afternoon light, men, oxen, and horses moving sluggishly around them. The humidity of the season had settled in the valley, and everything alive appeared to be swimming in a slow trance through cloudy water. Only the little river was filled with vitality — Father Gstir could hear the sound of it — as it picked up and tossed light that came from a sun barely visible in a milky sky.

He saw all this, but he also saw how it would be later, with crops and orchards growing in the cleared areas, and with painted houses and barns, and with gardens sprouting flowers. He beheld all that was there in front of him, and all that he believed would be there in the future, and he knew he was home.

Father Gstir was not unaware that most landscapes looked better from on high — from a distance — than they did once one was presented with the banalities of their details at a close range. Despite this, he dismounted from his horse and ran eagerly down the track that led to the valley floor, his cassock flapping, his fists punching the air. As he ran, the normal passage of time either collapsed or expanded (he was never able to accurately determine which) so that the surprisingly delightful aspects of the terrain through which he passed impressed themselves on his memory, as if he had been looking at them for a long, long time. Rock outcroppings and shallow caves suitable for the statues of saints, bubbling springs that were surely holy places, towering deciduous trees miraculously overlooked by the axe — important trees: oaks and chestnuts — delicate green ferns, and an array of colourful wildflowers in bright emerald grass all caught his attention as he rushed by them. When he burst into the muddy and now quite startled domain of the millers who had set up near the little river, he was gasping with joy. "You live here in this beautiful valley, this shoneval," he told two men who were so whitened by flour that he almost believed them to be angels. "God be praised!"

The younger of the two men smiled and held out his hand. He was long-limbed, fair-haired, with a well-chiselled rectangular face. His skin glowed opalescent as a result of its coating of white dust, and the folds of his clothing shone. As he moved toward the priest, a chalky cloud rose from him into the sunlit air.

It is at this moment that the spinster herself quietly enters the story, for the young man bathed in flour who stood smiling and holding out his hand introduced himself as Joseph Becker, and Joseph Becker was eventually to become her grandfather.

Son of a Bavarian miller, Joseph Becker
had been lured to Canada at the age of
twenty because of his passion for wood and
the rumours he had heard about an unlim-
ited supply of this material in the forests of
the New World. After his initial dismay at
finding nothing but cleared land in the
southern regions of Canada, he had
pushed steadily northward until he had
reached the bush through which Father
Gstir would soon trudge. But even there
the trees seemed to disappear before he
could fully appreciate them, lumbering
being the chief capitalistic enterprise of the
time. He was searching for perfect blocks
of carveable limewood, or basswood as he
would learn to call it in Canada. In his
imagination he had already carved ornate
altars from the trunks of the massive trees
he had read about before departing from
Bavaria. From the ages of fourteen to nineteen, he had been apprenticed to a stern
old woodcarver in his native town of
Ottobeuron, but by the time he was nineteen he was becoming impatient with his
master's reluctance to permit him to carve
anything larger than putti. Still, Joseph had
to admit that under the older man's in-

struction he had learned well and now knew how to use various chisels, the combination of delicate and forceful hammer blows employed to encourage flesh to emerge from wood. He had also become a master of polychrome and could work with gold or in an array of colours.

In Canada, however, he had had next to no opportunity to make use of his training for anything other than recreational purposes, and time for recreation did not come easily. For a while he worked in the very lumber camps that destroyed the trees he cherished. But he could not bear to accept employment in the sawmills, where once, and only once, he witnessed the massacre of a tree trunk large enough for a beautiful sculpture of God the Father Himself. Soon his frustration and almost physical pain, his feeling that the very saints and angels he would have carved were murdered, and his knowledge of the terrible ordinariness of planking combined to make it impossible for him to take an axe to a tree ever again. He left the lumber camps and began to work at his father's old trade of flour milling in the nearest town, moving north again only when the opening of a gristmill in a valley surrounded by new, raw German homesteads permitted him to do so.

Flushed and panting and filled with wonder, Father Gstir came to an abrupt halt directly in front of the tall young man whose pale, powdered demeanour made the priest believe for one dizzying moment that he might actually be in the presence of the angel Gabriel.

Then the divine being spoke in the voice of a human. "Hello, Father," he said, gazing at him with benevolent curiosity. "Are you looking for bags of flour?"

"This village," gasped Father Gstir, his arms opening as if to embrace the valley, "this is why I am here. Suddenly I understand why God spoke to me in my mind, why I have been sent here."

Joseph Becker glanced at the sawmill, the gristmill, the log bunkhouse, and the few shanties that stood near it. "We aren't much of a parish," he told the priest, "though families arrive presently from Waterloo County. And," he added, "there is no church."

The priest was staring with great intensity at the stream. "Such marvellous water!" he enthused. "From what miraculous spring does it emerge?"

28

"Springs all over here," Joseph pointed to a limestone outcropping on the opposite side of the mud track. "There's water all over. Hard to find a dry spot to build a shed. These springs bubble up when you least expect them right under the floor."

"Holy water," said Father Gstir, and then remembering the golden liquid of his homeland he added, "Perfect for a brewery." He turned and looked up toward the height from which he had first seen the valley, the same hill where two decades later sun would shine through coloured windows of an established convent.

"A church up there," the priest said, pointing, "made of logs at first and then, in time, a stone cathedral." He continued to gaze at the hill. "Or at least a large stone church," he added, "with a magnificent bell."

Joseph was amused, even intrigued, but not at all convinced. "The people around here aren't much interested in religion. Most of them are in the backwoods cutting down trees," he said.

"Then we must make them interested." Father Gstir paused and placed his hand on his forehead, considering. "We'll begin with a Corpus Christi procession," he said slowly, turning briefly away from Joseph while he assembled his thoughts. "Colour, pageantry, perhaps singing. We'll visit every corner of the valley, flush them out of the forest. Pageantry . . . in this place pageantry will be the answer." He moved a few steps closer to Joseph. "How many parishioners would you say were within a day's walking distance?"

"A hundred, maybe two hundred, but . . ."

The priest interrupted, "Do you know anyone, anyone at all, who might be able to carve a crucifix or the Blessed Virgin?"

Later Joseph Becker would tell his granddaughter that at that moment he shared Father Gstir's belief that to be in this unlikely valley had been part of a great plan, a key to his own destiny.

"Yes, Father," he said. "Yes, I do."

Father Gstir applied for and received permission from the bishop of the sadly neglected diocese of Hamilton, Upper Canada, to remain in the place he would call Shoneval among the almost entirely German settlers of the incongruously named Carrick Township. (The single Irish family in the vicinity had successfully argued that because the English had changed the name of virtually every city, town, and

30

hamlet in their homeland, they ought to be given the privilege of affixing this Celtic moniker to lands ruled by the British crown.) At first the priest slept in the bunkhouse with Joseph Becker and all the other mill workers, but his presence put such a damper on the men's usual banter about women and their constant drinking of homemade whisky that in short order they built him a not uncomfortable log shanty.

These were grateful men. They knew they had much to thank God for. Had they remained in Germany, for instance, they would likely have been soldiers by now, committed to fighting a number of petty yet deadly wars, the exact rationale for which no one was able to keep straight in their minds. They regretted the absence of a suitable number of women, but they were happy to be alive and not starving. They sensed God had treated them reasonably well, and they respected the priest as a result.

Shortly after Father Gstir had installed himself in his new quarters, the bishop wrote to inform him that his request to stay in the valley had miraculously coincided with the arrival in Guelph, and in Hamilton, of six missionary priests from

Europe who could now administer to Catholics in the rest of the territory. He was, however, to remain in contact with three or four nearby German villages about which the bishop had heard ominous rumours of planned breweries. Father Gstir, reading the letter to Joseph Becker, glanced up with fondness at the nearby crystal stream.

"Procession, church, bell, brewery," he announced. "These are our priorities."

Of the four, Joseph maintained that the men were only interested in the last. "We have only a sawmill and a gristmill," he reasoned. "You have no parishioners. How can we have a church?"

"The procession will bring the parishioners," the priest assured him. "You must begin work on the crucifix."

And so in the low light of high summer mornings and evenings, before and after his work at the gristmill, out of a huge tree trunk grudgingly donated by the sawmill owner in order to rid himself of the pestering priest, Joseph Becker began to carve the body of Christ. He had brought his most beloved chisels with him from Bavaria, and made his mallets himself from scrap lumber found in the yard. But it was with an axe that he first approached the wood, loving the idea that he could use the instrument for creation rather than destruction. Stripped to the waist, his muscles polished by his own sweat, he skilfully chopped out the rough shape of a slender man whose slightly raised arms were extended as if to embrace the world. This was pure labour and he enjoyed it as such, his heart pumping, blood rushing to his back and shoulders. The following week, as the face and feet and ribs emerged from the beam, he remembered and recognized the joy of carving, the miracle of turning wood to flesh. By the time he began to fashion delicate details — facial features, creases in the fingers, nails, and thorns — he was almost brought to tears by the poignancy of what he had made. In the final stages, even the toughest mill workers were removing their caps before entering the hut he used as a workshop.

Each day in the gristmill he had been aware that in the nearby sawmill enormous virgin trees, trees from which hundreds of beautiful sculptures might be made, were being fed to the teeth of the saws. Now late in the afternoon Joseph was permitted to shake the flour from his clothes and continue with the work of coaxing muscle and bone and sinew out of wood grain. At night by the soft light of the bunkhouse lantern he brushed curled shavings from his sleeves, dropped his trousers on a planked wood floor, and lay down on a cot made from timber and bark beside men whose lungs were filled with sawdust.

It began to seem as if his whole life were made of wood.

Years later as a very young woman, his granddaughter, Klara Becker, would experience similar sensations in her own workspace, which had once been her father's blacksmith's shop before he gave up in the face of all that heat and effort and had his horses shod in town. She would begin to understand the joy and oppression of the material needed for the task. But only in the moments when she could permit herself the luxury of carving, the moments when she was not making something for someone else to wear. In the early part of her adulthood, before she was changed by loss, her life seemed to be a minor war fought with a chisel and a needle, each tool demanding her time and attention, the shortness of her busy days suggesting she should perhaps commit to one profession or the other. And finally, how uncomplicated that war would seem in the face of the two real wars that would follow, the war with Eros, and then the Great War itself.

As the days shortened and huge flocks of pigeons and geese flew southward, passing noisily over the roof of his shanty, Father Gstir began to write a series of impassioned letters to the Central Direction of the Ludwig Missions at Munich. Reasoning that if he were to make these epistles lively and entertaining he might more quickly reach his goal, and knowing his countrymen's fascination with the trackless wilds of the northern New World, he decided that the Lord would forgive exaggeration if the exaggeration in question resulted in the building of a church. He described, therefore, terrifying encounters with wild beasts — particularly bears — "which approached in such great numbers that they crushed the large trees in their path," and with wolves the size of horses "whose howls filled the night with such noise that a conversation between two men was impossible to hear." He told of trees with trunks so wide it would take a healthy man ten minutes to circumnavigate them. When he made mention of the mill workers, he described them as hard-working, pious Bavarians whose desire for a house of worship was heartwarming to behold. "They will, of course, supply all labour free of charge," he predicted with optimism. "But where," he wondered, "are we to get money for stone and," he added, "for a bell?" He had also envisaged an attractive rectory but felt it prudent not make further demands at this stage.

In November, once the frost had hardened the ground, Father Gstir saddled his horse, strapped his portable altar to his own back, and attempted to negotiate the unreliable tracks to the outlying farms to disseminate the news of a magnificent Corpus Christi procession held the following June in the beautiful valley after which Shoneval had been named. The majority of the settlers he visited had but dim memories of this kind of pageantry, and many had no knowledge at all of the feast days of the church. But most had lived in isolation for so long that the announcement of any kind of collective experience was met with interest, and all promised to attend.

As he tramped wearily over the frost-covered mud, leading the horse that had developed a fear of the ice in the many potholes, Father Gstir fretted over the details. He knew that Joseph would successfully complete the large crucifix and the statue of the Virgin that would be carried in the procession, so his mind was at ease in relation to this. But someone in the procession was going to have to be splendidly robed, and that someone was himself. After making several inquiries along his route, a woman surrounded by whining children told him that the twenty-year-old daughter of a settler near the village had worked as a seamstress in a tailor's shop in one of the southern towns. Interestingly, like Joseph Becker, she too had brought her most cherished tools with her to the wilderness, in her case scissors and embroidery needles. (The spinster always experienced a slight thrill of recognition at this point in the story, for the handsome young woman who agreed to embroider Father Gstir's spare vestments, and who promised to contact her old employer about the donation of heavy red cloth, was her grandmother. "It was a Corpus Christi procession in the backwoods," Joseph Becker would tell his granddaughter, "that brought together the chisel and the needle.")

How young they were then, the carver and the seamstress and the priest, all dead by the 1930s, by the time Klara and her friends in the convent would recall and cherish the story. Younger than the spinster, and younger too than any of the nuns. But the backwoods was no place for even the middle-aged, as everyone was necessarily engaged in the act of turning one thing into another, an occupation that required an athletic form of labour, a labour that never ceased. The carver transformed barley into flour and wood into statues; the seamstress made bedsheets into altar cloths; the men in the sawmill helped turn forests into wastelands, while the farmers attempted to turn wastelands into fields. The priest was hoping to turn a barren hilltop into the site of a pilgrimage church whose bell would ring out to an established village and whose song would carry over beautifully cultivated fields. All of them were trying to force western culture into a place where it undoubtedly had no business to be. It was hard work.

As the winter progressed, more and more wooden European ships — ships that brought a few sacks of mail and cargoes of human beings in a westerly direction and a few sacks of mail and cargoes of lumber in an easterly direction — were tossed on unfriendly seas. It wasn't until March that Father Gstir finally received an answer from the Central Direction of the Ludwig Missions-Verig at Munich. The gentlemen, who had been delighted by the Bavarian priest's portrayal of life in the wilds, were full of questions regarding hunting and taxidermy. No mention was made of the church or the bell, but there was mention of their benefactor, Ludwig of Bavaria, who "had great interests in the wild beasts of the northern hemisphere" and who, having read Pater Archangel's letter, was now requesting that the "good arctic priest" trap three or four polar bears of highest quality and snowy whiteness to be shipped to His Majesty's property, where they would be tamed and then permitted to roam at their leisure through the Sauling; the mountains and the distant plain.

Father Gstir was not deterred. He had made contact with the monarch, the great king of architectural endeavour, the patron of difficult projects in preposterous locations. Surely His Majesty's desire for polar bears would diminish when he thought about the magnificent stone church Pater Archangel planned for the wilderness. Was not Neuschwanstein being designed for an inaccessible stone pinnacle in mountainous Bavarian wilds near Pollat Falls?

And were there not plans for a vast hunting lodge in another improbable spot? Father Gstir determined that in his next letter he would suggest — with great respect and humility — that, unlike the German treasury department, God the Father would smile on all of Ludwig's architectural creations were the king to make a contribution toward a church for Bavaria's exiled sons and daughters, as well as, he added, a bell for said church.

The reference to the polar bears had given him a number of ideas for the Corpus Christi procession, now only three months away. "An inventory must be made," he told Joseph, "of all the animals in our surroundings."

He had entered the carver's workshop just as Joseph was to begin work on the Virgin Mary — now with the approach of spring there was again some light before and after his shift at the mill. The large crucifix was completed and leaned against the wall. Joseph had not decided whether he would paint it and if so where he was to get gold leaf for the nimbus.

"All of the domestic animals, I mean," the priest continued. "Horses, pigs, cows, and a donkey. We must have a donkey for the procession. Christ entered Jerusalem on a donkey. Do you know where we can find one, Joseph?"

"I do not," replied Joseph, running one long finger across his jawline while staring at the block of wood from which the Holy Mother would emerge. "Shall I colour my statues?" he asked.

"Yes," said Father Gstir, "it will do the people good to see colour. And what are we to do about music?"

Joseph said that the Irishman responsible for the township's Celtic name played a sort of violin in a rather frenetic way. "It sounds somewhat like Bach," he said, "but played much too quickly." He took off his hat and shook wood shavings from the brim.

"And are there singers?"

Joseph recalled certain drunken evenings in the bunkhouse. "Sometimes the men sing," he reported tentatively. The songs they knew were quite inappropriate but might be modified. "One of the men has an accordion."

"Wonderful!" exclaimed Father Gstir. "And what is the Irishman's name?"

"O'Sullivan . . . Brendan. A farmer and a carpenter."

The mention of carpentry brought Father Gstir's imagined place of worship

41

back to his busy mind. He described his plan to interest King Ludwig in the church. But Joseph was skeptical. "He will never see it, this church," said the carver. "He will not be interested because he will not know what it looks like."

"O indeed he will," maintained the priest. "Indeed he will see the church, for you will carve a small model for the procession, and then we will send it to Munich." He smiled benevolently. "You may leave it unpainted. And before we send it," he added, "the church will be carried at the head of the procession by the children who will eventually worship in it."

"I have only three months!" Joseph threw his hands up in exasperation. "How can I work in the mill every day and then do all this carving for you?" He had no idea he was describing the division of labour that would determine the rest of his life, that he would always be employed at least half of the time to ensure survival while never — even for a day — letting his hand stray far from a chisel.

"You are not carving for me," replied Father Gstir. "You are carving for God."

The spinster was a woman called Klara, named at her grandfather's suggestion after the saint who attached herself to Francis. But as a mature woman in the early 1930s, Klara was not averse to being called "the spinster." She liked the sound of the word, the way it flung itself out of one's mouth and thrust itself, bristling, into the day. She was eccentric, as spinsters are meant to be, but she was forgiven this by the nuns and most of the village because of some unhappy events in her early life. When she burst into meetings of the village council, demanding a war memorial, the esteemed councillors soberly waited out the storm, then, after the door had banged shut behind her, remarked on her early sorrows. They talked about how she lived all alone, up there at Becker's Corners on the farm behind the church with only the odd hired boy to help her with her livestock, or the storing of winter firewood, or the requirement that four or five pails of water be hauled each day from the pump to the summer kitchen. Their assumption that she was "geist-ridden" — old enough at almost forty to be surrounded by ghosts —

was true enough, but what the men didn't know was that this affliction gave Klara enough spiritual company to make her life quite full. And as for keeping herself busy, the spinster had tailored the splendid jackets of everyone in town.

Klara had her memories, a cemetery full of dead family members, a village from which most of her schoolmates had fled, a brother who had vanished, an ancient religion replete with narrative, the knowledge of the village's mythology, two difficult skills learned from two masters (her mother and her grandfather), friends in the convent, and a solid sense of how to keep her mind intact, despite the constant loneliness. She had also the possession of something that only a very few spinsters have: independence and a past.

She was aware that most unmarried women in her village, and in the villages surrounding hers, had always lived auxiliary lives. Called in to look after the household when one of their more fortunate sisters gave birth to a child or hovering by the side of the sickbeds and deathbeds of elderly relatives, a spinster's career was often one of service to those whom nature had dealt with more fairly. They had no particular past because no man had felt moved to consider them, for whatever reason, as an object of romance or, failing that, as a useful object of domestic labour in married life. But Klara served no master; she alone determined the tasks she would perform each day. And when she was quite young, romance had disturbed and illuminated her life, had cast its light and its shadow over her for one intense, confusing season.

She did her best not to dwell on this any longer, feeling that to remain absorbed by a personal past of a romantic nature was unbecoming to a woman of her age. Better to be outdoors herding her white cows or harvesting apples, or indoors tailoring a suit jacket, washing windows, sweeping up. Or at the church polishing pews, or in the cemetery tending the plants around the family plot.

In her twenties it had been a fierce, unspoken sorrow, this past, catching her off guard during the day, causing her to dig her nails into the flesh of her palms, or taking her quite unexpectedly back to scenes so tender she could be locked in them for long periods of time, could find herself standing quite still, completely absent from the task that had been occupying her hands. This frightened and appalled her — so much so that she began to train herself in the art of stoic apartness, a separation from her former self. She had been a good pupil in this endeavour and began finally to behave normally as a spinster, keeping the past at a distance, on the other side of the fence, of her skin.

Only once in recent years had she given in to it, and this had caused her to do something quite odd on a moist summer day, one that was uncharacteristically misty for the season. All week, inexplicably, she had permitted scenes from the past to buzz around in her head until, by the time Saturday arrived, she began to believe that, like the fog that was everywhere except indoors, she was not really inside the house of her mind. Or perhaps it was that unlike the fog she was in that house and nowhere else. She decided then to let the outside atmosphere into her rooms, and she opened every window, every door, and watched the white, odourless smoke crawl over threshold and sill, curl around the legs of chairs, and spread itself over tables and beds. She unlatched cupboard and closet doors and pulled open drawers in various dressers so that the fog touched even her most intimate underclothes and crept around her dead mother's good dishes. When the whole house had turned opaque, she realized suddenly that her actions had gone well beyond the bounds of eccentricity permitted a spinster. She slammed shut windows, doors, drawers and cupboards, and washed her face with cold water — for she now found that she had been weeping — and promised herself nothing of this nature would ever happen again. There would be no more unpremeditated dives into personal memory. She knew this was nonsense, of course, that there was nothing at all one can do about something one can't forget. The more it is pushed away, the more it stays stubbornly planted in the rich soil of a life's narrative. Dormant, perhaps, but ready with the smallest provocation to burst into full flower.

Despite a total change in the weather, the dampness in Klara's empty house had lasted for several days.

The house, which was Klara's childhood home, had not always been empty. Once, there had been a father and a mother. Once there had been a brother. Each had left a trace of himself or herself in one room or another: a pipe, a set of suspenders, a jewellery box, a hand mirror, a small pair of good Sunday boots. And each had left something unresolved in Klara, words spoken, or not spoken, or words spoken in anger. Each had left an empty chair at the table.

It had taken her mother, Helga Becker, five years to die. When the actual physical sickness set in during the last six months of her mother's life, Klara realized she had known since the age of ten that some dark thing was growing slowly larger inside the woman who had given birth to her. When at fifteen she was told about the cancer and how it would soon kill her mother, it seemed to Klara that, like the dimension of her brother's absence that expanded at the close of each new day, this tumour had been gradually filling her mother's skull, slowly pushing the light and the life out of their house.

After Klara's brother had been gone for a full year, and her mother's fits of weeping and formidable tantrums had ceased, a new, clipped practicality appeared to enter her. She seemed then to be perpetually angered by the superficiality of a world that could continue on with its business in the face of the total dematerialization of her son. It was during this time that she began to teach Klara the art of tailoring, but without tenderness, as if she felt that her young daughter were part of this conspiracy of ordinariness and ought to be provided with some business to get on with. This phase was followed by greater and greater withdrawal, punctuated by terse statements suggesting that her husband, Dieter, was to blame for the boy's disappearance and therefore, by association, responsible for her own unhappiness, though she never spoke of Tilman except when making these allegations. When the subtle accusations were overheard by Klara, they terrified her, for though she had never said so, she felt that the real culprit was herself, that any blame ought to be aimed at her. In the end, though she left school and nursed her faithfully until the instant of her death, Klara no longer loved her mother but was able to muster no argument against her that did not circle back to her own actions.

But it was neither this nor the grief that accompanied it that Klara had been remembering the day she let the mist into the house.

When the land around Shoneval was cleared of trees and stumps and boulders by loggers and mill workers and farmers in the middle of the nineteenth century, several things began to happen. The stumps were used for fences, some of which, though not many, could still be seen in the vicinity of Klara's farm. The boulders were gathered to make the foundations of houses and barns and various other buildings, and endured as memorials to the frame structures that once surmounted them. The trees, of course, if not used for building, made the journey to the sawmill, where they were subjected to the mutilation process that had so disturbed Joseph Becker. Excess rainfall, which was once thirstily consumed by the great forests, now had nowhere to go except downhill to collect in the depressions among gentle hills. Over time the lingering moisture produced new swampy areas where, in the beginning, willow trees flourished until they were killed by an overabundance of the liquid that had originally encouraged their growth.

It was the swamp nearest the farm that Klara had been recalling, the swamp frozen over in winter, its dead willows sparkling with frost. A scene not unlike one of those unfurled at a travelling medicine show. A scene not unlike those she had heard were painted on the walls of the

Swan Room in one of King Ludwig's Bavarian castles. A scene filled with stillness and the anticipation of dance.

Had she allowed it, Klara's mind could still paint it, shining branch by shining branch: the dark perfect ice under a sky of eye-watering clarity, the young man and the young woman skating there. They had not moved together as partners but had made a game of it, skating the way young children skate in a kind of indiscriminate, inconclusive chase, for they were not many years removed from childhood and it was childhood's echo that moved with them across the ice.

It had been late in the afternoon. Balanced on a hill behind them, the setting sun appeared to be tangled in the twisted forms of a stump fence, its rays colouring the steam of their breath a soft orange. Though they had known each other most of their lives, they were suddenly uncomfortable with each other and confused by the impulse that had sent them off to skate in this strange place, alone, while the other young villagers were filling the pond with laughter. Klara had turned suddenly and they had crashed together, had fallen, as if killed in combat. Then they had lain quite still on the ice, mysterious, and knowing

51

something neither could speak about.

Klara remembered the warmth of his neck in the cold, his skin on the inch of her bare wrist between her mitten and her coat sleeve. His face had undergone a change, his expression becoming serious, the dark eyebrows gathered together as if he were puzzled or annoyed. In retrospect she believed that her face would have changed as well though she couldn't have known that at the time.

After that afternoon he would tramp up to the farm in the evenings and sit on a chair in the kitchen, his legs apart, his arms resting on his knees, his eyes on the floor between his feet. "Silent Irish," her father called him though they knew his name was Eamon, for the young man came from one of the very first Irish families who had been drawn by their faith to the Catholic settlement that was developing around Shoneval. Eamon didn't speak at all for the first few months, and Klara herself said very little. But she wanted talk, some sort of declaration or interpretation, an explanation perhaps for the waves of dread that accompanied her attraction to him, for the subtle anger his coming to the farm each evening seemed to cause in him, and in her, for the way he appeared to endure the hours near her as if they were punishment.

At night she would kneel by her bed and pray that he would speak to her. "One word," she would whisper, "one sentence." She had never in her short life been this perplexed by anyone. And she had never confessed him. What would there have been to say? "We fell together on the ice, Father, and have been angry with each other ever since." There was no sin in that, except the anger, and therefore no resolution beyond the suggestion that one or the other should apologize, but for what Klara did not know.

While he sat in silence, evening after evening in the large farm kitchen, Klara performed her domestic duties noisily, banging stove lids, rattling dishes in the pan, slamming the bottom drawers of the hutch cupboard. The kitchen was hers, really, had been so since she had turned fifteen, since her mother had died. She believed she resented this foreign intrusion into what she had marked out as her own territory. Until this moment there had been just her father and herself, night after night, their habits and conversation a hymn to predictability.

The grandparents walked over from their

own farm sometimes for a Sunday meal. Once or twice a year the new Irish priest visited, and some of the Sisters had come for tea. But there had been no raw energy in these rooms since her brother disappeared in their childhood. And she had become comfortable with being the sole custodian of youth in the house.

The weeks passed and Klara was no better able to explain the suffocating tension that seemed to enter with Eamon through the door, how his presence made the clocks tick louder and louder in a silence that grew like a lengthening shadow. Her father read the paper or a book near the stove and sporadically announced a surprising bit of news he had discovered in his reading or a change of farming practice he had heard about in town. The boy answered monosyllabically. The rustle of the paper, the creak of the Boston rocker set Klara's teeth on edge.

She was nineteen years old then. Until the accident of her uneasy and inexplicable connection with this boy, she had been happily spending her days engaged in the two professions she inherited from her mother — housekeeping and tailoring — and the one pastime she had learned from her grandfather — woodcarving. The first two activities gave her full run of the house; her sewing and cutting taking place in the sunroom over the porch, and most of her domestic duties, save the weekly dusting and waxing of the parlour, occupying the large kitchen. The moments of solitude with scissors, needle, chisel knife, or ladle — all much-loved tools — and the easy companionship her work led to — fittings and fashion consultations, shopping, and meals — were cherished by her. Each occupation fed the other, making her life, ironically for a tailor, seamless. Her handling of household objects gave her a greater knowledge of the shape and weight of things, and her measuring and fitting gave her much information about the structure of human anatomy, information she could in turn put to use when carving wooden saints. And the saints, themselves, she believed, bestowed grace on all the work she undertook to perform.

She made the saints in a small wooden building that had once been the farm's blacksmith shop. The old oven served well now to warm the air in the winter and to heat up the pots of horse-hoof glue Klara sometimes used to fasten the arms on her attempts at larger figures. Even with the door closed, the one south-facing window allowed her enough light to see what she was doing. The building's small size and its separation from the house gave the whole exercise the atmosphere of play; carving was the reward that she permitted herself when her other chores were completed. Pure pleasure came to her then as the fashioning of her wooden people was connected to neither the necessities of survival nor the need to bring cash into the household.

When she was a child, her grandfather had taught her how to whittle a small piece of wood, though it was really her brother, Tilman, that the old man had his eye on. He had hoped the boy would develop enough skill to at least make repairs to the church altars, if not fully embrace the profession of woodcarving, but Tilman's attention span proved to be short when he was indoors, while Klara howled and stomped in the workshop until her grandfather reluctantly handed her some wood and a knife and showed her how to cut away from her body so she would not harm herself.

In the beginning, Klara made toy animals: horses, pigs, and cows. Then she began to create more exotic species, beasts she had never seen except on advertising cards: leopards, giraffes with exaggerated necks and spots, or rhinos with horns. Dolls were a logical next step, and since her mother was teaching her how to sew, she made elaborate wardrobes for them from scraps she gleaned from the sunroom floor. She had a tendency to hoard her work at this early stage. Once, however, she made a complete Noah's ark for her brother at Christmas, but because he had vanished by then, he never came into his old room to play with it. It remained at the back of the closet where she had placed it, untouched, practically unglimpsed, except by Klara herself, who checked now and then to see if he might have returned unnoticed to play with it in the night. Finally, when she was almost thirteen, filled with an indignation she didn't even attempt to interpret, she took the dusty animals and their houseboat to the kitchen stove and dropped them into the fire, two by two.

The saints began to emerge when Klara entered adolescence and had been confirmed at the church. Then shortly after her mother's death she conceived the notion of making a life-sized statue of a medieval abbess — perhaps a saint — with a generously pleated habit. She would use what she had learned about cloth from her mother's and, to a lesser extent, her own tailoring. Her grandfather would teach her what he knew about carving drapery. Her father would provide the wood for her when he cut log lengths for the next season's fuel and brought them by sledge to the yard in midwinter.

Between the ages of seventeen and nineteen, Klara experienced contentment as she never would again — though, because she had not at the time known the restlessness of desire, she would come to acknowledge this contentment only in retrospect. Now when she sat cross-legged on the table in the sunroom cutting cloth, or when the chisel she held bit into the wood, there was a splendid animal unconsciousness about her, a fulsome sense of well-being. It never occurred to her to change her life. She was young, reasonably skilled, and in confident control of her surroundings. But when Eamon broke into her world, insisting by his stance and his silence that she make a space for him there, some part of her considered this an act of vandalism. She would never fully forgive the way he trespassed into her tranquillity, just as later she would never forgive his determined act of truancy.

★ ★ ★

The days lengthened, the snow began to melt, disclosing rough patches of the dark earth that had been ploughed the previous autumn after the harvest, and still each evening "Silent Irish" climbed the hill toward Klara's kitchen.

By now Klara was in a blistering, tight-lipped rage whenever he was in her presence, and much of the time that he wasn't.

"He's courting you," her quiet, sombre father told her with an uncharacteristic wink.

"I'm not interested in being courted by the likes of him," Klara snapped, her face filling with colour. "I'm not interested in being courted."

Dieter Becker shrugged his shoulders as if it mattered to him not at all. But the next clear, bright evening, after Eamon's arrival, even before the boy had seated himself in his customary place, the older man excused himself and walked out to the barn.

Klara had her back to the door, was lowering a tall stack of plates into the warm suds of the dishpan when she felt the whole atmosphere change by the fact they were alone together. She stared hard at the two skimpy lilac bushes she had planted last fall in the yard. Knowing she was never going to be able to turn around, she could feel Eamon's gaze touch her like a warm hand between her shoulder blades. There was no sound at all until finally she heard his footsteps on the floor, and then the sound a chair makes when a body is settling into it.

If she could manage to turn around, she decided, if she could just manage to do that, then she would be able to see things as they were, everything in place in her kitchen: a mat by the door, a damp tea towel thrown over a chair, all the reassuring furniture of her life undisturbed by his presence in her world. The thin branches of the lilac were bending to the left in a sudden evening breeze. The low sun, fiercely brilliant in the centre of the windowpane, was making her eyes fill with water. It was becoming almost impossible to continue to scrutinize the yard.

She turned finally, her hands glistening, drops of water clinging to the ends of her fingers. The room was dark in contrast to the brightness beyond the glass. Eamon was merely a featureless shape on a chair near the stove. Klara's intention was to cross the room and leave by the woodshed door, leave him alone in the kitchen with his silence and his stubbornness, but she paused for a moment while her eyes adjusted to the shadows in the twilit room. After she had taken two or three steps, Eamon leaned forward and grasped her damp wrist.

This one simple touch freed the storm of speech that had been building in her mind for weeks, setting in motion a savage interrogation. She hurled the words — almost hysterically — into the air. "What do you want? What right do you have, what . . . what are you doing here, and why don't you speak? What makes you think anyone wants you to come here?"

He was still holding on to her wrist. He said nothing.

Klara looked at his hand, the large-knuckled awkwardness of it on her slender arm. She made a sharp movement as if to pull away. Then she clenched her fist and jerked her arm in the direction of his chest so now it was as if he were holding her at bay. "Why do you never speak?" she pleaded. "Say something!"

They remained locked like this, obdurate, combatant, for several moments until Eamon flushed and tossed Klara's arm back toward her body as if it were a broken branch he were removing from his path.

Then he was out of the chair.

"And what is it you would have me say?" he asked, his voice half broken by anger and sorrow. "What can I possibly say to you?" He swung toward the door she had been planning to exit from, stopped as if he might have added one more word to his own question, then strode through the woodshed and out across the damp snow in the yard, his head down, his hands thrust into his pockets.

The shaft of setting sun that had so troubled Klara's eyes was now on the chair where Eamon had been sitting. He had forgotten his jacket. Klara's arm remained near her stomach, where it had come to rest after Eamon released it. It looked like a foreign object to her, something that was not now and had never been connected to her body. She watched with some interest as colour gradually returned to the white marks his fingers had left on her skin.

The next night he didn't walk up the hill at all.

And she waited for him.

"Where's old Silent got to, I wonder?" asked her father, looking up at her over the tops of the glasses he wore to read in the evening.

"I'm sure I don't know," Klara replied. "But it's good to have our house back to ourselves, I'd say."

"He was no trouble sitting quietly in the kitchen." Dieter looked at his daughter with fondness, amused by her petulance. "I'd say it's a good change to have a young man come into the house."

Klara didn't answer. She had been looking through the glass panel at the top of the door that led to the side porch, and had been distracted by the appearance of a figure far down the road. But whoever it was had gone off on the path that led to the village before she could accurately determine whether it was Eamon.

Some of Klara's temperament had been inherited from her grandfather. Whenever she looked at his serene face she could never believe that he had once been moved by any kind of passion. And yet he told her that as a young man in Bavaria he had been thought pious because he was known to break down and weep in front of altarpieces, and in the presence of statues of the Madonna or the saints. But it wasn't the Holy Spirit that had touched him; he was a worshipper of graven images, a lover of wooden skin. Sometimes, particularly when he was locked in a visual trance in front of a piece by the great sixteenth-century carver Tilman Riemenschneider, his tears would be those of joy and frustration. He would adore the figure itself, the long thighs, the branching streams of veins on the inner arms, but he would be driven almost to despair by the knowledge that he would never be able to cause such vitality to enter wood.

By the time Father Archangel Gstir came into his life, Joseph Becker was a craftsman of great skill — the priest thought him wonderfully gifted — but he himself was aware of his own limitations, and often when he was alone with the work he was doing for the procession, he would feel the tears begin to sting his eyes. For several agonizing minutes he would curse the God who had given him just enough of the gift to understand what he lacked, the same God that had permitted him to be carving at the outer reaches of the world among people who would be able to comprehend neither his ability nor his limitations. He would be forever a perfectionist incapable of achieving the quality of perfection he worshipped in the great master's work. And his granddaughter had inherited from him a need for order, a sort of corollary of perfection.

Klara had also inherited a tendency toward the kind of anger she had seen increase daily in her mother after Tilman's disappearance, and had incorporated into her own personality, as well as into her work, the sense of superiority with which her mother rode through the unworthy world that had taken her son away.

Helga Becker had always insisted that the service she performed was tailoring, and that it was as different from dressmaking as medieval tapestry-making was to pillow-slip embroidery. "Any fool can be a dressmaker," she had told Klara. "Anyone capable of looking in a woman's magazine and stitching two hunks of cloth together." But tailoring, she had maintained, required talent, skill, and patience. "And you are not just covering something up," she had said. "You are constructing something with shape and weight and volume. A garment that is *tailored*. Just because I'm a woman doesn't mean that I can't be a tailor. And don't call me a seamstress either. Anyone who can hold a needle can be a seamstress."

As an orphaned girl, Helga had been trained by the woman who would eventually become her mother-in-law, and she had strongly objected to the older woman's modesty. "Imagine," she would say to Klara, "your grandmother calling herself a seamstress right up until the day she died, when she could plan and cut and sew circles around those men in Goderich calling themselves tailors. And she did so much for the church. In my opinion, in his old age, Father Gstir was better dressed than the Pope."

Klara's mother had made good coats and jackets for almost everyone in the village, and travelling suits for the women, though hardly anyone took the journeys these outfits were designed for. She drew the line at men's trousers, for decency's sake, but reasoned that this was no great loss as men were apt to buy the readymades down at Hafeman's store. "They'd buy their suit jackets there too," she had confided, "if they didn't have to face me looking at them in such sad get-ups. Me, who can make a fine figure out of the sorriest of them with my tailored waistcoats. I've been the making of most of the men in this village," she asserted, "and a great number of the women as well."

It was true that the citizens of Shoneval were as well attired a congregation as entered a Catholic church anywhere in Ontario, especially in comparison to the collection of ragged folk that had shivered inside the first log church constructed in Father Gstir's day, folk who had neither the time nor the money to think about whether they wanted or needed waistcoats and travelling suits. Now it was a fine sight indeed to see such well-appointed people climb the hill to mass, then descend that same hill again to make the traditional Sunday visit to Der Archangel. In the early days the good Father had led his little flock down to the brewery for the customary tankard after mass. When the tavern was completed shortly after the consecration of the large stone church in 1881, Father Gstir had been greatly moved when the innkeeper elected to name the new establishment after his confessor.

Klara, skilled with a needle from childhood and a marvel with scissors from her adolescence on, had taken over her mother's business at sixteen, after Helga had been dead for about half a year. At first the men were shy of her, this young girl with the shining golden hair, but gradually they had relaxed in the face of her businesslike, formal, almost superior manner.

"Men are the most vain creatures on God's earth," her mother had told Klara, "even farmers. They claim they don't like to dress for Sundays, but they're just like peacocks once you get a coat on them. Add a piece of silk braid to the coat and there's no living with them.

"And remember this," she had added, "all men like to believe they have fine figures . . . even though next to none of them have. Tailors . . . good tailors cause magical transformations to take place. A good suit jacket creates an enviable illusion so a fine tailor is indispensable — mostly because of male vanity. Those farmers could no more create this illusion themselves than they could make palm trees flourish in their winter fields. You, therefore, will be indispensable."

Indispensable or not, Klara gave two hours of each day to sewing in the winter and sometimes up to four hours in the summer when the light lasted well into the evening and she was able to work after supper. She had, as a result, a good collection of "show" garments, the ability to complete projects well and on time, and a much cherished bank account of her own. None of the other young women she knew, with the exception of two or three nuns, were as independent as she was, and the knowledge of this contributed greatly to her as yet unrecognized contentment.

Eamon didn't walk up to the farm the next night either. Or the night after that. Or in the weeks that followed. Thankfully, with the lengthening days, her father became too busy in the fields after supper to ask about the boy. And Klara herself had her sewing to attend to. But now it was as if she were always waiting for something or, worse, as if she were searching for something she could barely remember. All those who were gone from her life haunted her, but imprecisely, never really materializing into brother, or mother, or lost friend. It was as if, against her will, her mind had decided to develop a philosophy of absenteeism, so that the tree felled in the yard five years ago or the broken platter she had tossed into the farm dump last summer now suddenly became grave losses, though she could not call to mind a branch or stem or leaf or the specifics of a china pattern. She stormed through the house for days looking for a pair of kid gloves that had belonged to her mother, finding them at last in the attic, dried and yellowed by the heat of several summers.

I have not paid enough attention, she thought, looking at the two wrinkled pieces of leather that were so disturbingly like the human hands they were meant to cover. When she picked them up, the leather fingers curled softly over her own, as if someone were attempting to press her hand. The palms and the ends of the thumbs, she noticed, were slightly soiled.

Klara stood alone in the dim light of the attic, her serious face partially lit by one low window. "I have never," she whispered, closing her fist around the gloves, "I have never paid enough attention."

Sometimes, during the howling winter nights of the first year Father Gstir spent near the gristmill and the sawmill that would eventually become the centre of Shoneval, he would surprise himself by becoming discouraged. He had never seen such weather, was not precisely certain that the performance of the elements was natural even in this northern place where no Christian had chosen to live before. Drifts climbed up the outside walls of his cabin and pushed their way under his wooden door. Snow swirled around the glass of his one window until it became completely covered with a thick rind of frost that could only be chipped off with a knife. His bible was glued by ice to the table, the table was glued by ice to the floor. Washing — either his clothing or himself — was unthinkable and, although the idea of sweat was unimaginable, he was not unaware of his own body odour and that of Joseph's when he was visiting, an odour that he decided was somehow even more rancid in cold air than it would have been in warm.

When he was alone on these nights he

consoled himself by thinking of his royal benefactor's castles. Though he knew very little about them, he imagined their architecture, their absurd constructions, their rooms of fuchsia and turquoise, the music in them, the pageantry. He saw them rise — against all odds — on the pinnacles of such extraordinary mountains that, in his more rational moments, he suspected did not exist — not in Bavaria, not anywhere. He knew that Ludwig's preposterous stone bouquets of towers and arches were in no way connected to God, that they celebrated almost all of the deadly sins, but still he loved them harder for their insistence on the secular.

As he sat practically embracing the iron stove from which little heat seemed to emanate despite its insatiable hunger for logs, one castle after another would swell and fade in his head, the way the sound of a great bell expands, holds volume and tone for a glorious moment, and then recedes like someone walking toward and then away from you. Linderhof, Neuschwanstein, the huge follies built first in the king's mind by his love of German mythology and by his imagination and later constructed on mountaintops by his peasants and his will. Before Father Gstir left Bavaria he had heard only rumours of plans for these palaces; they could not possibly have been completed in the intervening time. And yet here they were, fully embellished, draped, and painted in the mind of a cold priest huddled in the heart of a Canadian forest.

He talked about the castles with Joseph one night in February, both of them sitting side by side on a rough wooden bench with their boots on the fender of the stove. "What would your thoughts be on a great work of architecture perched so high no road could reach it?"

Joseph, more practical, pointed out that such a work of architecture could not be constructed without a road to bring in men and materials. His long hands appeared to be shaping the road, carving the men and the materials as he spoke.

"Perhaps the road . . . this impossible road . . . might be sealed up afterwards," Father Gstir ventured, "so that one could do nothing more than gaze at this marvel from a distance."

"But King Ludwig would want to live at least some of the time in his castles." Joseph sniffed the smell of scorched leather in the air, then removed his boots from the heat source. Each night the men moved their feet back and forth in the vicinity of the fender, having to choose between numb toes or burnt footwear.

"Yes," said the priest, placing his own boots on the floor, "he will live in them and there will be roads for him to come and go, and for supplies to be carried in. Chocolate. His Majesty has a terrible fondness for chocolate, which would, of course, be brought from somewhere else." Father Gstir paused, bent forward to examine the sole of one boot, then added sadly, "We have no chocolate here, which is a shame. No chocolate at all, Joseph."

"No chocolate at all," Joseph agreed.

"What I have in my mind, though," Father Gstir put another log in the roaring stove, "is a work of architecture that has no function, a chambered sculpture, if you like. One left entirely alone after it is built. One that perches on its mountain and lets the elements play with it, lets sun and shadow and nothing else into its rooms. The odd mouse, I suppose, might visit. Or birds, once the windows begin to break."

"No repairs?"

"No repairs. As one standing in the valley looking up year after year, I should like to see how this construction decays, how long it takes before it becomes a ruin. What would go first, do you think? The windows, of course, blown out of their casements by mountain winds. And then quite possibly the doors. After the roof goes, then there is no hope. Rain, snow begins to eat the plaster, the beams. After that it becomes a ruin, and there is no turning back. It is the same with almost anything that remains abandoned. Friends, sweethearts, places, homelands, houses, and this castle in my mind. After a certain period of time the roof goes and there is no turning back. Still it is important to see what kind of a ruin remains, for it is my contention that only the greatest works make beautiful ruins."

"Perhaps you are right." Joseph walked over to the table and opened the bottle of whisky he had brought with him. He poured a glass for himself and one for his friend, who, as always, refused it at first but would succumb to the temptation sometime later. "Perhaps you are right, but no man could live long enough to see it."

"God would see it," said the priest, "and it would become dear to him. No whisky for me," he waved his hand dismissively at the glass. "I don't drink whisky."

Joseph smiled. "Yes, you do," he said,

"but if you wish it to warm by the stove for a moment or two, that's your business."

"Beautiful ruins are the skeletons of fine architecture, I would say. They show us that the edifice had good bones from the beginning."

"You don't have this in mind for your church, I hope, this disintegration, this process of ruination."

Father Gstir laughed. "Not at all. Not, at least, in the beginning. But I want it built with strong bones so that if hundreds of years from now . . . if it is ever abandoned . . . it will become a wonderful ruin up there on that hill."

"Always remember the bones," Joseph Becker would say to his granddaughter after relating this story. "They last the longest and explain the life history of people, monuments, sculpture. Without them everything else falls apart. With them the inner secret of each structure survives. Too many carvings have no bones, so termite and woodworm can destroy them utterly . . . or weather, or war. Think always when you are working of the strong ribcage of your abbess, think of the long bones in her thighs. If you don't keep them in mind they won't be there and then she will be nothing more than drapery and skin, beautiful in its folds and gathers but always verging on collapse. When the bones are perfect, skin and cloth move over the frame the way grass and trees and streams adorn a mountain, making it this particular mountain, or that. Still when we look at it we see a mountain . . . not an alpine pasture or a waterfall. The bones, you see, are what we remember."

Klara had never seen a mountain and made this point to her grandfather. He had walked out of his barn workshop then and had returned with a small boulder from the nearest field. "This will be your mountain," he had told her. "Take it home with you and keep it near your carving hand."

When Klara later told the story of Father Gstir's belief in ruins to the nuns, she took the boulder her grandfather had given her to show her friends. One Sister felt she should anoint the boulder with holy water. As she did so Klara, watching the liquid run down the surface of the rock, felt she could actually see the European pastures and waterfalls her grandfather had carried with him in his mind.

Klara's brother, Tilman, had known nothing at all about the circumstances of his birth or, to be more precise, the circumstances of his conception. Certainly it was not the kind of information one would impart to a child, but had he had contact with his mother or his father after he was twelve years old, would they have been likely to tell him this story? It is doubtful, sexual congress between one's parents being a topic usually avoided by those parents and their children alike. Besides, the moment was one that, if remembered at all, was recalled with a hint of shame, representing the first instance when the young man and the young woman who would become the parents of Tilman (and later of Klara) revealed to the other something of the broken and sharp-edged side of their natures.

Dieter Becker had never been a hunter, and yet when approached in November of 1892 by some other young men in the parish, he had agreed to meet them the following Saturday at the edge of the same swamp through which Father Archangel Gstir had tramped almost a quarter-century before.

The day in question had begun for Dieter in cerulean darkness; a passel of knife-point stars in the inky morning sky could be seen through the window glass, but there was no moon. After bacon by coal oil lamp, he shouldered his seldom-used shotgun and left his young wife, Helga, preparing to make sweet tomato pickle with the late crop that had ripened in her garden. Already the slop pail was filling with skins boiled off the surfaces of ripe fruit, and the air of the kitchen was rife with a sweet, acid smell.

By the time the bright, low light of the day was at its most intense, Dieter had proved to his companions that he had a prodigious natural talent with the gun that he had only hours before learned to use properly. He had found that he could predict the exact angle of a flight path determined by panic or the movements of a swimming bird duped by a decoy. The sport came to him with such ease that by the afternoon he had tired of it, and grasping a half-dozen or more birds, he made his excuses and set off for home. He had tired of the sport but not of the flush of excitement his success had pumped through his veins, and he anticipated, with great pleasure, the delivery of the bleeding trophies to his wife.

He entered a humid kitchen whose windows had been fogged by hours of boiling pots and into which crept the muted red light of the early sunset. His normally blue eyes were blackened by enlarged pupils, and the smell of blood was on him. Helga, to her embarrassment, recognized his lust, and for the first time in her marriage felt desire rising in her own body. After he threw the brace of birds on a wooden chair, the husband and wife stood face to face in the dwindling light, like silent enemies. Then they fell groaning to the floor beside the stove, where they struggled to extract this new terrible pleasure from the other. Helga could see, as she and Dieter beat against each other, the wing of one not quite dead bird methodically slapping the pine planks, yet by the time they had finished, the feathers were entirely still. The image, though she never spoke of it, stayed with her all through her pregnancy.

Within twenty-four hours all relations between the couple would be enacted with the same courteous affection that had become a part of their marriage. Dieter never hunted again but dreamed, nonetheless, some autumn nights of dogs that were not his own bringing trophy after trophy to his feet.

Though Tilman knew about pathmasters, had seen men working at maintenance, and had been told by his father about earlier days when the trees were felled and the stumps removed, he could almost believe that the roads were natural phenomena like rivers or forests. Maps themselves couldn't hold his attention, and yet the interlaced branches of a tree outside his window, a spider's web — even his sister's braided hair — were like *wanderkarten* to him, one line leading the eye to another, and then another. The large tartan made by the concession lines and the King's highways was just a logical extension of this, so that to his mind the lane that extended from the barn to the edge of the farm had been put there not as a temptation exactly but more as an invitation that should be accepted now and then.

He feared the disappearance of the roads due to lack of use, could imagine them vague with weeds, then lost forever in the texture of woods and meadows. As a much younger child he had been made aware of this possibility when a path he had beaten from the house to the creek filled in with wildflowers during a late-spring week when his parents had succeeded in convincing him to go to school. This had terrified him so much that his sleep had suffered and he had woken with a start far too early each morning, rousing the rest of the house with the shrill, relieved announcement that the lane that ran from the yard to the concession line was still there, had not been erased during the night.

School had been impossible for him. The road that had taken him there passed beneath the three large windows of the schoolhouse, and teams of horses and the odd passing delivery wagon made him feel that he himself might be moving backward while they were progressing forward. He could not learn to read or write or even how to remain in his seat. The white marks on the blackboard frightened him, as did the fact that the desks were bolted to the floor. No one, nothing could make him stay, neither the schoolmaster's switch nor his father's harsh words, though the boy made the attempt, over and over, to attend, walking sometimes halfway to the schoolhouse before turning and running back to the farm. Eventually he was permitted to remain at home on the farm, where he roamed the lanes the workhorses took to the back fields or followed the paths the cattle had made through the woodlot. The appearance of the truant officer had seemed to his parents to precipitate his first full-blown departure. But it was really the sight of migrating birds sweeping across the sky and the low angle of the silver October light that had caused him to leave, though no one would ever know that for certain but himself.

That first time he had moved south as if by instinct, had slept shivering in barns on the edges of Ontario towns named after great European cities — London, Brussels, Paris — and eventually on the outskirts of villages that wore the names of spas or palaces — Leamington, Blenheim. At times, like an animal on the verge of hibernation, he would sleep for two or three days, but finally hunger would awaken him and drive him toward the more industrial centres of Woodstock or Chatham and the bins of garbage stored behind brick hotels filled with commercial travellers. It was at this point that he became aware of his own magnetism — something he had never thought about before — how it affected the adults on town streets, how it made them want to give him things: a doughnut perhaps or a stick of candy. Once, responding to his angelic face, his tattered clothing, and his almost ethereal thinness, a woman crossed the street and handed him a basket of groceries without saying one word. He feasted for days, delighted by his luck. But if anyone questioned him, asked where he came from, where he was going, or what he was doing, he would disappear before they finished speaking, making certain to turn a corner or slip into a woodlot so they could no longer see him.

He received comfort, warmth, and information from animals, from the horses and cows with whom he often slept and from the great congregations of birds whose numbers multiplied as he moved deeper into the southern part of the province. The honking clamour, the panting noise made by beating wings had pulled him down the flat, dusty roads of Essex County until the birds abandoned him in the marshlands on the edge of Lake Erie. There he stood weeping among bulrushes as tall as himself while flock after flock set out across an expanse of water that stretched as far as the horizon. It seemed to him then that he had come to the edge, to the end of the world.

No matter how far he had travelled, Tilman had never been lost. As long as he was on a road or beside a creek or a river, he knew he would eventually find himself in a recognizable situation. *Stay near something that leads to something else* was his motto, and *Always know which street gets you out of town* was his creed. He would later claim that when there was no sun to guide him he could determine by certain smells which direction the wind was coming from. But this unfordable body of water suggested chaos, an end to the pattern of the roads, the beginning of the idea that there might be nowhere else to go. Repulsed by the overwhelming quantity of liquid, he turned away, began a trek northeast.

Tilman had returned, at the end of this first journey, to a home that was sombre under a weight of grief, the search parties having given up in despair two weeks previously, his mother, father, and sister dressed in black. His father had whipped him then, for the first and the last time, but in a halfhearted way, the act really being an expression of relief.

That winter Tilman taught himself how to read by making use of the pictures and captions in a Butler's *Lives of the Saints* that Father Gstir's successor, Father Gallagher, an Irishman, had given to the boy when he had shown some interest in a reference the priest had made to the Voyages of Brendan in a sermon after mass. And each day he walked back and forth to his grandfather's farm and the old man's workshop, where, occasionally, he could be coaxed into mastering some basic carving technique. It seemed to his parents that with these efforts at self-education he had begun to settle. But when great numbers of birds began to pass over the house in the spring, he began a journey north. This time he was halted not by the obstacle of water, though there was a plethora of lakes in the vicinity, but by a wall of dense forest. Roads were what pushed him forward, and past the town of Lakefield, the roads petered out in a tangle of bush. This disappointed him, but at least the forest was on solid ground, suggesting that some sort of track might be made through it. And the spring journey had not the urgency of the one taken in autumn, did not carry with it the feeling that, if not taken at all, an important life-giving part of him would be extinguished.

After that his disappearances were sporadic, and shortlived, and did not involve much distance. Often he would walk to a neighbouring town, where he would linger for a few days and news of him would be relayed back to his father's farm by milk wagons or by the rural post. When he returned, most often at meal time, he would slip unceremoniously into his seat at the kitchen table. With time his family learned that it was pointless to ask him where he had been.

It was his mother who had sensed that he would someday leave forever, and that his disappearance would take place in the autumn during the same hunting season when he had been conceived. She knew she couldn't bear to lose him. When he was home she would rise sometimes six or seven times in the night to check his room. At the table, noon and suppertime, her face drawn with exhaustion, she would often threaten him with unspecified punishments were he to go missing again. As the summer progressed she insisted he should not leave the yard, then the house, and eventually she tried to confine him to whatever room she happened to be in. Tilman responded neither to her questions nor to her attempts at incarceration and intimidation but looked at her with confusion on his perfect face, once enraging her with what she believed was insolence when he invited her to come along with him on his next "walk." Despite his wife's insistence, Dieter refused to beat him again after this incident, sent him instead to his room in disgrace, then turned to her and said, "You might try some kindness, Helga. Some kindness might make him want to stay." Later, slipping into her brother's room, Klara offered to go with him since her mother would not. But Tilman refused the gesture. "You're too small," he said, "and you'd get your dresses dirty."

Though infuriated by the notion that it was she that Tilman was trying to escape from, and barely speaking to her husband as a result, Helga Becker made some attempts at enticement. As if trying to redesign her son's character, or to hold his body in one spot, she made more and more severely tailored, formal clothes for him, going so far as to add gold buttons and piping, and once even a velvet collar. Tilman wore these costumes briefly, walking stiffly around the house on the day they were presented to him. But always he appeared the following morning in his old dungarees and a torn flannel shirt. At the beginning of September, Helga reverted to interrogating the boy mercilessly about his thoughts and plans, and when he wouldn't answer, she wept openly in his presence. At the end of the month during which he turned twelve, and after one or two more brief absences, his mother became convinced that his permanent removal from her life was at hand. She pleaded with him to stay. By the beginning of October, the tension in the house had become unbearable.

When Dieter began the autumn ploughing, he encouraged the boy to accompany him to the fields. This Tilman did for a while, walking beside the slow, stately procession of the four large, dignified workhorses. His distressed mother, watching this from the kitchen window, had the premonition that when the last furrow was finished, the boy would be gone. The grandfather had failed to interest him in any carving projects. He had grown even more silent at the table, and had taken to looking early in the morning out the south windows of the rarely used parlour, as if there were something there calling to him, something that no one else could see.

The birds arrived suddenly and in great clamorous numbers, descending like dark rain into distant ponds or sailing noisily overhead like storm clouds moving in a strong wind. Helga panicked and locked the door of Tilman's room one morning while he was still sleeping, but he escaped by the window — how, she never knew — and appeared as usual at breakfast without a word to her about what had taken place. Later that day she took the boy's measurements to the blacksmith and returned with a hinged iron harness attached to a long iron chain. She wept and pleaded until her husband brought a cot to the woodshed, then she stood beside him while he nailed the chain to the door jamb.

"Only," she said, "until winter comes. Only until then."

"The boy will not submit to it," Dieter said. "He will not put it on."

"I can't lose him," Helga turned from her husband and ran her fingers almost tenderly along the iron links. "I won't permit that to happen." And then when he didn't answer, she added softly, still not meeting his eyes, "He'll be able, this way, to be outside. It won't be like a prison."

"Are you mad? A person in chains is always in a prison," Dieter stepped in anger toward the door.

She clutched his sleeve in her hand.

"You must make him wear it," she said desperately, almost hysterically. "You must force him to put it on."

"And how am I to do that?"

Dieter and Helga stood face to face: he breathing quickly, wanting to escape to his fields, she looking past his shoulder at the horizon that had so often enticed her son. Each hated the other and themselves for their part in Tilman's confinement. "You're bigger than he is," Helga said finally.

When Klara had been sent to bed in her room upstairs after a supper filled with a silence so profound she would recall it later as a fifth person at the table, Dieter coaxed his son into the woodshed. Golden light from the kitchen lamps entered through the connecting door, and silver light from the partial moon shone through one cloudy window.

"You're to sleep here now," he said to the boy. Only the foot of the cot was visible in the block of light entering from the kitchen. "You'll be our guard," he explained, "for foxes in the hen house."

"Do I have to shoot them?" asked Tilman, who had begun to undress. He was fond of foxes.

"No, no shooting," Dieter placed his hand on his son's shoulder, "but leave your clothes on. You may be required to be up in the night, just to yell at them."

The boy climbed between the flannel sheets. Dieter could see the harness. It was hanging from a hook on the opposite wall where a slice of moonlight appeared to have chopped the iron bars in half.

Tilman was pleased by the proximity of the outdoors. "I'll like to sleep here," he said.

His father did not answer but left the connecting door slightly ajar when he walked back into the kitchen.

A dreaming child is like a weed underwater, each limb languid, heavy beneath a depth of sleep. Dieter was able to position and then close the harness around Tilman's frail ribs and shoulders without disturbing his rest. Only once, with the sound of the lock clicking shut, did his eyes fly open, but he was not really awake and the lids lowered again one second later.

The next morning, however, everyone in the house was hurled into consciousness by the terrible sound of Tilman's howls as he flung himself to the end of his chain again and again. Around him his own dog ran in large, free circles, barking and snapping, as if the boy were already a stranger in the yard.

Helga would never recover — not from his imprisonment and not from his escape.

For the first few days on the chain the child would not eat at all, though his mother baked his favourite pies and stirred lumps of chocolate into mugs of warm milk. On the third day, he called repetitively for food and ate ravenously as if storing energy or building strength. Klara tried to talk to him in the yard, but he wouldn't answer, and even while gobbling stew or eating porridge his eyes remained fixed on the horizon.

Dieter, unable to bear the sight of the boy straining at the end of the chain, or the sound of his cries, left the house before dawn and returned to it in darkness when he hoped all were asleep. On the fourth night something growled at him when he crossed the yard, and he realized that Tilman had not gone indoors to sleep though the season was well enough advanced that there was a hard frost on the ground.

Dieter sat down on the stoop beside the

curled form that his son made in the dark. He tried to touch Tilman's shoulder, but the boy twitched away from him.

"Tilman," he began, "your mother is half mad with worry about you, and me too, wondering what will become of you if you go off again. Would you give me your word that you'll stay?"

The boy began to whimper.

His father continued, "How will you look after yourself? How will you learn to be a man?"

There was nothing but silence now from Tilman, as if he might have decided to listen. His father put his head in his hands and, after a few moments, looked up at the stars. "Tomorrow we'll fetch Father Gallagher, and if he says you should stay, and you promise him that you will, we will set you free."

Dieter heard the chain rattle somewhere in the darkness. Tilman had shifted his position. He had stopped whimpering, but his father could hear him breathing, quick and sharp, near his elbow.

"You see," he said to the boy, "we are all tied to a place." He coughed into his hand. "We're stuck to it. What if I were just to up and leave? What if I were just to wander off? Then who would keep the fields?"

"There's fields everywhere," said Tilman quietly.

"And everywhere," said his father, "there's a man keeping them."

The boy said nothing more. Somewhere in a nearby pasture filled with shadows and silver, a horse whinnied.

"Will you stay, son?" his father asked. "Will you just stay home? Will you promise if the priest says so that you won't go off again?"

Tilman took the chain in his hands, then scrambled to his feet. He ran back and forth in an arc at the far end of the moonlit yard until the taut links cut across his father's shins. "I won't stay," he called fiercely toward the house. "I want to go," he screamed. "I *want* to go!"

The next morning Tilman's howling started at the same moment as the birds began to sing, at the first suggestion of light. His cries were taken up by dogs all over the county — a kind of relay of despair — so that sleepers ten and fifteen miles away were unknowingly disturbed by the boy's anguish, their last dreams of the morning being those of confinement or attempted escape.

His mother writhed in agony in the

sheets, her hands against her ears. Klara, in her small white room, sat straight up in her bed, then ran across the hall, down the stairs, and out the front door, before she knew she was awake. She circled the house until she found Tilman thrashing in the yard at the end of his chain, flecks of foam at the corners of his mouth. His eyes were unfocused. He didn't see her at all.

"Stop it!" she screamed, flinging her body into his path, her fists pummelling flesh and the iron that encircled it. "You're bad, you're bad, you're all gone wrong!"

He stopped then and looked at Klara as if he'd never seen her before. She could see the harness rising and falling as he panted. He smelled of stale sweat.

Whirling away from him she ran into the house and used the pump at the sink to fill a large pot, then back in the yard she tossed water at him as if to quench the fire she sensed was in his bones. "Stop it!" she yelled again, and in her confusion and sorrow she threw the empty pot against the house. "You're bad," she sobbed. "You never stop being bad."

Tilman stood still, panting and staring at his ten-year-old sister. "I've stopped," he said, and then her name, "Klara."

Her feet were numb. The grass was crisp

with frost and the morning cold caused her teeth to chatter.

Upstairs, in the sudden silence, the exhausted parents tumbled again into a deep well of sleep.

He repeated her name, Klara, as if he'd never said it before, as if she'd never heard it before.

Every one of his ribs was bruised, the skin above them covered in plum-coloured blossoms. When he pulled up his shirt to show this to his sister, it was as if he were exposing his heart.

She winced and turned away. The colour of the morning in these few moments had changed from grey to golden.

Tilman pointed to the blacksmith's shed. "A hammer," he said. "Get me the hammer with the claw foot," and then her name again, "Klara."

She loved her brother, loved his beautiful face, even when it was contorted by rage, by fear. She fetched the hammer, then looked at the squint of concentration around Tilman's eyes as he pried from the door the large bent nails that held his chain. He twisted away from her, leaping down the lane that led to the road. She returned to her room and stood at the window watching her brother growing smaller and smaller in the distance, heading west with the newly risen sun on his back. She placed her inner arm on the window frame, pressed her forehead against her wrist, and counted to one hundred in order to let him get away. When she lifted her head she could still see him, his shadow twice the height of a full-grown man stretching out in front of him, his chain trailing behind him like print on the page of the road, like the end, or the beginning, of a story.

May of 1914 turned to June of 1914 and still Eamon stayed away from the Becker farm. Klara's father made only one remark about the young man's continuing absence, a remark that Klara suspected was delivered in order to save her pride.

"I expect the men at O'Sullivan's farm are just about as busy as we are here these days."

Klara said nothing. She hated his attempts at cheerful excuses. This desire to make ordinary all that was dark and unfathomable was a weakness in her father, a habit that had in the past stood in sharp contrast to her mother's anguish, her mother's fury. But he was also a man who, after his son's disappearance, would do anything rather than risk one more drop of rain falling into the ocean of his own concealed despair. He had in constant effect an unshakable policy of neutral appeasement.

"Almost haying time," he added, while his daughter pretended not to be listening.

They parted then, he leaving for the crops, she climbing the stairs to sew. She had been working every evening as long as the light lasted in order to finish a groom's waistcoat for Albert Stechley, and a satin gown and a veil for her neighbour, Katrin Erb, his bride-to-be. Klara's agreeing to work on the latter garment came dangerously close to dressmaking and would have shocked her mother, particularly because the fashions of the day inclined toward frills and laces and away from the strictly tailored.

"A good suit is all a woman needs for a wedding," her mother had always declared. "Anything else is mere frivolity."

The bride's dress was to have a line of buttons descending in a perfectly straight row down the centre of the bodice to the waist, but because the gown hooked at the back, these were to be for decorative purposes only. The bride herself would have been contented with buttons covered by the same satin fabric as made up the rest of the dress, but Klara had determined that a little picture, or symbol, by which the day might be commemorated should decorate the buttons. A flower perhaps, or the sliver of a new moon, or an open fan. For all her hidden passion for such details Klara was nevertheless a great believer in uniformity; there would only be one symbol or picture repeated. The choice would be difficult.

On this summer evening then, Klara sat cross-legged on the smooth surface of the large table in the sunroom surrounded by a semicircle of mother-of-pearl buttons, her back curved, her chin on one fist, her free hand picking up and then returning to its place one small object after another. Every now and then she lifted her head and squinted across the room in the direction of the tailor's dummy and the unfinished gown that adorned it, then resumed her study of the buttons. Years later she would still remember the images before her that night: the profile of a woman, a rampant lion with a marcasite eye, the moon, a star, several flowers, a spider, an apple, a cross, clasped hands, a fleur-de-lys, a maple leaf, a book, a coat of arms, a crown, a ruined tower, a bird, a pair of birds, an urn, a broken column, and a sampling of geometric shapes.

The top of the table that Klara sat upon, though over two feet wide, was made from a single board taken from one of the trees of the virgin forest that had filled the parish during Father Archangel Gstir's time. This irreplaceable woodland had been felled with alarming swiftness, had been floated down rivers to sawmills, loaded on lake boats, then shipped down the St. Lawrence River to the Atlantic Ocean. There it had been conveyed by schooners to an island on the other side of the sea, an island referred to as the Motherland. As a result of the Motherland's insatiable hunger for lumber, sawmills had opened all over Upper Canada, had flourished, had made small fortunes for their owners, and had closed and fallen into ruin — in the space of thirty years. All that remained now of the vast army of trees were vestiges in certain pieces of pioneer furniture and the odd oversized floorboard in a country house.

On that June evening, Klara sat on a slice of what had once been an extraordinarily large tree. The evening light moving through the window made an exact shadow of her head and shoulders in profile on the opposite wall.

She had almost decided to use the button with the twinned birds when she heard footsteps on the stairs. At first she thought it was her father, who might be wanting a book from the pile he kept beside his bed, but it wasn't long before she identified the sound as unfamiliar, tentative. The climber hesitated on the sixth step, then apparently descended to the fourth, which Klara recognized by its creak. (In the future Klara's foot would never touch that spot again without her mind remembering.) At least a minute passed before the person on the stairs began to ascend once more, and this time the footsteps were swift and purposeful.

Klara knew who it was, she *knew who it was.* And yet this knowledge did nothing to abate the shock of seeing Eamon O'Sullivan standing on the threshold of her sunroom tailor shop.

Characteristically, he said nothing.

"It's been six weeks," she heard herself declare in exasperation. "Six weeks — and now what do you want?"

He remained silent, staring at her from the doorway. Klara saw that small drops of sweat had beaded near his hairline.

In the midst of his silence and his scrutiny she felt the old anger returning, and she flushed and looked away from him. She dug her nails into her palm and counted to ten, not wanting to lose control. But it was too late, and she found herself confronting him with her scissors in her hand. "If you don't say something," she told him, "I'll stab you with these scissors. I *mean* it, Eamon. I'll cut your throat."

She didn't mean it, of course, but she was somewhat unnerved by how much she almost meant it. She held the scissors pointed toward him like a gun. "I'm serious, Eamon," she said. "I'll cut your ears . . ."

"I've come for a coat," he announced.

The hand that held the scissors dropped to Klara's side. "Oh," she said, "the coat. It's hanging on a nail in the woodshed . . . to the right of the door."

"I spoke," said Eamon. "I said something." Klara could see colour enter his neck and climb up his face toward his hair. "But it isn't my jacket that I'm after. I want you to make a waistcoat for me."

"Do you?" She was secretly pleased that he acknowledged her skill, aware of the necessary connection her sewing would make between them.

He nodded, not looking at her.

"I'll have to measure you," Klara said slowly, the horror of this now entering her mind. Then she looked him in the face with skepticism and said, "You don't have the money for it, do you?"

He pulled a wad of bills out of his pocket, walked across the room, and flung the money on the table. "I've been working these two months at the brewery," he told her.

"The brewery," Klara repeated.

"Yes, and farming too."

Klara could not meet his gaze. "What colour do you want then?" she asked.

"Red."

Klara had never made a red garment in her life. In fact, it was doubtful she had ever seen one, the costumes in her world being almost always black, white, or grey. "There is no excuse," her mother had said, "for flashy colour. No good can ever come of it." Then she took the bright pink hair ribbon that Klara had bought with a few pennies her grandfather had given her and dropped it into the stove. "Are you sure it's red you want?" Klara asked dubiously.

"Red," Eamon said again with great certainty.

"You can't have a red waistcoat."

"And why can't I?"

"It wouldn't do at all. No good will come of it." Klara was horrified. She remembered that while she wept for the burning satin her mother had lectured her on the subject of subtlety and taste.

"I want it to be red," Eamon asserted.

"Burgundy perhaps . . ."

But he held his ground, was not to be dissuaded.

Vanity, Klara thought, which according to her mother was the most common of the deadly sins, or at least the one most often exhibited in the presence of tailors.

"My hair is black," continued Eamon. "My eyes are green. Red goes well with both."

Klara hadn't known his eyes were green, and was too uncomfortable now to confirm what he was saying. Just like a peacock, she thought.

"Maybe," Eamon said softly, "maybe you don't know how to make a red waistcoat." Gaining confidence from the argument that he believed he had won, he was now able to look her in the face.

"Of course I do," said Klara. "What possible difference could the colour make?"

"None at all," Eamon grinned. "So you'll make it red then?"

Klara sniffed, crossed the room to a set of shelves where she rummaged in a wooden box until she extracted a light brown measuring tape and a small black notebook. "I'll have to measure you," she repeated.

Eamon, apparently exhausted by conversation but still smiling at his victory,

106

slumped on a stool at the opposite end of the room.

"Stand up," Klara said.

He stood.

"Stand up straight."

Eamon squared his shoulders and thrust out his chin.

Klara approached him. "The first measurement," she said, "is the neck."

She placed the cool, flat tape on the back of his neck, drawing it together just over his Adam's apple. She could feel his breath brushing her cheekbone as he repeated the words "the neck."

Klara wrote the number of inches in the small book under the heading *Red (!) waistcoat for Silent Irish.* "The next measurement is the bodice," she informed him as she pushed her thumb against the hollow between his collarbones, then slid her fingers down the tape until it reached his homemade leather belt.

"Are there more measurements?" Eamon asked while Klara was writing.

"Oh yes, many," she replied. "The next is the width of the chest at the shoulders." She measured and recorded the information. "Then the width of the chest from beneath the arms. She could hear his heart beating and, to her consternation, her own. "Turn around," she said.

He turned.

She pulled the tape across his shoulders, surprised at their width after the slenderness of his torso. "Turn back," she told him as she wrote again in the book. "Now the arm."

They were facing each other again. Klara ran the tape down Eamon's arm.

"Do you know," he asked, his voice breaking slightly, "do you know that your hands are like doves?"

Klara cleared her throat. "The waist," she whispered, choosing to pretend she had not heard him and thanking God silently she had never made trousers.

"You," he said, "with your neck like a swan." This statement was delivered when Klara had both arms around his middle and her cheek near his beating heart. "You who'll have nothing to do with a man like me."

With shaking hands Klara recorded the measurement in her book. In her mind she ran out of the room, down the stairs, across the orchard, and into the cedar woods. "I'll have to measure your hips," she said uncertainly, keeping her gaze directed at the floor. "I'll have to do that for the fit to be right."

He seemed not to hear her. "I'll die of this," he told her. "These words about you running and running through my mind."

She bent toward him, fixing her eyes on the dark printed numbers.

"And me remaining silent for months and months, tasting the humiliation of knowing that once I spoke you'd be gone from me like a startled bird."

Doves, thought Klara, looking at her own hands. *Doves*. She looped the tape around the back of him and pulled it tightly across his hip bones. Now she seemed to be moving in a dream, through water.

He put one hand on her hair. "Your hair," he whispered.

The panic in her was enough to make her wish for his old silence, her old impatience. Still she straightened and looked into his face. Green eyes.

"Do you never think of me?" he implored.

"Never," Klara whispered. She was unaware that she still held the tape, taut, at the front of his body.

"I'll die of this," he said, and kissed her on the mouth.

Klara found that she was kissing him back and the surprise caused her throat to constrict. She let the tape fall from his hips and brought her hands up to her face. "Why, *why* must you have a red waistcoat?" she gasped, though it wasn't at all what she meant to say.

Eamon drew quickly away, then began to pace back and forth across the room. "I'll leave the country," he declared, "and you'll not recall me for a moment. On you'll go with your life, sitting by another man's fire, while I'm an outcast moving from town to town, desperate at the very thought of you. I'll die in the winter ditch like a dog."

He crossed the room and placed his hands on either side of her face.

"But the waistcoat . . ." she began.

"Is for my funeral," he finished her sentence. "Make it well."

Then he bolted from the room and thundered down the stairs, leaving Klara shaking as she attempted to write his measurements in her little black book.

She lay awake all night, flat on her back, sweating under a quilt made from scraps of broadcloth and feather stitched with scarlet embroidery thread. The quilt was much too heavy for the season and she wanted to remove it, but she was immobilized, paralyzed by the enormity of the experience in the sunroom. Her mother's declarations concerning the frivolity of the female sex ran through her mind. *That girl doesn't have the sense to come in out of the rain, doesn't have the good sense God gave a goose.* The few times she almost dissolved into sleep Eamon's face bloomed on the edge of a dream and hovered over hers until she wanted to claw it out of the way. She was certain the scent of him had followed her into the bedroom.

The thought of his desperation caused tears to fill her eyes. Then, inexplicably, she would find herself pounding the mattress on either side of her with her fists. Where in the world was she to get red broadcloth? She would have to send to Toronto for it, or maybe even farther, maybe as far as Montreal. French people — her mother had disapproved of French people — often wore flamboyant clothes, flashy colours.

She tried to remember everything she could about him — from church, from school — but he had always been so quiet there seemed to be nothing to retrieve. Like her, he had been quick and capable in the classroom, but because he was a few years older, there had not been the usual competition between them. His family, she knew, was a little less tidy, a little less organized, and somewhat poorer than most in the predominantly German village, and Klara recalled her mother attributing this to their Irish background. His own mother went to mass more than was good for her, though Klara's mother had to concede that with five children there was much to pray about. He had four sisters, all younger than himself.

He had never really run with the other boys, though they had seemed to like him well enough, and he them. Preferring solitary activities and being handy in his own way, he had been a prodigious maker of kites and could be spotted on breezy days far off in the hills with something ungainly pulling like an angry fish on a string he held with both hands. Often his less successful projects could be seen as tattered and forlorn as ghosts tangled in the bare limbs of winter trees. Once, Klara had found a kite in early spring, soiled by mud and half-covered by old snow, out behind her barn.

Klara rolled over on her side and suddenly remembered something. When they had been children, at the time when the whole village had been speaking of her brother's disappearance, Eamon had told her that he could help her send a message

112

to Tilman if she wanted. She had followed the boy home from school, and had gone with him into a plain brown shed. Suddenly she had been surrounded by the anxious movement and quavering noise of penned birds.

"You write what you want to say on this piece of paper," he had said, producing a scrap from his pocket, "then I'll tie it to a bird and send it off to Tilman."

The birds were swarming around their feet like a dirty grey river. Klara was disgusted by them, and suspicious. "How will the bird know where Tilman has gone?" she asked.

"They've flown everywhere," Eamon assured her, "and they've seen everything. I'll talk to this one," he pointed to a bird with brown markings that was pecking at his boot. "I'll talk to him and tell him to look for your brother."

Klara prepared her message on the windowsill of the shed in the dim light. "Dear Tilman," she wrote with a pencil from her schoolbag, "Please send me a letter with this bird." She knew better than to ask him to come home. "I made you a present," she wrote instead, hoping to entice him. "See if you can find it."

"I've been training them for a year,"

Eamon told her. "I have eighteen of them now."

Klara handed him the paper and watched as he rolled it up and fastened it to the bird's leg. Outside the bird flew off into a cold winter sky.

When she asked a few weeks later, Eamon told Klara that the bird had returned with the unanswered message still tied to its leg. She didn't know which boy to distrust more: the one who always went away or the one who sent messages that could never be answered.

I will die of this, she thought as the beginnings of birdsong entered her room and then realized with bewilderment that it was his voice saying this, speaking in her mind. At the first hint of light she rose from the bed to look out the window. The yard was a sensible grey colour, not a hint of red in it, but there was an ominous band of hot scarlet on the eastern horizon. Having no idea how she was going to live through the day, she didn't dress but descended the stairs instead in her nightgown and bare feet.

In the kitchen she made a pot of coffee and drank two cups. Then she went outside and bent over the rain barrel to wash her hair. Two crows were shrieking at each other from pine trees at opposite ends of the yard. She couldn't decide whether they were engaged in a quarrel or an exchange of ribald jokes, but everything about their tone suggested sarcasm, insolence.

Your neck like a swan. Klara hated herself for permitting the phrase to enter her mind as she drew her hair up from this same neck. She remembered that she had threatened to kill Eamon with the scissors, then began to imagine the coat she would make for him. This led to an image of his black hair and earnest green eyes, the look of a red garment, a white shirt under it, and his pale throat rising out of a collar. There was something about his own neck, but she couldn't say exactly what it was. Klara flung her head back, and the water from her hair soaked her nightgown, which clung to her back like a membrane. She recalled that her wrist had rested on his neck for a few moments when they had fallen on the ice, and she blushed at the memory.

All day she was alone with herself in a way she had never been before, looking inward, aware of each emotional shift. When she dressed that morning she stared at her body for the first time in a self-conscious way, as if it were someone else's body altogether, the nipples hardening under her gaze. Then she put on her cotton summer clothes, and a smock, and left the house for her workshop. Once there she circled the roughed-out form of the abbess for some time without once being moved to pick up the chisel. The thought of Eamon clung to her the way the wet nightgown had clung to her back, and it seemed that there had not yet been invented an exercise that would help her peel him off.

Finally, in the heat of noon, she unrolled her pattern paper on the sunroom floor and began to map out the shapes Eamon's measurements suggested. All sounds were exaggerated, by her exhaustion and her preoccupation: the crackle of the paper, the squeaking of the pencil as she pushed hard against it. The house had recently been invaded by mud-dauber wasps — harmless enough, they didn't sting — but they browsed in her vicinity, indolently, their long legs hanging in the air like frail threads. Her wakefulness felt more like drunkenness and drowsing. She crouched over the paper on the floor and considered hidden pockets for the inside of the garment. What would he protect there? She drew the darts with great concentration, frowning as she calculated their width and how they should taper, then she drew in the pieces of the pattern until the paper was filled with curved lines like a map. Eventually she lay on her stomach, her shoulders echoed by her drawing of his larger ones, her arms on the drawing of his sleeves, and fell asleep.

When she awoke in midafternoon, and when she rolled up the large piece of brown paper, she was amazed to see that she had pushed the pencil so forcefully into the paper that the pattern she had drawn remained incised on the pine floor.

That night as she teetered on the edge of sleep, Klara heard music so achingly sad, so astonishingly pure and clear, that her entire body was alert to the sound. She walked furtively over to the window, as if she feared she might awaken a number of unfamiliar ghosts or alternative selves. She saw then, far off in the blossoming orchard, under the light of a partial moon, a small narrow shape with bent arms raised like wings. The wind was down, so the fiddle music seemed to be the only element awake and moving in the night, as if all the grief in the world were distilled into this thread of sound whose destination was her window. Eamon's father often played the fiddle at weddings, or at the tavern, and Eamon himself had once played "O Tannenbaum" at a school Christmas pageant. Klara knew all this. And yet, by the following morning, she had almost convinced herself that the music and the figure in the orchard had been merely an unsettling dream.

Then at breakfast, after her father had left the table, and while she sat gazing absently out the window with a half-finished bowl of oatmeal cooling in front of her, Klara saw something white begin to twitch, then launch itself skyward from the brow of the hill behind her father's cow pasture — one of Eamon's kites, though Eamon himself was hidden from view. The oddest-shaped kite she had ever seen, it nevertheless flew well in the early-morning breeze. Klara found herself smiling as she realized that he must have used his mother's bedsheets or muslin curtains in an attempt to make the object look like a bird. A swan. A dove.

The next day Klara awoke full of shame, sleep having manoeuvred her into the rational past, away from this preposterous present. She had allowed Eamon's foolishness — his dramatics and his antics — to make her dreamy and idle, she decided. She was determined to get back to work on the wooden statue, to finish it by the end of summer, hoping that the combination of the work and the purposefulness and energy she wanted to carve into the woman's face might strengthen her own character. The nuns had told her that any medieval abbess would necessarily have had to be practical. Apart from the day-to-day business of running an abbey, some had even delivered sermons, and some had actually lectured to bishops, cardinals, popes! She immediately banished the image of the scarlet apparel these dignitaries brought to her mind. But she would attend to the business of the waistcoat as well, completing it as soon as possible. It would be a task like any other task, and when it was accomplished she would be done with it. And done with Eamon too.

She wanted to squeeze him out of her life, the way a dart tapers an article of clothing, the fabric loose and supple at the place the needle enters, completely conquered at the point where the thread ends: an accommodation, on the one hand, and a complete disguise, on the other, of what were unmentionable body parts. A breast, a buttock. Or parts that were only slightly less unmentionable: the place where the waist on a woman blossomed into a hip, or a shoulder rising toward the neck. *Neck like a swan,* she thought, then squirmed away from the reminder.

How had he managed to twist her attention, swing it round in the direction of his face, his long silences, and now his abrupt reappearance, that one kiss. Klara had read about passionate embraces, but in the books she loved they had always taken place out of doors, in English gardens or on sweeping moorland, not in a tailor's workshop nor, for that matter, in a village like Shoneval. She had imagined that one day she would be approached by a man who would want to touch her, but in her imagination this individual was mature, worldly, could never be a boy she had known from school. No. He would have to come from somewhere else, from Europe, from Britain. She felt she had been abducted by Eamon in the midst of a journey to this other, unknown person, that he had cast a spell on her thoughts so that like his birds they would always return to him no matter how far they flew. Perhaps the carving would free her from this. She recalled with pleasure and relief certain periods of intense concentration when it would be as if she had fallen down a wooden well or had become lost inside a wooden cave, as if the world and its complicated inhabitants had disappeared, the only relationship in her life was developing between her and the figure emerging from the block. By the time you finish even the smallest figures, her grandfather had told her, you must know all about them: their habits, their weaknesses, what they had for supper yesterday, who their enemies are, where they spent last night. She had laughed then, but Joseph Becker remained unsmiling. This was the only way, he maintained, that one could make a statue live, make it affect those who came to look at it.

She decided to visit her grandfather now, wanting to borrow the delicate chisels she could not yet afford, chisels that would more precisely render the medieval woman's face. She also wanted, under the circumstances, some instruction on concentration. But before she left the house she leafed through her catalogues until she found a good red worsted material that could be purchased from a firm in Montreal. Reeling at the expense, she nevertheless wrote a letter ordering the required yardage. Then she untied her apron and left the kitchen through the adjacent woodshed where her brother's folding cot remained leaning against the wall in the shadows of the farthest corner as it had done for almost a decade. Feeling the sun on her face and hands as she walked down the lane that led to the road, her spirits lifted somewhat.

How beautiful the day was! Shoneval, finally at the peak of what Father Gstir had envisaged as its destiny, was filled with the flowering trees and shrubs of June. Lilac, spirea, cherry, and apple. Klara couldn't help but notice the opulence of the display. As she walked past the brewery she could feel Eamon's presence behind the soft yellow of the windowless brick wall. Even the small river that was the brewery's driving force seemed to speak of him, its voice melodic, emotionally charged, the water moving and shining. Klara shook herself and walked away — though the bright afterimage remained behind her eyes as she walked past Hafeman's store and up the hill toward Father Gstir's magnificent church. When she cut through the cemetery she paused to cross herself at her mother's grave, then wandered through marble stones and iron crosses to the fence that marked the beginning of her grandfather's property. His fields and pastures. His apple orchard. And the tidy Canadian farmhouse that was never a home to him in the way that his barn workshop was — for it was in his workshop that he preserved Europe. To enter this cluttered space was to taste, for just a moment, the flavour of everything he had lost. Markets and cathedrals, medieval cities whose spires stood like a bouquet on the horizon, and rivers over which arched bridges of such beauty that the old man's eyes filled with tears whenever he described them.

Klara stood in the doorway of the barn and watched as her grandfather worked. Everything about him was hunched and crooked from years of bending over various kinds of labour. The gristmill, the farm, and always this carving. He was bowed toward a relief panel with reverential affection, chisel and hammer in hand. As long as Klara could remember, her grandfather's fingers had been twisted and arthritic. And yet his hands were large and strong, with veins and sinews like a net of ropes rising from the skin. And his gestures, when touching wood or making a conversational point, were tender yet assured. He turned from his work, to look at his granddaughter, and his face lifted into multiple creases, as if the drapery of his many carved saints, prophets, apostles, and evangelists had taken up residence on his supple skin.

As Klara entered the barn, a lamb lying near the work table scrambled to its feet and cantered out into the yard. "Now look what you've done," said her grandfather, but not unkindly. "It took me all morning to coax the little devil in here."

"Was he a model?" Klara asked.

"That too," said her grandfather, "but also I was keeping him from your grandmother's spirea bushes. One more bite and we would be having him for dinner Sunday night." He began to clean the chisel he held in his hand with a cloth. "How is your abbess?" he asked. "Have you finished her yet?"

Klara did not answer but crouched down instead to look at her grandfather's latest carving. He had completed more than half of the spokes of radiance that emanated from the relief of the holy lamb's body. The floor around the piece was littered with spirals of paper-thin wood. "No," said Klara, still examining the piece, "I've had tailoring to do."

" 'It were noble occupation for ingenious youths without employment to exercise themselves in this art.' It was Dürer who said it."

Klara rose and crossed the floor to a small, partly finished altarpiece. She used her skirt to polish the hat of one of the figures where sawdust had gathered around the rim. She could not see how the statement applied to her — a wood sculptor, and a woman. Her grandfather, however, loved to tell how the year Tilman was born a book of Dürer's writings became available through a university in England, and how he had travelled all the way to Toronto to purchase it. It had contained, among other things, instructions from the great master on how a boy might be raised toward becoming the maker of "great, far reaching, and infinite art." This was seen as a highly auspicious sign by their grandfather and, after Tilman's birth, he lectured his daughter-in-law mercilessly on the subject. It was suggested that "the child be kept eager to learn and not vexed" and "that he dwell in a pleasant house so that he be distracted by no manner of hindrance." Dürer had never been mentioned in relation to Klara's upbringing and this had not gone unnoticed by her. But, in

125

truth, a few years after Tilman's disappearance, her father had forbidden any reference to the book in his house, knowing that each time the grandfather quoted from it, the boy's absence became more palpable, and his wife more vengeful. Once, after the book had been brought out, Klara's mother turned to her twelve-year-old daughter with madness in her eyes and whispered, "Why are *you* still here? Why don't you run away?" The grandfather had snapped the book shut then and had taken Klara by the hand out of the house to his own farm, where she stayed for several weeks under the care of her quiet grandmother. Everything in her had wanted to go home, believing that by staying with her grandparents she *had* run away, that she had proved her mother right. But her grandfather would not relent, and as neither parent came to fetch her, she began to believe that all of the adults surrounding her were complicitous, wanted her somehow to be gone.

Still, she loved and admired her grandfather and wanted to learn everything she could from him, so she patiently listened to him on the subject of Tilman, the subject of Dürer, knowing that he would be unable to mention either name anywhere

126

else. But today he veered briefly from the subject, the teacher in him stepping forward. "You must remember about the face," he was saying now. "This abbess would not be a pretty woman necessarily. She would be strong, a true leader. On the rare occasion, popes and cardinals might have even taken counsel from her."

Klara wandered around the barn picking up one tool after another. She did not want to admit to her grandfather that she didn't know which chisels to ask for. He would never let those he had brought with him from Bavaria out of his sight, had never permitted anyone other than Tilman to touch them, though in truth the boy had not entirely taken to the carving. But he was generous with his more prosaic tools, the ones he had purchased in this country. He watched his granddaughter slap a mallet against her palm as if testing its punch.

"My tools from the old country I will give to your brother when he returns," he said, "but you may have all the mallets you want."

Klara was silent. Her brother's existence was barely believable any more. She had ceased to be curious about his whereabouts. It wasn't as if he were dead exactly, more as if he had never been born. In the earlier days when he disappeared for only short periods of time, Klara faintly remembered weeping, and pestering him to tell where he'd been. She also remembered frantic games of hide and seek where with pounding heart she would struggle through the bush lot calling and calling Tilman's name, certain that she would never find him and that by agreeing to play she would somehow be held responsible for his disappearance. Now, looking back, she thought about the oddness of this child's game, how the seeker would lean against a tree, arm lifted, forehead on wrist, in an attitude of despair, enduring the one hundred seconds that would allow the other to successfully dematerialize. She also recalled following the boy through the village to their grandfather's barn, where the old man would patiently explain, for Tilman's benefit alone, the various tools and then would demonstrate an assortment of cuts and flourishes.

Klara moved to the east side of the barn where stood her grandfather's masterpiece, the one he had never been able to part with, though he had said it would go to the church when he died. The Virgin of Mercy stood with her arms slightly raised, her open cloak sheltering a small crowd of devotees, among them Klara's brother as he was last seen, a child of twelve. Whenever he could her grandfather included a likeness of Tilman in his carving, hoping perhaps that the God for whom he carved would interpret this as a petition or a prayer. He will never be forgotten, thought Klara bitterly. We can't even speak of him, but they will never forget him.

To her grandfather she said suddenly, "Tilman has been gone a long, long time, you know. Perhaps . . ."

"You remember," the old man broke in, "what she did? Your own mother. A terrible thing. After that . . . after he escaped, is it any wonder he would go away for a longer time."

"It wasn't his fault," said Klara.

"He would have a broken heart from being chained like an animal." Her grandfather shook his head sadly. "A broken heart."

Her grandfather had been the one to diagnose Tilman's wanderlust during the boy's first disappearance. While everyone in the parish had walked through the fields and had beaten their way through forests and swamps, while ponds and rivers were dragged and prayers were offered up to

Saints Nicholas and Lambert, while masses were said and candles were lit, Joseph Becker never once gave into the belief that his grandson was lost forever. His daughter-in law took to her bed in despair, his son abandoned his fields, and his own wife moved into the household to look after little Klara, who was practically forgotten in the panic. And still the old man held to his position that the boy would return. Four months later, when the six-year-old did return, sauntering into the house at nightfall without a word of explanation and taking his usual place at the table, announcing he was hungry, it was Joseph Becker who had the sense neither to question nor scold him.

Everyone else believed, in the beginning, that the boy must have been abducted by tinkers, who without a shred of evidence were always blamed for such things. But Tilman quickly put an end to these fancies. "I went for a walk," he said and then, when pressed, "I followed the road." He showed little interest in further detailing his adventures and eventually, when questioned, developed the good-natured evasiveness Klara would later encounter in him. The family was forced to surmise, by certain French phrases that had crept into his vocabulary and an ability to make omelettes from hens' eggs, that he must have gone as far as Quebec.

"He is a wunderkind," the grandfather would explain. "Often they develop wanderlust." It was a state almost common among boys in Bavaria. These children were considered cursed in some ways, but mostly they were thought to be blessed as they had often proved useful for guarding wandering flocks in high, distant summer pastures. "They are wonderful climbers," Joseph had told his worried son and daughter-in-law, "and good singers. Sometimes they become poets. Often when they become men, they settle. Tilman here," the grandfather put his hand on the boy's blond head, "Tilman will settle, and he will become a carver."

Joseph had tried repeatedly and unsuccessfully to interest Tilman in making a small figure-in-the-round. As he lectured him on the merits of limewood and as he repeated Dürer's instructions for the six attitudes of the human frame, the boy had stared absently at a bas-relief panel in the corner. Thinking that the child was fascinated by the "S" curve of Saint Sebastien's body and by the hundreds of arrows projecting from it, the old man carried the panel into a shaft of sunlight that shone through the door.

Tilman ignored the suffering saint but ran his long, tapered fingers over the texture of the distant landscape behind the celebrated martyr. "Teach me how to make that," he said.

Klara, having heard this story several times, resolved even at her young age to always concentrate on figures-in-the-round. Her grandfather had told her about the famous, sacred statue of the Infant Jesus of Prague, about its "garderobe" filled with dozens of dresses, and about the two jewelled crowns. "It would be almost the same size as your biggest doll," he told her. Though he had of course never seen this wonder, he pencilled a picture of the small sculpture on a piece of scrap lumber. Klara was delighted by the idea of a boy doll, holy or otherwise, wearing dresses, and she set to work immediately carving the body from a section of an abandoned porch pillar and making the dresses from her mother's scraps. But something else about the story had fascinated her: her grandfather said there was a legend about the monk who created the holy statue, that he had had a vision of the infant Jesus while working in his garden and had wanted to make a likeness but couldn't complete the face. "He couldn't complete the face," Joseph said, speaking mostly to himself, remembering, "until he allowed each detail of it to enter his heart. He had to revision it, you see, had to see it again, but not with his eyes, with his heart."

"How did he finish the statue?" asked Klara. "When did he do the face?"

Joseph looked at his granddaughter in surprise. He hardly knew he had been speaking aloud. "After hoping for a long time, he had another vision, a vision of the heart . . . with everything clear and joyful but at the same time terribly, terribly painful. When it was over, he was able to finish the face in minutes."

He sighed, came slowly back from the Bavarian workshop where he had trained as a boy and first heard this story, and turned toward his work table, away from the rapt little girl who had been listening and the quiet boy who had not.

Tilman had proved, in very short order, to be a genius of distant views, a kind of miniaturist when it came to detail but concerned with phenomena so far away their specificities dissolved into texture when

133

looked upon by an unpractised eye. Despite his grandfather's best efforts, he remained unmoved by either narrative or personality. He turned away from the facial expressions and gestures in his grandfather's carving as if embarrassed by them, as if he had been caught spying on another's intimate moments. Looking always beyond the drama imposed by the figures in bas-reliefs, he pointed to the swells of hills, or the stipple of forests, and moved by cloud formations looming over polished horizons. Wise man that his grandfather was, he encouraged this, allowing Tilman to use the smallest and most delicate tools he had brought from the old country: twist augers, gouges and chisels, miniature calipers. He taught him how to make the suggestion of a pine forest behind the spires of a distant hill town, and then how to render the much removed hill town itself. He described the towers and walls and "the Münster" of the city of Ulm, a city he had seen only once when he was not much older than his grandson. And then, because he could not stop himself, he spoke of the linden trees that were used by the boy's namesake, Tilman Riemenschneider, and by the other great wood sculptors during the miraculous flowering of the sixteenth century. Altarpieces, he told the boy, with tracery so delicate and fine you would swear the artists were descended from spiders. Figures, he enthused, in attitudes so rife with emotion one wept with joy or sorrow — sometimes both — just to follow the lines of limbs and drapery with one's eyes.

By the time the old man had reached this point of the lecture, Tilman would have turned away, drawn himself inward, would have become distant from his grandfather's passion. But Klara, who was playing with wooden scraps near the door, Klara, to whom no enthusiastic remarks had been addressed, never forgot her grandfather's words.

Once Tilman had discovered what it was he wanted to carve, he excelled at every landscape project he undertook, completing the small panels in an astonishingly short time. Sometimes he added herds and flocks and even the odd series of fences to the scene, but the grandfather learned that the appearance of these details often foretold the boy's departure, as if even anonymous references to human activity suggested an intimacy that Tilman simply wasn't able to maintain.

★ ★ ★

Despite her tidy appearance and orderly conduct, Klara had wanted her grandfather or, failing that, the Sisters of the Immaculate Conception to tell her everything they knew and anything they could imagine about the lives of the saints her grandfather carved, particularly about their lives before sainthood — moments of sin especially fascinated her. She suspected, for instance, that her namesake, the famous Chiara of Italy, had been in love with Saint Francis, and had left her parents' comfortable home in order to follow him, and that the many pious works of her strict, contemplative life would have been enacted as bids for his approval and affection. She believed (even more heretically and secretively) that the Virgin Mary had been in love with the Holy Spirit, and that she had spent the remainder of her days pining for this spirit and longing for another miraculous union.

The nuns, sensing a current of passion and imagination running beneath Klara's serene expression and good deportment, suggested a course of study that included much reference to female saints who had been abbesses rather than those who had been visionaries or martyrs, hoping that the practical side of the young girl's nature would be encouraged by their example of hard work and selfless attention to others. Klara's idle hands, they suspected, might be the Devil's playground.

The lamb had begun shyly to inch its way back into the barn. "Come," said Joseph, holding out his hand, "come back in here now and stay out of mischief. If the old woman sees you with flowers in your mouth, you'll be eating parsley and mint on Sunday." The animal stayed near the door, looking at Klara warily. "Oh, she's all right," said her grandfather. "She won't hurt you."

"Would my abbess ever have been in love?" Klara asked. "I need to know for the carving, for the face."

Joseph Becker looked skeptical. "Of course," he said wryly, "for the carving. Perhaps you should be asking such questions about the Irish saints."

Klara flushed but said nothing. Her father, she now knew, had been speaking about Eamon's visits. She imagined him laughing and winking as he described the boy.

"Father Gstir always claimed the Irish saints were the most passionate," her grandfather continued. "Passionate believers, passionate travellers, passionate scholars, passionate speakers. Might they not have been, at some time during their lives, passionate lovers as well?"

In the spring of 1868, the young Joseph Becker had worked on the model of Father Gstir's church in the early-morning hours, beginning by the light of a lantern, then moving outside when the first glow of dawn became strong enough for him to see by. He made use of leftover cedar shingles from the despised sawmill and horse-hoof glue that he kept simmering on his stove during the few short hours he was able to sleep. He had never done this kind of work before, but as a boy had admired the gorgeous branching of Veit Stoss's lacelike sculptural work and so was able to understand the beauty of a structure through which a breeze might be able to blow and light might be able to shine. The beauty of line, and then the clear air.

Father Gstir was full of instructions — mostly concerning the Gothic style he had decided was right for his project. The nave, the side aisles, the radiating chapels, the tracery, and the bits of coloured cloth meant to represent splendid stained glass. A tympanum! Could Joseph carve a minia-ture Christ in Majesty? Should there not be buttresses? Flying buttresses?

Joseph, overworked as he was, refused to make miniature altars, miniature statues of the Virgin.

"But we will need money for the interior as well," Father Gstir said, "for the altars and the magnificent pulpit. And you, Joseph, you will be the carver of these wonders. What about the baptismal font? Ludwig must know that we need money for all of it."

"I am only one man," said Joseph.

"Think of what you will learn," enthused the priest.

"I only wanted to carve limewood figures. I have never wanted to make a toy church."

"We'll need relics," said Father Gstir, ignoring this last statement. "Yes, we must have relics. I will apply to Rome immediately for relics." Weather, the entity that in this terrain was the most impossible to dismiss, sprang immediately to mind. "We will need protection from storms and particularly, because of the church's high elevation, from lightning, so I will write to Rome today for relics of Saint Sebaldus and Saint Vitus." Father Gstir slapped his cheek. A smear of blood remained on his skin. The priest seemed lost in thought.

"Saint Narcissus," he said at last. "We must have protection from insect bites as well."

Joseph was beginning to feel he needed protection from Father Gstir. "I will not make tiny relics," he announced.

The priest was shocked. "Make relics?" he cried. "Only God and the saints can make relics." He crossed himself.

"Perhaps you should hire a saint to make this toy church," said Joseph under his breath while removing a pot of bubbling glue from the stove.

"I heard you," said Father Gstir, shaking his finger in the direction of his friend, "but remember, this toy church is a model of the house of God!"

Both men were silent for a moment. Then the priest spoke again. "And we will need a bell," he ventured. "We will need a little iron bell for the model. The king must understand that the church is incomplete without a bell."

"A bell," muttered Joseph. "In this whole territory I have not seen one bell."

"First a small one, then a large," said the priest.

With a thin brush, Joseph began to apply glue to the edge of the miniature porch.

"A cowbell!" said Father Gstir. "That will be just the thing."

"Too large."

"A goat's bell then."

"Have you seen any goats here? I have not seen a single goat since I left Bavaria."

"I will write to the bishop in Hamilton for a small bell," the priest announced, undaunted. "He will surely find one." He opened his arms and lifted his smiling face toward the morning sun that shone through the window of Joseph's workshop. Then, abruptly, he turned and looked at the younger man. "You must not be discouraged," he said. "The little church will come easily to you. And the finishing touches of your Virgin and your Crucifixion. I will pray to Saint Olaf and Saint Blaise, both patrons of carvers, and the little church will practically finish itself."

Four weeks later, in the middle of June, on a bright, clear morning, the one hundred and fifty-seven souls who made up the parish of the Township of Carrick began to emerge from the northern forest on a variety of tracks. A number of the parishioners had two or three unfortunate-looking animals in tow, and some of the women carried infants in their arms. But what they had left at home were shanties and huts that barely kept out the cold, greasy fireplaces, animals too sick to travel, buried babies, mud, and a bone-chilling fear of the dispirited native peoples whom they had all but forced out of the vicinity — though one or two Ojibway had joined the crowd on this morning to see what the fuss was about.

And what had these people in mind to see? Few knew, other than they were going to witness *something someone had done*, a project completed for reasons other than survival, which, to a settler, would seem an act of pure madness, likely to result in sudden death. That anyone, even a priest, would waste valuable time in this terrain making a parade, would cause painted objects to be carried around in the company of a group of sad backwoods animals, seemed to them to be so absurd that they couldn't resist the novelty. None of them had ever been to a fair, or a dance, or a strawberry social. Few had even spent time at their neighbours' houses. And many had never even set eyes on their fellow citizens from the southern part of the province, some of whom were arriving by buggy at the same moment, on the better though still rough track that came up from

Goderich and spilled down toward the two mills of the officially unrecognized village of Shoneval.

The splendidly robed Father Gstir, who had solemnly taken his place at the head of what he hoped would soon be something resembling a Corpus Christi procession, held aloft on top of a pole the model church Joseph Becker had finished to the last tiny cedar shake on the miniature roof. When the good Father pivoted to bark orders to the assembling participants, he could hear the tinkling of the bell the bishop had sent from Hamilton by special messenger just days before. Behind the priest, flushed with pride, stood one of the larger mill workers, who had secretly completed a model of a brewery while Joseph was working on the church. After some discussion, Father Gstir had agreed that this small edifice might also be carried on a pole in the procession. He, himself, had taken note of the suitability of the bubbling streams of Shoneval for the making of beer and was happy to hear that the men had been praying for anything at all.

When the mill workers got wind of this, a burst of activity ensued during which the men engaged in hasty and considerably

144

less than skilful model-making after hours, creating renditions of structures they either remembered fondly from their pasts or fervently hoped would appear in their futures. All claimed to have been petitioning God and the Blessed Virgin for such architectural works, and so what could Father Gstir do but agree to their participation in what was becoming a very colourful Corpus Christi procession. Some now carried the fortified farms of their Bavarian childhoods, some carried the castles they remembered standing on distant European hills. One carried a dovecote, one carried a medieval wash house. One man, whom Father Gstir had presumed to be the least religious of the lot, carried a convent and another, who came from Munich, carried an opera house. Two men who had clearly worked together on the tavern model now stood arguing over who should be permitted to carry it, and one thin, ascetic-looking mill worker carried a brightly painted, turreted, and gargoyled building that only he, and God (whom he had been petitioning for same), knew was a brothel.

Joining them now was the unhappy collection of pasture animals loaned by the settlers for this festive day, many having been driven as far as fifteen miles through the bush. Almost all of them, at the priest's suggestion, had been decorated after a fashion with berries and grapevines and wildflowers. One cow was so completely covered with ears of Indian corn she appeared to be wearing a complicated suit of armour. Several tired-looking horses were complaining and shaking their heads, attempting to remove the wreaths their owners had attached to their bridles.

Two powerful mill workers struggled with Joseph's crucifix, and four more held aloft the Virgin and Child on a platform they carried on their shoulders. Much earlier in the morning the Irishman had begun to play a series of reels, and, as the hours wore on, he was able, with the help of an accordion player, to incite the singing of songs not altogether appropriate to the occasion.

What with all the building of model architecture, and talk of music and festivities, and rumours of sumptuous outdoor altars being created for "popish and pagan worship in the woods," news of the procession had reached as far as such civilized and somewhat industrialized centres as Listowel and Stratford, and just as Father Gstir was attempting to instill some order into the proceedings, the bell on his church jingling angrily, a contingent of grim-faced Orangemen dismounted from carriages and strode purposefully toward the crowd.

Father Gstir, who had never seen an "orange man," naturally enough believed that, if and when one appeared in his life, he would be dressed in pumpkin-coloured clothing and, as a result, readily recognizable. He therefore welcomed these vibrantly sashed visitors warmly and told them how delighted he was by their intention to add their splendid drums to the musical element of the procession, despite the plethora of Gaelic invectives their appearance had caused to issue from the mouth of the fiddle player. The Orangemen were placed somewhere near the middle of the parade, and after a minute or two of confused hesitation, they fell in line, agreeing amongst themselves that their participation could only be beneficial.

Years later Joseph Becker would entertain his granddaughter with stories of this day: how the procession had visited the four outdoor altars, one situated in each corner of the acre that would hold the church and the graveyard, made by Father

Gstir himself from cedar boughs. He described how one of the Orangemen had insisted that the white horse that had pulled his carriage should be unhitched so that she might enter the parade (and how that horse, in full view of the crowd, had been mounted by one of the backwoods horses, who turned out not to be so tired after all), and how the entire gathering had feasted on picnic lunches at the site of the future church.

Three months later a log church, built by the mill workers, stood on the spot, and near the springs in the valley, an enterprising couple lured to Shoneval by the procession were beginning to build a brewery. The Orangemen, full of fellowship and food, had announced before leaving that they would return each June at the feast of Corpus Christi, Father Archangel Gstir blessing them as they stepped into their carriages and rolled away toward the south.

Klara found the notebook lying on the floor of the shop. Someone had tossed it into her workspace while she was not there. She could almost hear the slap it would have made as it hit the worn boards of the floor, her abbess the only witness to its delivery.

A triangle of intense sunlight brought it to Klara's attention now as she opened the door. The leather cover was the same colour as Eamon's belt — handmade by him. Embossed on its surface was the word "Songs."

She picked the volume up and let it fall open in her hands. The words were small, printed in pencil, many of them misspelled. The random lines her eyes lit on read thus:

A black frost has withered my heart
She has taken the light from the hills
*   of Cloonaughlin*
And I and my life are apart
The lake is a shield of mahogany darkness
The colour, the weight of her hair . . .

Klara snapped the book shut and stared

hard into the stern face of the abbess, the face she had refined with her grandfather's chisels just the day before. A combination of panic and despair sang in her blood, and when she put the book down on the work table she saw that the shape of her fingers had been printed on its cover by the sweat of her hand.

The windows of her little shop were thick with spiderwebs. "Don't remove the spiders," her grandfather had told her. "They are just being who they are and have always loved, never harmed wood." But suddenly she needed a clear view, needed light and air. As she scraped the book over each pane of glass, the old webs clung to it, a gauzy, pale membrane encrusted with sawdust. Klara opened the book again and read, *It's you who has left my heart shaken, with a hopeless desperation as before you I stand.* She felt her throat begin to constrict with emotion. Such anguish on the page. Whose mahogany hair, the rich colour of the cover of this book? Why this abandonment, loss? The savagery with which these anguished words cut into the mind! She'd heard nothing, she'd seen nothing like them before. And a whole book of them.

She placed the volume on a table, stood

staring at it with her fingers lightly touching its edge. Then she picked up a chisel and the mallet and approached the sculpture. Squatting beside the wooden abbess, she began hastily to carve a fold into the swelling hem, breaking a piece of the skirt in the process. There would be a flaw now forever in the piece, Klara realized. She threw down her tools, snatched the small book from the table, and walked out the door.

Far back behind the woodlot, the farm midden was a spreading mound of discarded medicine bottles, broken wagon wheels, pottery shards, rotted fenceposts, and rusting bedsprings. Klara tossed the book onto the heap, then walked resolutely away from the spot. On the stoop of the house she changed her mind, sprinted back across the field, through the woods, lifted the book from the top of the heap, and stuffed it in the bodice of her work apron. The stove was a better alternative, she decided. What if her father went to the midden, found the book, and read the offending verses?

The book stayed where it was, near her heart, all through the preparations for the evening meal. At the table she asked her father for the first time about his courtship of her mother, then immediately wished that she hadn't, afraid the question might be interpreted as a kind of confession on her part.

Dieter, however, was obviously pleased by her curiosity. "She was our hired girl — we got her from the nuns when she was six and I was seven," he told his daughter. "So it seemed I'd known her all my life. The nuns had already taught her how to sew, which pleased mother." He paused here and leaned back in his chair, remembering. "I suppose I felt there wouldn't be any need for a courtship on account of us always knowing each other. I do recall, though, that one day I was surprised by the fact that she'd become beautiful. Until then, she would have been just like a sister."

Klara wanted to ask how a brother would feel about a sister, her own experience having been cut so short, but she didn't want to stop her father now that he'd begun to talk.

Dieter held his empty fork in his hand while he looked inward. "I took her with me to the fall fair in Listowel. We went in the wagon, alone, all the way there and back again. After that everything changed. She seemed to expect me to marry her, though all we'd done was ride out alone together. Or maybe it was me expecting to marry her." He plunged his fork in his food and began to eat again. "Anyway, it happened. We got married. And then a few years later Tilman was born."

The mention of the boy brought silence back into the kitchen as surely as if both Klara and her father had forgotten how to speak. Even now, all these years later, there was nothing that could induce Dieter to enter Tilman's vacant room, where the small jackets and trousers still hung in the closet and a book about Saint Brendan's voyages, which Father Gallagher had never had the heart to reclaim, still lay on the table. And under the table, side by side, stood a pair of good black Sunday boots, as if the boy had just taken them off after mass.

Several times during the evening Klara remembered that she had intended to burn the book, but with her father in the room she reasoned this could not be accomplished. All through the washing of the dishes, while she scraped the remnants of their meal from their plates and lowered crockery into the suds, the words ran in her mind, becoming constant, like the sound of a brook that passes near a

153

window. *It's you who has left my heart shaken*, and *I and my life are apart*. Her father looked at her quizzically from across the table. "What is it, Klara?" he finally asked. "Are you feeling poorly?" The book right there against her heart, and sometimes, to her utter amazement, the knowledge that it was there brought tears to her eyes.

She didn't burn it, of course, but during the next few days she moved it from one hiding place to another, all over the house. First she wedged it behind the tin boxes in the pantry, then among her underclothes in the upper drawer of her bedroom dresser. One afternoon she secreted it in the wooden lap desk that had belonged to her mother. At each change of location, against her better judgment, she allowed the book to open to one page. *No life have I, no liberty*, she read, *for love is lord of all*, and *She slipped away from me, with one star awake, as the swans in the evening move over the lake*. She knew she was like a small frantic animal desperately moving from place to place with an acorn, and the analogy did not please her at all. She wanted her uncomplicated life back. Each time she opened her workshop door, the abbess scowled at her in disapproval. In her sunroom, she finished the bridal dress listlessly, paying little attention to the joy expressed later by the young woman who came to fetch and pay for the finished product.

A week after she found the book, a bolt of fine red worsted material arrived from Montreal. This pleased Klara more than she would have liked to admit, and she walked home from the post office with the brown paper parcel clasped like a large tablet against her chest. This waistcoat would be a worthwhile endeavour; she would make it beautiful, if only to be finished with it and finished with the one who had demanded it.

She had seen Eamon two days before as she passed in front of the brewery (and while she was still under the book's influence). *The minstrel boy has gone to war,* she had read earlier in the morning, *in the ranks of death you'll find him,* and then, *O false are the vows of woman kind, but fair is their fair bodies, I would ne're wud ha' trod on Irish ground, had it not been for love of thee.* The combined fragments of the two songs had had a dire effect on her disposition, had made it impossible for her to concentrate at all. She had walked, mesmerized, out of the house and down the road toward the village. *I'll die of this*, she remembered Eamon saying. *In the ranks of death you'll find him*, she thought, *in the winter ditch like a dog*. The small round pools the villagers called kettles shone in the basins of distant green hills. The shadows of leaves shook on the edges of the dusty road. Klara staggered under her sadness as if afflicted by a startling illness or sudden deformity, an inexplicable crippling. Yet she was at a loss as to how to console either herself or him, the one she now knew was drowning in sorrow. She couldn't prevent herself from imagining her own hand touching the side of Eamon's grieving face.

As she passed through the village, she saw him outside the brewery, happy in the company of some other young men, his head thrown back, his laughter filling the air. And he didn't notice her at all. He had tricked her, she decided, everything he had done was part of some cold, cruel game that he could now laugh at with his friends. She felt her own coldness return then, and the wish that she had never come to know him.

And now today, coming back to the house with the bolt of cloth hugged close to her body, Klara hardly expected to see Eamon sitting on the stoop of the wood-shed, but there he was. He brightened when he saw her, but she remembered his utter unawareness of her when he was with his friends and she brushed by him, her skirt sweeping over his shoulder. He stood, then followed her through the door into the kitchen.

"You have something of mine, I think," he said.

"Yes," she said, laying the parcel on the table, keeping her back to him. "Yes," she said again, "the cloth came today."

He placed his white hand on the brown package. "I mean my book."

"Oh it's yours, is it? I wondered." Klara was very busy now, moving randomly from place to place in the kitchen. "So how did it come to be in the workshop then?"

"I put it there."

Klara shook the blue tablecloth in the space between them. "Why would you do that, I wonder? Well, it's gone now." She couldn't look at him. "I burned it."

"You burned it?" Eamon sat slowly down in her father's chair at the end of the table.

"It was just lying there. Whoever owned it seemed to have thrown it away." Klara glanced furtively in Eamon's direction.

He looked stricken. "They were my father's songs — the ones he remembered from Ireland. I wrote them down for him because he didn't know how."

Silence. Klara noted his paleness and softened. He was looking at the floor, then back toward her with confusion in his eyes. "My father's songs from Ireland," he repeated. "I'd made a cover for them, of leather."

"Eamon," Klara walked closer to where he was sitting, put one hand on his shoulder. "Eamon, I didn't burn the book."

Eamon looked up at her, his expression relieved but still wretched. Then seeing the beginnings of tenderness in her, he visibly relaxed.

"I didn't burn it, but I couldn't read those songs."

"Why?"

"Because," she moved one hand in an agitated way through her hair. "Because," she swung away from him, opened the lid, and shoved some kindling, for no reason, into the stove that was not lit in this season.

"Because?" he prompted.

She threw her arms down to her sides. "Eamon, how could I read them with all that suffering and dying for love?"

He smiled. "Then you did read them."

"Only bits. Why was there so much un-happiness in them?"

"Love," said Eamon definitively.

"And people die of it?"

"Only when its unreturned, and even then sometimes they just drink a great deal instead of dying. Or they write poems. Or they sing those songs and drink at the same time."

He told her then that his father had songs about the Cummeragh *struth* and about another, larger river called the Aoine, and in each song the singer was torn with grief at having to leave behind the banks of these streams, parents, friends, and green fields. Mostly the songs blamed the tyranny of the landlords, the British Empire, and swore allegiance to the cause of freeing the beloved and shortly to be abandoned country, the country and the Empire that had caused his father's anger. But sometimes the exile was connected to a passion for an unapproachable woman, a passion so hopeless it became a sweet sorrow in itself, an unrequited romance the only resolution of which was the impossible death of love.

Klara was quiet, then she said very

softly, "Is that why you said you'd die in the ditch like a dog, that you'd leave the country . . ."

"Sometimes I feel like a dog," he said darkly.

"A laughing dog," said Klara, flushing at the memory. "I saw you laughing, Eamon, with your friends outside the brewery. I think you'd forgotten me altogether, that's what I think."

He wrapped his arm around her waist, and the slight weight and warmth of this was telegraphed to every cell of her skin, a bewildering rush of apprehension and pleasure.

This was the way it was going to be then, this road she was going to have to walk. She would be always thinking of him so that he would be beside her even when he wasn't there, making her joyous or miserable, but always, always controlling the colour of her days. Klara, who since Tilman's departure and her mother's collapse had been a singular being, was now terrified by how this one person could so utterly disarm her, cause her emotions to swing in all directions. Yet there it was, and she could feel herself falling, straight through the fear, toward him.

Years later Klara would tell a middle-

160

aged man who listened carefully to each word she said that at that moment Eamon had waltzed with her in the kitchen, such was his happiness at seeing the misery on her face, misery that told him she had fallen in love with him. It was right then that the young man had pledged himself to her, right then that he had used the words "forever more." It was an odd moment, Klara would explain to the large, grey-haired man — the misery, the joy, the words, the waltz, the sudden knowledge that the possibility of pain would be part of their communion.

Now she walked into the parlour, removed the book from a dresser drawer, returned to the kitchen. Bringing the leather up to her face, its smoothness against her cheek, she inhaled the animal scent, then placed the volume in Eamon's hands. "I'll read more later," she said, her hands and voice trembling, "when I can."

What she never admitted, not to the grey-haired man, not to herself, not to anyone, was that there had never been a waltz, there had never even been a declaration, that all the pain and delight she later thought of as dancing was made known to her simply by the expression on the young man's open face.

June of 1914 was followed by a summer of beauty, warmth, and calm — a summer that would be mythologized all over the western world in the years to come. In Shoneval, insects attacked not one green leaf of the swiftly growing crops, animals fattened in dew-soaked pastures, parishioners attended mass regularly and confession infrequently (there being, apparently, few sins to confess). The brewery prospered, the nuns embroidered, and the Archangel Tavern developed a clientele — Eamon among them — of fine singers and fiddle and accordion players. Several new artesian wells and springs were discovered. The dissolute bell ringer at the church became surprisingly punctual. Hafeman's store extended its terms of credit. Despite the fact that almost everyone distrusted them, three telephones were installed in the district.

Klara worked in the mornings on the wooden abbess and during the afternoons on the waistcoat promised to Eamon. In the evenings she walked out with him down dusty roads, or through orchards, or across the cemetery. Often he was silent, as was his nature, but now they remained physically close, hands and shoulders touching or with his arm across her shoulders, so that quietness became a connection rather than a separation. Occasionally they would sit facing each other on a log as if it were a seesaw, as if they were small children, their hands flat on the bark, their eyes locked, entranced.

Eamon was a beautiful young man. Klara loved each detail of his face, the fringe of black eyelashes and the perfectly shaped eyebrows that some might say were wasted on a boy. The unblemished jewels of his green eyes, the fine pale skin lightly dusted by freckles, the small white scar on his temple, and his full, expressive mouth. She had leaned forward once to touch his lips lightly with her fingers as if they were unusual flowers she had discovered and wanted to remember the texture of. He had taken her hand then and kissed her palm, her wrist, a gesture surprisingly mature and tender in one so young, so new to the experience of romance.

Sometimes he talked about his father's homeland, how its spirit had been broken by the English, or how his parents worried about the abandoned cabins of their childhood, knowing the thatch would be gone from them by now. "When the thatch goes," Eamon told Klara, "even stone walls begin to fall into ruin. How sad those walls must be, and so many of them. People who have to leave, they just open the door to the wind and walk away. Soon after the gales bring rain into the house."

By July it seemed that every one of Klara's senses had opened to the light of the long, long days. The scent of freshly chiselled wood in the shop, or of cloth in the sunroom, the taste of salt on new potatoes, the coolness of a damp cloth on her neck in the morning. In the church there was the smell of incense, the buttery glow of candles, blocks of geometric light richly coloured by stained glass, and the precision of white altar cloths. All this gave her joy. But, shaken by the thrill of this boy's touch, she was vulnerable now to things that in the past she might have ignored. Anything at all, a sharp word from her father, the sight of a newborn calf, even a flower wilting on a stem, could bring tears to her eyes.

In her workshop, the face of the abbess softened to such an extent that Klara's grandfather became concerned.

"This abbess," he said, "is too young. And far too cheerful. She looks as if she has spent most of her short life dreaming in a field of flowers. No man would accept advice from her. No pope would listen to her for one minute!"

Klara was stung by this criticism, but only briefly, and the tears cleared in minutes. All the rest of the day she was thinking of the moments when Eamon's arm was on her shoulder or his hands were in her hair.

Late on certain afternoons, after work, Eamon and Klara would remove shoes and stockings and step into the bed of the clear-running creek that drove the machinery of the brewery; Eamon with his pant legs rolled up and Klara carrying her skirt in front of her thighs as if it were a sheaf of wheat. They followed the path of the water into an area surrounded by thick brush and cedar, lifting their legs over fallen logs and pushing aside the branches of aspen and poplar that grew near the bank.

Eventually they would reach a series of pools, each slightly larger than the last. The final pond, which had water deep enough for swimming, was ringed by willows around its circular edge. Eamon, covered with sweat from work, would immediately throw off his clothing, then would flail with much splashing into the water. Klara, shyer, removed her own clothes on a bank behind a willow and stepped into a deep area protected by a curtain of green leaves where Eamon was unable to see her.

"I'm coming in there," Eamon would tease. Then he would dive under the surface and emerge in a fountain of water, claiming that he had glimpsed Klara's legs. She lay on her back and looked up through soft green, or she stood waist-deep in the water and floated her open hands on a dark surface covered with echoes of light. The shadows of leaves were like bruises on her skin.

There was a kind of communion in this separate baptism. Though they couldn't see each other or touch, they were connected by the pool and by laughter, by the pleasure of the chilled water on warm skin, the shadows, the breeze. Later, as a mature adult, Klara would never swim, fearing the memory of this joy. But now when they scrambled from the water and dressed in their private green worlds, it would be as if they were preparing themselves for some inevitable, profound ceremony, a reunion of partnership. Eamon would shake his head like a young animal to remove moisture from his hair and then lean down to where Klara was lying on the bank to smooth out her long yellow mane to dry on the grass. They never knew how they had decided upon this daily ritual, but it became a necessary luxury, a significant part of their unspoken code.

On one such day as she stood in her green water hut, a startled Klara, hands held to her head to protect herself from the noise, watched between two long strands of willow as Eamon, who had just entered the pond, threw his head back and looked at the sky, his face lit by the full flood of the sun and then covered briefly by a swift, clamorous shadow that changed for the space of a breath the colour of his skin and the colour of the pond. She continued to stare as he climbed swiftly up the bank, struggled unselfconsciously into his trousers, unknowingly permitting Klara her first full view of his oddly delicate naked self. She remained, shivering, behind the green shield, her arms crossed protectively over her breasts, having registered the places where his black tufted hair interrupted white skin and how his sex shone between his legs. Then she moved quickly toward her clothing and dressed herself as the catastrophic noise sputtered and eventually stopped altogether. A great calamity had occurred, she knew. Something fierce and dire had fallen from the sky.

Before this day only birds, clouds, the rising moon, the setting sun, shooting stars, and Eamon's kites had moved in the sky, all occupying air with dignity, discretion, and at least a degree of silence. The racket might have been made by a bellowing Lucifer angrily approaching earth after being thrown out of heaven or the dusky flying monster from prehistory that Klara had once seen in a forbidden book about the evolution of man and nature. This was the first time in Klara's life that anything other than familiar, comforting sounds had entered her afternoons. And this was the first time in her presence that Eamon had turned his attention away from her. She was made briefly aware — though she hardly acknowledged this — that intrusions from the outside might be capable of removing him, of taking his mind and then his body permanently away from her.

When she stepped furtively out of the woods and into an open field she saw, near the opposite fence line, two men, one of whom was Eamon, standing beside a contraption apparently constructed of sticks and canvas. The stranger wore a tight-fitting helmet and stood quite still with his hands in the pockets of a leather jacket. Eamon, by comparison, was walking in busy circles around the now silent apparatus, pausing here and there to touch some part of it as if he did not quite believe it was real.

Klara called to him, wanting him to forget about this uninvited machine that had, she felt, already come strangely between them. But Eamon beckoned to her enthusiastically and, as she came nearer, shouted at her in an almost hysterical voice, "Klara . . . come look . . . an aeroplane!"

"An aeroplane," she repeated stupidly, quietly to herself. She knew about them, of course, but had thought they would be more seraphic, graceful. In her imagination they had been white, gliding and silent, a miracle lifted by wind. This machine looked, as she approached it, more like some ill-designed gadget from the mill or the brewery. And it smelled of grease and filth.

The pilot turned to her as she walked toward them and explained that he had run out of petrol on his way from Owen Sound to a fair at Goderich. Klara stared at his leather boots, which were cracked and covered with oily stains. She realized she had left her own boots at the pool and self-consciously covered one foot with the other.

Eamon was running his hands lovingly over the propeller. "My God," he said, "this is the most beautiful thing."

"She could use some tidying up," said the pilot as he opened one hinged part of the nose. "There's so many fairs now I hardly have the time. Can I get petrol in the village?"

"I'll show you where there's a tank by the mill." Eamon was examining the instrument panel.

"Good, and then I'll take you for a spin afterwards." The pilot looked at Klara, at her hair, her breasts, her bare feet, "and then I'll take you up."

"No," said Klara firmly. "Thank you."

"You'll take me up?" said Eamon incredulous.

"Sure, why not?"

"Don't go, Eamon," said Klara. She didn't want him floating through the clouds, no longer anchored to their own village landscape, to the earth. She wanted to be lying on her back beside the pool with him smoothing her long hair out to

170

dry in the sun, the familiar grass surrounding them both.

"This is a miraculous day," he was
saying. "What if I hadn't been here? What
if I'd been somewhere else?"

The pilot laughed. "No miracles happen
without petrol," he said.

"It's just a machine," Klara bent down to
seize Eamon's sleeve as he attempted to
scramble under the wings. He had never
paid this kind of attention to anyone, anything except for her. "It's just a machine,
but for all I can tell it's dangerous. Please
don't go up in it."

Several small boys had arrived on the
scene, gasping with wonder and physical
exertion having run across five fields after
spotting the machine in the sky. Now they
stood panting and chattering. One tried to
shinny himself up into the cockpit.

"Get down from there," shouted the
pilot, "and don't touch anything." He
glared fiercely in the direction of the children, then turned to Klara. "You stay
here," he said. "Don't let those little
buggers anywhere near it."

Klara was silent, shocked. She had never
heard anyone use a word like "bugger" before. She watched as Eamon accompanied
the leather-clad figure over the fence and

171

down the road. She wondered what was familiar about the costume and the short, thick body of the pilot, and then remembered. He looked suspiciously like one of the demons her grandfather had carved in a *Last Judgment.*

The boys were laughing and crawling under the carriage.

"Get out of there," snapped Klara. "You heard what the man said. I can tell you right now you wouldn't want to make the likes of him angry."

There was nothing Klara could do to prevent Eamon from riding in the aeroplane, and so while the pilot was filling the machine with petrol, she began to walk away.

"Aren't you even going to stay and watch?" Eamon called after her, his voice high and strained in disbelief.

She didn't answer but kept striding toward the wood where she had left her boots. While she was tying her laces, she heard the machine start up. The noise shook the leaves of all the trees around her and seemed to leave visible fissures in the atmosphere, lesions that affected Klara's vision in a disturbing way, making her believe that she would never see anything

172

whole again. As the aeroplane brushed over the top-most branches, she crouched on the ground and bent her arms over her head. When she once again returned to the open, she watched not the aeroplane but the way the children, like metal filings, were being pulled by the magnet of the circumnavigating machine around and around the field.

Eventually the apparatus landed and set Eamon free. He was in a state of great agitation. "Wasn't that something," he kept saying to no one in particular. "Wasn't that something!"

After the beast had once again hurled itself into the air and had droned into the distance, Eamon turned to Klara and began to talk excitedly. He told her that everything looked so small from that height he could have held Shoneval in the palm of his hand. "You became so tiny," he said. "I could hardly find you." He could see that shingles were missing from the roofs of most houses. Sheep were white dots, cows were black-and-white dots. Old Hammacher's rows of corn weren't straight. "I waved back when you waved," he said, carelessly throwing an arm over her shoulder, "but you probably couldn't see that."

Klara had not waved, she didn't tell Eamon this, but she had not waved. He had mistaken someone else for her. She had become interchangeable. He could not see her. This adventure had nothing to do with her.

She remained silent all the way back to the farm, removed his arm from her waist, walked apart from him, thinking for the first time about the separate paths that unfolded behind them and defined their differences: varying landscapes and the dissimilar patterns of their habits, their family lives. It had occurred to her that it might take years or might be impossible altogether to fully comprehend or untangle the complexities of their unrelated pasts. Despite the briefness of their lives, the similarity of the roads they walked each day, the weather patterns they shared, his mind held thoughts she might not even be aware of, never mind interpret. And now this seductive apparatus, fully embraced by him, utterly rejected by her. She felt that if she touched his hand and spoke now, Eamon might not have been able to hear her, the remembered furious noise of the flying machine cooling the warmth of her fingers and erasing each word she would have said.

★ ★ ★

In the middle of August and after many fittings, Klara finished the waistcoat. There had been much discussion with Eamon about whether the braid trim should be black or scarlet until finally Klara was convinced by him that he had, indeed, wanted a waistcoat that was *entirely* scarlet. The evening he came to collect the garment he burst into a room tinted orange by dusk and kissed Klara, first on the neck and then on the soft skin of her inner elbow. She held the coat open for him and he manoeuvred his body into it, then solemnly buttoned the front. The setting sun shone through the window and brought out the red tints in his black hair — even his eyelashes reflected light. Klara had never seen anyone so beautiful.

He grinned at her and opened his arms, but she shook her head. "I just want to look at you," she said.

He walked back and forth across the room with his eyes locked to hers.

Vanity, she thought but this time with admiration. She had lit candles for the previous four weeks to Homobonus, the patron saint of tailors. She had wanted the waistcoat to be flawless.

"It's perfect," said Eamon, laughing, his

175

face illuminated by the sun.

Klara felt as if she were bathing in the copper light that drenched the room, felt that each time she inhaled, her blood-stream became luminous. She was practically suffocated by radiance.

"Eamon," she said, testing his name, the shape of it in her mouth.

He did not answer but walked across the floor toward her, removed the coat, folded it carefully, and placed it on the seat of a ladder-back chair. Then he looked at her shyly, as if there were something of great importance he meant to tell her but couldn't bring himself to say. Stepping closer to Klara, who was made motionless by his nearness, Eamon for the first time tentatively moved his warm hand down the side of her neck, over her collarbone, under the cotton fabric. She was able to see his face become flushed and one vein beating at his temple.

When his fingers grazed her nipple, she gasped and drew back, frightened by the new nerve connections that were like plucked strings resonating in her belly, her inner thighs. "No," she whispered, "I can't . . ."

But his mouth stopped whatever it was she meant to say, and she became aware that he was undoing the buttons on the front of her dress, the clasps of her camisole. Then they were holding each other, locked together, staggering against the chair, which overturned so that the splendid coat lay discarded, a prone torso beside them where they fell on the floor. Klara cried out once, in pain, then felt herself sink into an unrecognizable ache of tenderness. She would remember this forever, this act they called sin, her body boneless, some new vine flowering in her veins. And then when it was over she recalled the afternoon they had skated on the ice, how they had fallen there.

They dressed quietly, avoiding each other's eyes, private in the wake of the experience. Eamon picked up the coat and smoothed it over his arm. Then he reached forward and grasped her hands.

"Is it all right, Klara?"

"Yes," she said, and then more firmly, "yes."

"We'll be married," he said. "We'll get married."

"My father . . ."

"He'll live with us . . . we'll live here."

Klara said nothing.

"He'll want what makes you happy," said

Eamon. "Whatever makes you happy."

Klara was thinking about the curve of Eamon's shoulders, the fine white skin there, the unfamiliar dark hair she had seen when he had clambered out of the pool toward the aeroplane, how there had been just a glimpse of it when they lay together. Then she had closed her eyes again.

"Would you want to be married to me?" he asked.

"Yes," she said. "Yes, of course." It surprised her now to realize that she'd never, even once, thought about marriage, the future, as if she would be caught in this lush, youthful summer forever. Would she confess this sin? Would Eamon? She didn't want to whisper about it in the dark of the confessional, and she didn't want Eamon whispering about it either.

"We're in love," he was saying, the first time he had used the word. A statement? An excuse?

"Yes," said Klara, moving slightly away from him, then righting the chair, the scraping sound of its legs on the floor loud, intrusive. She was alarmed by the sensation of an unfamiliar liquid travelling down her thigh, that and the fact that the chair and all the other familiar objects in the room seemed altered, arbitrary, and out of place though not one thing in the physical world had changed. Then she heard the sound of her father's boots in the woodshed. And his slow, steady progress through the downstairs rooms of the house. He had returned from the neighbouring farm where he had gone to buy some eggs and was calling her name as he passed through the parlour.

"I'm up here," she called back, only then thinking that he might have returned sooner, and that if he had he likely would not have been noticed. "Eamon has come for his coat."

Eamon and Klara exchanged glances, embarrassed by an awareness of a possible discovery. Suddenly Klara was able to imagine the act as if she had been a witness rather than a participant, as if she had stood outside herself and watched the senseless awkwardness of their lovemaking. She felt that she had been ushered by Eamon into a heated adult world where men and women clutched at each other, wrestled, collapsed on the floor. Then the moment passed and they embraced, Eamon burying his face in the warmth of Klara's neck.

But the outer world was not to be ignored. "Come down," Dieter Becker was
calling. "Come down and bring Silent Irish
with you. There's news. War has been declared."

In June of 1869, when the second Corpus Christi procession had completed its one-mile tour of the church grounds, Father Archangel Gstir rose from the long makeshift table where he had been enjoying the baked goods of his female parishioners and gazed around the cleared acreage. He held up his hand to quiet the festive crowd gathered near him and then signalled to those of his flock seated on the flat round surfaces of stumps left behind after the trees for the log church were cut. When he was certain he had everyone's attention, he bent down and, with some difficulty, lifted a wooden box from the ground. He turned his back on the crowd, placed his burden on the seat of the chair he had just vacated, and, swivelling back and forth, began to place on the table, one after another, the twenty iron railway spikes that had been brought to him the previous day by a tinker who worked the roads of the surrounding territory.

"These," Father Gstir announced, "are the beginnings of our great stone church."

Mill workers and farmers then rose from their own chairs and walked around the perimeter of the little log church, pacing out the enlarged dimensions of the imagined stone foundation. Father Gstir paced with them, pausing every now and then to hammer a spike into the ground. When this task was completed, he returned to his box and removed from it loop after loop of red ribbon, one end of which he tied to the stake nearest the spot where the front doors would eventually open to the congregation. Then, slipping the ribbon through his fingers as he walked, looking for all the world as if he were about to take part in a May Day celebration, he tied the ribbon in knots around the heads of all twenty iron spikes.

That spring enough fieldstones had surfaced under the ploughs of the farmers to make an adequate start at the foundation. The bishop was summoned, the cornerstone was laid and blessed, and oxen, horses, and a team of thirty volunteers provided the labour. By September, the resulting rectangular structure, six feet wide, looked as if it were an uncommonly large garden wall enclosing the yard of the log church. Goldenrod and Queen Anne's lace blossomed around its base; squirrels occasionally ran along its top. Work begun the following spring increased the height of the structure to such an extent that only the braver children were tempted to shinny up the stone walls.

How long the construction seemed to take! Despite donations of limestone from newly discovered local quarries, and lime from local kilns and sand from local pits, and many thousands of feet of hewn timber from local lots, money was still needed for the sandstone buttresses and the hundreds of running feet of lintels. Sometimes during the miserable winters that inevitably followed the industrious summers and autumns of this period, when snow threatened to completely bury the limestone walls, Father Gstir would almost give up hope. Then, on a clear day in February or March, a messenger would be seen climbing the white road from the village, a brown envelope sealed with wine-coloured wax in his hand, and another two or three thousand thalers would be added to the fund.

One of the largest of these spontaneous donations appeared during the bitterly cold winter of 1880. Father Gstir, in a letter of effusive thanks to the Ludwig Missions-Verig and to the royal benefactor, described the skeins of snow blowing against the limestone walls and through the empty

Gothic windows. *Like angels,* he wrote, *these trailing white clouds look to me like angels visiting our church.* By the end of summer, he predicted, we will have a roof, now that there is money for the slates. He apologized for the lack of polar bears, which, he claimed, had moved farther north because of the increasing population of the village.

In early August of that year dozens of healthy young men — men who in Europe would have made fine soldiers — gathered at the site of the church and ascended a multitude of ladders. In the space of a month, working in the evenings after a full day of agricultural labour, they had completely slated the roof. Each night, when darkness fell, they descended to earth, walked down the hill to Schmidt's Creek, and threw off their clothes in order to bathe. Everyone in the village could hear the sound of their laughter through open summer windows.

The same group of young men came to the church grounds in late September. Under the shelter of the soaring timbered and slated roof, by the light shining through newly installed window glass, they began, quite carefully, to dismantle the small structure that had until that very moment served as the community's place of worship. Then they took that structure, log by log, out the front door of the new stone church, leaving the planked floor, the pine pews, and an altar carved by Joseph Becker surrounded by a margin of bright green indoor grass. The work took all day and was eventually completed by the light of the harvest moon.

Father Gstir, who presided over the project, was most moved by this last act of labour connected to the building of his church, moved by the solemn expressions on the faces of the men as they carried the past through the doors of the future, how they stacked the timber so tidily in the northeast corner of the lot, where it would not interfere with anyone's view of the present. It seemed to him as if he were watching time itself being carried in the arms of youth, and as if the pile of logs being assembled in the moonlight was a kind of monument that both celebrated and mourned the receding past.

No one in Shoneval wanted to enlist. This reluctance would be later attributed to the German background of the village by a simplistic but effective propaganda machine designed to make people in

Canada increasingly aware of racial and ethnic differences. The truth was that nobody wanted to enlist because they had spent the Sunday afternoons of their childhoods listening to grandparents count their blessings — the most important of which was freedom from armed conflict. Large portions of the elder population had left behind war-torn Bavaria in their youth precisely for this reason. Even more had left behind the constant deadly squabbles over Alsace. They had not abandoned ancestral homelands, endured the misery of a pitching ship, battled armies of trees and insects, watched their spouses and children die wretchedly and far too soon only to see their grandchildren return to the battlegrounds from which they had fled. In Shoneval, news of the outbreak of war was publicly discussed for one day, and since that day was Sunday, Father Gallagher preached a pointed sermon on the first commandment, "Thou shalt not kill." Afterwards everybody descended the hill to the customary tankard that was always enjoyed at the Archangel Tavern each Sunday after mass.

And yet one young man with a red waistcoat far too warm for the season had seen something in a back field just a month ago, something that would turn his mind toward the conflict and determine his fate. No visitation of the Blessed Virgin, no choir of angels, no vision of the Infant of Prague could have moved him more than the shuddering, noisy machine that had descended unceremoniously into his life.

A few weeks after the news reached Shoneval, Eamon told Klara that he felt compelled to go, "and who knows," he added, "if I go they might let me fly an aeroplane . . . they will be crucial from now on in any war. Then when I come back I'll keep one in the barn."

Klara's response was one of sudden, cold fear. How could he step away from her now, place an ocean between them, put himself and their love at risk, and all for the love of an airborne toy? Since their encounter in the sunroom, Eamon had visited her nightly, entering her room by way of the chestnut tree that grew near the window, then slipping into her bed, her arms. His body was her body now; she barely knew where his anatomy ended and hers began. She had learned the whole geography of his bones and flesh, the taut ropes of tendons at his ankles and behind his knees, veins branching from his crotch to his upper thighs, his firm, smooth upper arms, and sharp hip and shin bones. She knew how to curl into the hollows of his adjacent torso, how to entangle her legs with his when she was stretched out at his side. What made him want to remove this physical warmth, this rapture and comfort from her? In the heat of these summer nights often they were so tightly connected by sweat that when he rose to leave he would break the seal their damp skin had made. Was it possible that he who had coaxed her into this trance of intimacy would now shatter it all?

In his own kitchen Eamon's Irish father told him that no son of his was going off to fight for England, and that if he chose to do so he would be a son of his no more.

When Eamon reported this to Klara on an August day thick with heat — when he told her this in an outraged voice, certain of the injustice, courting her sympathy — she crossed the kitchen and slapped his face with such violence that tears sprang into his eyes. "You're a fool, Eamon O'Sullivan," she hissed. "A fool and an infant. I want nothing more to do with you."

She had opened, had given too much of herself to him. Now all of his decisions wounded her. She watched as the shape her blow had made appeared on his shocked face, the way the anger entered his expression. After the screen door banged behind him, Klara went out to her workshop, bolted the door, and worked on the abbess for the remainder of the afternoon, sharpening her tools to make the woman's features and the folds of her garments angular and determined. She ignored her father's fist on the door, and his pleas for dinner. She ignored her visiting grandfather's entreaties. When she finally emerged into moonlight and heat, even the trees and buildings seemed to shrink under the angry grief of her gaze. As she climbed the stairs to her room she felt the temperature rise. These were the dog days of August, the day's heat never left the upper floors of the house, pushed back any relief that wanted to enter by way of breezes through open windows. Klara undressed, fell face down on the bed, and remembered with sorrow that just a week before, Eamon's sleeping face had rested in the hollow of the same hand that had just struck him.

And yet when she was awakened an hour later by the sound of a carefully lifted window, the sense that she had been betrayed by him returned and she quickly covered herself with the sheet and told him to leave.

"For God's sake, Klara." There was fear now on his always readable face. He held out his arms to her.

"Don't," she whispered, her knees drawn up, her face hidden on the sheet that was covering her arms and shoulders.

During the preceding weeks she had been delighted by his spontaneous nocturnal appearances, the hint of danger, the melting pleasure she could never associate with sordidness or sin. Now she could imagine that after his departure, shame would enter the emptiness he left behind.

"We'll get married," he said, "before I leave."

He had thought it was that.

She looked up at him, astonished. After this mutiny, this certainty of chosen absence, marriage seemed impossible to her. How could he not know that? Moths were now coming into her room, flying toward her lit lamp. "Close the window, Eamon," she said.

He believed this meant she wanted him to stay. He let down the sash quietly, not wanting to waken, to alert her father. Then he crossed the floor and sat near her on the bed.

A moth had landed on her cheek, but she did not wish to expose even her bare arms to Eamon, so she kept the sheet wrapped tightly around her torso like a shawl, like a shroud. He leaned forward and gently caught the insect in his cupped hands, then quietly opened the door and released it out into the hall. When he walked back to the bed, she turned her face away from him.

She should never have trusted her own passion, this animal that paced around the edges of her character. She was right to have been wary in the beginning, suspicious of the sound of its first unrecognized footstep. Now she believed that ever since that moment she had known that she would be somehow betrayed by it — even when it had felt like a light, almost transparent being, sensitive to every nuance and current of connection with this young man. But now it had become a heavy brute, tenebrous, unmovable, weighted by dread. This dark removal, this adventure in absence, chosen by him. She almost hated him for the pain its anticipation brought her. Reaching for a box on the table by her bedside, she opened it and pulled tight the amber necklace she kept there, snapping the string, beads spilling across the sheets and bouncing on the floor.

Eamon had given her this gift. "I don't want this any more," she said quietly.

The bruised, wounded look that came over his face would be recorded by Klara's mind and would be carried there for years to come. The string of bright beads, he had told her, were to remind her of the twenty brightest days they had spent together, and a promise of twenty more, and then twenty more, infinitely. Even in old age she would be able to call to mind the sound of the word "infinitely," the music it had made, coloured by the slight Irish accent in his mouth — a word that whether shouted, sung, or spoken sounded always like a tender whisper. When she broke the beads, she had been throwing all the bright days away.

But now, as Klara shifted and one final amber bead clattered on the wood floor, Eamon stood before her, his face flushed, his shoulders hunched, as if cringing in the wake of a physical attack. Then he had straightened and stood briefly, powerfully, above her in the room. "I can only hope," he said as he moved toward the window, "that you'll love me better when I get back."

After Eamon had gone, Klara walked through the silent house lighting lamp after lamp in the midnight gloom. Then she extinguished these same lamps one after another, her mind concentrating on how it was possible to control the intensification, the reduction of brightness, how one could make it blaze, then lower the wick, pull the damper down, or how one could let it simply diminish by degrees. She felt utterly defenceless in the face of his desertion, permanently fixed within the dimensions of a house. And all he had to do was walk away. Something she would never be able to do.

Not long after it was consecrated, miracles began to be associated with the church. There was the miracle of the establishment of the Convent of the Immaculate Conception at Shoneval shortly after the church was completed. There was the miracle of the multiplying congregation as people came from far and wide to see the church and to receive the Holy Sacrament. There was the miracle of Joseph Becker's continued carving despite the enormity of labour attached to the running of his farm and the fact that he now had a wife and a family. And then finally, in 1885, there was the miracle that Father Gstir had been waiting for.

The great church had stood for four years on the hill in Canada, surrounded by a skirt of specially planted pines, its splendid belfry visible five miles away, the dark blue of its slate roof echoed by the softer grey-blue of its stone walls. At sunset it threw its impressive shadow down toward the Archangel Tavern in the valley. At sunrise it darkened the bright white sheds that Joseph Becker had built to protect the outdoor altars when they were not being used for the Corpus Christi or other more spontaneous processions. Above the porch, the many-coloured eyes of its rose window looked out over an increasing number of cultivated fields and behind its nave a cemetery gradually grew in size.

On a clear weekday in October of 1885, Father Archangel Gstir, who by now was reaching the age of retirement, sat on the front steps of his church admiring the staggering display of autumn colour that poured through the air from nearby maples and carpeted the hills that surrounded the village. When the approaching wagon caught his attention, he noticed that it carried a crate so large it could have held a milk house, one of Joseph Becker's altars, a small chapel, or, for that matter, another wagon. For the first time since the church's consecration several years before, the good Father experienced the thrill of anticipation. The wagon could be heading to one of the farms being cleared to the north, it could be delivering a kitchen stove to the Becker household, or it could be approaching the church. Soon he had to conclude that the latter was the case, and by the time the wagon reached the lane he was standing at the top of the church steps to meet it.

Four men drove toward him, two sat on the vehicle's front seat and the others leaned their backs against the blond wood of the box. They stood on arrival, and after lifting several long boards stacked beside the crate, they made a ramp to slide their burden to the ground. There it settled deeply into the manicured, pebbled path that Father Gstir, just weeks before, had installed in front of the church steps.

"What is it?" he asked. "Is it for me?"

"It's a heavy son of a bitch, whatever it is," a red-faced man replied. Then he remembered where he was. "Sorry, Father."

After the crate was torn apart by crowbars and a prodigious amount of straw was thrown to the winds, the beautiful bell was revealed, its bronze surface glowing in a muted manner like the tanned and stretched hide of a great animal. It was as tall as the men who had unpacked it and who were now running their hands over its surface and exclaiming with surprise. "It has something written on it," one of them shouted to the priest.

"What does it say?" asked Father Gstir, who was standing very still at the top of the steps.

There was a pause when it became evident that only one of the men was able to read. The literate workman squatted beside the bell and crawled around its circumference reading the inscription slowly and with some difficulty, syllable by syllable. *Dulcis instar mellis campana vocor Gabrielis.* The man glanced toward the priest. "Is it Latin?" he asked. "What does that mean?"

The priest's entire body was trembling. "It means . . ." he began. His voice faltered. He wiped his brow. "It says," he continued, "I am sweet as honey and am called Gabriel's bell." Then, to the astonishment of the men who stood before him, Father Gstir sat down on the front steps of his church, put his head in his hands, and burst into tears.

That which he believed he had most desired had finally been delivered to him, and yet he could hardly bear to look at it, scarcely bear to speak of it. The bell stood before him, as enigmatic and beautiful as he had always imagined it would be, wholly itself in the morning sun, waiting it seemed for the ascension that must occur before it could use its honey-sweet voice.

And yet the priest could not look at this treasure, kept his face in his hands, not wanting perhaps to let the moment of its miraculous arrival pass, not wanting to enter into communion. Father Gstir on the steps of his church, overcome by the emotion of a wish granted.

But after the interval of the averted glance came surrender to the oppression of the real. When the priest composed himself and raised his face, it was not toward the bell that he directed his gaze, not toward the men who stood in embarrassed silence at the foot of the steps. Instead he rose to his feet, turned his back on the bell, and looked up toward the empty belfry through which a sudden autumn wind was blowing a flock of multicoloured leaves. And after that the world abruptly returned, and he understood that the details of how to manage his heart's desire were going to have to be considered, arrangements were going to have to be made. The bishop would eventually have to be summoned to bless the bell. Some sort of winch would have to be constructed to hoist it up to its rightful place in the tower. And then it must be maintained, must be made to ring joyfully, or toll solemnly. The very fact of the bell's presence, the very fact of its solid existence, exhausted the now older but not yet elderly man. The profound responsibility of it. He must cause it to make gorgeous proclamations, to make predictions, to celebrate, to mourn. Gabriel, after all, was the angel of the annunciation, the angel of miraculous pronouncements. The honey voice must continue to be heard through all the unpredictable weather of the coming days, the weeks, the years.

That night as he sat in front of the fire in the comfortable rectory built for him just one year before, Father Gstir felt himself sinking into his chair as if the weight of the great bell had settled on his thighs and shoulders. He attempted to negotiate the indistinct path back to the Europe of his youth, to remember just what was entailed in raising a bell to its place in a church tower and how the bell should be positioned once it arrived there. Various terms such as "headstock," "strike note," "timbre," and "the flight of the clapper" entered his mind. Sonority, he knew, was something to be considered, but he couldn't quite remember why or how. He recalled one bell ringer he had known in Bavaria saying something about "percussive grandeur" and then making reference to gudgeons. What on earth was a gudgeon? There would have to be wheels. There would have to be discussions concerning acoustics. Was there anyone at all in this wild country with whom one could carry on such discussions? Father Gstir rose painfully to his feet and walked out into the clear autumn night. The bell was barely visible in the dark, but when the priest's eyes finally adjusted to the gloom, the object in front of him looked solid and dour as if all of its bronze surface was concentrated on the act of pulling the night's chill into its bulk. The priest shook his head, turned, and walked despondently away, through the door of his rectory, down the hall, and into his bedroom, where without pausing for his customary evening prayers he fell fully clothed upon his bed.

The next morning when a crowd of excited villagers climbed the hill, they were surprised to find their spiritual leader neither in the vicinity of the bell nor inside his church. "And so I was elected to look for him in the rectory." Joseph Becker would tell his granddaughter decades later. "And there he was," the old man would continue sadly. "His eyes wide open but with no life in them." A stroke? A heart attack? Who could say, there being no medical experts in the vicinity. On the bedside table was a scrap of paper on which was written in a shaky hand, *I committed the sin of covetousness. Pray for me. The bell . . .* Joseph crumpled the note in his fist and stuffed it in his pocket, told no one about it. "But I did pray for him," he said to Klara much later, "and I did make all the arrangements for the bell."

Father Gstir did not know, therefore, that eight months later while the bishop was blessing the safely installed Shoneval bell, King Ludwig of Bavaria, the bell's royal donor, was forcibly removed from his palace at Neuschwanstein and driven to Schloss Berg. Declared insane and placed under house arrest, the plump and now mostly toothless monarch hoped for a peasant uprising to set him free. But the peasants, though fond of their king, were too pragmatic and too overworked to revolt. So, twenty-four hours later, while Father Gstir's congregation lit candles of gratitude and said prayers for the continued health of the ruler who had contributed so generously to the construction of one priest's dream in the wilderness (then lit candles of mourning for the same priest), the deposed King Ludwig walked into the lake at Schloss Berg and drowned. He left in his wake some effusive castles, a number of highly imaginative follies, operas by Wagner that would have never been created let alone performed without his financial and moral assistance, and one marvellous church in the wilds of Canada, his connection to which would be entirely forgotten.

As if Klara's life had been an oversized garment that she had allowed to billow uncontrollably out into the winds of the world, she now drew it back toward her solid physical self, fold after fold, then fastened it with the firm, strong belt of her will. She felt that if she did not speak of Eamon's departure, and if she made it known to her father and her grandfather that she would not tolerate enquiries, she would soon recover from the overwhelming feelings of loss that attacked her late at night and early in the morning as she lay under the covers of the bed in which, until Eamon had come into her life, she had always slept alone.

She put away everything connected to the boy: the studio photograph he had given her, the amber beads she had swept from every corner of her room, the pearl promise ring she knew was all he could afford. She put away certain articles of clothing she had worn when she was with him: a muslin blouse, a few bright hair ribbons — even the tape with which she had measured him and the scissors with which she had cut the red cloth. She pulled her yellow hair severely, almost painfully, back from her face and wound it into a knot at the base of her neck in response to her knowledge that Eamon had liked her to wear it falling down her back. She re-arranged the furniture in her room and placed the bed so that she could no longer see the window. And still she could not forget how the young woman she had been just months ago always moved into the part of the bed that still held Eamon's warmth after he had crept out that same window.

One morning in late September, Klara rummaged in the attic until she found a picnic basket that had come into her mind when she had lain awake the previous night. She picked it up and carried it with her out of the house, away from the farm. She climbed up to the church and passed through the iron forest of the cemetery just as the bell with the voice of honey tolled ten o'clock. Not even stopping to glance at her mother's grave she continued through the cemetery's back gate and down a sharp incline toward the kettle pond where she and Eamon had collided and where she had first felt the warmth of his neck at her wrist. Over half a year later they had picnicked at this spot, though neither of them had ever spoken of the winter day, the ice, the fall. The food they had eaten had been carried in the basket Klara now held with two arms in front of her, as if it were a burden much heavier than it was.

This was to be the last of him.

She placed the basket on the water. It floated easily, bobbing near the shore, surrounded by the bright circular ripples caused by its own round shape touching the water.

From her pocket she removed a small matchbox. She struck one match against the side and held it against the basket. For a moment she thought about how inconsequential fire appeared to be in the full brunt of sunlight. Barely visible in the glare that knifed toward her from the water, it illuminated nothing and threw no shadows. Love was like that, she told herself, just like that, when you looked at it in the ordinary light of day.

"Remember this, Klara," she whispered aloud.

The dry old wicker ignited immediately, and in no time at all the fire had sailed away from her and was floating in the centre of the pond. Klara watched the conflagration until it was swallowed by liquid. Then she walked away.

The last of him.

Now she believed she was done with it, that she had accomplished what she wanted. What she wanted was never again to be torn from sleep by love, never again to be awakened by grief.

Putting herself on a rigid schedule so that each waking moment was filled with activity, Klara worked in the kitchen filling Mason jar after Mason jar with preserved fruit as if she were gathering sustenance for a life of constant winter. She also darned and reinforced all of her father's socks, whether they needed it or not. When asked why she was doing this, Klara met her father's puzzled look with a steady gaze and said, "Frugality," a word she knew that he and everyone in their community approved of.

In the shop, in the space of one week, she had worked with such concentration on the abbess, and for so many hours, that she considered the sculpture to be finished and announced this fact with great satisfaction to her grandfather. But when the old man came to see the allegedly completed figure, he was not pleased.

"Too hard, too angry," he said after a long, contemplative silence. "She looks like she's a fishwife, a shrew. There is no authority in that. No priest would have listened to a word she said, never mind a pope."

She thought about her brother, Tilman, how she had given him the means to be free of the house and how he never returned, and she almost understood her mother, for the first time, what had driven her to imprison him. Only the old men could be counted upon to stay, wanting warmth and comfort from women. The young were bred to run away, to flee toward that which was not so easily known: the open road, a piece of machinery, toward anything but the disclosure women demanded of them. Even her father, as a younger man, had left his fields reluctantly at dusk, driven in the direction of the house by various forms of hunger. And once there, Klara now suspected, he would have resented his own surrender to the tyranny of the feminine, so that each morning his resumption of duty was an act of escape.

It was all one long, exhausting game of hide and seek.

★ ★ ★

All over Ontario boys were being worshipped and wept over as they covered themselves in khaki and marched toward a collection of similar brick train stations, part of a massive reverse migration. As if engaging in an act of revenge, Europe had demanded that the grandsons of the impoverished hordes that had left her shores a few generations before now cross the ocean to mingle their flesh with the dust of their ancestors. Blanketed in flowers, surrounded by song, accompanied by pipes and drums, young men departed from farms and factories, offices and banks, schools and churches as if enchanted, their faces smiling and oddly vacant. A fuss of this magnitude had never been made over them before — these farmboys and schoolboys and youthful labourers — and for the first time they felt themselves to be larger than life, a force so sweeping and elemental they were on the verge of forgetting their individual names. The word "we" sprang so easily and so joyfully to their lips that the word "them" would not be long to follow.

In the small, unimportant village of Shoneval there was an experience of a slightly different nature as only one young man, dressed in a red waistcoat far too heavy for the perfect weather, walked out of town without fanfare, carrying a small suitcase he had been forced to steal from his father's attic. His mother had packed him a simple lunch but had not embraced him before he left, his father would not speak to him at all, and his girl had dismissed him as a fool. Still, he kept his mind on the sky and convinced himself that when he had won the war in his aeroplane, his father would look on him with pride and Klara would love him again — better than before.

His path would have been dusty and hot — he might have slung the waistcoat over his shoulder after a mile or two — and as time passed the familiar scenes of his youth and childhood would give way to the similar but less familiar fields and woodlots on the outskirts of the neighbouring towns and villages. Perhaps someone going to market would have given him a lift and he would have shared the straw for the space of several miles with a calf bound for slaughter.

He would remember that the road he had walked in the dark each night to Klara's house on the hill from his house in the valley and back again had taken him over the rough bridges of what appeared to be two quick-running streams, but in fact it was the same Schmidt's Creek doubling back on itself, gathering momentum for its hasty progress past the brewery. He would remember that his father had compared this artery of water, unfavourably, with the little Cummeragh River that ran past his family's cabin in the Kerry Mountains, a river whose small brown trout had saved his antecedents from certain starvation during the famine. They had been poor, though not as bad as some — their walls were made of stone, not turf. Poor enough, however, that when Eamon's father had been born into the totally altered post-famine world, there was some talk of him living with his grandfather, a cartmaker in Cahirsiveen, in order to reduce the number of mouths at the table. The talk stopped when it became clear that the old man was so totally altered by years of privation that he would have to come to them to end his days near their own fire.

And so Eamon's father had grown up beside the Cummeragh River, and the dark lakes it flowed from, in a landscape of extraordinary beauty with no future in it until, at eighteen years of age, he had walked to Tralee, joined the crew of a creaking, overcrowded ship, and had sailed for Quebec, carrying the impossible fields, lakes, and mountains in his mind when he did so.

It was all his father talked about, this small stretch of geography, as if it were a woman he had wanted to marry and was forced to separate from. Letters still arrived from there, full of newspaper clippings concerning the recent political uprisings, full of humble pleas for small amounts of cash. These were sometimes hidden by Eamon's mother because she knew that her husband could not bear to ignore them, and they got by on very little themselves. Eamon had found the envelopes in the attic and had read the contents secretly and, though he was only ten or eleven, had worried about the fate of those who wrote them, knowing that his blood was tied to theirs and that the old country — the country they were writing from — was not free.

Though he was born in Canada, Eamon still spoke with a trace of the accent that so marked his parents' speech. He knew that Irish Catholics were not well thought of in Ontario — not now, not in the past. When thousands of them had arrived in the previous century, many dying of starvation and disease, all owning only the rags on their backs, they were considered to be dirty, lazy indigents who contributed nothing but their despised popish religion and dire epidemics to the New World. Now they were slightly more accepted though they continued to be looked upon with mild suspicion, and the campaign mounted against them by the powerful Orange Lodge remained in force. Oddly, it was the German immigrants, the sons and daughters of the country Canada was now preparing to fight, that were held in highest esteem, their cleanliness, blond hair, and clear eyes making them a welcome addition to Canada. Was it his Irishness, Eamon would now wonder, that had set Klara against him, the telltale trace in his voice? Nothing in him had wanted to remind her of his origins in the beginning and this, plus his shyness, had made it almost impossible for him to speak at all.

Last year, walking back from Klara's farm, Eamon knew that he had fallen into sharp sadness and speechlessness, and he resented the stubborn authority of his emotions that, each evening, had pulled him toward cold, dark, senseless journeys, toward the gold of the loved one's lit windows, and then the golden colour of her hair. Once he was inside her kitchen he was, admittedly, grateful for the stove's warmth and mesmerized each time by the way Klara moved while she finished her chores. Often, though, he had been so uncomfortable that he kept his eyes down and had listened instead to the sound of her footsteps brushing the pine floor. When her back was to him, and while his own hands burned as the chill went out of them, he had looked furtively at her hands placing clean dishes in the cupboard. He thought her hands were like white doves. Though he had never seen these birds, had dealt only with their cousin, the pigeon, there was much reference to them in his father's sentimental Irish songs. There was a moment that he had waited for each evening, a moment when Klara straightened her spine and reached behind her back to untie her apron. Everything about her then was birdlike. White doves and swans and skylarks singing wildly over the spot where some unlucky rebel boy was about to be exiled, or hanged, or shot.

At the armouries the efficient medical officer would inspect, in a manner terse and indifferent, the body Klara had caressed. No one in the room would have gasped, as Klara had, at the young man's beauty. One doctor, when being told by Eamon that he hoped the military might let him fly an aeroplane, might have smiled benignly at the guilelessness of youth, but this would have occurred absently and without real feeling.

Klara, on the other hand, throughout her long life, would never see or hear an aeroplane without remembering the pact Eamon had made with the sky.

The nuns in the Convent of the Immaculate Conception had told Klara when she was a child that, several months before the great church was to be consecrated, Father Gstir had sent a letter to his royal benefactor in Bavaria telling him of his joy. *All around me,* he had written, *the great trees of this wilderness seem to be shouting in the wind like a choir of green angels singing to the sky. I am only one man in this wild place, but surely, Your Majesty, you too would have felt my distant rapture — and that of the landscape — the day the last stone was mortared.*

How long, Klara wondered now, how long after the mortar set did the joy remain? When one embraces a moment of rapture from the past, either by trying to reclaim it or by refusing to let it go, how can its brightness not tarnish, turn grey with longing and sorrow, until the wild spell of the remembered interlude is lost altogether and the memory of sadness claims its rightful place in the mind? And what is it we expect from the sun-drenched past? There is no formula for re-entry, nothing we can do to enable reconstruction. The features of an absent loved one's face are erased one by one, the timbre of the voice drowned by the noise of the world. Fondly recalled landscapes are savagely altered; we lose them tree by tree. Even the chestnut tree outside Klara's window would die a slow, rotting death until it would fall one night in a summer storm when everything in Klara wanted it to remain standing, blossoming in spring, leafy in summer, the only access, she secretly believed, to the window of her former self.

When Klara heard the rumour at Sunday mass that Eamon was missing, she was at first unsurprised. Of course he's missing, she thought. He's been gone. . . . I haven't seen him for more than two years. The rumour would fade, she would never have to hear it again. Then, as if a foreign organism had entered her brain and body, she could physically feel an intensification of the passion that — ever since his departure — she had identified as the torment of being abandoned, and that she now suddenly knew to be dread, a terror of permanent loss. At her grandmother's funeral half a year before, she had looked down into the dark, wet combination of stones and clay as the coffin was being lowered and had turned away sickened and terrified. The old woman's death had saddened her, of course, but it was this hidden depth of unclean soil being exposed to scrutiny, this reminder that the pretty surface was only a disguise, that brought on her lightheadedness.

After his wife's death, Klara's grandfather abandoned his workshop and farm and moved to his son's house. The old man's Virgin of Mercy had finally made the journey across the fields to Father Gstir's miraculous church; he carved only small scenes in relief now that he was forced to work in the woodshed attached to the house. His grandson could still be found in each piece, but Joseph made him smaller than before and placed him farther back in the picture plane, where he stood distanced and looking away from the central drama as if he had been captured in the act of disengagement from the world. The old man was losing hope, was becoming resigned to the idea that he might never see his grandson again in this life. His wife recently dead, his friend Father Gstir buried for decades, the child of his heart and his hope gone from him, he understood the dimensions of loss.

That Monday morning, after he had

heard the news about Eamon from the proprietor of the hardware store, Joseph Becker returned to the house and paced the kitchen for almost half an hour, his son's pleading eyes on him. The war had gone on long enough that both men knew that those reported missing were not likely to be heard from again. Young men who had lost limbs, and could therefore not be reintegrated into the fray, had returned to their hometowns of Goderich and Listowel with reports of battles so deadly that afterwards there had been no hope of identifying their lost companions. Neither man could bear to tell Klara, but eventually Joseph volunteered and stepped slowly out of the house toward her workshop.

Klara had not said the boy's name aloud for more than two years and she did not say it now, but when she saw her grandfather — grim of face — walking without his coat across the snowy yard, she knew suddenly that the rumour was true, that it involved battles and bloodshed, that her hand would never again touch Eamon's warm cheek, that she had lost him forever.

When the old man opened the door and said, "Eamon," she would not permit him to finish the sentence.

"Stop," she whispered, her mouth losing

colour, the chisel she held dropping to the floor.

"Klara," he tried again, but she was past him in a moment and out the door. In the house, she ran up the stairs to the sunroom, where she searched furiously for any frail bits of Eamon that she might not have discarded: measurements, that one photograph — all that she had thrown away. And then she remembered, crossed the room, and stood for some time staring at the engraved shape of the pattern she had drawn — all that was left of him now — and she recalled what her grandfather had told her about the likeness of medieval knights in full armour being drawn with a chisel on their marble burial slabs. He would have only the traces of a waistcoat as a memorial. She folded to the floor, her hand near the spot where his heart might have been.

Later, she faced her father and her grandfather in the now darkened kitchen, the one lit lamp mirrored in the glass of a window, and the shape of the window a hard yellow rectangle on the snow outside. The terror of descent — his fall from the sky — had been in her mind all afternoon. And now her imagination insisted on details. "I need to know, was he killed in the aeroplane," she asked, "or when it crashed to the ground?" She had heard that men shot at each other from such things.

Her father rose to his feet and walked across the floor to where Klara sat on a pine bench near the wall. "Klara, there's thousands of them over there and maybe ten aeroplanes. He was a foot soldier. He would never have got anywhere near an aeroplane. I've heard his father thinks he was killed by the British because he was Irish. These explanations!" said her father emphatically. "He was killed by the war."

What her father was implying was unbearable. In Klara's memory Eamon rose shining from the pool and ran through the forest following the clamour, or stood with his head thrown back as the airborne machine shadowed his glowing face.

"It was an aeroplane that killed him," she said in a way that was both terrible and quiet. "It's what he went over there for." Then she walked into the seldom used, unheated parlour and shut the door. As she entered the room she was injured by the sight of her own live breath in the cold air.

Everything in her wanted her innocence back, knowing her girlhood had gone to the grave with a young man who had bewitched her with a combination of silence and song — that and the shock of his touch. The details of the last time she had seen him ran over and over in her mind. She attempted to reconstruct the scene, change the outcome, to melt, in retrospect, her own coldness. She wanted to make her self open up to Eamon, warm him with her embrace, to hold him so that he would no longer be missing, broken. The thought of his body, torn and mutilated, sent waves of panic through her, then waves of nausea until she burst from the front room and retched in the kitchen sink with the two men watching her. After this she staggered back to the parlour, locked the door.

In the dimly lit surroundings she watched her breath cloud the view of the mindless bric-a-brac and stern ancestral portraits. She listened to the slow beat of the pendulum clock, the stupid progression of time.

The next morning when the men walked into the kitchen for breakfast, they found Klara dry-eyed and bleak, with only one warning sentence on her lips.

"I'll not speak of this again."

Her grandfather and her father nodded and sat at their customary places at the table to be waited on by her.

221

The silence seemed to suck all the oxygen from the room, to intensify the heat coming from the stove, and the men soon departed for the coolness and clarity of woodshed and barn.

Klara then climbed the stairs to the sunroom, where she pulled down from a shelf near the table the brown paper she used for patterns. Lying on her stomach, on a sheet she tore from the roll, she used the flat side of a pencil lead to explore the floor beneath and slowly, slowly a white line in the shape of a pattern emerged. She was worried that there would be a break in the continuity, that part of the sleeve or the shoulder would be missing. But by noon she had it, and she rose unsteadily to her feet with her eyes blurred by tears and the potential for the perfect waistcoat rolled up under her arm. Her hands trembled as she wrote to the firm in Montreal to order a bolt of their best red worsted wool and enough red braid to make the trim. And buttons with harps on them, to celebrate his Irishness. The shaky handwriting on the letter paper looked like that of an old woman.

In subsequent weeks, though she occasionally tried to work on the abbess, Klara's mind anticipated the arrival of the cloth with such tenacity she felt she could detail each mile of its journey across the eastern part of Quebec, along the curve of Lake Ontario, and into her own territory. She believed that once she began to pull the scarlet thread through the wool, once she was involved in the act of reconstruction, some of her anguish would abate. But it was winter, and in her brief rational moments she knew it would be months before the brown paper package would arrive.

One morning she found herself staring for a long time at her abbess, hurt by the fact that nothing of what she herself was feeling was evident on the wooden face. Then she began tentatively to touch the mouth and eyes, making the subtlest of incisions with chisels the size of insects. An hour later she concentrated on the small amount of hair that emerged from the cowl. Her grandfather opened the door, then stood in front of the window between her and the light. He was silent for a long, long time before he opened his mouth to speak.

"I won't talk about it," Klara warned.

The old man sat on a rough stool and looked closely at the sculpture.

"Have you been to confession, Klara?" he asked.

"Yes," she replied, knowing that he would think she had spoken of it there.

She hadn't.

Joseph Becker ran his crooked fingers over the hair at the abbess's forehead. "She is too sad," he said finally. "Her hair, her hands . . . even her shoes are too sad. A woman this caught up with grief would be unable to counsel anyone at all." He pointed to the wooden cheek. "This line in her face has a life of its own, like a tear falling across skin. An abbess would never allow a hair of her head to be out of place, nor sadness to rule her life. You'll have to do something about that before you deliver her to the church. Father Gstir never would have stood for it."

"The church?" said Klara. It was the first time her grandfather had suggested the church as a destination for anything she had done.

"Yes," the old man said, "the church is the place for your abbess, but not, of course, until she has achieved sainthood."

"But I am carving an abbess, not a saint."

"Any work of art," said her grandfather, "must achieve sainthood before we set it free to roam in the world."

Three months later the cloth had arrived. Klara often stood beside her cutting table in a sorrowful trance, staring at the red material, unable to pick up the scissors, unable to thread a needle. It was easier, somehow, to work on the sculpture, easier to be away from the house. On a wet day in spring, rain was racketing on the tin roof her father had recently nailed on her workshop to replace the shingles that had begun to rot and then to leak, leaving an irremovable dark stain, like a birthmark, on the statue's left cheek. A miserable wind was forcing its way in through the cracks in the walls. She had been working on the fingernails of the abbess's right hand, but her own hands were becoming too cold to continue this delicate work. And she was dispirited, knowing that soon thousands of men who had survived the war would be returning. They would be returning and Eamon would remain where he was. Vanished.

Later when she told her grandfather in the kitchen she had given up on her sculpture, all he said was "This is too bad, Klara. Now there will be no carvers left in the family."

Joseph's first admission that he had abandoned the idea of Tilman, that he believed the boy to be irrevocably lost, shocked Klara. It occurred to her, though she didn't know why, that if her grandfather had let the idea of Tilman go, the old man would most certainly die, and quite soon. She walked across the floor to where he sat and clasped one of his hands. The history of the overwhelming labour of pioneer farming, the tools of woodcarving were all contained in this crooked warm package of sinew, vein, and bone. "Perhaps," she began, "perhaps Tilman is even now a famous carver in Europe. Perhaps he is making such beautiful things we can't even imagine them."

She didn't want her grandfather to let the boy go, she didn't want the old man to die. And in her heart she wanted Tilman to remain free, engaged in the life that was lived beyond the ordered walls of this farmhouse that so predictably echoed farmhouses all over the county. She realized suddenly that operating side by side with her grandfather's need was her own . . . this desire to believe in another vital reality, one she couldn't see. As if Tilman were a planet so far away as to be imperceptible, moving in a wholly different orbit, emitting an unseen, perfect light. If he were really gone then it would be as if the last vestiges of auxiliary mystery were abruptly removed from the world. "I think he's still alive," she said. "I believe he is the part of us that is learning the world."

The old man looked at his granddaughter — his blue eyes still piercing, inquisitive — and asked her what she meant.

She dropped his hand and brushed one long white forelock from his forehead. Then she straightened her spine. "I don't know what I mean, but I know I believe it."

"But not enough to continue the carving."

Klara heard the sound of her father's boots in the woodshed. She walked over to the soup that had begun to bubble on the stove. "I believe in Tilman," she said. "I just don't believe in myself. I seem to be disappearing, even when I am present in a room."

"Someday," Joseph said to his granddaughter, "someday something will happen and you will want to go back to the carving. You won't be able to prevent yourself; that's just the way it is. The world always somehow takes us back to the chisel. Something happens and we have to respond."

Her father, who had walked into the centre of this strange conversation, looked at his daughter's pale, tired face and thought, Poor Klara, I fear nothing will ever happen to her. But he said nothing.

"I don't know," said Klara, ladling soup into bowls. "I just don't know."

Before she had turned to walk out the door of her workshop for the last time, Klara had run the fingers of her right hand over the wooden face, which, she realized, would never be right, though oddly the stain had made the abbess seem more human. She looked into the blank wooden eyes and whispered, "I'm sorry I couldn't help you reach sainthood, couldn't help you get into the church." As she spoke she heard the steeple bell on the hill begin to call out the twelve hours of noon with its sweet, resonant voice and then a slightly higher ringing, with a thinner sound echoing it from the convent. For just an instant she visualized the nun and the priest, separated but still engaged in an act of communion, speaking together through their joint tasks. She envied them the joy of their faith, and their ability to communicate through this act of tolling annunciation. All her faith was gone and with it the desire for carving, for making something spiritual out of wood. With Eamon lost, she felt connected to no one.

She knew that all that remained of the texture of his skin was what she could remember with her own senses. But, as the months went by, she began to feel the past was shutting her out. Eventually, she knew all that would be left of Eamon would be bones and teeth scattered who knew where. Sometimes she dreamt of these remnants, dreamt herself wandering some distant battlefield, having collected his bones, which she carried in her arms like a bundle of kindling. But in the dream she was always searching because although she carried the miraculous package close to her heart, there was always a rib or a thigh bone she couldn't find.

Sometimes while she was sewing she thought for hours at a time about life beyond her walls. It was then she felt most like a ghost haunting the businesses and shops of the only community she knew, of no relevance to the actors in any of the small dramas that were unfolding. She who had recorded the body measurements of everyone in town, who knew their vanities, intuited their secret romances, could determine their mood during a fitting by gesture or posture, left absolutely no trace of herself in the minds of those she encountered. She knew she was a purveyor of costume, of disguise, a fabricator of persona, one who touched only the protective surface, never the skin, never the heart. She was beginning, as a consequence, to envy almost everyone she met, to envy their small preoccupations, their carefully kept account books, the way they stood on streetcorners talking about farm machinery, the weather, the price of a bag of oats, fully connected for the moment to these ordinary things. Her own connections continually slipped downstream, against the current, toward the swiftly disappearing past. What, beyond the most cursory, practical knowledge of fashion, had the present to do with her?

2

THE ROAD

Tilman had not paused at the bend in the road to look back at the farm. He had always enjoyed the far view of this familiar world, distance having knit together the disparate components of barn, orchard, pasture, and house into a satisfying whole — a picture he could take with him in his mind. But this time anger and fear drove him so rapidly forward he scarcely thought of anything but panic and motion. He was in full flight, passing swiftly through the scattered dawn mists of what would become a warm autumn day, breath entering and leaving his harnessed body, the chain scraping the pebbles of the road behind him. Despite the coolness of the early hour, his hair gradually dampened with sweat and turned from yellow to soft brown. He was twelve years old, was small for his age, but inside there lived an old man who knew the ways of the road.

He had learned the advantages of knowing several Protestant hymns by heart. This he had accomplished on a previous journey by crouching under an open church window one summer in the town of

Sebringville, concentrating fiercely so that the words, the tunes would enter him forever. On previous flights, whenever he was desperate he could stand on the corner of any street in any town and begin to sing "Unto the Hills," or "Rock of Ages," or "To Be a Pilgrim" in his beautiful boy's voice with his cap on the sidewalk in front of him and be assured that he would have enough pennies by noon to buy sausage at a butcher's, bread at a baker's. He had been powerful in his freedom then, delighted by the awareness that absolutely no one knew where he was and that those he met briefly — a shopkeeper, a matron dropping pennies in his cap — had no idea who he was.

Now with the chain rattling behind him, he avoided all human contact, not wanting the questions this evidence of imprisonment would undoubtedly raise. He kept to the country roads, lived on stolen hens' eggs that he sucked raw and unidentifiable food he was sometimes able to glean from the pigs' slop pail in night barns. The harness chafed his skin, he was half-starved, and by his third or fourth day on the road he had developed a harsh cough, but none of this was as bad as the chain attached to the woodshed door jamb of a house filled with intimates who could never understand him.

And yet, as the days went by, and because he knew he could never go back, each night as he shuddered under a stolen bundle of burlap bags, Tilman mentally reconstructed the home he had left behind room by room, remembering a particular detail of a sofa or chair or the grain or scarring on a table. He had loved the house; it had never — until the end — seemed like a prison to him. This time he had been too late for the birds, which had made his frenzied progress less urgent in terms of reaching a premeditated destination. But he was left feeling aimless and adrift, and the physical particulars of the house anchored him somewhat as a fixed point of departure, since he had no images to associate with arrival.

In early December, when it seemed he would never be warm again, he met an agitated figure — a bundle of quivering rags — on the road between Goderich and Clinton. He had been on his own for several weeks, long enough to become so familiar with the sound of his chain rattling behind him that he was instantly put on the alert when the sound ceased. He stopped and turned and saw a person behind him who was holding the last link with one crooked finger and who, when he tried to run, grasped the chain with two fists. Whoever it was reeled him in like a difficult carp.

"Who are you?" the figure demanded in a woman's voice. "What's yer name?"

He was close enough to her now that he could see clear blue eyes and a hawklike nose. The rest of the face was wrapped in scarves. A cap with earflaps covered the head.

"What's yer name?" the woman repeated. "Did you escape from a chain gang?"

The sound of Tilman's heart was so loud it seemed to be coming from outside his body. When he felt her tug on the taut chain, he began to shake.

"Yer just a kid," the woman said. "Think I'll call you chain-gang kid." She laughed and rattled the chain. "Do you like it, chain-gang kid?"

Tilman did not answer.

"The name, I mean."

Silence. The cold was enough to kill you. That plus the fear made his teeth chatter.

Without letting go of the chain the woman removed one of her several shawls and threw it over Tilman's shoulders.

"That'll make it better. You ain't been on the road for long, that's plain."

Tilman shook his head. His first response.

"Well, you won't get far with this thing draggin' behind you like the leash of a mad dog. 'Sides, we can sell it for scrap metal. My name's Crazy Phoebe," she said, holding firm to his chain with her left hand while extending her right.

Tilman put his own hands behind his back. He had always distrusted this strange gesture that joined adults to one another.

"Don't shake then," the woman said. "I'll shake your chain instead." She did this and laughed, breaking into a cough that lasted for several minutes while Tilman looked down at the road. "Giddy-up," the woman said when she had recovered herself. "Let's get goin'. Lucky for you I live in two places and one of them is junkyards, or at least them ones without them beasts from hell and has good owners. We'll get rid of this," she shook his chain again, "outside Goderich. Good junkyard there. Somebody'll cut her off yer at the junkyard."

They began to walk. After a long silence, the woman continued, "The other places I live is basements, but only at farms with cellar doors." They walked past the whole length of a prosperous-looking farm. "And good farmwives," she added. "Some women is hell. They's preserves in them basements been down there for years everyone's forgot. They's way back in the darkest parts hid by spiderwebs so as no one sees them, put there by some old granny whose all bones now in the graveyard. One year I lived entirely on strawberry jam. Fat as a dumpling when spring come." She peered closely at Tilman. "You could use some fattening," she said. "What yer been eating?"

More silence from Tilman. Each night at dusk he had slunk toward compost heaps and dumps. One day he had eaten nothing but tea leaves and potato peels. Another day he had drunk a half-bottle of Doc Chrighton's Grippe Reliever he had found among mostly broken and empty medicine bottles in a midden behind a woodlot. This had left him staggering and drowsy for two days. Since then the world had seemed slightly askew, and certain sounds — a dry leaf scraping over pebbles or a door slamming in the distance — had startled and disturbed him.

"Chain child," said Crazy Phoebe after a long pause, "you're not even a kid, you're a child. Kids roam in packs, as you'll find out once you're one of them. Chain child. Sounds better."

Now the chain hung slack between them as if they'd been skipping rope like he knew girls did, while chanting rhymes in a menacing minor key, in the school-yard. It was as if he and this woman were waiting for another song to come into their minds.

"Up there's the yard," said Phoebe after another stretch of silent walking. "Old Ham Bone there'll cut her off'n you."

Tilman could see only a seemingly end-less board fence, painted green.

"Knew old Ham Bone in my youth when he was still raising hogs, knew him before I was crazy. Knew his dog too."

"What's the dog's name?" asked Tilman, his first question.

"Saw Tooth," Phoebe answered. "Known old Saw Tooth since he was a pup out barkin' the bejeesus outta Ham Bone's piglets on the farm. Known him since be-fore I was crazy. Old Ham Bone give up the farm cause he didn't have no woman round there no more. Anyways, he always got blue when them piglets growed-up and had to be slaughtered. Saw Tooth got blue too. You know what happens to a growed-up piglet what isn't slaughtered?"

Tilman did not.

"Damn things get so big from overeating they can't raise themselves up on the hoof to get to the trough for no more slops so they starve to death." Phoebe shook her head. "Damn things," she repeated.

They were walking along the fence now, a fence so long it seemed to Tilman to divide the world in half, and a fence so tall Tilman knew there was no human being tall enough to see over it.

Finally Phoebe forced aside one large, loose green board and squeezed through the fence, pulling Tilman after her. He was not unaware that the regular entrance, which was wide open, was only a few yards off. "Always go in this way," Phoebe told him. She rearranged her several shawls that had become even more dishevelled when they caught on boards and projecting nails. "Always go out this way too," she added in a conspiratorial whisper.

Tilman looked around him at an array of rusting farm machinery, threshers, binders, hand and horse ploughs, pumps, gears, wrought iron, fire escapes, boilers, wheel axles, woodstoves, coal furnaces, and various unidentifiable bits and pieces. Behind two or three tangled lengths of iron he could see a wooden shack with a stovepipe projecting from its roof.

"Ham Bone," Phoebe yelled at the building. "Ham Bone, get out here and see. Phoebe's got a brand-new dog fine enough to make Saw Tooth pea green with envy."

The door opened and a medium-sized dog whose black-and-white coat appeared to be made up of moulting feathers sprang into noise and action. Tilman moved behind his female companion while a black-and-white blur made loud, furious circles around the two of them.

"Saw Tooth!" shouted Phoebe. "For God's sake, settle down. I was just fooling. It's just a tethered boy called Chain Child."

Saw Tooth shimmied over to Phoebe and licked her hand, then lay on his back while she caressed his feathered stomach.

Tilman was watching a large, red-faced man emerge from the open door of the shack and begin to walk toward them. "What the hell . . ." the man said when he saw Tilman's chain. "What the hell is this all about?"

"Don't know nothing about it, Ham Bone," Phoebe said while absently rattling the links. "Except think it should be off'n him."

"Jesus, kid," said Ham Bone. "Where did you get that chain?"

Tilman did not answer.

"Jesus," said Ham Bone again. Then he walked back to his shed and returned a few moments later with a hacksaw. "Hold still, boy," he commanded as he placed the chain on a nearby anvil and began to saw.

"What yer gonna do about that harness?" asked Phoebe when the chain was removed. "Can't have Chain Child wearing that harness for the rest of his life. He'll grow for sure, and that thing'll break his ribs."

Ham Bone sighed and went back to the shed for a smaller saw. When the lock was sawed open and the harness cast aside, the large man turned his attention to the woman. "Phoebe," he began. To Tilman's amazement he saw that the man's eyes were filling with tears. "Phoebe," he repeated, "where you been these last months?"

"No place near no hog barn," she said. "What you gonna give Chain Child and me for that good scrap metal? Also we is cold, and we need some place to warm up." She pointed toward the shack. "Let's go in there," she said.

Ham Bone leaned down and looked Tilman in the eyes. "You're mighty dirty, boy," he said. "You think you could find me a washtub out here with no holes in the bottom? Holes in the top is fine, but holes in the bottom is no good. You find me a washtub and we'll give you a bath."

This reference to domesticity put Tilman on guard. "I won't stay," he said.

"I won't stay neither," announced Phoebe.

"I know that," said Ham Bone softly. "I know that."

Tilman waited until the adults disappeared inside the shack. Then he twisted his upper body and flung his arms and legs about in all directions, delighted to be free of the yoke.

It was getting near dark when Tilman knocked on the shack door, having found a serviceable tub. Once he was inside, room temperature hit him like a furnace blast. Ham Bone had heated up a large can of beans, which they all shared silently. After this the man excused himself to lock up the yard and to fill the tub with water at the outside pump. When he returned he placed the tub on the woodstove. Tilman, experiencing warmth for the first time in weeks, dozed in his chair until Ham Bone used his own large coat to make the boy a bed on the floor. Some time later Tilman was awakened by Saw Tooth licking his face. The dog circled three times, then lay down at his side. From their place in the shadows, the boy and the dog watched the adults.

Ham Bone lifted the tub from the stove and tested the water with his hand. Then he stood and looked at the woman, who was slouching in a chair on the opposite side of the room.

"C'mon, Phoebe," he said.

"No," she said. "You ain't gonna get at me."

"I won't get at you," said Ham Bone softly, "but, Phoebe, you don't smell so good."

"I'm shamed by that," said Phoebe in a voice new to Tilman.

"It's not your fault," Ham Bone approached her slowly. "Let me take off these clothes, Phoeb."

"No," she replied but did not move away from him.

He placed a large hand on her head. "Phoeb," he said again as he began to unwind one of the several scarves she had tied around her head.

From where Tilman lay, everything seemed to be slowed by heat and by the orange light thrown from the coal oil lantern. That and the panting of the dog, whose warmth now penetrated the boy's left side.

"I won't let you take nothing off'n me," said Phoebe in her new voice, which had lost direction and meaning.

Ham Bone was removing her shawls, layer by layer. Tilman watched amazed as the woman who had rescued him became smaller and smaller. The dog sighed contentedly and put his nose between his front paws.

Tilman counted five skirts falling to the floor and still Phoebe was covered by clothing. But her surprisingly long, thin arms were bare now and hung limply by her side.

"What about that boy?" she said. "He ain't never seen a woman undressing, that's for sure."

"He's asleep," said Ham Bone. He removed a soiled petticoat and a camisole, and Phoebe's thin, white body reflected the lamplight and seemed to Tilman to shake off the darkness of the shadows around her. As a last gesture, Ham Bone unwound the final scarf wrapped tight to her head and a profusion of red curls exploded around her shoulders.

Tilman was just a child, but he knew that the woman he was looking at was younger than his mother. And he knew that she was beautiful.

"You didn't smell so good yerself," said Phoebe, "before I was crazy and you was coming in from the hog barns."

"No, Phoebe," said Ham Bone. "No, I didn't." He took her hand. "Come on," he said gently, "come on into the water."

"I won't set right down in it."

"No, that's fine, just step in there." Ham Bone crossed the room and took a rag from a nail on the wall, then returned to where Phoebe was standing in the tub.

The scene that unfolded before Tilman was one he would never forget. Years later when he came at last to love someone, the memory of this night would fall like rain into his mind: the gentle tenderness, the sound of falling water. He would remember the way the young woman's buttocks and calves shone when the man had put water there, and the glistening snails' tracks on her belly that, as an adult, Tilman would realize meant that she had borne a child. He would remember the tears on the large man's face as he moved the cloth under her breasts and down the insides of her thighs. And he would remember her utter submissiveness after all her protestations.

Now Phoebe placed her hands on Ham Bone's shoulders as he crouched before her and washed first one foot and then the other.

"How did I get to be crazy?" she asked, her head bent.

Ham Bone was silent. He wrung out the cloth, and the water sounded like a wealth of grief as it entered the tub.

"Will you come home, Phoebe?" he asked quietly. "You don't have to be crazy no more. We could take in the boy."

Tilman stiffened, preparing, as always, for flight at the suggestion of confinement.

But Phoebe refused. "I don't hold with homes," she said. "Homes is where sorrow is at."

Ham Bone took off his shirt and put it like a nightgown on her as she stepped out of the tub. Then he moved behind her and circled her waist with his arms, drawing her down until they were both kneeling, she on his lap. He pushed her slowly forward, then guiding her chin to her chest he brushed her red hair into the warm water.

"It feels good," Phoebe said, "this warm water on my head."

"I know," said Ham Bone. "I'll wash your clothes if you sleep the night here."

"You won't get at me?"

"No, but you'll eat something, and you'll spend the night here."

"If I was to let you get at me," said Phoebe, "we'd only have another baby what would die."

She began to weep.

Ham Bone held her. "I won't get at you, Phoebe," he said. "I know you'd only go away again anyways."

The next morning Phoebe shook Tilman awake while it was still dark. The boy scrambled nervously to his feet at her touch, then pivoted in the dark trying to determine where he was. When he saw the glowing coals of the pot-bellied stove, he remembered the warmth of the scene he had witnessed the previous evening, and the fact that the chain and the harness were gone, and he felt light-headed, giddy with new physical freedom.

Phoebe had covered herself once again with the layers of tattered clothing Ham Bone had rinsed out the night before and left near the fire to dry. All evidence of the young redheaded woman Tilman had seen were gone, buried under cloth. He could hear Ham Bone snoring in the corner of the shack.

"Hurry up," said Phoebe. "We got to get out of here before he wakes up."

Tilman, not knowing what else to do, headed for the door, though he knew the man was kind, not a threat. The dog stood watching them sleepily, then, evidently familiar with scenes of departure, groaned, walked in a circle, and curled up at the large man's side.

"We got to keep moving," said Phoebe as they walked through the junkyard. "You stay still someone'll put a cage on you sure as anything." She looked at the boy. "Guess you know that, don't you, Chain Child?"

"Yes," said Tilman. "Yes, I guess I do."

Tilman travelled with Phoebe for less than a week. Neither one being disposed to changing their itineraries for anyone, they soon reached that inevitable crossroad where Phoebe took it in her mind to head east at the same time as Tilman headed west.

The boy was no more than fifteen paces away from Phoebe when he heard her call to him. He turned on his heel and sauntered back to where she stood. The breeze had picked up and in the sky there was a suggestion of snow. Tilman was hoping to reach a town as quickly as possible.

"Just want to give you something before you head off for God knows where." Phoebe rummaged around in her layers of clothing. "Just want to give you the god-damned Royal Thunderer."

Eventually she unearthed a bright silver whistle. "Can you read?" she demanded.

Tilman nodded.

"Then read that." Phoebe pointed to some lettering incised on the surface. "Read it out loud."

"Royal Thunderer."

"Ham Bone give it to me in case someone ever wanted to get at me on the road." She laughed and shook her head. "No one ever liked me enough to try. It's all yours," she said, handing the object to Tilman, then turning to walk away. "And remember, just whistle."

He nodded and began to walk away. Then Tilman heard Phoebe calling him one more time. "I won't come running, though, not now, not ever."

"I know you won't."

"Try it and see. Count to one hundred, then whistle."

While watching the batch of rags that

covered Phoebe's back grow smaller and smaller, Tilman counted slowly to one hundred. Then he put the Royal Thunderer in his mouth and blew. A trilling sound pierced the air.

Phoebe stopped, stood entirely still for several moments, her scarves and shawls flapping in the wind. Without turning around she lifted one arm in the air, waved it around, then started walking once again.

And so began Tilman's unchained adventures on the road.

When he was more than likely thirteen or fourteen years old, Tilman lived under a bridge that crossed the Nith River in Waterloo County. He had been walking and running on the dusty concession roads for days, stopping to beg for food at the tidy Amish and Mennonite farms common in the region, a little frightened by the somewhat familiar German dialect spoken there. He was concerned that because he had travelled for so long he might have actually left his own country behind and entered a territory so foreign he would never again understand anything. Once, he had questioned a woman who had just given him a whole apple pie, which he had spotted cooling on her windowsill. "Canada?" he had asked. "Ontario?" The woman had not understood the context of his question but had asked his name. Hearing her speak English, his mind at ease, he ran away without answering, the pie held out in front of him.

It was around this time that he began to train himself as a runner, understanding that this was a skill useful to him in his chosen way of life. His legs were longer now, and they had filled out some in recent months. They were, of course, along with his hands, the part of his anatomy he knew best, mirrors coming infrequently into his visual experience and often startling him when they did cross his path in that he had so little acquaintance with the boy he saw in them. But his legs, though covered by his patched trousers, were familiar, a dependable place to rest one's hands or elbows and something to hold on to when crouching in a doorway or sitting at the edge of the road. He liked the firmness of his thighs, the boniness of his knees, and the reliability of his feet — despite his often desperate footwear. And he would never forget that it was his legs that had removed him from the place where he had been chained and had helped him escape chains of one kind or another ever since.

He ran along the spines of hills, along fence lines, through the narrow green hallways of tall corn. He ran on old settlement corduroy roads where the ribs of the logs on which they were built passed under his feet like waves, or on farm lanes that had a bright green band of grass between the two tracks of beaten earth. He ran on railway tracks, pacing his stride so that his feet never once missed a tie, and across trestles with such swiftness and confidence that he was disturbed neither by their height nor by the moaning sound of a distant whistle. He ran around baseball diamonds at the edge of villages on early-summer mornings before anyone else was awake, back and forth on Great Lake piers at Owen Sound or Goderich by moonlight. While he was in Waterloo County he drifted, once, into the city of Berlin and was seen by a policeman at dawn running down King Street after a good breakfast at the garbage bin behind the Walper Hotel. Having mostly avoided heavily populated areas, it had simply never occurred to Tilman that a policeman would be awake at four-thirty in the morning, but when he discovered that one was pursuing him he ran faster than he had known he could, straight out of the city, heading north until a kind of oxygen euphoria infused every cell of his body, stopping only when he could see nothing but trees and fields, having no knowledge that the policeman had given up after two blocks.

A few days later Tilman came upon the bridge. Hot, dirty, and thirsty, having run just that morning past the villages of Bamberg and Wellesley and Nithburg, he had seen the river lying like a bent silver arm in a valley half a mile away and had taken a narrow road to reach it, descending a hill so steep that he didn't see the bridge until he was halfway down the incline. Made of iron girders and shaped like the back of a large animal whose skeleton was being presented to the boy in profile, every part of the structure delighted Tilman. He ran back and forth over its planked floor, across the shadows of its steel beams several times, though he was breathless and covered with sweat. Then he tore off his tattered clothes, climbed up on one of the iron railings, and jumped into the green-brown water beneath, which he had figured would be deep enough for the plunge. Floating on his back and looking up at the sky, he was able to admire the bridge from below, the way the sunlight shone between the planks and how the whole framework sat so squarely on its cement abutments. It was then he realized that, with scrub bushes on either side and the incline of the bank, the positioning of the southern abutment created the perfect shelter, the perfect hiding place, and he decided to make it his home.

It was a good summer. The view from

the bridge was extensive in all directions, hills and fields and orchards being cut into geometric shapes by the angles the steel girders made, and the sound of the water was soothing. Tilman was up before dawn during his first few days at the bridge, skulking around the sheds and the dumps of neighbouring farms to get orange crates for furniture and empty cans and bottles for tableware. Once, he took a fishing rod that had been left leaning against a railing of a back porch. He kept it for a week, then, well fed and filled with guilt, he returned it to the spot, placing two freshly caught trout on the doorstep as a kind of payment. It was then that he first saw the border collie that wagged his tail vaguely as a greeting before ambling casually in the direction of the smell of fish.

After that it didn't take the dog long to find the boy, to scramble down the bank and shimmy into the cave Tilman had made for himself. The dog approached the boy with courteous discretion, his ears down, his tail moving in circles. Tilman thought of calling him Saw Tooth but named him Buster instead, changing it only when the dog responded to a faraway human voice calling for Shep. Shep arrived at least once a day, sometimes much more often. No one else knew the boy was there, even though, because he needed food, the Amish farmers spoke in Pennsylvania Deutsch about the beggar boy who was sometimes found with his hands out at their back doors, and the usual attempts were made by women to capture and tame him.

Tilman sat under the bridge all summer watching the refracted light from the river tremble on cement and wood, memorizing the shape of the opposite bank, and listening to the sound of wagons and tractors rattling on the planks above him. He walked the river in both directions, passing by cows and the occasional horse but never meeting anyone else. These outings were considered adventures by him, but he preferred the cool shade of the cave, his view of engineering and of water, and of fragments of woodlots and fence lines. He liked also the way the dog stayed beside him, panting and alert, his ears and nose twitching in response to the subtlest changes in the atmosphere.

Having looked at the river for so long, Tilman was able finally to understand the language of water: quiet water, and water that speaks. He knew the slow, almost imperceptible sigh of it during weeks of drought, and its more aggressive babble after four or five days of rain. When it was swollen, full of itself, the river was most likely to offer surprising gifts: a perfectly fine and much-needed pair of boots tied together by their laces on one occasion, a toy boat on another, and, as the season progressed, apples fallen from the trees of neighbouring orchards.

He loved the bridge with a child's love, the way a boy will love a tree house in the yard or a clubhouse in a scrub lot. But he loved it too in a way peculiar to his own nature, because it gave him shelter without closing him in. There were no impenetrable walls, no doors that might contain locks. Air and light flowed through it, all the landscape's openness was visible from it. And always below him there was the river, solemnly moving and changing, going somewhere else.

Tilman knew the river was heading west. At the end of August, a week and a half of torrential rain made it hurry in that direction. Then, in the middle of September, a small punt came bobbing swiftly around the bend a quarter-mile upriver, and Tilman and the dog ran down to the bank to meet it. It caught on a log about fifty feet from the bridge and the boy leapt toward it, delighted by the fact that it had a rope attached to its bow. This he tied to a steel ring embedded in one of the cement abutments, and then he spent the rest of the day gathering branches to hide it from potential thieves. Its appearance seemed like a miracle, for Tilman was aware that soon he would have to follow in the wake of the migrating birds, and now he would have a vehicle for the journey.

He floated away in the middle of September, leaving the dog barking wildly on the beloved bridge and leaving too all the various textures of the undulating terrain that had become so familiar to him. He had had, though he did not know it, his first encounter with intimacy, his first experience of knowing something, anything, so well and in such proximity that he would never forget it. He had seen the bridge in every kind of summer light and darkness, knew the sounds it made when it supported wagons or motor cars or the odd bicyclist. Years later he would be able to close his eyes and see the exact patterns of rust on steel, the distinct black-and-white markings of a dog's coat, or the way tall grasses bend in a breeze near the margins of a river, and when he recalled these details he would experience also the ache of loss. He had taken all these things into his heart and had voluntarily left them behind, the way he imagined that Phoebe had left Ham Bone. Nothing had kept him there, and so he loved the place harder as he let it go. His first true home growing smaller and smaller, its bones black against the sun as he sat facing the stern of the boat the river had given him. He shouted goodbye to the bridge and yelled words of praise to Shep, who hurled himself down the bank to follow the punt to the edge of the farm. Tilman knew the dog had been trained not to leave the property, so he was forced to call out one last word of farewell to him before a bend in the river removed them each from the other's sight. He realized that these words of leave-taking were the first sounds he had made in weeks, that his voice was harsh and rusty as a result, and choked as well by tears.

Each autumn Tilman had followed the birds to the flat marshlands of southwestern Ontario. Situated on the northwest shore of Lake Erie, these reed-filled areas swept around the long curve of bays or moved out into the body of the lake, forming their own uncertain peninsulas. Or they journeyed inland, taking the edge of the water with them so that early settlers were sometimes surprised to awaken to a new damp world of frantic cries, beating wings, and singing frogs, as if the lake itself had made a decision to push both them and their recently constructed log houses farther inland.

Farther east the land stabilized, and here prosperous farms developed in full view of the water. Tilman knew the back screen doors of every solid red-brick farmhouse along the narrow highway called the old Talbot Road, and their front doors as well with the beautiful sunburst transoms, though he knew better than to knock there. He was familiar with all the barns, their granaries and mounds of hay, and had visited some of these wooden cathedrals so often that certain animals seemed to acknowledge his arrival with pleasure.

Occasionally Tilman was permitted entrance into one of the brick fortresses. This would happen when a gentleman farmer's wife or a kitchen servant along the route would attempt to adopt him, to entice him into the domestic fold with hot food, a comfortable bed, and clean clothes handed down from their own or their mistresses' children. Much later he would tell a friend that he particularly remembered the painted hallways of these places, how itinerant painters had worked the prosperous line, leaving behind them walls filled with distant blue landscapes quite different from the scenery anyone was likely to see in southwestern Ontario. After a few days of leaning on newel posts and losing himself in the drowsy ease of far-off imaginary mountains and nights spent in starched white sheets, he would become anxious and, inevitably, one early morning unable to sleep he would run off into the darkness.

The men always assumed he was an escaped Barnardo boy, one of hundreds of orphans sent from England to Ontario farms to work as hired hands. Tilman had found it best never to argue with an adult opinion of his condition, having learned during his time on the road that it was always safer to have an explanation for what one policeman had called "chronic vagrancy." Sometimes farmers offered him work in apple orchards or hay fields, and Tilman would keep the resulting coins in a handkerchief he had stolen years before from his sister's dresser drawer because of its flying birds pattern.

But he wouldn't stay long — never more than a week — preferring to move from orchard to orchard and in the summer and autumn refusing any employment that did not include a view of the lake. During high summer he picked strawberries with large crowds of migrant workers, content with his anonymity in the throng. He loved these mornings, dew silvering the low plants, stars of sunlight on the lake. And in the evenings, swimming in the lake washed the sweat from his skin and all the winter anxiety from his mind. He was content in the knowledge that he was connected with nothing, no one, that neither his presence nor his absence counted for so much that he or anyone else needed to be dependent upon it. The days moved by with the fluidity of a silk scarf drawn through a ring. No work in a field or a pasture was onerous to him; nothing compared with the panic and exhaustion he felt when scrambling for food and warmth and shelter in the winter.

He had been — so far — a road tramp, a child of farms and villages. In the winter he put himself up for any kind of adoption, and had been taken in by pastors and matrons, bankers and thieves, or under the wing of a series of adult tramps who taught him how to look forlorn, and how to beg, and had taken more than half of the profits for themselves.

In his sixth autumn on the road he had stayed so long in the tomato belt in Essex County that the geese were mostly gone from the shores of Lake Erie, and the lake had become too cold for him to venture into. Banners of shimmering gold leaves were streaming past the brick houses where he begged his meals, and the barns were full to overflowing with a successful harvest. One crisp morning a farmer asked him to stack the firewood an older tramp was splitting, offering him twenty-five cents, a meal, and a cot in the barn in return. He showed Tilman a wheelbarrow. "Take all that wood the Italian's split and put it in the barn. Mind it's neatly stacked." Tilman looked across the lane to the edge of the pasture where an olive-skinned man with curly grey hair was working like a tightly wound machine, his axe flashing in the sun, dark stains under his arms, though the day was cool.

"He's a queer one," the farmer remarked, "but one hell of a worker."

Tilman made two or three trips to the shed before the man chopping wood spoke to him.

"I'm not chopping wood," he said. "Don't tell anyone I'm chopping wood." He balanced a large piece of oak on the stump in front of him, lifted the axe high over his head, held the pose for a second or two, then slammed the axe into the flesh of the wood, splitting it into four equal pieces. "I didn't come down here to find Italians," he said. "I'm not Italian. There are no Italians in Leamington. I haven't been picking tomatoes."

"I seen lots of Italians picking tomatoes," said Tilman, "and lots what own the farms they're grown on."

"You must never tell anyone that," said the man, repositioning a log that had fallen from the stump. "And don't tell anyone that I told you not to tell."

Tilman had met many hobos on the road who were running from one thing or another: wives, children, the law. "I won't tell nobody nothing," he said. "What's your name? Mine's Tilman."

"Your name is not Tilman," said the Italian, making instant kindling out of another log. "It's not Tilman any more than mine is Refuto."

Tilman thought about this while he hauled a loaded wheelbarrow to the shed. By the time he returned, the man was sitting on the stump, wiping his face with a dirty cloth and drinking water from a pail. He rinsed his mouth and spat on the ground.

Tilman shook his head. "I think your name is Refuto, 'cause mine is surely Tilman."

"Who wants to know?" asked the Italian suspiciously. "And why?"

"Nobody wants to know except me."

"I didn't ask who wanted to know. I'm not chopping any more wood." Suddenly the man's eyes went as blank as the ones Tilman remembered from his grandfather's wooden statues. He remained utterly still, unbreathing, for two or three minutes. Then he inhaled deeply, his eyes snapped back into focus, he leapt to his feet, grabbed the axe, and attacked another piece of wood.

"Not . . . one . . . Italian . . . working . . .

here . . . chopping . . . wood!" he shouted. "Not . . . one!"

Tilman threw two pieces of split wood into the pile. "You look like one Italian to me," he said quietly.

"Who told you that?"

"No one."

The man rested his axe on the stump and stared into space. "This boy," he said, "did not say, 'No one.' "

Tilman picked up the handles of the wheelbarrow and marched off toward the shed. When he came back he addressed the man by name. "Refuto," he began.

"No," said Refuto, "my name is not Refuto. Who told you my name was Refuto?"

"You did."

"I did not."

"Well, you told me your name *wasn't* Refuto, which made me think more 'n likely it was."

Refuto selected a piece of cedar from the pile. The energy seemed to have leaked out of his argument, but still he looked suspiciously from side to side. "Just don't tell anybody," he said.

"Refuto," Tilman began again.

"No," said Refuto.

"Refuto, are you crazy?"

"I'm not crazy."

"Are you starvin'?" Tilman had seen older hobos hallucinate and start to rave when they had gone without food for a long time . . . or when they were suddenly without alcohol.

"Not starving," said Refuto.

"What's the matter with you then?"

"You didn't ask that."

"Aw, c'mon, I did so."

Tilman was feeling irritation, a barely remembered sensation, one he had not experienced so far on the road. Almost all the other sentiments and passions had visited him: fear, affection, happiness, agitation, excitement, very occasionally boredom — but not since his parents had sent him to school had he felt irritation. He pushed the wheelbarrow over to the growing pile of wood. Refuto's axe whistled through the air, then smashed through wood over and over, as if the man were an oversized mechanical toy. Tilman noticed Refuto was shaped almost exactly like a bear.

"You sure can split wood," said Tilman. "So you don't have anything the matter with your arms."

"What arms?" said Refuto. "Who says I got arms?"

Tilman sighed and trudged back to the shed with a full load. "I'm not hauling wood to the shed," he called over his shoulder. Then he laughed and picked up his pace. Behind his back he could hear Refuto laughing too. By evening they were the best of friends.

The day, much like the days Tilman's grandfather had experienced half a century before, had been one devoted to wood: hardwood, softwood, cordwood, kindling. At one point Refuto called out to Tilman, "This isn't beautiful basswood some fool has me chopping for his fire," and the word "basswood" made something in Tilman's memory twitch and jump.

His grandfather's workshop. The distant landscapes he had made on a flat, golden-brown plane by cutting into the wood pictures of the smallest trees and hills and pastures anyone could imagine. He remembered the pleasure of it, the pleasure and the pride. He dropped the handles of the wheelbarrow. "Did you say basswood?"

"No, I did not say basswood. Who wants to know?"

"Let me see it," said Tilman.

"Jesus, look out for the axe."

It was basswood all right, Tilman recognized it from his childhood. He remembered his grandfather telling him how the great sculptors of Riemenschneider's time had been required to apply for its European cousin, limewood, one tree at a time, from the controlled forests surrounding towns such as Nuremburg and Ulm, how sometimes during times of scarcity, they had dropped to their knees in front of the municipal authorities and begged and wept. Limewood. Basswood. His grandfather said they were almost the same, though not quite, basswood being somewhat inferior. Tilman, carrying a full load of this material into the farmer's shed, recalled that his grandfather could read wood, was able to determine from the grain how a piece might crack or warp as the moisture departed from it, where the flesh of it might glow when it was rounded, glazed, and rubbed, and how it would catch the light when coaxed into a particular shape. The old man had taken the boy outside one winter night and had pointed to a barely discernible cluster of stars in an otherwise vibrant sky. *"Caela Sculptoris,"* he had said. "Our own constellation — the carver's tool. Not the brightest but still placed in the sky by God to honour a humble profession." Tilman had not looked for it since. Tonight, he thought, I'll look for it tonight.

But in the evening the wind that had all day long thrown the last of the yellow leaves into the lake began to push dark clouds in from the west, and Tilman and Refuto went early to their bunks in a small barn filled with the racket that rain makes on a tin roof. While Refuto muttered to himself about all the plans he didn't have for tomorrow, Tilman began to carve — with a broken-handled knife — a faraway forest on a flat piece of basswood he had rescued from the shed.

The knife, which he had carried all over Ontario with him in a burlap bag, was much too dull and unsuitable for the job at the best of times, but eventually a recognizable woodlot began to appear as a result of his efforts. When Tilman looked up from his pastime, he could see Refuto's shadow huge on the opposite wall, cast there by the lantern the farmer had loaned them for the night. Tilman, who was much more fond of animals than he was of human beings, was pleased by the bear shape it made.

"There's a bear in the stars," he told Refuto, "as well as a carver's tool."

Refuto shook his head, presumably in disagreement.

"You chopped every bit of wood on the

place," Tilman ventured, "so there'll be nothing for us to do tomorrow. Looks like we'll be moving on."

Seldom, in fact never did he take to anyone the way he had inexplicably taken to this impossible man.

"No, we won't," said Refuto.

"So where'll we go?" Tilman continued. "It's getting winter soon. We'll have to go to some town."

"Hrumph!" said Refuto, his most positive statement so far.

"I know some towns that are good," said Tilman. "Chatham, Sarnia. Not too far. And good."

"There are no towns," said Refuto.

"There's towns everywhere all over with women who'll give a kid a supper. I've been in big brick houses. Once I lived a day in a mansion."

Refuto sat silently on the edge of his cot and stared at Tilman while the boy scratched away at the wood and leaned forward to blow the shavings onto the floor. Once, when Tilman looked up, he saw there were tears in the tramp's eyes. "I don't have a son about your age," Refuto said. "And this boy," he added, leaving Tilman wondering exactly which boy he was referring to, "can't he carve."

★ ★ ★

It was Refuto who introduced Tilman to the world of the trains. More comfortable with silence than with speech, the older man proved to be an excellent teacher of movement. He showed Tilman the precise steps necessary to mount a moving boxcar, how to position oneself for comfort, camouflage, and safety when riding the rails, how to make and read the symbols that were always left by tramps on water towers near the railway stations.

This calligraphy, these pictures delighted Tilman. "You're not supposed to have a picture all your own," Refuto told him. His personal mark was three circles in the shape of a bearlike snowman with tight curls on the head and a cross intersecting the torso to indicate to all who might want to know that Refuto had never been there. Tilman created a drawing for himself that looked somewhat like a pennant in a strong wind, but which the boy knew was the shape the carver's constellation made in the night sky. Refuto also demonstrated the correct approach to another hobo's campfire: a skilfully balanced performance combining an air of deference with that of confidence. Head up, arms down, shoulders curved, faint, wistful smile. Many of the other tramps knew and liked Refuto, whom they greeted with lines such as "It's *not* Refuto" or "Well, if it *isn't* Refuto." Some of them preferred to call him "Naysayer Nick."

"What's this Nick?" Tilman asked.

"My real name is not Nicolo Vigomanti. Refuto is not the name I got on the road."

The man and the boy crossed the country twice, emerging from boxcars after long, rumbling sleeps in towns named after animal bones, flowering plants, glaciers, berries, Greek gods, or a bend in the river. They were thrown off the train twice in Saskatchewan, near Moosejaw on the way out and Touchwood on the way back. Tilman, who had remained unaffected by the Rocky Mountains beyond being disappointed somewhat that they did not resemble the hallway murals he remembered from his brief stays in large houses, was thrilled by the open expanse of the prairies, where he could see barns, grain elevators, farmhouses, and the onion domes of lonely wooden churches — all so far away that he knew they would never interfere with his enjoyment of them. He could see thunderstorms on the horizon that would never dampen his clothes. And by the time they were on their way back east, he could stand in the sun and watch snow squalls twenty miles away, for each night now was colder than the last.

Tilman continued to carve the piece of basswood he had taken from the farmer's shed, often working in the thin slice of sunlight that entered by way of the partially open boxcar door. Refuto occasionally glanced at the boy's handiwork but never commented. Still, Tilman's constant energy seemed to activate something in the older man, some latent need for labour brought about by his tremendous strength and a realization that with winter would come long, empty days with only a kid and the cold for company. One day as they sat in the slanted light of a late November sun on a bench outside a rural train station, Refuto began to talk about employment.

"I'm not going back to work," he announced.

Tilman had to agree it didn't appear that he was.

Across the tracks the winter sun was climbing a pine tree branch by branch. Tilman and Refuto had managed to beg some day-old bread from the town baker, and a woman near the tracks had given them some cheese. Refuto munched thoughtfully for a while before continuing.

"I'm not going back to making those cast-iron woodstoves that no one wants to heat their houses any more."

Tilman began to pay serious attention. Each year at this time he became more and more interested in heat.

"You've never been to the city."

"No," Tilman admitted. Three times with Refuto he had to switch trains in Toronto. And one of those times they had wandered briefly into the huge marble palace of Union Station, but they had never gone into the city itself.

"You do not know that there are two cities quite near to each other."

Tilman did not. He looked quizzically at Refuto, surprised that three times in succession his companion's negative statements had coincided with reality.

"Toronto and Hamilton," Refuto continued.

Tilman began pacing up and down on the platform. He was worried about how to put himself up for adoption. It had been five years since he had left home, and suddenly other people's mothers opening the doors of their houses viewed him with suspicion rather than pity. He had become, without knowing it, a powerful-looking young man — almost an adult. He had forgotten when his birthday was but knew by the passing of each summer that he must be somewhere near sixteen or seventeen years old. He had grown hair on parts of him that, to his mind, had no business having hair, but he was afraid to ask, even to ask Refuto, what this might mean.

"We're not going to Hamilton," Refuto shouted at him from the bench. "You can be sure of that."

"Hamilton," Tilman repeated. "Not Toronto?"

"Nope. That other city. The one nearby."

Refuto's re-entry into the Italian district of Hamilton rivalled, in some minds, the return of the Medicis to Florence.

He took Tilman down the Guelph Line Road through the villages of Cambellville and Flamborough. As they walked and occasionally hitched a ride in a delivery van or farmer's wagon, the last curled yellow leaves were being blown from the maples that bordered their route. The wind was bitter and held the promise of a hard winter in its teeth. When they reached the edge of the long limestone escarpment that cuts through this part of Ontario, they were able to stand at its height in the town of Ancaster and look out over the industrial city of Hamilton and the filthy yet beautiful indentation in the coastline of Lake Ontario known as Burlington Bay.

"That isn't one big stinking mess," said Refuto, "and it wasn't once lovely, I suppose."

Tilman thought it was gorgeous right now, this bird's-eye view of factories, docks, and houses. A whole city you could hold in the palm of your hand. He wanted to carve a bas-relief with all of the smoke-stacks included, and all of the boats out on the water.

"Great big stinking mess!" exclaimed Refuto in a surprisingly forthright manner. Then, as if to correct himself, he looked sideways at Tilman. "Don't tell anyone down there that I said that up here." He paused. "Us up here and them down there and they don't know it yet."

As it turned out he was wrong, for in the third storey of an industrialist's house built up on the escarpment in order to avoid the air pollution caused by the factories in the city below, a second cousin of Refuto's was hanging wallpaper in a bedroom so luxurious it even included a telephone. At the instant of Refuto's declaration, this paper hanger, who had been looking out the window and wondering, concluded that it was indeed his cousin Nicolo Vigamonti, and he telephoned another cousin — a greengrocer — to tell him what he had seen. Every woman in the neighbourhood saw the greengrocer once a day. By noon, the whole community was on the street, looking up at the escarpment.

Tilman and Refuto stood for close to half an hour on the edge of the escarpment and looked down at the city that the boy knew instinctively must hold the man's family. The people in this family might or might not be happy to adopt a boy for the winter, but they would certainly want Refuto back for the rest of his life. Tilman felt that this was an uncertain and significant moment. Refuto might just as easily decide to turn back, to go to Guelph and hop a train. Or he might decide to enter that other city, the one with the marble train station, where no one knew either of them.

It was the end of November, and though it hadn't yet snowed heavily, there was frost everywhere. Tilman's extravagantly patched coat was wearing thin. This was the only time of the year that architectural structures of any kind appealed to him.

"Steel town," Refuto eventually spat out bitterly. "I killed a man," he announced, almost as an afterthought.

"You couldn't kill a man," said Tilman.

"I did and there's no point your denying it," Refuto sniffed angrily. "This man was my brother."

"He was not!" Tilman abruptly became aware that, absurdly, their roles had reversed and he was the person carrying the burden of denial.

"I killed him with steel," the older man

continued. "I stayed in the stoveworks, making a parlour stove called The Persian Warrior. I don't even know where Persia is, do you?"

Tilman did not.

"There was a job for more money at the steel mill. And I made him take it. He had more children so I forced him to take this job, this money. We argued all night, and finally I said he would not be my brother if he did not take the job, so he said he would take it if I would get the next one that became available. A week later he didn't come home. After three days I went to the mill to ask. He was killed by a steel beam, they said, but they did not know who to tell." Refuto glared down at the city's smoking chimneys. "Do you know why they did not know who to tell?" he asked in a low voice.

Tilman shook his head.

"They did not know who to tell because my brother's name was not listed on the payroll."

"You're saying they weren't going to pay him."

"Oh, they were going to pay him, but instead of his name they had the word 'foreigner' listed on the payroll. When no one came, they buried him in the potter's field.

They threw him out like trash."

"Then there wasn't any mass said for him at his burial," said Tilman, remembering now the church and the masses he had attended with his family.

"Who wants to know?" asked Refuto warily, as if frightened by all he had disclosed.

Tilman had learned long ago that Refuto expected no answer to this question. He noticed that white caps were developing in the bay and that the exposed trees on this rise were entirely bare of leaves and were bending in the wind. Christ, he thought, it was cold on this hill. He looked at the older man standing beside him, the torn expression on his weatherbeaten face, and for the first time it occurred to Tilman that Refuto was afraid, afraid that he might not be able to find a job, afraid that his abandoned family would reject him.

"Listen," Tilman said gently to his friend, "anything you want is possible. My grandfather knew a priest once who built a gigantic church in the wilderness — right in the middle of a forest — a stone church. With a bell. And my grandfather carved the altars out of wood, just like he was in Europe."

The older man nodded. "This is why I

have not almost returned," he said.

Tilman looked at Refuto quizzically.

"I have not almost returned because of the carving."

"The carving?"

"I have a son about your age who wants to carve angels with Juliani, who does the tombstones. He is hoping to be apprenticed." Refuto pulled out a dirty handkerchief and blew his nose loudly. "I also have younger daughters," he added.

"Why did you leave them?"

"Because I could not put the burden of a killer on their shoulders. Or put the killer's body beside that of their mother at night." Refuto's eyes took on the opaque quality Tilman had noticed the day they met. "Foreigner," he said, "on the payroll he was listed as foreigner. He didn't even have a name. At the stoveworks I didn't have a name either. I was, he was, a not-person."

Tilman was quiet. Then he said, "I had a mother and a father. A sister too. But I couldn't stay. Then my parents got this harness and they put it on me while I was asleep." Tilman was looking straight ahead as he spoke, as if he were talking to the city, to the lake. "They put me on a chain so I wouldn't leave."

Refuto looked at the boy's profile, his large face filled with horror and compassion. "Oh no," he said, "they didn't. They couldn't have chained you."

"Yes." Tilman shuffled his feet on the frost-hard ground. He didn't often allow himself to think of his confinement, his escape. He had a sadness for the parents he had lost, and now suddenly felt a deep love for the little girl who had set him free. When he closed his eyes, he could see her running at him across the morning yard. Then he thought of Phoebe, another agent of liberty. "A man who loved a woman cut my chain off," he told his friend.

The older man turned to the boy at his side. "I should not go down there," he said quietly. "You should not tell anyone that I showed you this city, that we stood here looking down at it."

"You didn't kill anyone . . . not your brother . . . not anyone. The factory killed him." Tilman began to walk straight ahead on the road that descended into the city. There were at least twenty smokestacks in his view. Refuto hesitated, then followed, his strong legs making it easy for him to catch up. "Your family will be glad to have you back," said Tilman.

"No, they won't," whispered Refuto,

though without any real certainty.

The last word, always.

Tilman entered a crowd so tumultuous that had he known of it in advance he might have taken Refuto's suggestion and stayed up on the hill. Refuto — or Nicolo Vigamonti — was related to almost every Italian in the district. All of his relatives and most of his friends had congregated near the greengrocer's on a street lined with similar-looking brick row houses fronted by an infinite variety of recently harvested gardens. The community was there to witness Vigamonti's miraculous and much-prayed-for return. The weeping and embracing that ensued caused Tilman's nerves to jump. Through no fault of his own he was swept with the crowd into an overheated house where Mrs. Vigamonti was being revived — she had fainted when she heard the news — by a flock of chattering elderly women and by her own young daughters.

"I did not mean to leave you," Nicolo shouted at her across the din.

She continued to weep and to finger her rosary. Suddenly the room became very quiet. Tilman watched as the darkly clad widowed sister-in-law approached

Nicolo. She placed one hand on his cheek. "I am so happy you have come home," she said.

And the room exploded into Italian and English cheers as her brother-in-law embraced her, his beard soggy with tears. Then he struggled through the crowd to his wife and his young daughters. "I thought I was a killer and a not-person," he told them, while the smallest girl hugged his knees.

The widow embraced Tilman, who surprised himself by saying, "Sorry for your trouble," something he remembered being said at funerals by the few Irish families in Shoneval. An olive-skinned boy about Tilman's age hovered near Refuto and eventually touched the man's arm shyly. Refuto put his own arm around the young man's shoulders and pulled him across the room. "This is Tilman," he said. "He can make things. He is a friend to me, Giorgio, and soon to be a friend to you. He'll show you how to make woodcarvings."

Giorgio continued to gaze at Refuto's face. Tilman could tell that he was filled with joy, practically speechless in the wake of his father's return.

"I have made, already, marble carvings while you were gone . . . of an angel. The man at the gravestones has been teaching me how."

"This boy, we could never keep him from watching Juliani at the gravestones. So this is good. But Tilman will teach you how to carve wood, which will not be as expensive."

For the first time the two boys exchanged glances, sized each other up. Tilman was taller than Giorgio, but Giorgio was larger boned, more powerful-looking. Yet there was curiosity, not hostility, in the son's gaze, and Tilman sensed that it would be safe to come to know him.

That evening Tilman ate a meal larger than any he had ever consumed before. A rich, dark soup was followed by an assortment of slippery noodles in which he indulged himself to such an extent that he almost couldn't finish the subsequent meat course. When a piece of yellow cake soaked in syrup was placed in front of him, Tilman began to believe that the whole community must be fattening up for the winter, that they would likely not eat again for weeks. He was filled with pleasure, intoxicated by nourishment.

After the presentation of the new babies of several second cousins and the funeral photos of the recently dead, the family's attention turned to the boy who had so recently entered their midst. The robust Mrs. Vigamonti, now thoroughly recovered, threw her hands up in despair after a close inspection of Tilman's clothes and physiognomy.

"Too skinny and too dirty," she announced. "Needs scrubbing down and fattening up." She looked sternly into his face. "Where's your mama?" she asked.

"Dead," said Tilman, unknowingly telling the truth.

"I found him out there," said the man now called Nicolo Vigamonti. "He let me talk." Nicolo shook his head, then looked around the room. "I've been gone," he admitted, "but Tilman told me to come back." He shook his head again. The crowd of Italians was sombre and attentive. Nicolo addressed the room. "I feel now as if my head is clearing in four directions at once." He turned to his wife. "How did you manage, Lucia, with me gone?"

"Giorgio took your job at the stoveworks." She folded her arms and looked firmly at her husband. "They are hiring more men."

"This is good, Lucia," said Nicolo, a hint of shame in his voice. "Tilman and I will go down there tomorrow."

"Am I old enough?" asked Tilman suddenly.

Giorgio once again examined Tilman's crop of blond hair, his height, his recently broadened shoulders. "You're old enough," he said.

Despite the fact that he was required to appear at the stoveworks each morning at 7 a.m. and to remain inside its walls until early evening, Tilman did not mind the large, clamorous interior of his new workplace or the work itself, which seemed — for the time being — fascinating. Nicolo had announced early on that Tilman could carve wood, "trees, and the smallest, farthest cities," he enthused, and soon Tilman was asked to make scenes for the elaborate wooden pattern moulds that provided not only the shapes of the stoves but any added decorative elements as well. While several Italian stokers stood behind him happily shouting words of praise in their beautiful language, Tilman deftly executed the tiniest branches on the tiniest trees, little noticing the irony of this in relation to an iron woodstove called The Forest Eater.

The stoves he came to know were made in all shapes and sizes, attempting in their own cumbersome, heavy way to imitate marble fountains, sinuous statuary, oversized porcelain vases, exotic four-legged animals, chariots, thrones, and canopied beds. The Forest Eater was itself reminiscent of an early Renaissance writing desk, but unlike the other stoves and presumably in deference to its name, it had bark-covered stumps for legs and roots — rather than paws or hoofs — for feet. Tilman made one forest for its side panels and another — this time with a medieval city nestled in its midst and a stretch of meadow in front of it — for its door.

This work took him several weeks. When the casts were finally made and multiples of the completed object were seen in the works, Tilman suffered for some time from the sin of pride, as did Giorgio, who had designed the stumps and the roots and the huge acorn for the top.

"What will happen to our Forest Eater, I wonder," Giorgio mused as he and Tilman ate the lunches Lucia Vigamonti had packed for them. "It is most certainly a parlour stove," the dark-haired boy continued, "and so will seldom be lit. I predict, therefore, it will not burn down many houses."

Tilman allowed that it was comforting to know this.

"Though it is mostly stovepipes and chimneys that are the real problem," said Giorgio, "the stoves themselves are supposed to be on fire."

There was a damper on the door of The Forest Eater, just below its meadow, and when this damper was open its future owner would be permitted a view of the red glow of the fire inside. Tilman would like to have seen that. The final touch.

Giorgio then went on to describe the few burnt houses he had seen in his lifetime, with the family's stove or stoves standing guilty and unharmed among the ashes.

"They are that strong, our stoves," he said proudly.

To his surprise, Tilman was able to live inside the rowdy hysteria of the Vigamonti family for almost four years, loving the food and enjoying the unintrusive companionship, earning a reasonable salary at the stoveworks and helping to supplement the household income by paying room and board. Every now and then he disappeared, sometimes for up to two or three weeks, but he always returned and was welcomed back both to the house and to his job. Giorgio had quickly become a friend, and Tilman missed his daily companionship when, after a few years, Giorgio left the stoveworks to work full-time as an apprentice to Juliani the tombstone-maker. Once he had a chisel in his hand every day, it took the young man no time at all to outstrip his master in skill, and soon he was signing the elaborate tombs of industrialists. The stern marble faces of these men can still be seen in the graveyards of Hamilton, though they have become soiled over the years from the soot produced by the factories that made them rich enough to afford tombs of this nature. Now and then Tilman would visit his friend at the monument works, and finally Giorgio taught him one or two things about carving marble. Though the blond boy still preferred wood, there was, he had to admit, something satisfying about making hills and forests appear on the surface of such apparently unyielding stone.

Nicolo slipped easily back into the role of family patriarch, sometimes taking Tilman aside to offer him one or another of his older daughters — two of whom had become high-spirited, attractive young women — in marriage. But the girls were too much like sisters to Tilman, and he could never imagine one of them engendering in him the tenderness, the muted passion, he would never forget Ham Bone harbouring for Phoebe — his sole idea of true love. He had thought about love now and then, but could only imagine it for himself as something that would take place from a distance, a kind of courtly worship of a beautifully made far-off object. He preferred the camaraderie of men, camaraderie that was neither inquisitive nor physically close.

As for Nicolo, he now lapsed back into his paranoid negativity very rarely and only when he was extremely agitated. This happened just twice during Tilman's stay. When massive layoffs began at the stoveworks and many of Vigamonti's younger relatives and friends — Tilman among them — found themselves out of work, Nicolo became restless and distressed, talked about returning to Italy, to a country where heat was not needed, a country where he could keep a garden all year to feed his family. It was not long, however, before this problem was solved by the second event to cause Nicolo distress.

"It's not war that has been declared in

Europe," he told the blond-haired and the dark-haired young men one evening in August. "You will *not* have to go," he said as tears filled his eyes and the boys jumped to their feet with excitement. "You will *not* have to go."

3

THE MONUMENT

Klara had become a particular kind of women one saw now and then in villages the size of Shoneval. Immediately recognizable as spinsters in both dress and posture, they favoured dark cotton dresses with small prints and sensible black laced shoes. Although they were always slim and kept their spines rigidly straight as they walked down the street, they appeared ageless, sexless, and ill-humoured. If they weren't schoolteachers, they often lived, as Klara did, near rather than in the town, on a piece of inherited property once worked as a family farm, the fields of which were now rented out as pasture for the animals of neighbouring farmers. In order to supplement this meagre income these women frequently, as the term "spinster" suggests, engaged in some activity related to cloth or clothing; they took in laundry or, like Klara, they sewed. They were known to have roots deep in the town's pioneer past and therefore commanded the respect such things still engendered at this time in these communities, though, beyond that, being the end of their line in a society mostly tribal, they had no real social life.

They were often, perhaps as a result, very pious, attending mass more than was strictly necessary if they were Catholics or acting as caretakers and cleaners of the Protestant church if they were not. They were almost always eccentric in some way or another. It was now more than fifteen years after the war had ended, and Klara's father and grandfather were both lying beneath wrought-iron markers in the cemetery behind the church. Her insistence on running the farm alone was perceived to be exactly the kind of eccentricity expected of a spinster, though it would have been interpreted as madness in a widow.

Each morning Klara could be seen walking into town — through heat in the summer, rain in the spring, and snow in the winter — where she quite consciously engaged in a few minutes of conversation with the keeper of Hafeman's store. This she did because she feared that, living alone, her sanity might begin to suffer were she to have absolutely no concourse with other human beings. Every third day she visited the nuns in the convent, where her desire to tell, or be told, stories concerning Shoneval's early days was indulged. Then she walked back to the farm, where she carried out the routines of her existence:

feeding her three cats, sewing the seams of the current garment, tending to her old horse, and taking pleasure from looking out the window at her own four cows.

She hadn't so much lost her looks as forgotten them. And there were few in the town interested enough to remind her that she had once been a beauty. Each morning she rose, washed, put on one of those dark cotton dresses and an apron, and laced up her shoes. The mirror was used by her to make certain that no strand of hair escaped the severe knot she tied each day at the back of her head. Or to make announcements to herself about the weather. Once or twice a day, if the circumstances warranted it, she would approach the oval above her dresser and deliver, as if a message of great importance, statements such as "The wind has stopped" or "It has rained for far too long." Sometimes at twilight the white fenceposts at the bottom of the lane looked like a procession of ghosts approaching her gate.

At night her body sometimes attempted to awaken distant memories, but her mind would have none of it. This was going to be her life, this routine of daily tasks and chores and prayers. Whether she was happy did not seem to be important. As for affection, it was given to her cats, and more recently to the four large dignified animals occupying the field nearest the house — the field she had kept for herself, and for them.

Klara had seen her first white animal in a painting on the side of Kiefer Erb's barn, where normally a portrait of a perfectly ordinary Holstein was displayed. Klara thought for a moment that someone in the night must have come along and painted out the cow's dark spots. A few days later the words *Erb and Son* were added above it, and below it Klara read *Home of the Wissemburg White*. (The Erbs' ancestors, she knew, had emigrated from the town of Wissemburg and so had decided to name the cow on the barn after the faraway Alsatian town they had never seen.)

Klara was perturbed and fascinated by the painting and finally was compelled to confront Kiefer Erb one day in the store.

"Is there such a thing?" she asked bluntly while the man was deep in thought near a variety of roofing nails.

"What's that?" he asked.

"The white cow you have on your barn, is it real?"

Kiefer smiled, always happy to talk about his prize. "Oh, it's real, all right,

Miss Becker," he raised an eyebrow and exchanged glances with the storekeeper, "but I'm surprised you didn't notice. It's not a cow, it's a bull. A special bull — Charolais — from France. Best breeder in Ontario, I figure." He paused, considered, then couldn't resist, "Someone you want serviced?"

This kind of humour was often employed at the expense of spinsters, who men assumed were starved for sex, but rarely, it's true, were these jokes told in their presence.

The shopkeeper smiled sheepishly and reddened. But Klara refused to be embarrassed. "Where did you get him?" she asked.

"Quebec. Cost a fortune. But I figure he'll earn his keep."

That summer Klara saw the bull glowing in his pasture each day when she walked to town, his colour creamier, warmer than in his portrait. Unlike others of his species he showed neither curiosity nor hostility when she gazed at him from her side of the fence. In fact the only thing he seemed to be interested in was the bell in the steeple of Father Gstir's church. When it tolled, and particularly when it tolled for a long time at noon, the beast would raise his head in a regal fashion and there would be something in his manner that suggested a sorrow nobly borne. Klara imagined that he was homesick for Quebec, a place where, she had heard, there were numerous Catholic churches and therefore, it would follow, many wonderful bells. Most of the time, however, he appeared to be distant and preoccupied, as if he were trying to solve the puzzle of how he came to be standing in an Ontario pasture surrounded by unfamiliar spotted females.

Klara adored him, loved even the soft sound of his name, *Shar-oh-lay*. Interesting to her too were the rumours, soon strong around town, that he had refused to mate. Even his portrait was proving to be ambivalent, the white paint beginning to peel after the second or third of August's thunderstorms. In early September she noticed, passing by Erb's farm, that the red paint covering the rest of the barn appeared to have erased Wissemburg's penis and to have eliminated the words beneath the painted beast that identified his home. Several black spots had been added to his neutered snowy side. On the Erb mailbox there hung a humble sign advertising the fact that a bull was for sale.

Klara was mad with joy, the word

"Charolais" ringing like Father Gstir's bell in her mind. Her grandfather had left her a small legacy, and she happily parted with over a quarter of it to buy the sturdy white animal. The rest of the money she sent to Quebec and soon Charolais' loneliness was assuaged by the appearance in his new pasture and proximity in the winter barn of Charlotta, a fine, soft-eyed white Charolais cow.

Charlotta calved in spring. Twins. In late winter of the following year a certain amount of incest took place and Klara sold the offspring for what she considered to be a handsome price, trying not to think too long or too hard about what would become of the "wee ones." Kiefer Erb, jealous at her success, made suggestive remarks all over the village about Klara's relationship with the white bull, but as no one had the nerve to repeat them in her presence, they had no effect whatsoever on the pride she felt at seeing the animals increase in number and at being able to care for them herself, doing the job as efficiently as any man.

Despite this, in the evenings when she had stopped working in the barn or sewing a jacket for someone else's husband, Klara could not get over a feeling of distance, a sense that she was not only separated from the community in which she lived but also that she was becoming oddly disassociated from the trappings of the only home she had ever known. Often she became vaguely irritated with one physical object or another, or mildly antagonistic toward a whole room. Those brass candlesticks, she would think, they just sit there and tarnish, or That parlour, what good has it ever contributed to the world? Each Sunday after mass she indulged herself by reading a newspaper, *The Goderich Star Sentinel* or, if she could get it, *The London Free Press*. The wealth of stories contained in these journals both stimulated and disoriented her, making her wish that something would happen in her own life, then making her fear that such a wish was capable of changing her current neutrality for discontent.

Klara could manage the maintenance of only the first row of trees in what had been a substantial apple orchard when her father was actively running the farm. But, even so, the other trees — though twisted and wild and bearing only puny, worm-ridden apples — still blossomed splendidly along with their pruned and plucked cousins, adding a pleasing balance on one side of the house to the field of white cows, calves, and one bull who grazed on the other. In the autumn Klara faithfully harvested all of the apples from the four well-kept trees, giving some as treats to the animals and hauling the rest by a wagon attached to her very old horse to the cider mill near the brewery.

It was a late afternoon in September of 1934, while she was perched dangerously close to the top of the pointed ladder with one hand grasping a perfectly round McIntosh apple, that Klara spotted a stranger with a pack on his back, limping slowly up the long lane that led to the house. Tramps had begged at her door before and she had always given them something. Today it would be apples and whatever other scraps of food she had lying about. She sighed, let go of the apple she was holding, and began to descend the ladder. But on the third step she stopped. There was something she had recognized in the shape of this man's head and, even from this distance, in the placement of his ears and eyebrows. She stood entirely still and gazed at her hands, which were wrapped around the grey wood of the ladder, then unconsciously lifted one of them to smooth her hair, for the first time in over a decade becoming aware of what she had become, of how she would appear if the man in the lane turned out to be Eamon. He was making painfully slow progress, swinging his right leg stiffly forward before permitting the left to join it, but with each step the spark of recognition was fanned toward flame in Klara's mind. She experienced terror then: pure, cold, and immobilizing. It took an unimaginable strength of will for her to climb again two rungs of the ladder in order to be concealed by the leaves of the tree, leaves that she noticed had begun to twitch in a sudden shift of wind.

Klara stood on the ladder and tried to remember the appearance of the woman to whom she spoke each day in the mirror, but she could call up only an uncertain image of tidy hair. The man had entered the yard now and was lurching toward the back door. Without a fraction of hesitation he lifted the latch, hauled his bad leg over the threshold, and disappeared inside. Klara recalled evenings two decades past when Eamon had sat sullenly in the kitchen. If it were him, would he choose the same chair?

Sometime later she came back to herself and found that she was standing perfectly still on a ladder, hiding in a tree, and she felt infantile, stupid. Her insteps ached and there was a sliver in her palm that had lodged there when she had slid her hands too quickly up the side of the ladder in her panic. Dusk was falling, and she was trembling slightly. The chill in the air was causing this, she decided, her old practicality returning. Klara thought about the man who had sauntered casually through her door as if he were a family pet. What could this possibly mean, this assumed right of passage? She quickly descended the ladder and began to march toward the house. Inside, the vaguely familiar stranger was sitting at the table eating bread and cheese.

He was not Eamon.

He was not Eamon. Grief rushed at Klara like an avalanche, as if someone had seized her from behind and had suddenly thrust her head into coldness and darkness. She was physically assaulted by it. There was no breath remaining in her body.

"Don't be afraid," said the man, his eyes a mirror of her own. "Is it Klara?"

Not taking her eyes off the stranger she sat down slowly, unable at the moment to answer even the most simple question about her identity. Her self had slipped out of her body and was floating somewhere above the long grass she could see from her window. Black-and-white images of the carnage of the war from her father's newspapers were passing swiftly through her mind, as if she had been a country senselessly invaded — passing through her mind though she had no memory at all of ever looking at these pictures. She stood up and then sat down again, became aware of the stranger's face looking at her with concern and slowly, like oxygen returning to the bloodstream of one who has almost been strangled, she began to re-inhabit the room. But she knew she would never recover. This man was not Eamon. Eamon was dead.

The man had crossed the room now and had put his hand on her arm, was bending toward her and looking with confusion into her face. "I'm sorry if I frightened you," he said. And then again, "You are Klara, aren't you?" He was so close to her she could feel his warm breath and smell his sweat.

Klara did not answer.

"Oh God." said the man, turning his face away, "how could I have expected anyone to know me. I'm Tilman. I lived here as a child. Is it still the Becker place?"

Klara stared at him, a look of such profound shock on her face it was as if the man had slapped her. She stood up suddenly, took his shoulders in her hands, and pushed him roughly back, causing him to stagger awkwardly against the old pine table.

Then Klara flew at her brother with her fists.

Tilman stood still and received the blows. She attacked his arms and chest. He stopped her only when she began to kick, fearing she might injure herself when her foot met his wooden leg.

That evening, while an exhausted Klara soaked her bruised hands in a bowl of cool water, the brother and sister sat at the table and talked. Tilman explained little about where he had been before or after, but he did talk about the war, making reference to his artificial leg and telling her about the great battle in which he had participated until he was wounded out.

It was being fought on all levels, he told her, under the ground, on the surface, and in the air. It was the craziest thing, he said, pure bedlam. And the casualties were huge, overwhelming, though in the end the Canadians had taken the ridge. Afterwards hardly anyone who had participated and survived could remember anything about it, except chaos.

"Which battle was it?" Klara wanted to know.

"Vimy," said her brother. "Vimy Ridge."

When Tilman returned from the war without his right leg, news had preceded him concerning his ability to work with wood. His sergeant, secretly impressed by the small, flat scenes the young man had worked on in the boggy trenches, had noted his talent on some form or another and this piece of paper had made its sluggish way through the network of military bureaucracy. After Vimy — the days and nights in the underground tunnels, the chaos of the battle, the grenade, the shattered leg and subsequent hurried and sloppy amputation — he had asked in the hospital, when he was finally able to talk, for limewood and a knife. "Quite a whittler!" a doctor had scribbled on an otherwise purely medical report, and that too had wended its way toward the governmental department that was being hastily assembled in the nation's capital to deal with permanently damaged soldiers.

Thousands of wounded veterans were returning, many missing limbs. The government was in a state of mild panic. Various opinions were offered about what was to be done with these mutilated young men, the most common being that they should not be permitted to sink into shiftlessness, sloth, and self-pity. Eventually an otherwise dull and unpromising civil servant made a name for himself by suggesting that as most of the boys were still on crutches with one hollow pant leg blowing in the breeze, some of them at least might be gainfully employed making wooden legs for themselves and others like themselves in a factory designed for this purpose. A building that had been used until very recently in the manufacturing of wooden porch pillars, and was therefore splendidly outfitted with saws and lathes, was discovered in Toronto, inspected, thought to be just the ticket, and rapidly purchased by the department. It was much too large for the operation the government had in mind, but that problem was quickly solved by the same civil servant, who suggested the handicapped workers could be housed in dormitories above their place of employment. (No one had thought about how these young men were to get up and down the stairs, but that was a problem for another day.) When Tilman's case came up, the two references to carving were met with great approval by the committee that had been formed to compile a list of suitable candidates. Tilman's name went to the top of this list.

Tilman had hated the factory, hated the rigid legs and feet he worked on all day, and had utterly despised his own bogus limb. In the overcrowded and often panic-stricken hospitals at the Front, each sloppy amputation had been sloppy in a manner all its own. The result was that to each order that reached the workers was attached a complicated and in some cases unreadable set of measurements, which somehow would have to be transformed into a three-dimensional form. After a day filled with the problems of construction geometry, bad meals served in the adjacent cafeteria, and struggles with inadequately maintained machinery, the young men, Tilman included, would clump painfully up the stairs to the dormitory. Here at night Tilman's dreams of burning his own wooden leg would be interrupted by the shouts of nightmare-ridden men who had not even begun to recover from the trauma of the war. Some of these same men could be heard crying themselves to sleep after lights out.

In many ways Tilman had been a model soldier. Used to sleeping in mud and rain, cooking meals in the open air, and by nature enjoying looking at things from a great distance, the army seemed to him to be just a slightly more dangerous variation on his tramping life. (Before and during Vimy he had often been a sentry, usually volunteering for the position, preferring the dangerous exposure to the congested camaraderie of the trench.) Even gross physical mutilation and death were no surprise to him as many tramps he had known had lost their limbs, or their lives, leaping into or being thrown out of moving boxcars — or by carelessness when riding the rods. But he was greatly disturbed by the unhappiness around him, by the meaningless slaughter of confused boys who were homesick in a way he had never been homesick, and he was repelled by the claustrophobic conditions of the trenches and the tunnels at Vimy. But even these dim passages seemed to be leading toward purpose and change, however misguided and misdirected. This factory, this pathetic attempt to patch up afterwards, this effort to reconstruct limbs and lives in a closed space was closer to hell than he had been since the chain. Had he the use of both legs, or even had his wooden leg caused him less discomfort, he would have bolted. As it was, he knew he could never survive his old life on the roads, so he stayed where he was, fed and housed and employed, gradually growing physically stronger, and tentatively entering, for the first time since the Vigamontis (and undoubtedly with some of the skills he had learned there), a community.

Like Tilman, most of the other men in the factory had nowhere else to go. Wives, girlfriends, in some cases even mothers and fathers had withdrawn in horror at their physical condition. If the men had worked in offices before the war, old employers had claimed they were not able to find a position for them. Physical labour was out of the question. Most of the men were too broken in spirit anyway to re-engage in anything that predated 1914, could hardly remember who they had been before the catastrophe, as if from now on they were to be stalled in a peculiar atmosphere of both stasis and transition. One former tramp commenting on his purgatorial life called himself a limb-bo rather than a hobo. The expression seemed a perfect moniker for the place in which they all lived and worked. Tilman carved an elaborate plaque with the name featured in large letters. It was hung on a wall at one end of the dormitory and was the first thing most of the men saw when they awakened in the morning.

After two years or so, Limb-Bo became a place of gradually declining activity, and in three years' time the orders for artificial legs were down to a trickle. Not everyone in the country needed a prostheses, apparently, and the war amputees had all been serviced. As hastily as the department had opened the factory, they now firmly closed it down. Satisfied that they had done all that they could to rehabilitate Tilman and his colleagues, the same government that had called these young men so earnestly to arms now cast them unceremoniously out into the streets.

All this was told to Klara as she and Tilman sat at the wide table in the kitchen after a meal of bacon, cabbage, potatoes, and applesauce. Only one small, dark stain had blossomed on the cheekbone under Tilman's left eye, but Klara continued to soak her hands, having received the worst of it in a battle with only one side fighting.

"They'll be all right tomorrow," she replied when her brother asked repeatedly about her hands. She and Tilman had barely taken their eyes off each other, the need for knowledge was that great. Klara could see in Tilman's face just vague traces of the flawless blond boy he had been, mostly in the clarity of his eyes that were still a piercing blue and in the shape of his mouth. The rest of his face had changed utterly, was rough, lined, and in places faintly scarred, though whether by battle or by the rigours of the road she couldn't say. "What did you do," she asked, "after the wooden legs?"

"I stayed in Toronto, begging on the streets and sleeping in the missions for a few years." Tilman picked up his pine limb with both hands and moved it to a more comfortable position under the table. "It wasn't any good, though, after the war. I wasn't a kid any more, and there were so many vagrants in the city that people just became immune. Some of the boys pretended to be sick, or really got sick and went to the veterans hospital. Some of the country boys went home — if their families would have them. At least that way there was an address for the pension. I never had an address so there was no pension for me."

"You could have come here." Klara tried to imagine her father and her grandfather's response to a wounded veteran returning from the war. A grown man with a hardened face and untidy brown hair, not a golden child.

"I wasn't ready to. Even after the war, I wasn't ready to."

"What Mother did . . ." Klara touched her brother's arm.

"It wasn't that I was afraid of that, I just hadn't forgotten it. I remembered everything about that time, about them doing that to me." Tilman looked out the window, past the reflected kitchen and deep into the September night, silently recalling his distant imprisonment. "Why did Father let her do it? Why didn't he just stop her?"

There was nothing that Klara could say that would answer this question. "He spoke of you, you know, when he was dying," she said.

Tilman settled back in the chair, his expression softening somewhat. "But he was part of it . . . he agreed to it. I think he even put the harness on me."

"I don't know," said Klara. "But he was filled with regret. It was obvious he was always filled with regret."

Both were silent for several moments. Then Klara asked Tilman how he managed to survive with his wooden leg.

"I was used to it by the time they closed

the factory; I got around pretty good. But I couldn't do the trains any more. So I hitchhiked. The army jacket helped. And the medals."

"You won medals!" said Klara, preparing to be proud.

"Only one, for some supposed enemy activity I spotted while on sentry duty. But one of the fellows I worked with in the factory was so disgusted with everything — the war, the stupid legs, he threw his own medal in the trash. I fished it out later, figuring it might come in handy. You use everything you can on the road," he said. "It's part of what we hobos call our professional code."

Klara lifted her hands, dripping, from the bowl, stood, and crossed the room to a linen towel that hung near the stove.

"The Kitchen Queen," announced Tilman, not looking in the direction of the cumbersome iron contraption.

Klara laughed. "The stove," she said. "Did you remember it?"

"Not really," Tilman twisted around to examine it, "but I worked in a stove factory for a while."

"There can't be many of those left. Most people have gone to electric now."

"True," said Tilman. "I know a whole

family put out of work by that."

She gave him their parents' bed, believing that his childhood room would hold too many ghosts for him. She did not ask how long he intended to stay and knew instinctively he had not come back for the farm, despite the enthusiasm — perhaps feigned — that he showed concerning Charolais and Charlotta and his praise of her success with them.

"Do you remember this?" she kept asking the next day. "Do you remember?" She touched object after object in the house as if bringing them to his attention might make their shared childhood come into focus for her, if not for him.

"The curtains!" he exclaimed, glancing into the room that had once been his and later belonged to his grandfather. "I remember the curtains! I hated them closed, even at night." He looked at Klara and smiled. "Needed to see the view."

"Needed to get out the window, you mean."

"Sometimes."

He clomped behind her obediently from room to room and then down the stairs to the parlour. Most of their grandfather's woodcarvings had been commissioned by the church, and now they stood in various religious institutions in the south and west of Ontario. But a few modest figures, a Saint John the Baptist and a Saint Jerome, complete with writing desk and sleeping lion, were kept in this room.

"How did he die?" Tilman asked.

Klara glanced at her brother's face, which had the strained look of someone trying to remember a person they had lost long ago. "In his sleep," she said softly. "He just sort of wore out."

"Good, I'm glad he died like that. I remember him . . ." Tilman stroked the polished drapery hanging from the baptist's arm. "I remember him with fondness. I was sometimes happy in his workshop."

"He lived here after grandmother died. So he worked in the woodshed." Klara paused, "It wasn't quite the same. Would you want the tools, perhaps? He always thought . . ."

"I don't know about that," Tilman frowned slightly. "Tools stay in one place and . . ."

"Did you never carve again? He always kept one scene you had done." Klara did not tell her brother about the small boy that had appeared in every group of figures the old man carved. "He was always waiting for you to come back."

"I carved," said Tilman, "here and there. In the stoveworks I carved the pattern moulds for the decorative work."

Later in the afternoon, Klara took Tilman upstairs to the sunroom, her own bright tailoring shop. He stood in the doorway. "Mother's sewing room," he said. "I remember this too."

"It's been mine now for more than twenty years."

"So she died as soon as that then." Tilman's face underwent a change as the soft line of his mouth hardened.

"Yes."

"And it was because of me. I always believed I would be responsible for her death, one way or another."

"She died of a tumour," said Klara matter-of-factly. "You couldn't have done that. But she felt your loss terribly, and father said she never stopped feeling it."

"He talked about me?" Tilman sounded pleased, but there was still a tightness about his expression.

"For a while. Then he stopped. The way you do with a dead person."

"I wasn't dead."

"How were we to know that?" Klara looked away, unable to keep a brief twist of anger from showing on her face. "You could have at least let someone know you were all right," she said.

Tilman walked into the room and leaned against the sewing table, his wooden leg straight out in front of him. "It wasn't that I didn't care about them — or you either — I just couldn't come back at first, and then not coming back became a habit. Not coming back to anything . . . ever."

"Why now . . . what brought you back now?" Klara was staring out the window at a horizon she had seldom visited, the limit of her own known territory.

Tilman said quietly, "The business wasn't going so good in the past few years. And," he added, a hint of shame in his voice, "I'd nowhere else."

What business, Klara wanted to know. She'd heard nothing about a business.

Tilman scraped and clomped his way down the hall and returned with the sack Klara had seen him carrying when he first arrived. From it he pulled one wooden box, a rectangle eight inches long, six inches wide. On its surfaces were scenes carved in relief. Only the bottom was flat.

Klara picked it up and turned it slowly

323

in her hands. She saw a prairie with several mountains behind it, a view across water with a tiny "V" of migrating birds on the left and a peninsula on the right, a bird's-eye view of an industrial city, another plain with a freight train and grain elevators in the distance. The carving was detailed and skilful. "This is lovely," she said, "and you didn't even have a workshop."

Tilman looked surprised. "I don't know," he said. "I've never thought about needing a workshop." He paused. "People buy them . . . for a dollar. Or bought them. But not so much now with times being hard."

Klara continued to turn the box in her hands.

"I've done marble carving too. My friend Giorgio apprenticed with a man who made tombstones and he got me a job there. Giorgio is so good with marble he did all the angels in the graveyard and after the war he got interested in inscriptions. He tried to get me into lettercarving too, but I wasn't keen on it. I liked carving roses and willows sometimes." Tilman looked pensive. "But anyway I couldn't stay, and you can't take marble on the road. Giorgio could always settle into a job as if it would last forever, but when the hard times came, no one could pay for the angels any more. Last time I saw him he was living in some shack in the Don Valley in Toronto. Him and a hundred other men. He was a tramp, like me." He smiled. "I told him I thought I'd never see the day . . ."

It was the first time Klara had heard Tilman use this term in relation to himself Her father had used the word "tramp" with some disdain, but he had always given them something, a coin, some food, nevertheless.

"Giorgio's an Italian name, right?" she said.

"Yes. His father was on the road with me when I was younger. But he was only a temporary 'bo. So's Giorgio. Only temporary. He'd got a job overseas, or he thought he'd get one, working on some Jesus huge Canadian war memorial that's going to be built at Vimy, where I lost my leg in France. It's been in the works for years. The sculptor, Allward — the man who got the commission — is such a fanatic that it took him forever to find the right stone, apparently. Then they had to build a road, clear the site," Tilman walked over to the window. "That would have been a real treat," he said bitterly, "sort of like clearing a charnel house."

Klara could feel the nerves awaken in the skin of her back and neck. "Nobody from this place went to war," she said. "They all took agricultural exemption." She looked at the floor, not wanting Tilman to see her expression. "Nobody but one."

"Two," said Tilman. "I sure as hell went to war."

"Sorry." Klara began tidying her work table in the uncomfortable silence that ensued. Scissors to the left, patterns to the right.

"Could you use this?" Tilman asked, his voice softening. He pulled a slightly larger carved box from the sack. "Maybe for thread or something."

As Klara took the box in her hands she could feel tears entering her eyes. It had been years since anyone had given her a gift. "Thank you, Tilman," she said, turning the box on the table, keeping her eyes on it, embarrassed by her emotion. "Why didn't you go?" she asked quietly now, not looking at him, her fingers moving over the texture of the various landscapes. "Why didn't you go to this Canadian memorial?" There was a tiny bridge, very far away, on the part of the box she was looking at. "I would have gone."

"Why on earth would I ever want to go back there, Klara? I couldn't begin to tell you what hell it was. Think of this: Giorgio said it took five years to remove enough mines from the ground so that it was safe to begin construction. And even so, someone is blown up every few months. This Allward, the sculptor in charge, must be a nightmare to work for. He's had the commission for ten years and only now is he able to hire the carvers."

Klara was dropping spools of brightly coloured thread into the box he had given her.

"There's going to be names engraved on it, which is why Giorgio is so interested," Tilman continued. "But only the names of the eleven thousand who went missing in action in France. Giorgio wanted me to go because he said my leg went missing in action." Tilman laughed then but did not look at his sister, expecting her not to share the humour.

Klara was holding a spool of thread in her hand. "Missing in action," she repeated.

"Yes, you know, the ones they never found, probably because they were blown to bits. We found some — but only parts — nobody could tell if they were

Brits or Germans or even what colour their hair had been."

Klara dropped the thread in the box and slammed down the lid. Tilman, startled, jumped up and faced her. Then his eyes narrowed. "You have no idea how awful it was. Nobody has any idea."

"Don't tell me," Klara said. "Please, just don't talk about it."

"No," said Tilman, "you wouldn't want to know. No one does." He turned his back and hobbled over to the door. "No one over here wants to know anything about it."

The next morning Tilman was up early. Klara could hear him below making the fire, the stove doors clanking and the sound of water flowing into the kitchen sink. It had been a long time since anyone other than she had made these morning noises, and she allowed herself the luxury of listening to another prepare to meet the day.

She had slept late. For hours, long into the night, the man Allward and his memorial had been in her mind, and she lay on her back and whispered the name to herself over and over, terrified that she might forget it. Very early in the morning she had sunk into sleep, and she had dreamt of Eamon for the first time in years, a tender dream in which he had whispered the words "Now you can love me" as they lay together, skin to skin, in the very bed where she slept. "Now you can say it, Klara," he breathed the sentence into her ear. "Now you can say you love me." In the dream she thought it must have always been like this, and happiness touched all of her like heavy rain. She could smell his skin and feel his lips brush her face. "You

329

are filled with joy," he told her. She woke refreshed, as if her mind had been rinsed clear by bright water.

In the kitchen Tilman offered her tea, but she touched his arm and told him she had something to show him. He asked if she could wait until after breakfast, but she said no, she had waited long enough.

As they passed through the woodshed Tilman put his hand on the door jamb to which he had been chained so many years ago. Klara, walking ahead of him, stepped into the long, dewy grass of the yard. "No one scythes it any more," she explained. "Sometimes I tether a calf here to keep it down."

Tilman didn't respond.

"Sorry," she said, remembering.

Her shoes were drenched when they reached the lane that led to the shop. She stopped there to allow Tilman to catch up and noticed as he swung his leg toward her that the moisture had glued his pant leg to the surface of his artificial limb. How altered we are, she thought, how changed. But now the difference seemed wonderful, miraculous, for she knew that there was something else they recognized in each other, something cellular and deep that made all the muscle and skin of their external selves seem constructed, like Tilman's false leg.

"Do you ever wonder," she said quietly, "how it would be for us if things had gone the way they should?"

Tilman stopped walking and looked far off to the point where he could see one concession road intersecting another. "Things did go the way they should," he said, "for me."

How had it been for him, she wondered, moving away from the familiar and with all those impediments, a chain at first and the awful vulnerability of being an unprotected child in a world full of strangers. Then the war, and now this cumbersome prosthesis.

She guided Tilman over to the old workshop, handed him the hammer she had brought with her, and watched as he struggled to free the bolt that had been welded by rust to the rungs that surrounded it. A voyage to Vimy was unthinkable, farther than she could imagine. Yet, since the moment her brother had mentioned the monument she had felt as if the urge to cross the Atlantic had always been a part of her life, even as if she were familiar with the journey. Perhaps she had always wanted to go, always wanted to walk out the back door and know she was leaving an entire way of life behind, to see if there was another point of view, another narrative waiting for her in a landscape she hadn't yet experienced. But her brother's absence, and Eamon's dematerialization, seemed to have used up all the energy necessary to move forward, to keep going rather than turn back. It could be that Tilman's return brought with it the animation she had always believed she lacked. She looked at the sky and then at the pasture beneath it. The white animals in the field looked unreal to her now, like discarded phantoms, as if they had already been left behind. Or as if they belonged to someone else.

"What's in here?" Tilman asked after he had finally knocked the bolt sideways.

"Just wait," she answered, wanting his pure reaction.

He handed the hammer back to her, pulled the door through the thick weeds that prevented it from swinging open, and gasped in surprise, almost in fear.

In the light that shone through the east window of the small shop stood the abbess, her smooth, sightless eyes staring through a tapestry of spiderwebs, her two hands holding a network so thick it was as if she had spent the last decade creating a gauze map of the river systems of the world.

"Good Lord," said Tilman, "I thought for a moment she was real."

Klara clawed her way through webs into the interior of the shop. She seized an old broom from the corner and began to clean the sculpture with it, revealing an arm, a shoe, a draped skirt, almost as if she were painting a huge canvas. Dust rose into the shaft of light from the door and hung glittering there.

"Grandfather was one hell of a carver," said Tilman with admiration. "Thank the Lord the carpenter ants didn't get at her. How long has she been out here?"

"Grandfather didn't make this," said Klara. "I did."

"You made this?" said her brother in disbelief. "You made this by yourself?"

Klara stepped back from the figure so Tilman could see it better. "Grandfather taught me," she said. When her brother did not reply, she added, "It's not quite finished."

All Klara's carving tools on the bench were oranged by time and bathed in dust. "I'll show you," she said, seizing a medium-sized chisel and the hammer. "Watch."

It was as if the whole room were lit by her brother's amazement. Though she worked with difficulty as the tools were not sharp, and she was nervous and out of practice, a fold, nevertheless, slid down the skirt at the end of the tool.

"Jesus!" said Tilman, impressed.

"I can barely hang on to the chisel," said Klara. "It hasn't been sharpened for a decade. But, as you can see, I *can* do it."

Tilman, as if overcome by the largeness of the figure and the smallness of the space, stepped back toward the door of the shop. "Grandfather wanted me to make large figures like this."

"Yes," said Klara. "He had high hopes for you. When he was older he liked to believe you'd gone to Bavaria, that you were in some kind of workshop there, studying Riemenschneider, studying the masters."

"Meanwhile, I was over there trying to kill the Hun, not even thinking about their works of art. Sometimes our trenches were so close together I could hear the men talking, and I knew what they were saying because of Grandfather. Remember . . . he would speak to himself when he was working. He always treated himself as an apprentice, then gave himself instructions in German."

Klara quietly returned the chisel to the

shelf. "I've done no carving now for almost twenty years," she told Tilman. "Grandfather knew I had stopped. He said I would start again, that something would come along that would make me want to do it, that would make it impossible for me not to do it."

Her brother was a dark, silent silhouette in the bright rectangle of the door.

"I want to do it now, Tilman," Klara continued. "I want to carve. We should go to that man Allward's monument, where your friend is, in France."

Tilman was standing with his arms outstretched, one hand on either side of the doorframe. Klara could see his body swing forward as he began to laugh. She solemnly observed his mirth for a minute or two.

"I'm serious," she said when he had recovered himself. "I honestly think we should do it."

She had an answer for every one of his arguments, though the debate went on for days. *His leg?* He'd already travelled with it. *No money?* She would sell the animals, since she wouldn't be there to mind them. *Still not enough money and all of it hers.* They would do it mostly on the bum, and

335

he surely knew how to do that. *She didn't know how to carve marble.* She'd learn, knew she could. He, in fact, could teach her. *She's a woman.* It doesn't matter.

"It *does* matter, Klara," he argued. "You have no idea what happens to women on the road."

"Whatever it is, it won't happen to me."

Tilman told her he hated the ocean, that he had found the journey to the war almost as bad as the war itself, the feeling of entrapment had been that strong, that and his persistent seasickness.

"You came back . . . you had to take a ship to come back."

"Without a leg and with lots of morphia. I don't remember much." Why couldn't she understand, he wanted to know, that almost every aspect of that period of his life had been nightmarish? To him, France was a place of carnage, claustrophobia, and continuous bad weather. "And Klara," he added. "I'd been on the road, I survived it better than most."

Tilman crossed the night kitchen, then returned to the table, sat down, and hauled his wooden leg up to the seat of the adjacent chair. "Christ, this thing is a burden," he said. "Can't ever rest easy with it — except at night when it is on one side of the

336

room and I am on the other." He was silent for a bit, then he leaned forward, his arms resting on the table. He looked at his sister. "I don't like saying this because I believe in freedom and everybody being at least given a chance to do what they want — even if what they want to do is nothing."

Klara waited.

"But, Klara, I have to tell you this. You won't ever be able to work on that monument."

"I can do it. If they won't let me carve I'll do some other kind of work. I want to be near it. I'll do anything."

"No, you can't." He raised his hand to keep her from speaking. "You're a woman, Klara, and everyone else is men. Not one of them would hire a woman."

Klara looked right back at him. "I am harmless," she said, the last thing he expected to hear. She rose and walked away. "I wouldn't touch a hair on the head of any of them," she added as she left the room.

"Well, I'll be damned," Tilman said, laughing. He was certain the discussion had ended.

Tilman chopped wood every day for a

week, explaining to his subdued sister that when he met Giorgio's father, Refuto, the man could chop wood like a machine and he had taught Tilman tricks so that the work went faster. "At least I'll have been some help to you, Klara, before I go," he told her. "There'll be enough in the shed for winter by the time I've finished."

Klara was washing up after dinner and paid him no mind. After this she would climb the stairs to her sunroom, where she had been sewing for the past few days, quiet, absorbed, and distant from her brother. "And where is it you are planning to go?" she eventually asked, not turning away from the sink.

Tilman didn't answer but rose from the chair instead. "It will be cold tonight — a frost maybe," he said. "I'll go bring in the animals. They'll be happier in the barn."

"They can stay in the pasture," said Klara. "No need."

"No, I'll get them," he limped toward the door. "It's better that I do."

Through the window, Klara watched him dragging his leg down the lane toward the pasture.

She said "Vimy" and "Allward" aloud, hoping that even though he couldn't hear them, the words would penetrate his brain and stay there. She didn't want to see him limping like that on the concession road, going out to meet life and taking all of life with him. And she staying put, trapped in her constant place, the view from the window never changing except on those occasions when it framed a picture of someone walking away from her.

As she had each day during the past week, Klara sat cross-legged on the wide work table surrounded by pins and thread and scraps of cloth. It was mid-October, each day was fractionally shorter than the last, and there was a scurrying noise of squirrels storing nuts between the ceiling and the roof above her, a sense of urgency in the air. Klara was pleased to have almost completed the garment that lay draped across her lap, the arms hanging languidly down from the edge of the table.

People up and die, she thought, they up and die before they have their fill of the impossible. Her grandfather had died before Tilman's much-longed-for return. Father Gstir had died before the bell for his illogical church was blessed. Eamon, without ever laying a hand on a military aircraft. They all had approached their desires naked, simple and glowing, without artifice or disguise, their wide-open hearts an uncomplicated target for annulment of one kind or another. Renunciation was an option they never even had time to consider before they were rejected by experience and the light was cancelled.

This was not going to happen to her. She would court the impossible, but she would conceal herself, confuse the spirit of annihilation, bring no attention to her quest.

When she descended the stairs for the noon meal, she found Tilman rummaging in the pantry, making room for the large bag of flour he had brought from town. "Traded one of my boxes for it," he told her. "It should last you quite some time.

"What a relief," he added, stepping back into the kitchen, "to have been in a village not filled with widows and orphans. Towns all over Ontario are still carrying on about the war as if they knew something about it, naming streets and memorial halls after battles they couldn't even begin to imagine. Not in Shoneval, though," he remarked sarcastically. "The Germans here still look at me as if I'm a freak because of my leg. Refreshing."

"You said you sometimes heard the Germans talking in the trenches."

Tilman stood still for a while, remembering. "You know," he said, "it was peculiar, but they were talking about precisely the same things that the men beside me were talking about: girls, hometowns, food.

Sometimes I would forget I was listening to German because what they were talking about was so familiar."

"It's not what you think," Klara said, "about Shoneval. Some of the boys were keen to go, but parents and grandparents got them exempted for farming."

"Lucky them." Tilman began to walk back and forth across the room. "Except," he added, "they are all still here, in the same place." A look of faint contempt passed over his face.

"Sit down," said Klara, "stop pacing. You're not on the road yet. Just sit right there and don't move. I'm going upstairs. I've got something to show you. A surprise."

Tilman collapsed into the Boston rocker. "What kind of a surprise?"

"Wait and see," Klara called over her shoulder. "Just wait and see."

Klara undressed in the noon light of the many-windowed sunroom, no one to see her nakedness. She stood without clothing for several minutes, allowing the coolness of the air to touch her skin, to dry the sweat behind her knees and between her breasts as if all she had been until this moment were disappearing with the evaporation. Eventually she stepped into the trousers she had been tailoring all week and sat down to lace up the new shoes she had bought in the village. She stood and placed a dark hat on her head. Then she straightened her shoulders, dressed the upper part of her body, and descended the stairs.

When she entered the kitchen, Tilman sprang from the rocker, then stumbled, having forgotten about his leg. "What the hell . . ." he said.

Klara, dressed in men's trousers and shoes, white shirt, tie, complete with her father's diamond tie pin and a splendid red waistcoat, tipped her hat. Her father's gold cufflinks shone in the sunlight.

"What's all this?" Tilman's expression had changed from shock to suspicion.

"I am going to Vimy and you are too," Klara said. "You told me they'd never hire a woman, so I'm going as a man, as your brother."

Tilman continued to stare at her. He was not sure she looked like a man, but she didn't look like a woman either. She had pulled her hair up under the hat.

"I'll cut it," said Klara, noticing his gaze. Then she changed her mind. "No, I won't cut it. I'll keep my hat on all the time."

"What *is* this madness?" her brother asked. "It's like a religion, your wanting to go. If it's the carving you're after, stay here and make angels for the churches. You're good enough for that. I meant it when I said no man could do better."

"I don't want to make angels," Klara ran her hands nervously over the waistcoat. "I want to work on that monument. . . . You know how to travel." She stopped, let her pride slip. Then she said quietly, "I can't get there by myself, Tilman, I don't think I could do it."

Tilman stepped away from her, crossing the floor to the sink. He bent down so that he could see as much of the sky as possible. There was one delicate chevron of migrating birds, far off, but they were heading east, not north. They're practising, he thought, they're not departing yet.

Few birds crossed the ocean, Tilman knew, unless they were carried by the fierce, inescapable winds of storm, unless they had been forced to give up all control of direction, departure, arrival. The boat would be like the chain or at best like school, or like Limb-Bo. "I'm not going, Klara," he said, refusing to look at her. "I won't go."

Though he couldn't see her, an atmosphere of sorrow seemed to run like a river from the place where his sister stood. Tilman felt its strength flow over his shoulders, through the window glass, and out into the grey autumnal sky.

And then there came a loud crash as Klara swept her mother's good Limoges platter from the ledge of the china cabinet onto the planked floor. She stood staring at the shards for several moments, then with her voice choked by tears said, "I won't stay any more."

Tilman looked at her, amazed, frightened by this display of emotion. In her men's clothes with her slight figure Klara looked like the boy he had been — filled with the need for escape — and despite the fear his heart went out to her.

She stepped away from him as he reached over to touch her arm. "You can go, Klara, anywhere you want to and I'd take you there. But why this monument on the other side of an ocean I can't cross?"

"I *want* to go there," she said. "I want *you* to go there." There were tears streaming down her face just as there had been when Tilman had last seen her thirty years before.

Tilman's arm dropped back to his side as Klara moved to the farthest corner of the room, her arms crossed and her face red with anger and grief.

Her hat was askew and some of her hair had come undone. She looked as crazy and as vulnerable as the little tramp so popular in the cinema, though she knew neither how she looked or how the little tramp looked as she had never been to a moving picture.

"Ah," said Tilman, "so you're tired of your life here. That's it."

"I'm tired," Klara said quietly. "I'm tired of everyone leaving me, everyone going off on the road, going off to wars . . ."

Tilman stepped a little closer to her. "Who went off to the war, Klara? I thought you said no one went."

Klara was silent. Then she whispered, "No one but one, I said, no one but one."

"And where is this one now?" asked Tilman.

"He's dead." Klara sat down, took off her hat, placed it on the table. "He thought he'd be able to fly an aeroplane in the war. Father said he'd likely never even have seen one. I don't know how he died. He was just missing, gone."

"I'm sorry, Klara."

"It was a long time ago," Klara unhooked the top button of the waistcoat. There was a vacant stillness about her now.

"A long time ago. But I did it all wrong. I said things, things I was never able to take back. And now he hasn't even a grave. This Vimy seemed so . . . I've been foolish, I suppose."

"Not foolish," said Tilman. "You had a love, is all. I've never had a love . . . don't suppose any woman would have an old one-legged 'bo like me anyways."

Klara didn't respond. After a few moments she rose to her feet and said, "I'm going to lie down. There's soup on the stove if you want something to eat." She felt oddly stunned and empty, as if she would never care about anything again. A weighty drowsiness moved through her blood. She was certain she had just experienced the last of her passion, and she had let go of her will.

In her bedroom she allowed her men's clothing — the red waistcoat included — to sink like wilted foliage to the floor, and without bothering to remove the shirt or the cufflinks, she closed the curtains, crawled under the quilt, and collapsed into sleep.

A few hours later Tilman banged on her door.

"Okay," he said. "Time to get up."

Klara raised her head, alert as an animal. All the sleep had left her.

"And if I die of being on that boat, it's your responsibility."

Klara laughed, "I'll bury you at sea. You'll become a 'bo berg." She sat up in bed. "Tilman," she said, "Tilman, open the door."

He lifted the latch, entered the darkened room, and was startled by his sister flinging her arms around him. "You're real kin to me now," she said. "Until now I was never wholly certain it was really you."

"It was me, all right," Tilman said, stiffening. He stepped away from her. Touch to him recalled the cold, hard harness across the ribs, though he understood and was moved by his sister's gesture.

"First thing," he said, walking to the other, safer side of the room while keeping his eyes on his sister standing in a shirt that hung almost to her knees, "first thing you do is something about those clothes." He pointed to her arm. "Somebody would have those cufflinks in a second. You'd be rolled and beaten up. You look like a rich kid, which is worse, even, than looking like a woman. Better tear the jacket some, add some patches."

"I can't do that," said Klara. "Not to the waistcoat."

"Leave it at home then. Wear some other coat."

"I can't do that either. I'll carry it with me somehow." She knew it would break her heart not to wear the garment and to leave it behind was unthinkable. "I'll make something else, fast. I'm a good, speedy tailor," she said.

"Yes, you are," said Tilman, "but it's not your tailoring skills you'll be needing. It's your wits."

"I've got them too."

He smiled. "I dare say you do."

A few days later they took a slow, sputtering bus into the lakeside town of Goderich, where Klara made arrangements for the passage while Tilman, who had never paid for travel in his life, stood sheepishly at her side in the ticket office. They would take a Great Lakes steamer to Montreal the following week and once there would board an ocean liner bound for France. They had argued for hours about whether to travel on the bum, or whether to book a cabin. In the end they decided to hire an auctioneer to dispose of the old wagons, sleighs, and farm machinery in the barn. When approached by Klara, Kiefer Erb, the original owner, was only too happy to repurchase Charolais, to pay a good price for Charlotta and the calves, and to more or less tend to the old horse. All this added several hundred dollars to Klara's bank account. The barn cats and the kittens she gave to the good Sisters of the Convent of Immaculate Conception.

"He'll mate now," Erb had said, jerking his thumb toward Charolais and winking at Klara. "Now that he has a taste for it."

Four days after Klara bought the tickets, Tilman boarded up the windows, both downstairs and up, despite Klara's anxiety about his use of a ladder, and they spent their last few days in the house with lamps lit indoors at all hours. Tilman hated the sense of enclosure, but for Klara the lack of view and the golden interior light intensified the look of the rooms she knew she would not see again for a long, long time, and was growing fonder of as a result. How wonderful the far corner of the parlour, for instance, with its soft cushions, the dark wood of the bookshelf, and the rich warm reds and browns of the books kept behind glass panels there. And how lovely and still the pressed-glass goblets kept on a tray on top of the shelf. All this seemed more mysterious, and gorgeous, and distant than it had during childhood when she had been admonished not to touch books or glass, they being among the few treasures in the family's possession. Tilman made his way into town and came back with a large brass lock. Then, in the midst of fastening this to the workshop door he stopped, looked at his sister, and said, "Klara, this is crazy. Do you know how crazy this is?"

"No more crazy than living on the road for thirty-odd years. Look who's talking about crazy."

Tilman put his hammer on the nearby windowsill. "What are you going to do about your voice?"

"What do you mean?"

"How are you going to talk over there, even on the boat, without revealing you are a woman?"

"They speak French in France, perhaps I won't have to say much."

"Klara," said Tilman. "Seriously, you're not going to be able to talk at all."

Klara considered this. Male and mute.

She cupped her hand to her brother's ear and whispered, "We'll say I had a terrible childhood disease that affected my vocal chords."

"All I can think of," said Tilman, backing away from this physical intimacy, "is a disease that might have made your balls fall off. That's the only way any man would get a voice like the one you have."

"I beg your pardon," said Klara, taken aback by her brother's coarseness. "I was intending to whisper. There's no male or female voice in a whisper."

"You'll have to do it all the time."

"Yes, all the time."

"One more thing," Tilman whispered. "You better stop being shocked when people talk about their balls or anything else. As a matter of fact, you better start talking about them yourself."

"I will not talk about such things."

"Well, you better whisper about them then," he said.

Two weeks later, as they walked slowly away from the farm toward the village and the bus that would carry them to Goderich, it seemed both terrible and wonderful to Klara that she was departing with her brother, as if he had at last invited her to disappear with him into the world that had so often lured him away. She was still dressed in women's clothing — the skirt flapped against her shins and wrapped uncomfortably around her legs — and she looked forward to the change of costume, the change of self. Few spinsters would even consider anything as reckless as what she was going to do. She was surprised that her own mind could conceive the idea, could insist that she risk the adventure.

"It is astonishing that we have decided to do this," she said to her brother now, who raised his eyebrows and repeated the word "we" skeptically.

She didn't add, though she knew it to be true, that if she had permitted her life to leak away, day after day, in the same predictable fashion, pinning her hair up, sweeping her floors, washing her face, eating her frugal meals, it would be not only as if Eamon had never put his foot on the grass that surrounded Shoneval, had never gone off to the war believing that he was stepping into harmless ether, but also as if his skin had never touched hers, as if her own passion had never existed. As time passed and she had turned from young woman to spinster, it was as if — without any kind of memento mori and with no life to replace the story of him that, despite her best efforts, still held on to her heart — Eamon, his love songs, his hands on her young body had all been a dream, a fantasy concocted by her old maid's mind.

In the future, as a much older and much calmer woman, Klara would find that she wanted to know more about the man responsible for the huge Canadian monument in France, wanted to add to her own distinct memories some kind of chronicle of a life lived, of apprenticeships served, of tasks completed. The opportunity would arise when, after a few decades of almost complete silence, the sculptor Walter Allward once again caught the attention of his fellow Canadians by the simple act of dying. Then, for a moment or two, his accomplishments were revisited and his life was examined. Having read about his death in a small column in her local newspaper, Klara would begin a trek from library to library of the cities she was able to reach in a day's journey, reading back issues of magazines and the publications of Veterans Affairs, taking notes, examining the indistinct grey reproductions in art books published in the first decades of the century. There was never enough. Nevertheless, the information she would glean during these intensive searches would allow her to fill in the picture of the visionary man she had come to believe had transformed her life.

It turned out that for a man with such an uncompromising nature, Walter Allward had served a fragmented, yet fortunate and by times lyrical apprenticeship. His exhausted mother, able for a few startling moments to look past the chaos of her seven children toward what even she recognized as precocious marks on paper, sent him off for Saturday drawing classes at the Toronto School of Art. There he showed more interest in line than in colour, and more interest in pencil and charcoal when the opportunity to sample paint was given to him. His father, a carpenter, taught him the mechanics of wood construction: the care and use of tools, the importance of measurement, plumb bobs, and spirit levels. Indeed, some of his earliest memories concerned the trapped, quivering bubble of the latter instrument. He might have become a carpenter like his father, but his need, his desire, to control what should be built (and what should not) led him to spend five years of his youth as an apprentice draughtsman in the offices of an architect, until one day he realized that he would never be permitted to draught anything other than brick row houses were he to remain there permanently — a price he felt was far too high to pay for a limited amount of security.

There was a fissure in the brick city of Toronto, where he grew up, a deep, branching wound caused by a river and its tributaries endeavouring to scrape out channels to Lake Ontario and creating, after centuries of effort, a series of interconnecting ravines known as the Don Valley. The nineteenth century had left in its wake a smattering of mills and factories, breweries and tanneries in the valley — some of which were abandoned by the dawn of the twentieth century — but little else had been coaxed out of the wild. Smaller enterprises flourished there in Allward's time: market gardens, orchards, and apiaries. And here and there one might discover the huts of nature-loving hermits lending to its green depths in summer the feel of Pliny's country home, or Yeats' imagined Innisfree.

After leaving the architect, the young Allward descended each day into this unlikely verdant and humming world in order to work for the Don Valley Brickworks, where he had been employed to design and model the terracotta bas-reliefs that decorated the outside walls of the homes of the wealthy in the world above. This he did happily for a few years, using his wages to set up a studio in the city core. Eventually, the incoming commissions for statues of dead young women, elderly statesmen, and various allegorical figures freed him from the brickworks. He climbed out of the gorgeously blossoming valley on an evening in June and never glanced back. Except that it entered his dreams sometimes as a kind of alternative deep space that one could gaze into as if looking from a cliff above water while birds swam in an ocean of air. In some far and as yet uninvestigated room in his mind he had learned much from the valley about vantage points, about edges, about depths. He had learned that a valley can be used by industry, or can be used as a peaceful answer to industry, that it can provide shelter for several species of plants that would not have been able to survive in the congestion and exposure of the upper world, and that much of that which thrives in congestion and exposure would have languished near, or would have itself been killed by the music of nature. And then there was the question of whether any or all of this was worth preserving, worth protecting or fighting for. In his dreams sometimes the little orchards of the valley that he had walked through on his last ascent to the world above darkened with sudden armies.

During the first half of the war years, Allward walked to his studio like a ghost from the past who has no knowledge or interest in the present, fixed images of bronze figures in his mind, his preoccupation with casting larger and larger objects blocking his view of the carnage in the papers and the mourning of his neighbours. As if he were an arctic navigator determined to find the Northwest Passage, he was frozen into his own discoveries, unable to stop commemorating the might of the empire. Commissions had for some time been arriving at his door: a statue of Sir Oliver Mowat, the Alexander Bell Memorial, the memorial to the Boer War. His wife presided over his domestic life with efficiency and pride. He was a great man, still young, and yet too old to go overseas. Their children were, thankfully, simply too young to think about the war at all.

Who knows who or what shattered his indifference, or why, but the last years of the war came to him as a great awakening that let all the horror in, and he dreamed the Great Memorial well before the government competition was announced. He saw the huge twin pillars commemorating those who spoke French and those who spoke English, the allegorical figures with downcast or uplifted faces, and in the valley beneath the work of art, the flesh and bones and blood of the dead stirring in the mud. And then the dead themselves emerged like terrible naked flowers, pleading for a memorial to the disappeared, the vanished ones . . . those who were unrecognizable and unsung. The ones earth had eaten, as if her appetite were insatiable, as if benign nature had developed a carnal hunger, a yawning mouth, a sinkhole capable of swallowing, forever, one-third of those who had fallen. A messy burial without a funeral, without even a pause in the frantic slaughter.

Who were these boys with their clear eyes and their long bones, their unscarred skin and their educated muscle? How was it possible that they were destined to be soldiers? In what rooms had they stood? In what shafts of sunlight? Prairie grasses quivering beyond the old watery glass of farm windows. Snow falling softly on small uncertain cities, or into the dark lakes of the north. And all the footsteps they left in the white winter of 1914 would be gone by spring. The boys themselves gone the following autumn.

Nothing about the memorial was probable, even possible. Allward wanted white, wanted to recall the snow that fell each year on coast and plains and mountains, the disappeared boys' names preserved forever, unmelting on a vast territory of stone that was as white as the frozen winter lakes of the country they had left behind. Or he wanted granite, like the granite in the shield of rock that bled down from the north toward the Great Lakes. So sad and unyielding, so terrible and fierce in the face of the farmer.

The memorial was to be built in France, at the site of the great 1917 battle of Vimy Ridge, won with huge losses by the Canadians who had lived for weeks in tunnels they had carved themselves out of the chalky soil before bursting out of these tunnels on April 9 into a hell of mud and shrapnel. It was to stand near the Ypres salient on the crest of Hill 62, looking across the Douai Plain toward the coveted coal fields in the east and what were once lush fields belonging to peasant farmers to the west. After the war the French, in an act of reckless gratitude, had given one hundred hectares of the battleground to Canada in perpetuity, one hundred hectares of landscape that looked like it had been victimized by a terrible disease boiling through the earth's system to its surface. Almost a century later there would still be territorial restrictions on this land as active mines and grenades would occasionally ignite. And in the tunnels below, helmets and entrenching tools would continue to smoulder in the slow, relentless fire of rust.

Allward had watched the citizens of the provincial capital of Toronto stroll or hurry past his Queen's Park sculptures of colonial founding fathers without a glance; in fact, he had not once seen a passerby pause to examine the bronze faces of these men who had so successfully imposed Europe's questionable order on what had been their personal definition of chaos. After the brief ceremonies of installation, these statues in frock coats had become as easy to ignore as trees, fire hydrants, or lampposts. This would not — could not — happen with the memorial. It would be so monumental that, forty miles away, far across the Douai Plain, people would be moved by it, large enough that strong winds would be put off course by it, and perfect enough that it would seem to have been built by a vanished race of brilliant giants.

After he received the commission, Allward moved his family to a studio at Maida Vale in London, England, assuming that from there he would be able to travel easily back and forth to France in order to oversee the engineering of the project. He auditioned models for the figures of defenders, mourners, torchbearers, for the figures of peace and justice, truth and knowledge, often abandoning or substituting these individuals before the plaster models were cast or sometimes later, when he would change his mind throughout the night. He made hundreds of drawings of swords and wreaths, of pylons and of walls, always with the lead of his pencil sharpened like a weapon. In the end it was the imposing front wall of the memorial that obsessed him, the wall that would carry on its surface the names of the eleven thousand no one ever saw again.

In 1923, he began his investigation into dimension stone, his tour of the great quarries of Europe, his search for flawlessness. It was as if in his mind he had decided that the stone he chose must carry within it no previous history of organic life, that no fossil could have been trapped in it, no record of the earth's hot centre or the long periods of cold retreat that had crept across its surfaces in the form of ice ages or floods. An undisturbed constituent, innocent since its own birth, of any transient event, so that the touch of the chisel cutting out the names would be its first caress.

Nothing pleased him, not the warm stone used by medieval architects for the great cathedrals, not the cold stone used centuries later for great public buildings. He visited quarries in France, Spain, Italy, England; he investigated the possibilities of Canadian quarries, American quarries; he sent his emissaries off to distant corners of the world, rejecting their suggestions over and over until they quit his employment in despair. Two years passed, a sizeable portion of the money had been spent on the quest. *I have been eating and sleeping stone for so long it has become an obsession with me,* he wrote in response to queries on the part of the concerned War Graves Commission in Canada, *and incidentally, a nightmare.*

Eventually, news came to him of a vast quarry near Split in Yugoslavia whence the Emperor Diocletian had procured the stone for his baths and palaces. It was opened for the first time in centuries so that Allward could inspect it in the company of his engineers. Like the negative imprint of a great architectural complex, the deep outdoor rooms of the quarry shone with a blinding whiteness in the sun. Exhausted after months of travel, and after a full day of scrutinizing the face of the stone, a day in which he spoke not one word to those who accompanied him, Allward placed his hand and then his forehead against the quarry wall and wept. "At last," he is said to have whispered, "at last."

Before the stone could be shipped to France, a road leading from the Route Nationale on the Douai Plain to the site of the memorial had to be built. During the two years that passed in this employment Chinese workers young enough to have but scant knowledge of the European war were killed by mines hidden in mud, the noise of the fatal explosion like an insistent letter of reminder from the past. A rabbit warren of tunnels had to be closed and filled beneath the spot, a sunken rectangle had to be dug, and concrete had to be poured where the enormous foundation was to be installed. Body parts and clothing, bibles, family snapshots, letters, buttons, bones, and belt buckles were unearthed daily, and under the plot of earth from which the central staircase would someday rise, the fully uniformed skeletal remains of a German general were disinterred. In the seven years since the battle, several poplars had made a valiant attempt to take root on the battlefield, and some were now taller than a man. In almost every case when they were removed to make way for the road, bits of stained cloth and human hair and bones were found entangled in the roots. Once, a mine a half a mile away exploded, unearthing a young oak tree and the carcass of a horse, intact, activated, it would seem, by the fractional movement of the underground growth of roots.

While this was going on, Allward worked on plaster figures in his London studio or travelled to the continent to audition Italian carvers for the making of the great on-site sculptures — the male and female nudes that were to be executed on the base or high on each of the pylons. He made several voyages back to Yugoslavia to supervise the extraction of the stone at Split. Crossing the water to the white marble island of Brac, he entered a white stone world where men worked all day in white quarries, departing at night for villages composed so entirely of white marble it was as if they lived in their own mausolea. Back on the mainland, he spent days watching stonecutters ease the limestone from the earth with such gentleness they might have been handling bone china. When it came time to move the massive pieces for the pylons to waiting ships, the wagons used in the process were so heavy they broke the ancient bridge at Trau over which stone for palaces and parliaments had passed without incident for almost two millennia. Work had to be halted until another bridge was built. Time passed.

And then more time passed. The stone was coaxed from the earth, permitted to slide in a controlled manner down the mountainside. It then was taken — with great difficulty — over the Adriatic Sea, across Italy, and up from the south to the north of France. Eighteen thousand tons. Load after load. The final several tons were interred in the wrecked earth of Vimy for safekeeping against repairs, for Allward always anticipated breakage and ruin. And each minute of every day Allward's ambition rolled heavily, turgidly through his mind, as something he would have to work with since it could neither be buried nor moved.

Angry letters arrived from Ottawa demanding dates of completion, and then more letters arrived filled with threats of cutting back the funds. Allward replied with rage, claiming that no one but he was intimate with the memorial, knew what it meant, what it would be. I will be emptied, he thought, when this is over. I will have put every drop of my life's blood into this already blood-soaked place. The anatomy of everything — natural or built — obsessed him. Stems became pedestals for that which must be supported to survive. Rivers became carving tools scouring curved banks, acting on the earth through which they passed in the same way as a sculptor's gouge moved through stone. Human beings too were either an extension, a manifestation of his own skills, his own vision, or they were not. If they were not, he wasn't interested. If he thought they were, and they proved otherwise, he felt first betrayed, then furious. The personal couldn't hold his attention, he was driven by the idea of the monument. A sentence that did not make reference to its construction was a sentence he could neither hear nor respond to.

When more than ten years had passed, an increasingly hysterical government in Canada sent out emissaries to lure him home. The depression in the country had deepened, the tax base was shrinking. Allward kept none of the appointments these bureaucrats made with him. If they were in France, he was in England and vice versa. They eventually went back to Canada to report that the memorial was too advanced to stop now, that to suspend operations would be a diplomatic error impossible to overcome.

Visible from a distance of forty miles, the two massive, irregular pylons stretching toward the sky like white bone needles or remarkable stalagmites, even the skeleton of the memorial had become a feature of the French landscape. The Italian carvers were beginning to work on the figures Allward had cast in plaster in his London studio. The names of the eleven thousand missing men were being collected and the complicated mathematics necessary to fit these names into the space available on the base was being undertaken. The most recent set of figures had suggested that it would likely take four stone carvers two years to chisel the hundreds of thousands of characters into the stone. Lines, circles, and curves corresponding to a cherished, remembered sound called over fields at summer dusk from a back porch door, shouted perhaps in anger or whispered in passion, or in prayer, in the winter dark. All that remained of torn faces, crushed bone, scattered limbs.

When Giorgio Vigamonti was twenty-five and back from the war, he had almost immediately gone to see his friend and employer, the tombstone-maker Juliani. Things were still prosperous in a city such as Hamilton, a place dedicated to the fabrication of various kinds of metal, a city that had almost more than anywhere else in the country benefitted from the increased manufacturing brought about by the boom in the armaments industry.

Juliani had embraced the returning soldier and then, without pausing for conversation, had handed him a carving tool. He needed help, he said. Many of the wealthy and some of the not so wealthy wanted memorials for their dead sons, marble plaques for various churches, portrait busts for the cemetery or, if the home was ostentatious enough, for the hall. There was lots of work, he told Giorgio, and lots of money.

"How's your pal, Tilman?" he had asked. "Dead or alive?"

"I haven't seen him, but I've heard he's

alive. He was wounded out at Vimy. Lost a leg, so they say."

"Poor bugger."

"Yes."

"He was pretty good with marble but liked wood better, I seem to remember. Not a bad carver. Glad it's only a leg he lost. It could have been his right arm."

Giorgio was wandering through a room filled with half-finished projects, the pale faces of young men stared at him from every corner, and the chisel was hanging useless at the end of his own right arm. "What shall I do?" he asked.

"Words," said Juliani. "You're going to have to do a lot of words. Seems like everybody nowadays wants to express themselves. Used to be a name and the dates would do, but no more. You kill off a generation of boys and suddenly the whole world becomes interested in poetry. Sometimes, God forbid, they even write the poetry themselves." He told Giorgio that he had seen hardened capitalists approach his shop, a piece of white paper shaking in their hands, tears in their eyes when they read the trite verses aloud. It was almost always the men who came to him, he said, and oddly they had all wanted him to approve of their choice of elegiac lines.

Women visited the shop only if there was no man to do the job, and they were surprisingly less overtly emotional, often satisfied with the customary "king and country" epitaph.

"I don't know how to carve words," said Giorgio.

"You'll learn. I'll show you a couple of scripts, and you'll learn."

In the past Juliani himself had always carved the names and dates, and Giorgio had paid very little attention to him while he worked at this task, which seemed to one who was constantly busy with angels to be boring in the extreme. He hadn't been interested then, and he wasn't interested now. But he was eager to enter civilian working life and felt, therefore, that it was prudent to agree — at least for the time being.

"With any luck," Juliani was saying, "we'll get a commission or two for a war memorial from some village or another. Good money in that."

"And lots of words."

"Well, lots of names, yes."

And so Giorgio, quite reluctantly, began what would become a love affair with the alphabet. At first he struck a bargain with his employer that if he worked three weeks on words he would be able to spend two weeks on some image or another: an angel, a lamb, the face of a dead or missing soldier. To his great surprise, however, he developed — quite suddenly — a passion for the way words occupied the surface of stone, the placement, the depth, how the light affected them, and most of all their permanence. Even the mathematical calculations required for centring the words seemed to him somehow magical because they were so necessary. Without order, he came to know, the words would appear to be haphazard, unintentional, would lose the dignity that permanence demanded. He became fanatical about bevels and lines of incision, often in a temper for days about faults that even Juliani could not see. When the contracts for village war memorials began to arrive, it was he who negotiated with the mayors and councils, and he who carefully counted the number of characters necessary to honour the community's lost sons. These symbols in stone would be all that remained of this farmboy, that office clerk, this boy who had played in the town band. Inevitably a quiet relative or friend or sweetheart would stand at a respectable distance behind Giorgio while he carved a particular name. And when he had finished they would shyly approach the stone and run their fingers over the marks that he had placed there. Sometimes they wept as they did this.

For ten years Giorgio Vigamonti would concern himself with rendering the letters of the alphabet, and with the powerful emotions this alphabet had on men and women when it was arranged in certain ways. He had, during this period, almost married a woman from an Italian family, someone he had known for years. The great friendship between her family and his, and the fact that he was now making a reasonable amount of steady money, made marriage and a family seem like a logical next step. Then the bottom fell out of the market. The last of the war memorials had been completed, the rich had lost their fortunes in the stock market crash, and there was very little interest in memorializing anything at all. The need for angels and lambs seemed to have departed from the earth, granite was replacing marble, and few had the money even for granite. Juliani, who was by then an old man, was forced to let Giorgio go and not much later to close his shop for good.

Giorgio, out of work, out of money, and out of luck, said goodbye to his family and his intended, left the city of Hamilton. For a year or two he became a vagrant and sometime migrant worker, drifting around the world of the hobos, eventually ending up in the large shanty town developing in the Don Valley in the heart of Toronto. It was here that he was reunited with Tilman, and here that he learned about the huge Canadian monument being built in France. A former soldier told him about it, a mad, dishevelled pencil seller who really *had* lost his right arm. The memorial was to honour the thousands of men who had gone missing in France — the names of those who had disappeared in Belgium had already been inscribed on the Menin Gate at Ypres. Giorgio would never forget the way the pencils in the man's cup rattled as he gave him this news, as if they were an extension of the fellow's constantly shaking body. He could barely believe what he was hearing. "The government is really going to pay for all this?" Giorgio asked.

"So I've heard," said the pencil seller and then added under his breath, "the bastards."

A week later, after hitchhiking to Montreal, Giorgio was stowed away in the baggage hold of a steamer headed for Le

Havre, having unsuccessfully tried to persuade Tilman to join him.

"What could ever make you want to go back there?" Tilman had asked his friend. "Back to the scene of the carnage?"

"Work," Giorgio had answered, "and anyway my particular scene of carnage was closer to Belgium, not in this part of France."

"I wouldn't even *think* of going," Tilman said. He had remained unsmiling when Giorgio suggested he might find his leg there, at Vimy, where he lost it. But as Giorgio walked away, Tilman had called to him, "Look for me when you get back and we'll go see your father."

Giorgio had turned around then and shouted back, "Yes, we'll do that. But what you should do in the meantime is find your own family."

Tilman would always remember this, knowing, as he did, that in the final analysis both he and Giorgio had found the Becker family, or at least what was left of it.

Giorgio could barely imagine what eleven thousand names would look like carved on a huge stone wall surmounted by a magnificent monument. The texture they would make would be like no other surface, for words were like that. Even on impermanent, short-lived paper, even in foreign languages you would never understand, words had a presence unlike any other presence. They carried authority in a way no other collection of lines, circles, curves, and squares could. "Alpha and Omega," he would sometimes whisper to himself when he was working. "Moses and the tablets."

He was disappointed to discover upon arriving at the site in the spring of 1934 that another man would not be needed for the carving of the names for several months. At present, the list of men provided by the Ministry of Defence was being added to and subtracted from each day, as men believed to be missing turned up in the north woods of Canada, or in the tropics, or hidden in their attics. And every week or so a few other men would be reported as never returning to homes that had waited for them for years. Occasionally a body with identity tags would be found during the course of the work itself, when a landmine went off, or when a road had to be built, or a pit had to be dug. The boy in question would then be scratched from the list of the missing and his remains would be buried in a nearby military cemetery with the customary simple white stone engraved with a maple leaf and his name. Giorgio was told by Captain Simson, the overseer, that he might get a position as a carver, might be able to join the team of Italians who were currently hanging, supported by ropes and scaffolds, all over the vast pylons.

He would have to wait, however, until the man Allward returned to Vimy in a week or so, as each carver — even the stonecutters — had to be auditioned by him, and if Giorgio was to believe what Simson told him, the master sculptor was not easy to please. Still there was always work to be had, apparently, as each week a few Italian carvers would succumb to a combination of homesickness and the miserable weather, throw down their tools, and begin the journey home to Naples or Perugia.

Giorgio spent his first few days in the Picardie region, wandering in the countryside around the site, amazed by the colour green and the white, pink, and yellow blossoms in the orchards that had been planted since the war. So this was the celebrated French spring he had never witnessed during his years as a soldier. He could remember only the colours of flesh and of mud from that time; now there were tulips and daffodils in gardens, lace on the boughs of trees. After a day or two he began to feel uneasy, as if the display were somehow in bad taste in the face of what had gone before. There were those who were moved by nature's blanketing of catastrophe. He was not to be one of them. To participate in work on the memorial seemed to him to be the only acceptable response to what had taken place.

His own battles had been fought farther north — notably at Passchendaele and Ypres — but it did not take much of an act of the imagination for him to re-create how things must have been at the ridge, in the trenches that surrounded it and on the slope that led to it. What he had never before seen was such an extensive series of tunnels snaking like an underground river system beneath the fields of conflict. As soon as he could borrow a lantern, he walked the half-mile from the busy site of the monument to the entrance of Grange Tunnel and began to explore this subterranean hallway and the passageways that veered off from it. The rusting military detritus underfoot and the names and images scratched into the chalky walls recalled so vividly the human activity that had taken place there they caused his eyes to fill with tears.

Though born in Canada, Giorgio moved easily through the throng of Italian carvers at the work site, recognizing in them certain tribal similarities to the crowded community of his childhood and understanding the language his parents had spoken in their home. And the men themselves welcomed him as a lost brother, inviting him to camp secretly on the floor of one of the huts until he could be hired on and saving scraps from the mess hall so that he wouldn't starve while he was waiting. They were all eager for information about the New World — some had plans to emigrate — and they questioned him constantly. Was it unbearably cold? Were there many large sculptural commissions? Marble quarries? Giorgio hadn't the heart to tell them that, in Canada, most of the carving took place in humble shacks near the graveyard. And now even that employment was vanishing along with the money that supported it. Instead he gave the particulars of his parents' address to anyone claiming they wanted to go to

Canada, that and the whereabouts of the parish church.

During the day he walked around the partly constructed monument, surveying it from every possible angle, then climbing the stairs to the top of the massive base, where he looked out again over the strangely innocent countryside. He then turned to examine the few completed allegorical figures. A downcast middle-aged man and woman were placed at either end of the east side of the base — Canada's parents grieving for lost sons — and some other figures were in various stages of completion at the bottom of the two pylons. Giorgio was impressed by the enormity of the work, by the larger-than-life brooding presence of the figures, and by the massive architectural scale of the base and the pylons. Sometime soon, he was told, the man Allward would arrive and with him would be the largest sculpture of all: a female *pleurant* who would gaze down at the symbolic tomb that would be completed when the two carvers finished the marble cloth with which it was to be draped.

Giorgio made friends with the carvers who were working on a grouping of *Defenders*, whose stern marble countenances and firmly crossed arms he found almost comical. The men told Giorgio about the pale limestone that contained just enough ochre to make it seem warm rather than cool, about its long journey on the sea and over mountains to this place. Aphrodisa, they told him, was the name of this stone, like Aphrodite, they said, with her honey hair, her cream-coloured skin.

Giorgio looked at the figure they were carving, a powerful young man. The ribs and muscles of one-half of his torso were like the ploughed furrows of a field, the other half remained rough and primitive, the traces of the primary, harsh chisel work still explicit.

The older carver handed the young Canadian a tool. "You make an ear for us," he said, offering this command as a challenge — a challenge to the New World.

"It's the wrong chisel," said Giorgio, "and I'll need more than one. A drill also, and rasps." He was remembering the ears of angels, his time in the shop in Hamilton. Juliani had always referred to the tombs with angels as sepulchral monuments, elevating them above the common tombstone. Now Giorgio was being asked to add something to the largest sepulchral monument of all.

The second carver opened his tool box. "Use anything you want," he said.

Ever since he was a boy Giorgio had loved freeing the shell shape of an ear from the stone. What, he had always wondered, did angels listen to? It was, in many ways, the most delicate operation in the sculpting of a human body, more so even than the hand, though admittedly not as expressive. He looked for a long time at the location of the eye, the angle of the neck, and the shape of the skull. Then he climbed the ladder that rested against the figure's shoulder and began by using a small drill while his companions worked opposite him, smoothing the bent arm that, with its twin, folded across the chest. By the time the shadow of the pylon touched the bottom rung of the ladder, Giorgio was using a small rasp on the outermost fold of the ear, that part which to his mind most resembled a curling leaf. The other two carvers were now watching and praising him. *"Belissimo,"* they said and more than once, *"Bravo."* Then, suddenly, they were silent.

They had heard the sound of city shoes on the stone floor of the monument. Although the footsteps did not make an echo, there was the impression of an echo, and

384

something in the rhythm of the sound made one think of a sentence, a declaration. Even in his concentration, even with the rasp his primary concern, Giorgio registered the approach of one who was not wearing the customary gum-soled workboots, and he looked down from his ladder into the face of a tall, middle-aged man with thick eyebrows and a broad forehead. He was dressed in the kind of dark woollen overcoat that Giorgio remembered the rich men who owned Ontario factories wearing on their tours of inspection.

"Do I know you?" the man asked. *"Chi siete?"*

"I am Giorgio Vigamonti. You cannot know me. I have just come from Canada."

"From Canada?" the man was surprised. "All that distance. Obviously I have not hired you."

This was Walter Allward then. Giorgio was silent. He carefully placed the rasp beside the other tools he had lined up on the upper platform of the ladder.

"Why did you come? I expect to know absolutely everyone on my monument. And all of my carvers are Italian."

"I *am* Italian," said Giorgio, "but from Canada. I fought in this war. I fought with the men you are honouring here." He did not say that he had come because there was no longer any work for him in the country he had left behind.

Allward turned to the carvers, who had removed their white caps. "And what do you think of this Canadian? Why have you let him work on your man here?"

"He came from the New World," the older carver said, "and we wanted to see," he cleared his throat nervously, "we wanted to see what he could do."

"And," Allward glanced up in the direction of Giorgio, "and what can he do?"

"He can carve, sir," the younger man blurted out. "Look at the ear. You see, he can carve."

There was a community of workers around the memorial: English stonecutters, Italian carvers, and French labourers all going about their business. Giorgio liked this, was comfortable in the midst of activity. He was less at ease when he found himself alone with one other person in a closed space, for he believed those were the times when terrifying and secret extremes of love or violence could occur. But not here, not with this easy, understood collaboration, this fluidity of contact, and this wonderfully open space. The choreography that was unfolding around a project of this scale excited and moved him, every cell in his body wanted to participate.

Allward found Giorgio the next day sharing lunch with the two men who had given him the opportunity to carve the ear. "Hey, Canada," he called from the bottom of the steps. "Come with me."

"So it's Vigamonti," the master sculptor said to Giorgio as they walked toward the overseer's hut. "Vigamonti," he repeated. "So . . . did you know, Vigamonti, that the French call carvers like you and your friends over there *'practiciens.'*"

Giorgio did not. He kept his head down, sheltered from the wind. The sun that had given such explosive life to the blossoms had abruptly disappeared, and spring was frozen in its tracks by a cold front from the north.

"I believe it is not necessarily a term of endearment. It means no creative thinking, no artistic designing. Does this matter to you?"

Not knowing what to say, Giorgio shrugged.

"Your Italian friends over there have been trained since birth not to consider anything but skill . . . nothing at all but the perfection of skill. How about you, have you been trained to do that?"

Giorgio did not think that he had but maybe so. "I was apprenticed to an Italian gravestone maker," he said. "Most of the monuments were very similar, but once in a while we suggested something if the client didn't know what they wanted . . ."

"You will suggest nothing here," said Allward. "You will simply carry out instructions. What was your rank in the war?"

"I was a private at the beginning. Toward the end I was promoted to corporal."

"Why was that?"

"Sir?" Giorgio noticed that Allward's grey hair was standing upright in the wind, making him appear to be even taller than he was.

"Why were you promoted?"

Giorgio thought for a moment, then he spoke. "They said I was being promoted because I had served well, or something like that. But I think," he looked northward, toward Belgium, squinting, "I think I was made a corporal because I was neither missing nor dead, and almost everyone else in my battalion was. So I suppose I was promoted for staying alive."

"No heroic acts then?"

"No." Giorgio was looking at the familiar mud at his feet.

"Good. There will be no heroics here either, no spontaneous bursts of artistic licence. I've already done all the creative work."

"So you are the general and we are the troops."

"Something like that." It had begun to rain and drops of water were running like sweat down Allward's forehead.

"I came here to carve words. I'm especially good at that, at letter carving."

"We'll see about that when the time comes." Allward bent down and picked up a piece of a military belt from the soil at his feet. "When we first started working here, the whole vicinity still stank of death."

"I remember that. I remember that, during the war, even the few flowers we saw smelled of decay, like they were rotting."

Allward held open the door to the hut. "Ah yes," he said, "during the war they would have, I suppose."

When they were inside, Captain Simson, the short, plump overseer of the project, pushed a one-page contract across his desk for Giorgio to sign. "Welcome aboard," he mumbled. "Are you afraid of heights?"

Giorgio had never climbed a structure this tall so really he didn't know, but he answered in the negative.

"Tomorrow we'll be starting the uppermost figures . . . if we can get the studio up there, that is. We're going to begin to build it this afternoon . . . or we're going to try."

Allward was looking out the window at the memorial. He turned to Giorgio. "You know what I like best about all that stone?"

"*I* know," said Simson, who had heard it all before.

"What I like best about all that stone, Vigamonti, is that there is nothing putrid about it." Allward walked out the door, repeating the words "so clean, so clean" to himself.

And so it followed that Giorgio came to work in what the Italians soon called the *studio in ceil,* the studio in the sky. With his lunch strapped to his belt, he climbed the rope ladders and scaffolding each morning to the precarious elevated hut, full of wonder that his employment was actually to take place in the room that was part swing and part tree house. As he worked he sometimes sang, "When the wind blows, the cradle will rock." When asked

390

which opera the tune came from, he eventually sang and then translated into Italian the whole nursery song for the two other carvers in the studio, who were horrified by this English verse they believed must be about infanticide. Giorgio was pestered for the rest of the story: Who put the cradle up in the tree? Was the mother dead? Perhaps the child was the result of some passionate and forbidden union, or a princeling whose existence would upset the order of royal succession? A complete narrative developed in full view of the silent plaster models, while the men busied themselves preparing the work space that would enable them to transform these into stone.

One of the men was a genius with the pantograph, a kind of pointing machine that combined with Allward's precise calculations would permit the carvers to accurately tease the enlarged female figures of *Peace*, *Knowledge*, *Justice* and *Truth* first in rough and later in detailed form from the stone pylon.

Giorgio worked on the sensuous stone body of *Peace*, who, with her back curved and her face lifted, held a laurel branch up toward the sky at the very pinnacle of the monument. He had to resurrect everything he had learned about the female body from

carving angels — and what he had remembered from hasty encounters with women
during the war. This was a handsome,
strong, mature woman — nothing girlish
here — and as he worked he realized he
was beginning to fall in love with her, her
slightly opened mouth suggesting an inha-
lation of breath, and her attitude, almost
that of a swoon, which implied that she,
herself, had made the enormous effort required to climb to the summit of the
pylon, where she would stand forever
locked in the moment of victorious arrival.

The wind tore across the ridge some
days, shaking the studio and causing the
men to stagger like drunks under glass skylights drenched with rain. On other days
there was golden light, a view across cultivated fields to villages still only half reconstructed after the annihilation of a war now
more than fifteen years gone. The Italians
knelt on scaffolding erected inside the
studio and worked with such concentration
it was as if they were engaged in the act of
worshipping the human body.

Although he couldn't see them, it was
possible at times for Giorgio to hear airborne larks singing on the other side of the
thin studio wall. They provided a kind of
thrilling accompaniment to the heart-

breaking songs the Italians sang while Giorgio moved his chisel and then the palms of his hands over the stomach of the magnificent woman, the drapery that covered her slightly bent leg, or while he ran his fingers across the bones of her cool hand.

When they boarded the ship in Montreal in mid-November, Klara was covered by a coat, a vest, trousers, and a cap, having decided to change gender once she left Ontario behind. She had walked to the end of a pier on the St. Lawrence River with a bundle under her arm and, after looking guiltily around, had dropped her burden into the water. Moved by the sight of her familiar clothing opening like the petals of dark flowers in the river, she had wept a little at what suddenly seemed to her to be the death of her young woman-hood, a discarded body, floating away to-ward the sea, the arms of the black silk blouse extended as if still anticipating a lover's embrace.

On the trip from Goderich through Lakes Huron, Erie, and Ontario and even-tually down the St. Lawrence River, Klara had been amazed at the lovely composi-tion of each lakeside town, the layout of which, she concluded, must have been de-termined in the nineteenth century with the notion of an approach by water in mind. Port Stanley, Cobourg, Kingston, and the large city of Toronto; she had heard of such places, of course, but until now they had seemed too remote to be interesting. Even Tilman, disliking boats as much as he claimed he did, enjoyed the passing scenery that was close enough to convince him that, if necessary, he could swim to shore, yet far enough away that he could imagine carving the hills and spires on one of his wooden boxes. He became quite animated as they approached the city of Montreal, telling Klara that he had been there once or twice during his time on the road and remembered its cosmopolitan flavour. He knew some good flophouses too, he explained, where they could lodge for a day or two until they sailed. But Klara, who wanted nothing to do with flophouses, eventually persuaded him to stay with her in a small, inexpensive hotel on the river.

During the daylight hours Tilman disappeared into the streets and alleys of the city leaving Klara alone in their room watching the river traffic from the hotel window. As it neared time to board the ship on the day of their departure, an anxious Klara stepped out the door of the establishment to look for her brother. To her relief she soon spotted him under a nearby bridge, where he was standing around a fire with a group of vagrant men, all of whom had clearly recognized and accepted him for what he was, a temporarily reformed tramp. "The Frenchies are a more cultivated kind of 'bo," he had told Klara. "Better food, better wine, and more interested in looking around at where they are. They like nice landscape."

Not one of these hobos gave Klara a second glance as she beckoned to her brother, and she began, right then, to understand the freedom her costume gave her, a feeling of calm, similar to what she imagined men must experience walking unnoticed through the world.

"Goddamned ocean," Tilman complained when they were installed in the cabin they shared with two other men. "Who'd have thought anything would ever get me back on the goddamned ocean." Though they were still moving down the river he was already feeling dizzy.

"We're not even *on* the ocean," Klara whispered, "and you were fine on the lakes. Surely you can't feel sick yet."

"Don't perch like that on my bed," hissed Tilman. "Men never perch on beds."

The swell of the Atlantic in early November proved to be formidable. As soon as the river widened into sea, Tilman moaned, turned his face to the wall, and refused to rise from his bunk. Klara, however, was awestruck and exhilarated by the heaving expanse of water and by being buffeted by gusts and spray. She spent much of her time on deck, leaning on the rail with the wind in her face and her hand on her cap for fear of it blowing away and revealing her wealth of hair. Before the journey was over she would have to cut it, as Tilman kept insisting she should. But for the moment there was still some vanity left in her. As for undressing at night, she accomplished this by squirming under the sheets that covered her bunk. "My kid brother," Tilman had explained to the other men, "is bashful. Always had his own room. Mama's boy."

After ten days at sea, Klara saw the coast of France early in the morning through the porthole of the cabin where she and Tilman slept, and as if until that moment she had not believed she would set foot on that soil, she finally made the decision to cut her hair. With scissors in hand she made her way to the W.C., locked herself in one of the cubicles, and, wincing, began to slice off hunk after hunk, filling her trouser and jacket pockets with skeins of golden hair threaded here and there with silver. When she was finished she rubbed her head and was surprised to find the beginnings of the curls that, until now, had been straightened by the weight of her long mane. Then she placed the hat on her head and walked out to the deck. At this hour, it was not long before she found a private spot. Using both hands she tossed her shorn hair into the wind, and though some of it blew back onto the deck, most was swept away from her so quickly it was as if the elements were hungry, eager to help her assume her new role. As the ship moved forward, Klara did not see one lock enter the water. But for weeks afterwards she was still removing the remaining golden strands from her pockets and sleeves.

When the ship docked in Le Havre, Tilman rose from his bunk, hastily gathered their few belongings, and guided Klara out of the cabin up to the deck. Still holding her arm, he pushed through the crowd and hurried awkwardly down the gangplank, stopping only once to allow Klara to retrieve her cap, which had blown off her head. He grinned at her momentarily. "You finally took my advice," he said. "You cut your hair."

Once they were on the quay he almost immediately began to talk about nourishment. "Don't worry, I know how to beg in French," he informed his sister. "First house we scrounge some food."

They were surrounded by the sheds and warehouses of the port, which seemed oddly insubstantial in the grey morning fog, the dim November light. It was difficult to believe that there was a thriving town behind the cranes and machinery of the dockyards. Klara was suddenly disoriented, uncertain on stable land.

She doubted Tilman could speak French and told him so.

"Sure. *Messieurs, mesdames, je suis un pauvre, mais j'ai un coeur plein de la joie de Dieu. Dieu* means God. The Frenchies are all Catholics. All the 'bos in Quebec travelled with a rosary."

Klara pulled her own beads out of her pants pocket and showed them to her brother, who announced that they would be very helpful for begging.

"No one is going to beg," said Klara. "If you are hungry, we'll go to a restaurant."

"Good idea, lots of scraps out back."

"No, Tilman, we are going right *in* the restaurant."

Tilman stopped walking and looked at her in amazement. "I've *never* gone into a restaurant."

"Neither have I," said Klara. "But I've always wanted to."

"I wouldn't even go with the others during the war on leave, wouldn't even go to a café. I didn't like the crowds."

"Well, we're about to share a new experience together." Klara looked up and down the narrow, unfamiliar street on which they stood. She was unnerved by the strangeness of the architecture, the shutters that seemed to be closed against her, the thick, bolted doors. But she knew she wasn't as frightened as she would have been had she still been dressed as a woman. As they penetrated deeper into the city, the streets seemed to become older, darker. Brown water ran in the gutters and the cobblestones under their feet were blackened by a persistent cold rain. Eventually, Klara saw a plain painted sign announcing the Hotel Restaurant Richelieu.

"Okay, let's go there," she said, pointing.

"No," said Tilman, though he sounded less determined. Klara suspected that he was beginning to enjoy being managed.

★ ★ ★

Years later Klara would say that her brother, Tilman, unrepentant hobo, gave up the road because of a humble French restaurant near the docks in Le Havre, a restaurant where he first encountered *Coquilles St-Jacques meunière* and *Jambon d'Alsace à la crème.* "One mouthful," she claimed, "and he spontaneously recovered from a week and a half of nausea. He would have liked to make us stay at Le Richelieu because he couldn't believe there would be more of these miraculous establishments in the rest of the country. Eventually he would spend most of the money he made at the monument in a restaurant, running into town every time he had a chance. He insisted on moving to Montreal when he returned," Klara would announce to anyone who would listen, "became a real snob, worrying about freshness and texture. And *finally,*" she would add, "finally, he learned how to speak French."

They slept in a room above the restaurant, descending in the morning for bowls of coffee and milk, served with bread, butter, and gooseberry jam. The patron, who was also the chef, had ceremoniously embraced each of them when he discovered they were Canadians. His eyes filled with tears when he spoke about the war; two sons dead and every landmark he cared about reduced to ash and dust. Everyone, he said, had heard about the great monument being carved at Vimy, and about the perfect Yugoslavian stone. There was a train to Amiens, and another from there to Arras. Once in Arras they should stop anyone at all with a horse and cart, tell them that they were Canadians come to work on the great monument, and, he assured them, they would be joyfully delivered to the site. Then he gave them two *baguettes,* some goat's milk cheese, and a hunk of sausage, and sent them on their way, refusing all efforts on their part to pay for either food or lodging.

"Couldn't we just stay here for a couple of days?" said Tilman, and then when Klara refused, "How can you just walk away from that fish soup? We could have it again tonight." He was quiet and sulky all the way to the station.

On the train Klara worried about how she should manipulate the mask of her new identity. What did men think about that gave their faces expressions she knew had never visited her own? She had been surrounded by men all her life: her father, her grandfather. She had experienced the anger, the brief joy of courtship, and then the sorrow of Eamon's death. And she had at last become familiar with her brother. But she knew she had never been able to tunnel into the part of men that determined their posture and disposition. Eamon's feelings had always been disclosed by changes in his eyes, the line of his mouth. Yet the faces of the mature men she had known well had closed against the world, had become unreadable when they were moved or frustrated. Would she be able to keep her own face closed if the situation demanded? She looked at her brother's profile beside her. His blank eyes and neutral mouth gave her no information, no sense of what the men concerned themselves with when in a state of rest. Was he still thinking about the food? Or was he looking back or forward, remembering, or germinating the seed of a new future? "I've never gotten used to a seat on a train," he had said to her. "More comfortable with the boards in the boxcar, or even the rods. Only other time I had a seat I was on my way to slaughter with a bunch of other fellows all dressed the same.

Maybe it's that . . ." Perhaps, thought Klara, in spite of his placid demeanour, he was thinking of terror and blood. But who would ever know? These thoughts swam in her mind until the motions of the train made her drowsy, caused her head to droop.

Sometime later Tilman shook her awake. "Don't put your head on my shoulder," he said. "Men never put their heads on each other's shoulder."

As predicted in Le Havre, Tilman quickly located at the market in Arras a farmer with a cart who was delighted by the idea of being able to convey two new workers to the massive sculpture at Vimy six miles away. As they got nearer to the site the terrain through which they rolled became unsettling in its disorder, the farmer pointing out germinating trenches, muddy craters, barbed wire, shell holes. Acres and acres remained fenced off, posted out of human bounds as active shells and mines still littered the surface and hid in the depths of the earth. Each crossroad they passed through was defined by a mound of rubble where once there had been a hamlet, and almost always behind and on either side of this mound men still toiled at reconstruction. All this more than sixteen years after the troops had gone home, leaving in their wake a torn, unrecognizable landscape, a wind full of ashes, and the smell of rotting flesh. The most manicured and orderly spots now were the household gardens (growing only cabbages and endive in early December) and the military cemeteries, though, even there, the landscaping was in various stages of completion. But the grass that covered the graves was mostly green, ironically unscarred. Tilman would not look at the graveyards, stared straight ahead as they lumbered past these inappropriately tidy reminders of tragedy, these gardens of the dead. "I can't look at them yet," he told Klara, who had reacted with shock at the quantity of headstones and crosses. "Just, please, don't make me talk about it."

Above all this, on the horizon, rose the twin white towers of the monument, their shape distorted by five-storey-high scaffolding and canvas bunting. Klara touched Tilman's arm when the structure first came into view, but he drew away, reminding her that men usually don't touch each other's arm.

The wagon turned onto a splendid new

road lined with young Canadian maple trees, a few brown leaves of late autumn still clinging to their frail branches. Although Tilman and Klara were viewing the monument from almost a mile away, the structure had begun to dominate the entire landscape. Distant grey woodlots, this miraculous road, the ridge itself, even the stratified clouds in the sky leaned toward it as if a construction of this magnitude could not be ignored, even by the surrounding disarray, and even by nature.

As they entered the work site they were amazed by the numbers of horses, donkeys, the cumbersome cranes and lorries. "Just like the war," Tilman commented. Dressed in the traditional French worker's costume of overalls, jacket, and cap, several dozen men scurried like bright blue beetles along the scaffolding and across the frost-covered mud that surrounded it. A narrow gauge railway had been set up near the structure in order to more easily move horse-drawn cars filled with the stone that had been used for the base and the pylons. The wagon drew up near this, and the farmer turned to them and smiled and nodded. "Much working!" he said.

Tilman smiled back, descended awkwardly from the vehicle, and reached up and quite uncharacteristically shook the man's hand. Then he gave Klara a quick glance. "Let me do the talking," he said, gesturing toward the Quonset hut the farmer had pointed out to them. "I'll get us a job in no time."

"There's another Canadian here," Simson informed them. "Only one, an Italian Canadian, Giorgio Vigamonti."

Klara looked warily at the overseer. There was a dismissive, almost pompous practicality about him for which she was grateful. He did not raise his eyes from his desk.

"I know him," said Tilman. "That's why I'm here. That's why we're here, my brother and me."

"Allward will have to see what you can do before you can be brought on board. What kind of experience do you have?"

"I worked with Giorgio . . . but I'm not as experienced as him." He rapped his wooden leg with his knuckles. "I can't climb," he said.

"I gathered that," said Simson. "You'll have to work on the details at the base, if you are hired, that is. We need some help there. What's the matter with your brother, cat got his tongue?"

"Vocal chords destroyed by," Tilman paused, "a bungled tonsillectomy when he was a kid."

Klara could feel her face grow hot. Simson was looking at her now as if he knew there was something odd here, but he couldn't determine what. He raised his eyebrows. "What a pair: one can't walk, the other can't talk. What's his work experience?"

"Mostly woodcarving. He'd like to be an assistant, or something like that. He can do any kind of light manual labour."

Simson examined Klara for a disturbingly long period of time. "Well, he's small enough to be a good climber. He could go upstairs. Plenty of odd jobs up there. And that's where Vigamonti is." He led the pair over to the window and pointed to a wooden room affixed to the top of the left pylon. A long rope ladder that hung from it was swaying back and forth in the wind. "No need to audition to be an assistant or a polisher up there." He turned to Klara, "What do you say?"

She nodded, then whispered, "I'll do anything."

"Is Giorgio up there now?" asked Tilman.

"He is, but as you say, you can't climb,

408

and he won't descend until sundown." Simson was still looking at Klara's face. Not a trace of a beard. Maybe, he thought, the surgeon had cut something else besides the vocal chords. "Perhaps your brother here could climb up there with a note or something?"

"No . . ." whispered Klara, not wanting to leave her brother's side.

"We'll wait till evening," said Tilman.

Simson began to busy himself with a pile of papers on his desk. "Suit yourself," he said.

Three days later word spread around the site (where like Giorgio before them, Tilman and the small man known as Karl were being housed and fed by a few of the carvers) that Allward would arrive from London later that day to oversee the arrival of two new plaster figures that would be used as reference for the sculptures on the inside of each pylon. All the previous day Klara and Tilman had watched as men worked at fixing the studio in place. Some swung from ropes, like rock climbers, using their legs to push themselves away from stone and wood out into the air and over to another part of the scaffolding. Others lay on their stomachs on the studio floor with their arms hanging out of the canvas doorway hammering nails, using screwdrivers, while underneath them a pulley was attached to the bottom of the studio floor. Klara was intrigued by these acrobatics, but Tilman was appalled. When Giorgio joined them at noon, Tilman told his friend that for the first time since the war he was actually grateful for his amputation. "Thank God," he said, "I only have one leg. Otherwise that would be me up there swinging around like a suicidal monkey."

Giorgio laughed. "Listen to you," he said, "and after all that bragging you've done about riding the rods, leaping in and out of speeding trains."

Klara liked the sound of this large man's laugh, the warmth it brought to the chill December air.

That afternoon Tilman and Klara stood with Giorgio in a crowd of silent workers and watched as the man called Allward unpacked his latest creations. "There'll be hell to pay," Giorgio informed them, "if anything's broken. One of the *Defenders* had his nose knocked off coming over the channel. Allward almost didn't survive that."

410

Allward was brushing straw from the wing of a plaster angel. Behind him the monument rose like a pale, partly completed cathedral.

"*Charity*," said Giorgio, moving his head to one side to get a better look, "or *Hope*. I'm one of the angel men," he continued. "I'm going to get to work on them. Look," he pointed at Allward, who had uncrated another winged woman, straw blowing around him as if he were in the centre of a small cyclone.

There are certain visual occurrences that become tethered to memory, Klara would later decide, images that appear in the mind when one is sitting in waiting rooms or staring out train windows. If they are strong enough, they may bloom in the brain when one is making love or, perhaps, though no one really knows this, a few moments before death.

The raising by rope of the white plaster angels up to the elevated studio that was to be their home until they were reinvented in stone was, for her, a masterpiece of shape and motion that she took, unknowingly, deep into herself. The twisted rope beneath the breasts, the shadows of the wings moving up the marble pylons, the utter silence surrounded her, none of this would ever leave her. She had witnessed an ascension, an apotheosis, an act so fragile its perfection could be shattered by the smallest alteration in the direction of the wind. And when it was over and she looked at Giorgio, she could see that, like her own, his eyes were full of tears.

Allward had disappeared to the overseer's hut, his head in his hands, the shades drawn, and all his paranoia about the destruction of his work rampant in the room. But Klara had not noticed his departure. She was rapt, certain she had seen the expression on an angel's face change, become painfully alive when, for just one second, a cloud had hidden the sun.

"I only hire Italians," Allward told Simson and a silent Tilman, "and I hire them because they are the best, the most energetic, and the most skilled."

Klara and Tilman were standing in the overseer's hut the morning after the ascension of the plaster angels. The low winter sun entered through the window in front of which Allward was standing, his shadow stretching the full length of the room. While Klara shifted nervously from foot to foot, Tilman stood entirely still beside her, remembering that he really had no desire to be there at all, never mind a desire to be lectured to.

He had spent some time late on the previous afternoon wandering around the vastly altered battlefield with Giorgio trying to explain the situation as it had been in April of 1917. "A mess," he kept saying. "It was all a disaster."

"I thought Vimy was our great victory," Giorgio looked at Tilman, who was squinting in the face of the wind.

"That may be," Tilman said, turning to climb out of one of the craters, "but I don't think a single one of us who was there knew whether or not there was a victory. We barely understood where we were when it was all over. And let's not overlook the fact that thirty-five hundred guys died, and three times as many were injured. I didn't even hear about the grandness of the victory until the war was finished, and then I thought the fellow telling me had things all wrong." Tilman's expression tightened. "I never thought I'd ever be back here, that's one thing for sure."

"But here you are," Giorgio put his large arm around his friend's shoulder.

Because he was so fond of him Tilman endured his companion's warmth for longer than usual. Then he pulled away.

413

"Only because of my brother," he said. "I'm only here because he wanted to come."

"I didn't think you had a brother."

"No, neither did I."

"Look," Simson was saying now, his military side surfacing despite his healthy respect for Allward, "this man lost his leg fighting here at Vimy, fighting for his country. And he came all this way. Give him a break."

Allward sighed, handed Tilman a chisel, and, leaving Klara anxious and alone with the overseer, escorted him out the door toward some abandoned chunks of marble. "All right, let's see you carve a face."

Tilman hated carving features, but he had learned how, after a fashion, from Juliani. "I'm better at distant views, reliefs, that kind of stuff."

"There are no distant views on this hunk of rock. The distant views are all out there," Allward jerked his thumb over his shoulder toward the French countryside. "If you hadn't come all the way from home, I wouldn't hire you. But, I suppose, you can do some of the patterns on the base: fleurs-de-lys, shields, and the like." He put his hands in his pockets and surveyed Tilman's carving, which was less than impressive. "No danger of you wanting to do something original, you haven't got the skill."

Tilman was vaguely insulted, though he knew what the man was saying was true. At least when it came to stone. "Can *you* carve wood?" Tilman asked the tall man with what Allward correctly identified as impertinence.

Allward liked impertinence. "I've never had the desire to," he said. As he walked away, his long dark coat flapping in the wind, he pointed toward a triangular-shaped wall that flanked a staircase on the east side of the base.

"Over there," he called without turning around. "The Italians will show you what to do."

As Tilman walked slowly back to the hut to rescue Klara, there came over him a strong desire to bolt. Shields, crosses. The work would take a long time and would, in the end, mean little to him. Moreover, he was anxious because of his sister's disguise, which he knew would be close to impossible to maintain forever. But his own disguise as a dependable worker would be even more difficult to perpetuate. There were roads everywhere — some he could see from up here on the ridge — and around him were a number of tempting horses, had he only known how to ride them. Vehicles too, trucks, delivery vans, often stood purring nearby, their operators having briefly abandoned them to complete another task. It would be simple to climb into one of them, drive away. Then, as he rounded the east corner of the monument, he saw his sister leave the hut, walk a few paces beyond it, and lift her face to look at the pylons. From this distance he couldn't read her expression, but everything in her posture suggested awe, as if her small body had already been transformed, redeemed by the experience of arriving at this destination. He was strangely and tenderly affected by this, and he knew then that he would stay, stay as long as he possibly could.

Klara slept in a dormitory Quonset hut in a bunk next to Tilman. Fifteen other workers shared the space and filled the air at night with muttering and snoring, the waking hours with a cacophony of Italian sounds Klara couldn't understand. Often they could be heard singing when they returned from the mess hall or from the showers, and many of them stood unashamedly naked by their beds while sorting out the jumble of their morning clothing. Klara's sole knowledge of the male body had come to her as a result of learning Eamon, a pale-skinned, beautifully formed boy with a clear chest and a flat stomach. Now she saw everything that in the past she had only measured for suit jackets, and she saw much more besides: men with enormous pot-bellies and hair covering all of their bodies, and younger men, powerfully but thickly built. They were wonderfully unselfconscious lumbering about the room like large, friendly animals, often delivering long Italian speeches to the man they thought she was. Though they knew he didn't understand, and couldn't reply even if he did, Klara suspected it was their way of telling her — or him — that they knew he was different in significant ways and that they had accepted these differences. They were physically affectionate with each other in a way that women would likely never be. Klara admired this. There was a peculiar smell to the place as well that eventually she came to savour, something to do with sweat and dirty socks, these things and a kind of acid sweetness that she recalled from Charolais.

Tilman's friend, Giorgio, slept in a much smaller hut next door with the two other carvers who worked in the elevated atelier at the top of the pylon. Klara was grateful for this as she wanted, for the purposes of maintaining her disguise, no further intimacy with this friend of Tilman. There were occasions during the progress of the work when she was convinced that one or another of the men was examining her delicate, hairless hands with too much curiosity or was glancing far too often in the direction of her chest. And once or twice she caught herself just on the edge of saying something out loud. Her nightmares included scenes where she would find herself entirely undressed in the studio full of men. Tilman, sensing her anxiety, and acutely aware of his own, had tried to persuade her that they should tell Giorgio who she really was, confess her gender. He is entirely trustworthy, he had explained, and he would look out for her if he knew, would help them keep her secret. But she hadn't liked the idea, and said she wanted to be treated the same as everyone else.

"How can you be like everyone else," Tilman had argued, "when you have to whisper all the time?"

But she wouldn't be convinced, so remained quiet and discrete when working, whispering a word or a sentence only when a question was put to her directly, and keeping her back turned and her head lowered as much as possible. Oddly, without words, she began to open more to the perceived world. As if even the pores of her skin had enlarged in order to drink light, she began to retain in startling detail the visual images around her. The way the sinews on the men's hands moved when they held a carving tool, the concentration lines around their eyes when they squinted at the development of form in stone. How the men hovered in front of a line of chisels perfectly arranged on a table in order of ascending scale. And how, once they had made their choice they never changed their mind. Sandro, Alfredo, and

Giorgio, the musical sound of their names in a wind-rocked room.

They were finishing the figure at the top of the monument, a female allegory of peace, her back arched against the top of the pylon, her head thrown back as if she were succumbing to an invisible embrace, the laurel branch like a stone fountain in her raised hand. She was clothed only from the hips down, one leg emerging from the drapery; her upper torso was naked. Full breasts, the horizontal ladder of her ribs, and wonderfully formed shoulders and arms.

The men clearly adored her, referred to her as the *bella donna.* Each morning Sandro would take off his cap and greet the stone woman, whom he said that he knew well since it was he who had carved her features and expression. But the other men spoke quietly to her as well, glancing at her white face now and then while they sculpted her body. All day long she was invented and reinvented, changing under the chisels, which Klara handed up to the carvers, and under the altering angles of the light.

As the weeks passed Giorgio instructed Klara, explaining the use of chisels, rasps, and claws so that eventually she knew automatically which size the men might need, could sense by their posture and gestures when they required a change of gauge. He showed her how to use the pumice to polish finished limbs, always speaking slowly and patiently.

One day, shortly after the carvers began to work on the recently arrived angels, Klara whispered to Giorgio that she knew a bit about chisels from woodcarving.

"Like Tilman," he said. "You had a grandfather who was wonderful, I understand."

"Yes," she whispered. "He taught us when we were quite small children. He had high hopes for Tilman. But after he disappeared . . ."

"Your brother finds it hard to stick," Giorgio said. They had pulled the canvas aside and were sitting at the front door of the studio, thoughtfully chewing on the baguettes they were given for lunch, their legs swinging over emptiness. It was a cold, clear day in early March. They could see as far as Arras. "Sometimes he even ran away from us, his adopted family. But we all knew he would come back. And he was pretty good about jobs, the one at the stoveworks, and even when we were with

Juliani." Giorgio exchanged a wave with someone on the ground, then turned back to the person he knew as Karl. "How long do you think he'll stay here?" he asked.

"I hope he'll stay," whispered Klara, not really answering the question. "I hope so."

"Well, I'll be here, anyway," said Giorgio, sensing by the way this small man kept his features mostly shadowed by his cap that his companion was shy and reticent. Giorgio laughed now and made some kind of uninterpretable male gesture to his friend below.

Klara turned to look at him, to study his rectangular-shaped face in profile, the prominent nose and generous mouth, his large arm resting on a strong thigh. She couldn't remember ever coming to like someone this quickly, this fast. She almost touched his sleeve, the soft plaid flannel that emerged from his blue jacket, then remembered and pulled back.

He glanced at her suddenly, then grinned and scrambled to his feet, oddly light and agile for a man so large. "Back to work," he said.

"Yes," whispered Klara, "back to work."

Later in the afternoon Giorgio asked her to work with him in the far corner of

422

the studio, where he had begun to rough out the left wing of an angel. Klara was to fill a bucket with waste stone, then take it to the canvas door and lower it by a rope to the ground beneath. On one occasion, just before she was to proceed to the door with a full load, she amazed herself by asking Giorgio if he were married.

He tilted his puzzled face down toward her. Then he looked away and began to tap the chisel with the mallet.

"Do you have a wife?" she whispered. Giorgio was four rungs up on the ladder, working on the angel's shoulder. From where she stood, Klara could see the smooth curve of his throat.

"I came close once, but it didn't happen. Circumstances," he said slowly. "First the war, then the Depression. How about you?"

"No," she whispered. "No, not ever." Klara moved away from him — away from the ladder — to fetch the broom and dustpan.

"Tilman never told me he had a brother. You are how old?" He did not look at her, concentrating instead on the way the surface of the neck unfurled at its base to allow for a collarbone, a breast.

"Thirty-nine." Klara looked at the floor, stone chips and dust.

Giorgio threw his head back and laughed. "I'm forty-one," he said. "We still have lots of time for women, you and I."

Klara laughed out loud.

Giorgio stared at her, surprised. He had never known what to make of this brother of Tilman.

Klara staggered a bit as the studio shuddered under a blast of wind. She feared she had briefly released her hidden womanhood simply by expressing her delight in the phrase of another. Frightened, she drew this woman sharply back into her self, but couldn't pull back the scenario that was building in her imagination. She looked at her small hands, which to her embarrassment she could envisage undoing the buttons on her shirt in the presence of this man, although she couldn't even remember the shape and weight of her own breasts.

Giorgio turned back toward the sculpture. Klara felt a kind of tense silence settle between them, and she decided from now on to remain as quiet as possible in his presence. But all day long, after this, while Giorgio and the other men chatted in

Italian, Klara's inner voice continued to speak to her brother's friend. Do you see? she was saying to him in her mind, this looking inward unfamiliar in the wooden and canvas room. Do you understand?

She hadn't dreamt of Eamon for a long, long time, but in recent nights he had been strolling through her dreams, looking angry and distant, as if he no longer wanted to know her. In the past she had often had such dreams, attributing them to the difficult way in which they had parted. Now that she was standing on the soil of the country whose air he had last breathed, in the vicinity of a memorial that would bear his name, the memory of Eamon often came painfully alive in her mind. How did he think about her in the end, with longing, with indifference, or with hatred? Or was there, by the time he died, a French or English girl on his mind, someone who had been kind to him? It was she who had felt abandoned, when in fact she had closed toward him, had sent him away without even touching his hand. One morning after she'd had a dream in which Eamon behaved as if he had forgotten he had ever known her, Klara was told by Simson to help treat and polish the stone torchbearer that stood on the base of the monument between the pylons, directly behind the figure representing the spirit of sacrifice.

She had never been inside the lower studio, had no real idea of how the work there was progressing. But she remembered clearly the morning when the plasters for the lower grouping had arrived. She and the men she worked with had scrambled down from their eyrie to join the other workers gathered around the crate. It had been a miserable winter day, dry but overcast with a wind that cut through the blue cotton of their coats and overalls. A hundred yards or so from the place where the truck had stopped, some of the men had been busy digging a huge pit — it looked to her like a grave — where surplus blocks of marble were to be buried. Allward, she had come to know, always anticipated damage of one kind or another and wanted an excess of his treasured stone to be stored near the site for future repairs. But Klara remembered that for one brief, irrational moment she had thought that the figures inside the crates might be lowered into the ground rather than taken up to the monument. She also recalled an exquisitely rendered plaster arm, rivered with tendons and veins, holding a torch toward the sky, remembered finding herself running her hand gently across the neck of the torchbearer when she thought no one else was looking, then being admonished by Allward, himself, for this action. No one should touch the work any more than necessary, he had announced while Klara, her face flaming, stared at the pencilled instructions and mathematical calculations written in Allward's hand on the pale plaster arm.

"Everyone's being moved," Tilman told her now, "except me. I am still to work on the back of the base." Although his carving skills had turned out to be less questionable than Allward originally thought, Tilman was kept busy with decorative work: crosses and shields and, more recently, wreaths. This suited Tilman fine. He knew in any case he was mostly just putting in time, and besides, he had discovered for the first time in his life that he was interested in a paycheque, for Tilman had encountered in the restaurants of the town of Arras what he believed was going to be the love of his life.

Night after night as she lay in the bunk next to his, Klara would fall asleep listening to her brother telling her about the pleasures of eating French food. He would describe with great tenderness his experiences in the restaurant of the Hotel Picardie, when he first met *Gratin de homard au porto* or *Truffe St-Hubert,* or that particularly memorable evening when, quite by accident, he came to know *Caneton de la belle époque* in the company of *Flan de Lagoustines George V.* He would also describe for her the tablecloths, the napkins, the large silver-plate spoons, and the elegant china edged in gold leaf, things that, in a thousand years, Klara would not have thought could have held his attention. It all proved a most soothing lullaby for Klara, the soft cadences of the French phrases: *Écrevisses à la crème, Bouillabaisse Marseillaise, Grillades aux pommes soufflées, Poulet à la crème et à l'estragon* . . .

"Everyone's being relocated," he said, "because there's some big shot coming from Ottawa. Simson wants to have the lower figures, at least, completed by the time he gets here. Giorgio told me that the folks back home are getting impatient. It's all taking too long, costing too much money."

Klara was not sure she wanted to work elsewhere on the site. She had become comfortable with her co-workers, liked her surroundings.

"Giorgio's being moved to the names . . . which is what he wanted," Tilman was fussing with his prosthesis. "They've, so far, only made it to 'H.' But he'll only be there half-days. They still want him upstairs, working on the angels." He stood up now and smoothed his pant leg over the wooden limb. "I'm going into Arras for dinner tonight. Why don't you come with me? I'll treat."

"No, no, that's all right," said Klara. On the one or two times she had dined with Tilman she had soon tired of trying to keep up with his rapacious appetite.

On a morning in late April, Klara, who had been assigned to the lower studio, walked through its soft doors to be confronted with the beautiful stone sculptures of the two young men: one, *The Spirit of Sacrifice*, languid against a plinth, caught at the edge of surrender to unconsciousness, death, or complete dematerialization; the other, strong, alive, holding a torch toward the sky. The light shining between the pylons and through the skylight of this lower studio touched the arms, shoulders, and chest of the torchbearer, while his fainting stone companion, placed on a lower level, sank into shadow and became, himself, almost a shade. A tangle of ladders and scaffolding disguised the lower bodies of both youths, but the torso of the upper figure could be seen above this, sun from the skylight pouring over his chest and stomach like honey.

Klara gasped, let the canvas fall from her hand, and walked out onto the marble base of the monument, where she collapsed into a seated position, her head in her arms. She felt as though she might actually black out in the face of this radiance. She sat there for several minutes, swallowing air, attempting to focus. Then she pulled herself together, walked back through the studio door, moved behind the scaffolding, picked up the pumice, and, reaching through the scaffolding in a kind of trance, began to polish the torchbearer's feet. When she finally climbed the ladder and permitted herself to look carefully at the half-finished face, she touched the neck, her fingers moving across it in the same way that they had, three months before, the morning the plaster had arrived. She would have to wait for the carver to complete the sculpture before she would be asked to polish the features.

When the work day was over, she walked away from the studio with an idea as a companion. No one could disturb her relationship with it, no one could break into the plan. When she found herself alone with Tilman outside the mess hall, she could hear him talking to her and she could hear the sound of her own replies, but she knew she wasn't fully there, was answering mechanically. She had walked into an interior classroom, a dark school, where as if committing an act of robbery, she was gathering together for her own use everything she had seen the men do when they had chisels in their hands and all she remembered about the shape of her dead lover's head, the features of his long-absent face.

"What do you do with everything that is cut away?" she asked Tilman, thinking now about the negative space of stone sculpture, the stone that is discarded, thinking too about how she had thrown away huge pieces of her own early life, how she had tried to dispose of the memory of Eamon.

Tilman dug in his pockets and pulled out two marble shards that were shaped like the native arrowheads he had sometimes found in the fields after his father was finished with spring ploughing. "Some of the tourists, even ones who have lost family, friends, like to take away helmets, bullets," he said. "I prefer a souvenir of the monument, rather than anything that reminds me of that mess. You can have one of them, if you like."

"Thanks," said Klara, holding out her hand to receive the shards of stone. Then she walked away from him with the idea speaking in her mind and with the sharp piece of stone digging into the flesh of her palm.

His sister had no real knowledge of what the return to Vimy had meant for Tilman. Among the throng that had gathered to work on the monument, he would be the only man who carried the battle in his mind, who carried the scars of the battle on his person, and from whom the battle had stolen flesh. The lower part of his leg had been abandoned somewhere in this landscape — the thigh being amputated later. Now that he was back at the site, Tilman thought he should be able to identify the shell hole, that he would somehow be drawn to the exact spot where the mud had swallowed his limb. But the terrain was so altered by the time he and Klara had arrived — Allward had rebuilt the ridge itself to enhance the shape of the memorial — that he was disoriented by grass, and saplings, roads, and tidy grave-yards. He could never really believe that he was in the same place, even though after all this time the silent evidence of horror was everywhere. And yet, despite Tilman's in-ability to mentally reconstruct the terrain of the conflict, there was something in the at-mosphere, the way the light hung in the air, and in the direction of the wind that carried with it a grim reminder, a souvenir. *Souvenir.* The French term that appeared over and over, carved into the marble of civilian graveyards in Amiens or Arras, though oddly not in the military cemeteries. The word itself, which spoke of wrenching grief and loss, seemed to him to bring the sound of this wind with it, a sound like that of a bayonet slicing flesh.

When Tilman and his company had been preparing for the battle at Vimy, the claustrophobia of the tunnels had made him eager to volunteer for any kind of job that would allow him out into the open air. More comfortable with snipers than with confinement, and remembering all the training he had done as a young boy during the summer of the bridge, he begged to be made a runner, loved the freedom of speeding across mud, then leaping into trenches, the message delivered by his unshaking hand. He had felt swift and alive, impervious to enemy ammunition, invisible almost, because he was on the move; travel of any kind had always relaxed him. But during the two days before the battle, the tunnels had swallowed him again, and he was forced to stand upright for twenty-four hours in murky and constantly faltering electric light with a multitude of other sombre men, some sleeping on their feet, others whispering to themselves or to a mate, all anticipating the barrage and their own performance in the face of it.

Who were those boys he had stood beside on that April morning waiting for the command. *Joey, Jimmy.* He couldn't remember, remembered only the dark boy's flesh exploding under sleet and shrapnel. And the other turning to him, seemingly unharmed, his head cocked to one side, a puzzled expression in his eyes and the beginnings of a question on his lips. One word forming there. Something with a "W," Who? or What? Then the opaque film moving over the eyes, and the knees buckling.

Tilman had grabbed him by the sleeves as he sank, only then noticing the small dark circle at the temple. When he let him go, the boy fell backwards into the trench from which they had just emerged. Through the next twenty minutes of chaos Tilman froze in a crouching position with his back to the Germans. The boy's pale, dead face had stared up at him from the filth of this unclean grave, the question, whatever it was, still frozen on his lips, and the face itself lit by the glorious colours made by the hail of deafening ammunition that was part of the soon to be famous "rolling barrage." More noise, it would be said, than the world had ever heard before, the furious sound travelling across the English Channel, heard as far as London. More beautiful than any other form of fireworks that had ever visited the sky.

An unimaginable amount of death had come into Tilman's line of vision in the previous three years, and yet this one boy's demise stayed with him, perhaps because it was the last clear image he retained from the great battle during which he was wounded out. *Wounded out.* The term seemed to fit his life. He had been wounded out of his family when he was a child, his parents being unable to cope with his nature. There were times when he felt that he had been wounded out of life altogether, forced to live in a world apart. Even at Vimy, he had avoided the camaraderie of the tunnels, the sense of collaboration. He had volunteered for dangerous jobs, for night reconnaissance work, or as a messenger before the battle, simply for the relief of an exposed position. And it was because of this that he had become intimate with the wind, could recognize it now when everything else had been camouflaged by order. The wind remained unpredictable, impossible to control, often vicious.

Ghosts and marble and memory on the heights, and down on the plain, warmth and food and life. As often as he could, Tilman walked and hitchhiked through the wind into the atmospheric stillness of Arras, where, in his role as appreciator of haute cuisine, he had come to know Monsieur Recouvrir, the chef at the Hotel Picardie. A huge man, covered first in an ample layer of fat and then in his white chef's uniform, he had noted the strange Canadian's attachment to his restaurant and had been impressed by his interest in sampling even the most creative organ dishes that were almost always avoided by those who spoke English. Eventually he had presented himself at Tilman's table, and a few days later he had offered to take the Canadian carver on a tour of the kitchen.

Tilman had immediately responded to this aromatic workshop, the cauldron of potage murmuring on the gas range, garlands of onions and garlic in the vicinity. Recouvrir's hysterical and very thin sous-chef frenetically chopping vegetables, the round, red face of Monsieur Recouvrir himself beaming in the centre. The chef was like a calm, benign God, confident in the midst of creation, seven perfectly sharpened and polished knives near the plump flesh of his right hand, a semicircle of different-sized ladles hanging from the ceiling, making a metal nimbus over his hat. As the weeks passed, Tilman visited the kitchen on his days off, and in the long evenings, and while the chef's large body swayed as he stirred a sauce or while he leaned forward to roll out a perfect pastry, Tilman sat on a nearby stool, a glass of vin rouge in his hand, and began to talk about the war.

Monsieur Recouvrir understood very little of what the English-Canadian said and was therefore in some ways the perfect listener. Grave and sympathetic, he responded infrequently and only, therefore, to the names of battles he recognized. "*Ah, oui,*" he would say sadly, his wooden spoon stopped in mid-stir, "*la Somme.*" And once he repeated the word, "Verdun" with tears in his eyes.

One afternoon he met Tilman at the door and led him into the vacant restaurant. Sitting opposite him at the table, a pichet of vin blanc between them, he began to roll up his white sleeve. Tilman could see a red circle just above the dimpled elbow, and in the centre of the circle, a dark, sharp point. Recouvrir took a paring knife and, wincing, extracted a flat, bloody sliver of wet metal that he dropped with a clang onto a plate on the table between them. "Shrapnel," he said, knocking twice on Tilman's wooden leg. "Verdun," he added. The Canadian understood then that this kind man carried in his body fragments of the catastrophe of the battle of Verdun, fragments that now and then, like Tilman's own memories, worked themselves to the surface. He touched the plate where the blood was drying, then brought his fist down on his artificial leg. "Vimy Ridge," he said. "Vimy."

Recouvrir began Tilman's informal culinary training with an *omelette aux fines herbes*. A Québécois hobo had once shown Tilman how to make omelettes over an open fire when he was a boy, but Tilman was only too happy to receive the instructions again.

Standing with the stainless-steel bowl clasped to his round belly, Recouvrir said, *"Regardez"* while using his right arm to move the whisk in a winding, rhythmic motion. Then he let Tilman try to copy his actions, which he was able to do more or less successfully. The resulting shape of the eggs in the pan made Tilman think of a small yellow landscape in relief. He was so pleased with himself he wanted to frame the omelette rather than eat it. But Recouvrir roared at him goodnaturedly, *"Mangez, mangez."*

They strolled through the arcaded streets of Arras to the market, where the chef pointed out the roundest tomatoes, the fattest garlics, the most beautiful and aromatic cheeses, the plumpest chickens, gleaming trout, the small curls of pink shrimp. They visited the *boulangerie,* the *pâtisserie,* and walked back to the restaurant with their arms full of golden wands of bread and one small, round pastry, gorgeously decorated with quarter-moons of peaches and pears topped with bright berries, the whole surface glazed as though varnished.

When they returned to the hotel in the late afternoon, Recouvrir put his arm around Tilman's shoulders and guided him into the apartment that he kept at the back of the establishment. In the small salon Tilman sat on a burgundy chair near the fireplace while his new friend scurried around in the adjacent kitchen, called out pleasantries in French, some of which Tilman actually understood, and finally re-appeared with the pastry, fruit, dessert dishes, silver forks, and a bottle of Veuve Cliquot champagne all artfully displayed on a silver tray. He stood for a moment in the doorway, side-lit by the light from a window that looked out to a small garden, his face soft and unguarded, the tray and its contents gleaming in his hands, a kind of glorious Father Nature, Tilman thought, complete with bubbles and grapes and lustre. And it was while he was thinking this that he realized he had not flinched when the plump arm had touched his shoulder.

One morning not long after this, Recouvrir drove his rather battered Renault up the road lined by young Cana-dian maples, parked in front of the Givenchy Road military cemetery, and walked toward the work site, carrying in his hand a plate covered by a blue linen towel. Now and then he stopped to talk to French labourers he knew, as many of them came from Arras or the surrounding territory. One of these men directed him to the opposite side of the monument from where one could see the industrial town of

Lens, and so Recouvrir climbed the south-west steps, rounded the left pylon, and began to descend the left set of north-eastern steps, where several men sat on three-legged stools, engraving the names of the lost. Beyond them, at the front of the monument, he found Tilman carving a pleat in a flag that draped the empty stone catafalque meant to suggest the tomb of an unknown Canadian warrior. The noise of machinery in the vicinity had overwhelmed the sound of Recouvrir's footsteps, so Tilman did not hear him approach.

Recouvrir gently placed the plate on a nearby stone ledge, then crouched down beside the spot where Tilman sat without his wooden legs, which he had removed and placed against the casket. Recouvrir smiled at the Canadian's surprise and sensed his momentary lack of recognition now that he was not wearing the customary white outfit. He touched the fold that Tilman was carving. *"Merveilleux,"* he said. *"Tu es artiste."*

"And I have just completed this," said Tilman, pointing to the shield at the right of the drapery. He felt shy but not offended by the large man's proximity. Neither shifted his gaze from the other's face.

Recouvrir moved his hand back and forth across the unremarkable shield. *"Merveilleux,"* he said again, then took his hand away from the stone and placed it on Tilman's back, touching it with the same sweeping motion as he had the shield.

Neither man spoke for several moments.

Recouvrir rose, walked over to the ledge, and returned with the plate in his hand. He placed it on the catafalque. *"Pâté de Campagne,"* he said. *"Un cadeau,"* he paused, *"pour toi."*

That night Tilman, who had never made love to anyone, dreamt that he was being made love to by Recouvrir. Both were clothed, Tilman wearing his blue worker's jacket and overalls, Recouvrir in his chef's outfit but without the hat. They were alone in the Quonset hut, but Tilman was at first concerned that, because of the activity outside the walls, they might be discovered. "Why this?" he asked his friend. The large bulk of Recouvrir was silhouetted against the open window near the foot of the bed on which Tilman lay. The chef moved to one side to allow Tilman to look out at the world filled with singing birds and a multitude of trees in full leaf. He gestured toward the verdant, musical landscape that held traces of neither battle nor monument.

"Because I love you," he said in English, "and because," he gestured toward the open window and the world beyond, "I love this too."

In the dream Tilman was suddenly filled with an indescribable joy as a river made of leaves and grass flowed through the window and into the room where he slept.

When they undressed each other the following Monday night in Recouvrir's apartment behind the restaurant, Tilman was amazed to find beauty in his friend's enormous body, which was firm and round and clean, amazed too by the map of scars that made Recouvrir's skin appear to have been ceremonially patterned, like the engravings of South Seas tribal warriors that Tilman remembered from a book he had looked at as a child. The white marks left by the entrance and the exit of hundreds of bits of shrapnel covered his arms and chest and belly like tiny flowers or stars. "Like constellations," Tilman would tell him some months later, touching some of the groupings and naming them, looking for and finally claiming to have found *Caela Sculptoris*, his very own carver's tool, somewhere on the skin under Recouvrir's left arm. But on this first night, when the two men stood naked and facing each other, having touched each other tentatively on the head and hair and shoulders, Recouvrir moved his hand toward Tilman's hip. *"Explique-moi,"* he said, adding, *"s'il te plaît."*

Tilman showed him how to remove the wooden leg, and when Recouvrir knelt beside him to complete this task, Tilman remembered Ham Bone and Phoebe, remembered the kind of tenderness that transformed a crazed, ragged woman of the roads into a beautiful young girl, ennobled by love. And he knew that the love he had witnessed then was echoed here in this French room as two damaged, fragmented middle-aged men made each other fresh and beautiful and whole again.

Because he had no experience of a sexual nature, having always avoided proximity of any kind, it did not seem odd to Tilman that the hands and mouth and body that were providing him with this miraculous pleasure were those of a man and not a woman. What stunned him was that such joy could be part of human experience, could draw out of him the part of himself that had been left unmarred by either chain or battle. When he closed his eyes he saw the migrating birds that had moved him as a small child, he remembered his mother's breast. When he opened them again, he saw Recouvrir closer than anyone had been since then, closer than anyone except this gentle man would ever be again.

Klara woke on a spring morning before dawn. Five-thirty and the half-finished face of the torchbearer still burning in her mind. She who would eventually rub with powdered pumice his legs and feet, she who would polish the long stretch of his side. His half-finished face in her mind, the roughness of the one side, the wrongness of the other.

Everyone else would be sleeping for two more hours, and even then they would awaken reluctantly, a full day of labour their only reward for the reappearance of light. Klara left the hut dressed only in trousers and a shirt, not wearing the cap, thinking little about disguise, carrying her true self to the task.

She stepped, barefoot, onto the cool pebbles of the earth beyond the hut, then sat on a boulder and pulled on her boots, removing them again when she reached the ramp that led to the lower studio. The texture of the planks on her soles gave the ascent significance, purpose. When she pulled aside the canvas door, she saw that the dawn was just beginning to enter through the windows and skylights of the room, warming the flesh of the torchbearer and his dying stone twin and painting one section of the wooden floor deep shades of blood and rose, though enough shadows remained in the corners of the room that she decided to switch on the electric lights. She walked across to the table where the men kept their tools, chose a mallet, a medium and a small chisel, and several different sizes of rasps, then looked carefully at the stone youth. She would need to climb the ladder twice in order to deliver the tools to the platform beside the torchbearer's face. Once she began she might have to fetch something else. None of this concerned her, she was peeling back the layers that time had built around her visual memory, pulling the past across the vague landscapes of the intervening years.

How to recall the face of one who has died, a face that has been held in the inner eye and then, when the pain of this has exhausted the holder, pushed from the mind altogether. No matter how much it is cherished, an absent face that is a fixed point of reference becomes tyrannical, and tyranny eventually demands revolt, escape. Klara had fled from the memory of Eamon's face over and over, his bright eyes and perfect skin, now almost two decades younger and more perfect than her own. She had rationed the time she would allow herself to think about him, and by a fierce act of will had almost succeeded in turning him into a faceless ghost, until all that was left was the vaguely human, dark shape of his absence. A shadow thrown against an unforgiving wall.

Now she would have to remember the bones under the skin, the scar on his left temple, the beautiful, full mouth, his upturned glance and radiant expression when searching the sky for a kite, an aeroplane. Each detail. The two graceful wings of his eyebrows. How his hair fell when he threw his head back, the soft, slightly slanted contour of his eye. He had been only a boy, the inquisitive child he had been had never left his face. He must hold the torch aloft, yes, but because this figure would become Eamon and would be looking up toward his beloved ether, his expression must be one of astonishment and joy at finding himself, at last, forever reaching toward the sky. His arm illuminating clouds. She stood on the ladder, eyes squeezed shut, scraping these images from the deepest recesses of her memory as if using a sculpting tool on the inner curve of her skull. Then she began.

It was necessary for her to lean over the upturned face so that she was looking down at him as she had so often done as a girl, in haylofts, in orchards, in the sun-room. These scenes came back to her as she worked, and occasionally she felt as if she were falling into the ghost of an embrace, as if either he or she were haunting the stone. She was a novice with marble and she knew this. Hers was the almost impossible task of keeping her concentration fierce and divided at the same time between her long-vanished lover's remembered features and everything she had surreptitiously learned about the marble carver's skill. And so it was, while she was causing the eyes and mouth and expressions of a beloved farmboy's face, the tendons of his beautiful neck, to emerge from the blond stone that she realized she was carving one-half of Eamon's face with the tools Giorgio had taught her how to hold and to use. Giving little thought as to how the face would be explained when the others entered the studio in a few hours, Klara focused on the *ping, ping* of the chisel. Perhaps they would think it was an act of God, a miracle.

She began with the hair on the finished

side of the head, which was too long and straight to be Eamon's. She cut it with the claw, then choosing a small chisel she added several curls, knowing that by changing texture she was altering the colour as well, making the young marble man dark rather than fair. She thought of Riemenschneider, Tilman's namesake. Her grandfather had told her how the great wood sculptor had insisted that colour could be suggested without the use of polychrome, how he had wanted the wood or the stone he was using to describe smell, body temperature, colouring, narrative, and emotion as well as form. She adjusted the angle of the cheekbone, made the jawline softer, and the bones above the eye and at the top of the nose slightly less pronounced. Then she allowed the mouth, which must be sensual and flexible, to carry her hand into the virgin territory of the unfinished side.

Her own mark.

Once she began to work on the untouched side of the face, she remembered the pure joy of making art, how the self connected with the emerging form. She began to sing quietly, and the sound of her own voice was like liquid pouring over the stone.

She did not hear the squeak of the ramp under the shoes of the climber. She did not hear his step on the planked floor. It was only after she had smoothed out the shallow basin of the temple that she heard the voice, shouting. She froze. The chisel in her hand was poised to the left of a stone eyebrow. She slowly lowered her arm, and turned, and fell.

Allward stood looking down at Klara as she struggled to pull breath back into her body. "Who are you?" he demanded. "Are you injured?"

Klara knew she was bruised. The fall had knocked the wind out of her, but nothing else about her seemed to be damaged. "I'm fine," she gasped. "It's just the wind gone out of me, that's all," she whispered.

"Listen," said Allward, "I inspect the carving early each morning before anyone else is awake. *No one* is ever here. Who exactly are you and just what were you doing up there?"

"I'm Karl Becker," she whispered, rising now to her feet, knowing who she was speaking to. "I am one of your carvers," she lied. "I had hoped to get some extra work done," she whispered, "on the torchbearer."

Allward began to climb the ladder from which Klara had fallen. He scrutinized the marble features, then slowly descended, his face white with fury. "That's not my torchbearer," he said. "You've paid absolutely no attention to the plaster. You're ignoring the points."

Klara could not interpret the tone of the man's voice, the level of anger in it. She said nothing but was suddenly aware that she was not wearing her cap, that her blonde curls were painfully visible. She felt exposed and terrified by the exposure.

"Don't try to fool me," Allward said. "I tell everybody, *everybody* who works for me that there are to be no independent acts, no theatrical feats of originality."

Looking down at her boots, Klara remained silent, the sound of her heart pounding in her ears.

"You're not one of my carvers. You're some kind of vandal." Allward had begun to pace. "And you've ruined my torchbearer." He looked up at the sculpture. "I'll have to replace the head now," he said, "but, Christ, it will always look damaged. Where the hell did you come from?"

"You knew I was Canadian," whispered Klara. "My brother and me. Giorgio Vigamonti told you when we came."

"Well, Canadian, do you have a voice?"

"No," said Klara, "I lost it as a child."

"You're a liar, Canadian. I heard you singing in a woman's voice." Allward was glaring at her. "Do you dress up in women's clothes as well?" he asked sarcastically.

Klara walked over to him and seized the sleeve of his jacket. "Please," she said, "I'm sorry." Then, horrified, she covered her mouth with one hand, knowing she had unmasked herself simply by using her own voice, by forgetting to whisper.

Allward backed away from her. "So you *are* a woman."

"Fire me," she said, "but don't change the face." Klara was ashamed to realize she had begun to beg.

Allward sat down heavily on one of the stools the men had brought into the studio. Now that the sun had fully risen, the wind began to blow in from the Belgian coast and the canvas door began to scrape slowly against the floor like an animal stirring in its sleep. Outside the walls, the men could be heard shouting to one another on their way to breakfast in the mess hall, while he remained inside this makeshift studio with a damaged sculpture and a disguised woman. He looked at the body of the torchbearer and then again at the face, the alterations Klara had made. He had wanted this stone youth to remain allegorical, universal, wanted him to represent everyone's lost friend, everyone's lost child. He had wanted the stone figure to be the 66,000 dead young men who had marched through his dreams when he had conceived the memorial. Even in its unfinished state this face had developed a personal expression, a point of view. This had never been his intention. But he had to admit the work that had been done here in the early hours of the morning was careful, skilled.

"I think," he said to the forlorn figure in front of him, "you had better tell me what this is all about." His tone was still coloured by anger, but he placed a second stool beside his, then touched Klara's elbow and motioned for her to sit down. "Come on," he said, his voice softer now, "tell me what it's all about."

Klara's own voice in this studio seemed strangely high and thin, even to her own ears, and at the same time rusty and harsh from lack of use. A part of herself she had put aside, an odd revisited diction, which at the start didn't want to operate properly. "I can't . . ." she began. She did not sit down.

Allward raised his feet one rung on the stool, then rested his forearms on his thighs. "Could you tell me at least where you learned how to carve?"

"My grandfather taught me woodcarving when I was a child. This," she nodded her head toward the torchbearer, "this I learned by watching the men, by watching your carvers." She began to walk toward the door.

"Come back and sit down," said Allward. "Please."

Klara turned to face him but did not move toward the stool. Allward looked huge to her, even when he was sitting. The atmosphere of authority that surrounded him made her feel that she herself would always be a child in his presence, could never achieve maturity.

"Surely you must have known you would be discovered sooner or later. I'm just astonished it didn't happen until now." He put his hands in the pockets of his long coat.

"I don't know," Klara said, desperation in her voice. "I don't really know. But I'll go now, I'll go back to Canada. I'm sorry, I wasn't . . ."

"You don't have to leave." Allward looked at her closely. Dressed in the blue trousers and the man's shirt, with her short hair, she seemed ageless as well as sexless. It was hard for him to situate her in any of the usual categories reserved for women. "You can stay and work here for as long as you like," he continued, surprising even himself with this decision. "I'm intrigued by this, you going to all this effort, the voyage, the disguise." Turning his head to the left, he examined the sculpture again. "But I want to know about the face you were making up there. You must understand. He was meant to be everyone, all of them." Allward paused, a brief cloud of anger passing over his face. "You've changed that."

There was full sun now in the studio. Allward walked across the room and switched off the electric lights.

"There was a boy I knew . . ." Klara began. She broke off, her voice gone from her.

"Ah . . . of course," Allward settled himself back on one stool and pushed the other in her direction with his foot.

Feeling dizzy from the fall, the fear and the shock of being revealed, Klara leaned one hip against the stool and braced herself with her left arm. "It was a long time ago," she said.

"But it's never long enough, is it? How did he die? Did he die here?"

"No, not here." She was suddenly exhausted, no longer able to stop the words from pouring out of her. "There wasn't conscription yet," she said. "He chose to leave. I think I hated him for a while for the pain he caused me. Even after he was dead I couldn't forgive him for that, for choosing a war and death, for choosing that instead of me."

Allward was shaking his head. "They all believed, every one of them believed there would be something romantic about it, some notion of adventure. They all wanted it to be beautiful in some way, noble, I suppose. What they got instead was a living hell with nothing resembling beauty or nobility in it."

Klara was silent, looking at the floor. Then she spoke, "I don't know how he died. He just disappeared."

It was almost time for the carvers to begin their morning shift. One of the men pulled aside the canvas door and was about to step over the sill when he saw Allward and stopped in his tracks, surprise on his face.

"Don't come in," called Allward. "Come back in half an hour. And tell your friends to stay away too." The carver looked puzzled but let the door fall back into place. Klara and Allward listened to the receding footsteps for a moment or two and then Allward rose and walked back over to the ladder. He stood on the third rung and looked at the torchbearer's face.

The work was clean, assured. "You know how to carve," said Allward, not turning around, not taking his eyes off the sculpture. The face was becoming a portrait, he could see that, but beyond that the expression had about it the trustfulness of someone who did not know he would ever be missing, lost from the earth. This woman had brought a personal retrospection to his monument, and had by doing so allowed life to enter it. She had carved the uncomplicated face of prewar youth, children who were unaware they would be made extinct by the war. No subsequent generation, Allward suddenly knew, would ever achieve such innocence. Their kind would never come again.

He sighed and began to climb down the rungs. "We'll leave the face," he said, "but when you work here I want you to work as a woman. Forget the disguise, it's too much trouble. He was just a kid, after all.

You're a woman. And you can finish carving his face."

"Thank you."

"For letting you stay? It's not much."

"For letting me stay, yes, but also for giving me my voice back."

News of Karl's true gender was telegraphed around the site with a velocity that seemed to exceed the speed of sound. This information, combined with the knowledge that Klara had actually altered one of Allward's figures and had lived to tell the tale, gave her a kind of superhuman presence that caused the men to fall silent whenever she appeared. She smiled at this, then solemnly shook each carver's hand, hoping that this neutral gesture of good will would make them more comfortable with her, would allow them at least now and then to treat her as an ordinary colleague.

Her brother seemed, against all odds, to be more and more at home in Picardie. The rhythm of the work, his time in town, the emergence of the stone figures above him all now gave him pleasure. The fact that Klara had been unmasked, and that there had been no serious repercussions, appeared to have removed the last vestiges of tension from his mind. One day he took her aside and told her that he had decided that everything about this adventure at the monument was astonishing, miraculous, that it had been fate, after all, that had brought them to this place.

"And you hated boats," she said, teasing him. "And I thought you couldn't bear to work on shields and wreaths and crosses."

Simson had walked into the Quonset dormitory the morning after Klara's encounter with Allward and had stood staring at her for a full minute before speaking. "Allward wants your bunk moved to the office. Out of here, anyway."

Klara looked at Tilman. "I can stay," she said, "with my brother."

"Not according to Allward. He wants you out of here." Simson cleared his throat. "Now that you're a woman." He shook his head. "I thought I'd seen it all, but I guess I was wrong." He wasn't able to look her in the face, whether from embarrassment or irritation Klara couldn't tell. "So get packing," he said to her before abruptly leaving the room.

That afternoon Giorgio stepped quietly into the lower studio while she was working. When Klara turned on the ladder to see who was there, he looked up at her, grinning. "God, how amazing . . . your disguise," he said to her. "How did you manage it all this time?"

Klara's face became hot and flushed.

462

She didn't know what to say to him.

"I came to see your carving," he said, moving toward the torchbearer.

Klara remained silent but descended from the ladder and stepped aside. Then Giorgio, like Allward before him, stood on the third rung and looked at her work. Afterwards he walked back and forth on the floor in front of the statue. "You've made a portrait," he finally commented. "This is now much more than an allegorical figure. A sensitive face. This is the face of someone you know."

She still said nothing, then reconsidered. "It's someone I knew."

"Dead?"

She nodded.

"Sorry." Giorgio reached across the space between them and touched her shoulder. "Tilman told me long ago how you helped him get free when you were children. He always loved you for that, and somehow I suppose I came to love you for it too . . . this distant small sister I thought I'd never see." He looked into her eyes. "I'm sorry if you lost someone that mattered to you."

Klara could feel the heat of his hand through the flannel of her shirt. No longer wearing the cap, she felt self-conscious

463

about the short blonde curls on her head, felt neutered, ashamed.

Giorgio walked toward the door, then turned before leaving the room. "The carving is very skilled," he said.

"Thank you."

"I felt there was something odd about you, you know . . . I couldn't say what exactly. But Tilman had never mentioned a brother . . ." The sound of a distant hammering filled the silence that fell between them. Then, suddenly, Giorgio ran his hand over the short curls on the top of her head.

Klara stood utterly still.

"I'm doing this for all the Italians," he explained to her. "They're much too shy, but they believe that to rub the hair of a blonde person brings luck."

"Oh," said Klara, reddening once again.

"Well, anyway, it's good," Giorgio added, just before leaving the studio, "very good to hear your voice."

That night Klara sat on her bunk in the overseer's hut for a long, long time, not ready to undress for sleep, sorting through the details of the past two days and trying to assemble the self she was now. She glanced at Simson's desk across the hut, on which a number of bulky files were neatly arranged. One of them, she knew, must contain Eamon's name. She thought of all that had become dormant in her during the empty season of her young adulthood. Her body, once awakened, had gone back to sleep, folding in on itself, the skin recognizing only the change of external temperature, or the touch of cloth, or now and then a rush of fever or pain. Anything else she had simply willed away, refused to remember or even dream. Once or twice she had thought of her unborn children, but they were ghosts, gone before she could conjure them. In the early years men had approached her from time to time, but although she had made no conscious decision to remain true to Eamon's memory, in fact, had tried to push his memory as far away from her as possible, it seemed that when he had gone, he had taken all her desire with him.

Now she was made anxious by the discovery that in the presence of Giorgio, it was as if this lost desire had pulled aside the swaying canvas door of the studio and had stood grinning near the table that held the carving tools. She had begun to dream about this friend of Tilman after full days in the company of men and statues, dreamt, sometimes, that he *was* a statue she was working on, polishing his marble boots and overalls. Once she dreamt that she was measuring him for a suit coat. In the mornings she would awake confused and disoriented. And it had taken some time to reassemble her persona, to remember who it was she was meant to be. She had stood for three months beside him on the unsteady floor, a woman disguised as a thin man with pumice in his hand and marble dust on his clothing. Now that he knew she was a woman she felt middle-aged and unattractive. She found herself trying to remember what her woman's body looked like, whether there was anything left there that a man like Giorgio might receive as a gift. Almost immediately she was embarrassed by her thoughts, even the idea of presenting herself to him seemed to her to be presumptuous, bold, vaguely shameful. Desire was a word that had no place in the vocabulary of a spinster.

It took Klara three days to complete the face, though most of the essential work had been done that first morning when she knew she had been carving in secret, each gouge a private gesture. Allward came each

466

day to see Klara's progress, to see the completed head, and nodded at her to let her know he was satisfied. But he made it clear that she would not be carving anything else.

"You will remain an assistant on my monument," he said. "You are too dangerous with a carving tool in your hand. As you and I both know, you suffer from an excess of originality. And, anyway, you've already made your statement, as the saying goes."

So in the mornings she hauled water, stacked lumber, and swept up discarded stone chips and dust. And in the afternoons she climbed to the upper studio to hand tools to Giorgio and to polish those areas of the angel he considered to be completed.

As they worked, the talk flowed easily. He told her about the city in which he had lived for most of his life, about his large, rowdy family, the stoveworks, the tombstones. He mentioned the young Italian woman to whom he had been briefly engaged.

"You must have loved her," Klara said quietly.

"I don't think I ever really did. I was fond of her though. She has another man for a husband now." They laughed as they remembered their conversation about marriage, and Giorgio having asked her if she'd ever had a wife.

She told him about Father Gstir's church, and her grandfather's workshop, about the cows, and about her friends the nuns in the Convent of the Immaculate Conception. She couldn't bring herself to mention Eamon, as if to say his name aloud in the presence of this man might expose her as a sexual being, on the one hand, and prove her disloyal, on the other. She would keep Eamon — his bright spirit — in the darkest part of the centre of herself, like a secret lantern. She would keep her own young self there too, to make him stay. Were he released, if he became no longer her secret or something other than her secret, she feared his light would be scattered by the winds of the real world.

Giorgio threw his head back and laughed when he heard about the cows. His white teeth, his brown face. "Good for you," he said, his hand once again on her shoulder. Then he became serious. "There is absolutely nothing," he told her, "like the carving of names. Nothing like committing to the stone this record of someone who is utterly lost." He described the reactions of the people who sometimes came to see him do this in Canada.

They were again sitting at the entrance to the studio, looking out over the beautiful fields whose patterns had been determined a thousand years ago, fragmented by the war, then reassembled in recent times. If you overlooked the dimpling of the craters, which were now covered by green, you could, from this elevated position, easily believe that the calm landscape had never known battle. And yet, each year, war's detritus was plentifully unearthed by the blade of the plough. One farmer had told Giorgio that since the war he had discovered at least fifty small bibles — French, English, and German — in the plot of earth where he grew his turnips. And often these bibles were found in the torn and decayed pocket of a military uniform, along with a mud-soaked photograph or a stained and unreadable letter from home.

Late one afternoon Klara left Giorgio working alone on the drapery that covered the angel's right leg and descended the ladder until she reached the base of the monument. It was a Friday and the site was deserted, the men having quit at four to go into town with their paycheques. Tilman, she knew, would be looking forward to a gourmet dinner in the company of his new friend. She stood for a moment or two surveying all the signs of hastily abandoned labour, shovels in mounds of earth, a discarded lunch pail, a cart halfway down the narrow gauge track. Then she pivoted and walked back to the ladder, climbed slowly up to the studio. Giorgio stepped away from the sculpture as she entered and turned to her with a puzzled look.

She stood with her hands clasped nervously in front of her and her eyes down, her heart thumping; she could not look at him. Neither of them said anything for several moments. He high on the scaffolding, she on the floor. "Do you understand?" she finally whispered, raising her face up to him, "*Do* you understand?"

He climbed down from the angel then, walked across the room that rocked slightly under his feet and hers. "Yes," he said, touching her hair and her neck and face, then running the fingers of his right hand along her collarbone. His hands were rough and calloused, his gestures gentle but purposeful. She responded to the first, wonderful unfamiliarity of another's fingers on her own skin.

"I understand," he was saying. "I understand."

In his Maida Vale studio in London, Allward had built the plasters, employing a process Byzantine in its manipulations of space, on the one hand, and dependent on scientific and mathematical accuracy, on the other. First he had made simple gesture drawings in the presence of the model, attempting to find the pose that would most perfectly describe *Hope* or *Honour, Peace* or *The Spirit of Sacrifice.* He explored the most minor alterations in the line of a jaw, the setting of a shoulder, the bend in an arm. He lifted a cheekbone by a quarter of an inch, fractionally increased or decreased the circumference of a thigh, changed the weight of the body from the left to the right foot, and then back again.

When he believed that the attitude of the figure was set, he would make one formal drawing, busy with measurements, then begin to build the figure in clay. It was during this process that he felt most like a child playing with mud and at the same time most like God the Father creating

Adam. When the dark grey, vaguely ominous clay human was modelled, Allward would approach it with wet plaster, and rags and burlap, and then more wet plaster until it was completely covered in a rapidly setting white cloak that, when removed, provided the perfect mould for the final pouring of the ultimate plaster.

Most of the sculptures were to be placed against the various walls of the monument and were therefore not executed entirely in the round. Before they set, it was necessary to brace them at the back with wire and crisscrossed wooden beams and to constantly add more plaster and rags to the rear of the piece. Allward loved this tattered, unfinished side almost as much as the smooth flesh of the front, was pleased, for instance, that evidence of his own palms and thumbs would be left like frantic signatures behind the serenity of the flawless, fragile figures that emerged.

Once this theatrical act was completed, however, and the figures stood beside him pure and clean in the studio's light, Allward would begin to become anxious about how the carvers — with the help of the pantograph, the pointing machine — would transform them into stone. Like a scientist who has just discovered a new formula, he made endless calculations that — along with copious verbal instructions — he recorded in pencil on the thighs and arms of the white men and women. He drew the placement of the limbs of one figure like maps of peninsulas on the flesh of its neighbour, adding to the sketch phrases such as "arm of *Hope* should cross here" or "knee of *Peace* comes in at this angle." He was pleased by the sight of his own handwriting on the smooth white surfaces, felt finally that this, along with the handprints at the back, ensured that something of himself was present in the crates that would eventually take the pieces across the English Channel and then overland to the site, the wind-scoured, silent battlefield he kept, always, in his mind. London never really came into focus for him, was known only by the differing intensities of light in the studio, the way the rain beat on the skylight.

He fell in love over and over again with the clay and then the plaster renditions of the young women he created, though never with the models themselves, who seemed too actual, too specifically human to be fully interesting. For the young men, once they had evolved into the perfection of plaster, he experienced huge compassion, knowing that he had caught them just as they were letting their individual personalities go, beginning to understand that they were part of a collective, moved by the lunatic actions of war.

As the years passed and the monument came close to completion, the world beyond Allward's walls was beginning to forget about the tragedy of a distant slaughter. The grief was losing its sharpness, could perhaps bruise, but could no longer really cut most hearts. Rarely now did women weep in their beds for a man whose face and body they had known in the teens of the century, or for a child the earth took back too soon. Allward began to feel like a vessel into which the world's diminishing sorrow was poured for safekeeping, and the weight of it was heavy on his bones. He put as much of this intense responsibility into the reflective and powerfully sad figure of the mature male mourner, the curve of his spine and the desperate inwardness of his downcast face, but his own grief was less focused and contained more anger. There were no words to express this, only the impressions of his hands in the disarray of cloth and plaster behind his beautiful plaster people, the exact measurements on the muscles of their arms. And the pencil drawings of the gestures of one on the limbs of another.

When they descended from the upper studio that afternoon, Giorgio drew Klara into the lower workspace to point out these delicate pencil lines on the plasters of the two youths that had been used to carve *The Spirit of Sacrifice.*

"It's as if Allward wished there to be a relationship between his sculptures," he said to her, "as if he were trying to invent a way for them to express affection, as if he were giving them instructions on how to touch."

They had embraced once again then in the shadow of the torchbearer, Eamon's face looking away from them, toward the sky.

Even in early summer, particularly in bright, clear weather, the nights in this part of France could be cold enough that the combination of their dark chill and the heat of the earth that had all day swallowed sun would produce a thick covering of morning fog. Then Giorgio would insist that Klara come with him to the upper studio for the first few moments of the day. They would climb a ladder that disappeared into white vapour, a ladder that would allow them to enter the strong sunlight that shone on the studio floor. Giorgio poured two cups of coffee from his Thermos as they sat in the open doorway with their legs swinging fifty feet above a surface of thick, quilted mist, the pylons thrusting their marble arms through this like the architecture of heaven. Beneath the place where Klara and Giorgio sat, odd sounds — a whistle or the crunch of footsteps in gravel — would reach them from a world they couldn't see. When the fog began to fragment under the assault of the sun, the spires of churches would appear first, and Klara and Giorgio would attempt to guess the names of villages . . . Souchez,

476

Thelus, Neuville St. Vaast. Then the tops of woodlots would emerge like gardens growing in snow, followed by the tile roofs and the chimney pots that had been so recently reconstructed.

On one such morning, Giorgio and Klara were looking over the plain at patches of townscapes that had only recently become visible through the mist. "These are our priorities," said Klara after mentioning that the church was always the first building to be repaired. "Procession, church, brewery."

"Pardon?" Giorgio looked confused.

"One of the first remarks to be made by Father Gstir about my village. Both the church and the brewery were the result of a Corpus Christi procession."

"With such an auspicious beginning, I hope they are both still there."

"They are. Maybe someday I'll show you."

They could see now the medieval roof timbers of one or two distant houses that had not yet been, and might never be, restored. "Like the brown bones of ancient skeletons," said Klara. "It's so easy to see that they were hewn by hand when you look at them closely. The irregularity, the marks of gouges and planers. To think that

477

the hand that did the work has been gone for six hundred years, though the wonderful thing about wood and stone is that they always hold traces of those who have shaped it."

One night after dinner in the mess hall, Klara and Giorgio met outside among the debris at the base of the monument, then walked down the new road past the scrubbed, sanitary reconstructed trenches in the direction of Grange Tunnel.

They waited near the entrance until they were certain the landscape was empty of witnesses. Then they descended to the labyrinth beneath, Giorgio walking ahead with a blanket over one arm, his lantern illuminating in an arbitrary manner graffiti, rock carvings, the handle of a stretcher, helmets, bully tins, old pipes, and bits of electrical wiring. There were surprisingly clean white signs on the walls, pointing to the 42nd B.H.Q., or to the officers' room, or the telegraph office, and finally one indicating a passage on the left that led to the old brigade sleeping quarters. Here the bunks remained intact, and in the corner on a makeshift table stood a basin and pitcher filled not with water but with the dust of nineteen silent years.

"I found this room last week," said Giorgio, "when I was exploring. I wanted Tilman to come with me to explain these tunnels, but he would have none of it."

"He hates enclosed places like this," said Klara, who did not know that her brother had been confined here before he lost his leg.

Giorgio placed the candle on a shelf near the most trustworthy bunk and unrolled on the dirty surface the clean blanket he had carried over his arm. He turned to Klara then, who was near him in the partial gloom. "I'm sorry," he said, "that there isn't someplace nicer, warmer. But we'll have no visitors here."

Klara said nothing. She was frightened by the thought of the exposure that she knew was about to occur, frightened by the fact of her own body, grateful for the dark. What if he turned away, in disappointment?

But when — surrounded by the detritus left behind by an army of men who were on the cusp of death — they began to undress each other, their nakedness seemed fresh and new set against the rotting furniture and sweating rock and everything that was covered by the silt of the intervening years.

They were no longer young. Each was aware that they were uncovering a body that had walked through months and years of abstinence, a body that had relinquished all hope of communion. They touched each other's necks, as if to discover the life tremor there. Then Giorgio pulled Klara's head close to his chest; she could hear the sound of his heart. They made love quickly, Klara gasping, this new solid weight on her ribs and inner thighs, her senses being shaken awake. And then later, more carefully, until she believed her body, the candlelight, and the walls of the tunnels were all turning to water, and that she might drown in herself, in him. And all around them, stretching as far as the market town of Arras, the dank tunnels, like graves, out of which thousands of young men had rushed into the brimstone air.

"Love, in such a place as this," Giorgio said, finally.

Klara remained silent, curled precariously by his side on the narrow bunk, aware of the ancient springs, the feel of them pushing into her hip and shoulder.

The tunnels themselves were a kind of memorial. Sometimes after making love

Giorgio and Klara would walk the main passageways and then the tributaries that led from them as if they were explorers penetrating an unknown continent, travelling a river system they had yet to name. They moved the lamplight across the walls, reading and often recording in a notebook the inscriptions they found carved into the rock. *R.I.P. In Memory of the Sappers who fell at Vimy* was written in one spot, though whether in the midst of the battle or later, who could tell. A sculpted coat of arms hung over the words *in honour of the dead of the 42nd R.H.C.* Once Giorgio gasped, then drew Klara's attention to a section of a wall where a boy had scratched his name and *still alive and kicking* in the same roughshod manner as he might have decorated the surface of a pioneer desk in a one-room country school. Another name was inscribed next to this along with *untouched by whizzbangs yet.* Giorgio grasped Klara's arm. "I carved the letters of this boy's name yesterday," he whispered, pointing to the second inscription. He shook his head. "And the other . . . the other was found under the rocks when they cleared the entrance to Grange Tunnel. He was scratched from my list."

Eventually Klara began to view the

whole landscape, all the land given to Canada by France, the sky above, and the depths of the chalky earth below as part of an interconnecting system, one aspect of which could not survive without the other. The tunnels were like extended tangled roots reaching up to the monument above, feeding its construction by their very existence. And though the centre of the network was her carving of Eamon — who had never seen this particular battlefield — the heartbeat was surely her secret lovemaking with Giorgio, a life source pulsing deep in the earth.

At night Klara would lie in her bunk in the overseer's office, thinking of Giorgio two huts down, letting her affection for him wash over her like warm water. In her youth she had wanted to live inside her lover, to look out at the world from under his eyelids, to be constantly stretched out at his side. Then she had, unconsciously, resented the intrusion of this thought, resented her own preoccupation. The woman Klara was now, however, could walk out into the bright morning, happy in the shadow of the monument, exchange glances with Giorgio as they moved toward their separate tasks, and take the pleasure of this one look with her, its atmosphere surrounding her all through the day. And then there was the delight in the discovery that a woman of her age could still succumb to the warmth of passion, could feel this smooth, manageable desire, allow it to enter her life.

Klara spent most evenings with Giorgio now. She would leave work, run across to the hut that held the showers, which, as she had learned during the time of her disguise, were always empty at this hour. After this she sometimes dressed in the skirt and one of the blouses she had bought in Arras, but often she waited until after the dinner hour to wear these feminine garments as her appearance in them seemed to make the men uneasy in the mess hall. Walking across the green grass of a summer evening toward a chosen underworld, dressed as if heading for a dance or a movie, no longer seemed odd to her. She wanted the walled enclosure, the sense of removal from the world provided by the tunnels, the darkness, and the private circle of light from Giorgio's lantern.

"I have something important to show you," Giorgio said one evening as they lay on the sagging cot. "There are artists everywhere that no one knows about. You are one, I am another. But down here, even then, even with the rats and the blood, there were those who had to record experience. Let's get dressed. I want to show you."

Klara had begun to believe that his body was shaping hers, the way a bend in a river shapes the bank beside it with the caress of water and of current.

"I don't want to stop touching you," she said. "I don't want you to stop touching me." She loved the roundness and the warmth of his belly. His arms hardened by carving, and the tight skin that covered all of this. She didn't want to separate his skin from hers. They had held their arms up side by side, his dark and full, hers pale, thin, but strong from the work. She liked to think about the clothes she might make for him, had she her tailoring equipment with her. She liked to think about seams she might sew following the contours of his body.

Often she felt she might weep.

"No," he said, "come."

They dressed and walked with the lantern through the maze of tunnels, entering at last a room that someone had called Place de la Concorde. The whole labyrinth seemed a parody of the world above as soldiers had chiselled into the passageways and underground rooms the names of places they had been fond of, or places they had imagined. One oval space had been called Centreton Ball Park, and another Convocation Hall. What had these men carried in their minds? Had these references to the pleasures of the life they had left behind consoled them in the face of the damp and the lice and the certainty of death?

They passed a tunnel that veered to the left, then slanted upward toward the surface. "Tilman probably used this exit," said Giorgio, "when he volunteered as a runner. They wanted the messengers to burst out of here in full flight, hit the air running, unhampered by stairs. I remember that before the war he was a fabulous sprinter . . . kept the skill honed, for escape purposes, I guess."

"Then he lost his leg," said Klara, "and lost all that too. Poor Tilman, no wonder he loathes all reminders of the battle — those ditches lined with concrete renditions of sandbags, for instance. He says they look nothing like the real thing, that they are toy trenches for tourists."

"Tilman's right. If it's authenticity they're after, they should fill them up with mud and rats, pus and blood. But there is *some* authenticity left, down here, or at least the remnants of it." He took Klara's hand and led her into the darkness.

They pushed deeper into the tunnels, took a left and then a right turn, the chalk walls leaving white traces on their sleeves. Once, Klara tripped and almost fell over the wooden levers of an abandoned and badly decayed canvas stretcher. Often there was the crunch of thin rusted metal under their feet.

"Are you sure you know where we're going?" she asked. "Will we be able to get back?"

"Here we are. Look." Giorgio held the lantern near a carving in relief of a young face with a soldier's collar tight against the neck. "Who do you think he was?"

Klara moved toward the wall, looked closely at the carving. "How can we know?" she asked.

"I mean the carver," Giorgio coughed, bending over his fist the combination of the dank air and chalk dust of the tunnel, catching in his throat. Then he straightened and cleared his throat. "Look at the expression in the eyes . . . This is a face the carver loved. What do you suppose the carver was thinking?"

Giorgio leaned closer to the white chalk carving, moved the lantern back and forth in front of it. "He had compassion for the suffering of this face."

"Yes," said Klara.

She was turning to walk away when Giorgio gently caught her arm. "What was his name, Klara?" he asked softly. "Who was the boy you were carving?"

"I can't . . ." Klara began.

"Klara," Giorgio said, "I want to know you . . . everything about you . . ."

"No, I can't. Please understand. It's something I can't talk about to anyone." This she said remembering the moment she had spoken to Allward. But nothing in her wanted to bring Eamon into her connection with Giorgio.

Giorgio looked away from her, but even in the faint lamplight Klara could see he was wounded.

"Let's go back," he said, turning away, heading for the tunnel that led from this room. "Let's get out of here." He began to walk away, taking the light with him.

The air around Klara grew first dim and then dark. She knew he was hurt, angry. But she insisted on the ownership of her past. Since the day of his departure, Klara had never once said aloud the name of her young lover. She felt that to release the syllables into the air all these years later would be a kind of amputation, a violent removal of a part of the self. To present them to the man she had so recently embraced would betray, she believed, Eamon's bright, eager passion, would for the second time annul it. She wanted to crawl away from Giorgio now, to curl up somewhere in the dark, alone. But not here, not when the tunnels were not lit by love. She had only two choices: to stay alone in the dripping shadows of the underground labyrinth or to follow Giorgio, follow his light.

They parted awkwardly at the entrance to Grange Tunnel: Giorgio looking intently into Klara's face, she scrutinizing the uneven and still deadly ground of the surrounding territory. The innocent, she suddenly thought, were never aware that merely by strolling across grass they could activate a mine from the past. Just last week a horse had been killed by simply grazing in what appeared to be a benign field.

All the way back to the overseer's hut and for a long time after she had collapsed onto her cot near the window, Klara thought about the foolishness of a woman her age engaging in a love affair as if it were the most natural thing in the world. She imagined how the villagers in Shoneval would react were they to come to hear of it, how shocked they would be if they knew about the overwhelming response of her body in such awkward and arousing positions, the sounds she knew she had made once Giorgio entered her. They were both too old for this sort of thing; it could only end badly. And now this space between them, this unspoken name. A horse trusting a green field because his knowledge of fields had never involved injury, pain. A young man's unclouded love for her, complicated only by her own ultimate refusal to accept it. She had never been one of the innocent, had always predicted loss. "Eamon," she whispered now, in the dark, "Eamon O'Sullivan."

Reared in a household that on Sundays expanded to hold a hundred people, and on ordinary days never sheltered less than ten, Giorgio had become ubiquitous — though never fickle — in his affections. No person was to him too young, too old, too withdrawn or effusive to be interesting. He could recall with great fondness all the little girls dressed in white whose first communions he had attended, and all the old men at whose funerals he had wept. He had loved equally the hobos in the Don Valley, the labourers and artisans with whom he now worked on the memorial, and the soldiers with whom he had fought in the war. It had never occurred to him that one should, or that one *could,* focus all of one's attention on a single human being, though loyalty in romance was something he believed in. He had always assumed that were he to find a woman he liked well enough he would be faithful to her, and had in the past stayed close for periods of up to a year to one young woman or another. But the relationships had shifted to friendship as time passed, and it became clear that neither he nor the woman had experienced the inner connection that binds couples together even when they are apart.

He knew that Klara was different, that she was comfortable with long periods of isolation and would likely be given to infrequent yet passionate attachments. He admired this in her, this focus that had driven her to cross an ocean, carve the beloved face of one long dead in the stone of a monument. He suspected that she had been alone for so long she had forgotten what it was to be known, knowable, and he understood this. Still it hurt him that she would not disclose this important, tender episode from the past to him. He wanted all of her, was interested in every detail that had gone into the construction of her character, and it was this combined with physical desire that made him realize for the first time, and now into the middle of his life, that he had actually fallen in love.

Each day he rendered the letters of the alphabet that made permanent the names on the stone. Had he already, unknowingly, carved the name of Klara's young man while thinking of something else? Often he concentrated so fiercely on the precise bevelling of a character that his mind became empty of plans and memories, his thoughts circling around how the letter "M" resembled two houses touching, for instance, or the champagne glass look of the letter "Y." Had Klara walked to the wall once after he had finished a day's work, and had she run her fingers sadly over the shape of the loved words?

In the weeks since they had become lovers, Klara and he had met at lunch hour to sit beside each other on the west steps of the base while they ate their baguettes. In recent days, however, she had not appeared, neither there nor, as he had come to expect, at the entrance to Grange Tunnel after the dinner hour. He stared at her across the rows of tables in the mess hall, trying to read something, anything into her expression. At noon he walked by the studio where she was working and saw her sitting hunched and silent beside a half-finished meal. She glanced at him, then turned her face away. When he approached her and began to speak, she said, "Don't!" and then scrambled to her feet and walked hurriedly back into the studio.

He was devastated and in turn shocked by his response to her coldness. In subsequent days he carried the pain around with him like an infected auxiliary organ, of no use to body or heart. There was nothing that was not affected by it; he became withdrawn, taciturn, even in the friendly company of his fellow carvers. He had lived four decades in the world and yet he had never known that affection could carry within its warm centre the seeds of such appalling anguish. Even when his father had deserted the family for a year, Giorgio had believed with a child's trust that one day the absent parent, whose love, he correctly intuited, was being telegraphed from immeasurable distances, would re-enter the door and take his place in the family circle. Perhaps he should just hold on to the faith, the hope that Klara would once again soften toward him.

One day, unable to prevent himself from doing so, he spoke to Tilman about it. "What did I do wrong?" he asked, his voice whining and querulous. "All I wanted was for Klara to tell me about him." He stood with his hands in his pockets, his shoulders drawn forward. "What happened to the poor kid, anyway?"

"The war, as usual," his friend answered. Tilman pointed to an area about five hundred yards to the south of them where all day men had been planting saplings of various kinds. "It's sort of wonderful, don't you think, that all those trees were brought from Canada? One of every species, they say. All the provinces mixed up together. Wonder if they'll all survive? I'd like to see them grown."

Giorgio was not interested in discussing the trees. What were they doing planting trees in midsummer, anyway, he thought with irritation. Shouldn't they do it in spring?

"You know, Giorgio," said Tilman, responding to the uncomfortable silence that had fallen between them, "I wasn't there when the romance happened. It was such a long time ago . . . probably while you and I were making stoves. Remember The Forest Eater?" He smiled at Giorgio, then shook his head. "So much time has passed."

Giorgio found that he was now put off by his friend's remarkable good humour, the geniality that he had exuded for weeks. "This boy," he asked quietly, "was he from your town?"

Tilman nodded. "Klara didn't say much to me about it, but she did mention he lived near Shoneval." He stopped walking, swung his artificial leg back and forth as if exercising it. "I remember she told me she'd made him a coat or a jacket out of red cloth."

Giorgio waited. He was startingly hungry now for any information about Klara's past. He looked intently at Tilman, hoping for more.

"Sorry, Giorgio, that's all I know. Just that she made him a coat . . . Klara's quite a tailor, you know . . . and that he was from Shoneval." Tilman began walking again, turned and beckoned for his friend to follow. "Why not come into town with me tonight?" he said. "I'd like you to meet Recouvrir. We could have something to eat, a good bottle of wine."

Giorgio could see that Tilman was impatient to get to the Hotel Picardie. "I don't think so. You go ahead."

"C'mon." Tilman insisted, *"Canard à l'Orange,* a fine Bordeaux rouge . . . it will do you good, make you forget the past. It looked to me like you and Klara were curing each other of all that, anyway."

Four nights later Giorgio stood outside Grange Tunnel waiting until long after dark. The stars became vivid behind the monument, though its bulk blocked out large portions of the Milky Way. He could feel the night chill penetrate his shirt. It was always cold in the tunnels, but of course there he had had the warmth of a woman. The warmth of Klara. How the hell had it come to this? In his family, sorrow was always shared, almost celebrated, experience of any kind being considered a gift, a narrative that would be given to the community like scenes from an opera. *I have lived, I have felt this grief. Now you will live it, feel it with me.* He became aware of the subtle weight of the blanket on his arm, then thought himself a fool for standing in the dark holding this reminder of his brief, dying love affair as if it were a grey shroud.

As he walked back toward his sleeping quarters, he saw that the light in the overseer's hut was on, the curtain near Klara's bed drawn back. Looking through the glass of the door's upper panel, he could see that Klara's cot was empty. Gone into Arras with Tilman probably. Perhaps this Recouvrir, whoever he was, had caught her attention with his fancy French food, his bourgeois restaurant. He had thought it impossible that Klara might take another lover, but by now he was so tired and discouraged, so confused and vulnerable, he believed anything might happen. He stared hard into the functional room where Klara slept, its scrubbed linoleum and iron cot, as if he might find some evidence of this imagined, dark betrayal. Then, on the foreman's desk, just a few feet from where he stood, he saw a folder with *Master File* written on it.

It took him no time at all to open the unlocked door, to approach the file. For one moment he felt like a thief, or as if he might be betraying Klara's wish to keep her young man's name private. All he knew for sure was that the boy was dead. His name might be on a stone in a military cemetery or, he touched the cardboard cover, it might be in this file.

The missing, as he expected, were listed alphabetically, so it was necessary for him to read every town name in the adjacent right column. Grimsby, Maple Creek, Fernie, Clinton, Lévis, Vernonville, Rimouski, Colborne, Truro, Humboldt, Walkerton, Parry Sound, Lilac, Medicine Hat, Moose Jaw. Who were the settlers who had titled these places? Could they have imagined the names they had invented would lie, as the result of an immense slaughter, in an official document on a foreign desk? Vernon, Collingwood, Val d'Or, Nanaimo, Lunenburg, Kingsville, Swift Current, Trois-Rivières, Hull, Winnipeg, Alderville. Eventually his finger came to rest at Shoneval. But still he knew he must keep reading, for he was unaware that only one boy had left this overlooked hamlet for France. By the time he came to the final name, every cross-road, every city, every rural township, each Indian reserve, and almost all the concession roads in Canada had been present in his mind.

There was only one name with Shoneval beside it, and that name was Eamon O'Sullivan. Giorgio was filled first with relief, then joy. He and his fellow letter carver had only gone as far as the letter "K." The name had not yet been engraved. He carefully closed the folder, then laid his hand on it for a moment or two as if he were blessing it. As he approached the door he saw Klara coming toward the hut. She halted as if startled by the appearance of his head and shoulders framed by the door's small window like a portrait in the glass, the rest of the world a dark night around him.

He left the hut and walked toward her with his arms out and his palms up. I am guilty but remorseful, this gesture said. She had her hands in the pockets of her worker's jacket, and she stood entirely still with her head bent. Stars appeared to be raining down the sky above and on either side of her.

Giorgio stopped and stood with his hand on her sleeve. Even though his touch was tentative and held nothing but the loose fabric of the jacket, he could tell she was trembling. He smoothed her hair and to his great relief she didn't walk away. "I thought all of that was over for me, years ago, decades ago," she said.

"It's not over," he said.

"I'm not uncomplicated."

"No," he agreed, "you're not. But I won't try to force anything from you ever again. Your soul is your own. I should not have interfered. If only we can still meet."

Klara took one hand out of her pocket and placed it in one of his. "Do you not want a younger woman? What about children?"

"I want you."

They stood together silently for some time, the unlit tunnels beneath them, the monument, ghostly and still webbed with scaffolding, cocooned with canvas, a quarter of a mile away.

"Good night then," Klara said.

"I'll wait for you? Tomorrow night?" Giorgio was suddenly aware of, and slightly embarrassed by, the blanket that still hung over his arm.

Klara didn't answer but wrapped her

arms around his large chest before opening the door. Then she turned and, not looking at Giorgio, whispered in the direction of the monument the two words she had uttered only to herself. "Eamon," she said. "Eamon O'Sullivan."

Giorgio almost told her that he knew, then reconsidered, this gift from her being so purely given.

"Poor boy," she added. "He was so young." She paused. "And so much time has passed."

There are certain currents of air that have crossed the Atlantic, have become confused briefly by the intricate coastline of Cornwall, and then have been reassured, calmed by the salt moisture of the English Channel. When these currents find themselves over the land mass of France, they respond to this unfamiliarity by transforming themselves into large towering clouds, some of which look like monuments or castles or cathedrals. Were it not for their whiteness and total absence of attendant noise they might be mistaken for thunder clouds, but they bring with them no bad weather. They appear in pairs, one-half of the sky mirroring the other, as if making important statements about twinship, about collaboration.

Allward had studied these clouds, had watched them boil up behind the ridge on sunny afternoons. Even before the road was made, before the ground was cleared and levelled, he had decided they would be part of the monument, two soft gardens of mist to offset the hardness of marble, the toughness of grief. After months of vigilance, amazed by the predictability of these airborne wonders, he knew exactly where the memorial was to be sited: on the clean slice of the ridge, embraced on each side by the theatrical presence of vapour sculptures.

There are, of course, days when the marvellous clouds do not appear — though if he could have managed it Allward would have had them constantly present. Sometimes in the winter in Picardie a solid grey sky settles in for weeks on end. And then, very occasionally, in the summer and autumn, there will be days when the sky is a dome of piercing blue, as if clouds have yet to be invented. Days when the monument itself stands as if at the edge of the world, solid, confident, reflecting light.

And so it happened that one summer morning, very early, Giorgio woke just as the sun was making a faint red seam along the eastern horizon. The other men in his dormitory were snoring; one was mumbling a woman's name in his sleep, and Giorgio felt for a moment a deep connection with this Italian called Carlo whom he knew came from the town of Orvieto — a comrade in love. He dressed quickly in his overalls and blue worker's jacket and, boots in hand, walked in his sock feet across the planked floor, out the door into a world where light visited only the very tops of recently planted trees from Canadian forests. All so young now, hardly taller than a man's shoulders, but he hoped they would grow to be healthy in a land where they were never meant to be, in the same way that his own family had grown — with some difficulty, it's true — and had finally become rooted in a land far from the soil of their birthplace. He remembered his mother's struggle with the spindly wisteria someone had brought her from the homeland, how it hung, frail and listless, on the trellis his father had built near the back door, barely leafing in the spring until one year it burst triumphantly into blossom in early June, its flowers hanging like an overstated offering of pale grapes at an emperor's feast. And how his mother had wept with joy and told the family that she knew they were settled now in the new country.

When he looked through the window above Klara's bed into the grey stillness of the morning hut, he could see that she was sleeping on her stomach. She stirred when he knocked, lifted her head, and brushed the blonde hair from her eyes, confused by this interruption of her dreams. Then she smiled at him in a questioning way. He motioned for her to come outside, and she reluctantly threw off her blankets and put on her own overalls and jacket.

"What?" she said, emerging from the door. "Is there something wrong?"

Giorgio lifted his finger to his lips and then embraced her. He wanted no conversation at this time, wanted them to walk arm in arm over to the monument, up one set of stone stairs and down another to the part of the wall where the names gave way to untouched stone. Wanted them to walk to the west side, where the torchbearer was, then turn the corner to the south side of the base, where Giorgio had finished working the day before. The quietness was so profound that even tools abandoned the day before — wheelbarrows, shovels, carts on the narrow gauge railway, the tracks themselves — seemed to be sleeping. It wasn't until they reached the platform of the monument that the first bird began to sing.

They stopped for a moment and looked at the northeastern façade from which the scaffolding had only recently been removed. The monument was slightly backlit by the faint beginnings of day, its stone covered in cool blue shadow against a sky that was fractionally gaining in luminosity. Already several other birds had joined the first. Klara was shivering in the dawn chill, her shoulders drawn up to her neck. Both she and Giorgio were looking up at the pylons, at Allward's distant angels whose features and expressions were barely discernible on this dark side of the sculpture. Around their wings there was nothing but sky.

"This must be what night is like in heaven," said Klara.

"Night turning to morning," said Giorgio, taking her arm, guiding her around the pylon to the opposite view.

They arrived at the southwest side just as the sun broke through. Neither of them had seen the figures here so dramatically lit. Klara could barely move her eyes from the uplifted face she had illicitly carved, and the ribs, the strong, sinewy neck, the torso.

"He was like that, was he?" Giorgio asked gently.

"Yes, at times he was just like that," Klara moved closer to Giorgio for warmth. "But he could be sombre too. For the first few months he came calling, he didn't say one word. I thought I'd go mad if he wouldn't talk."

"Young," said Giorgio. "Shy."

"Yes, I suppose."

"But determined."

"Yes," Klara smiled, "determined and stubborn."

"Come," said Giorgio. "Come and see what I've been working on."

As he had hoped, the emerging sun was raking across the letters he had been carving. Beneath them his metal tool box shone. He pointed to the last name he had finished the day before. T O'Rourke.

Klara's eyes filled with tears, and her voice broke as she asked, "You are just about to carve his name then?"

"No," said Giorgio. "I'm not."

"But he must be soon. Here is some unfortunate boy called O'Rourke." Her hand briefly touched the stone.

Giorgio crouched over the tool box, opened the lid, and removed three delicate chisels and a small hammer from the top tray. Then he straightened and looked at her. "*You* are going to carve his name, Klara," he said, "and I am going to help you, show you how."

Klara felt the slight warmth of the new sun graze the top or her head, or thought she did. She did not move, immobilized by the tenderness of what was being offered to her.

Giorgio brought over his work partner's stool and they sat side by side with the morning sun touching the backs of their blue jackets. Placing the chisel in one of Klara's shaking hands and the hammer in the other, Giorgio wrapped his own larger hands around hers.

"We can only use the initial of the first name," he told her, "because of the space, which has been worked out to the last character, the last eighth of an inch."

Klara said nothing. Then, "I don't know if I can do this. What if I can't do this?"

"We'll take it slow," said Giorgio. "The curved letters are the most difficult, and there are only three of those in his name. We'll just make one mark at a time. Start here." He tapped the chisel in their joined hands very gently with the mallet, and the straight line that would make the left side of the letter "E" began to appear on the stone.

Klara knew this would be the last time she touched Eamon, that when they finished carving his name all the confusion and regret of his absence would unravel, just as surely as if she had embraced him with forgiving arms.

A shadow fell over the inscribed wall in front of them. "You can't go wrong," said Allward, who had been silently watching this small drama from the bottom of the stairs and had now made his way over to them, "as long as you don't engage in any heroic feats of originality."

The artist towered over the carvers as they twisted on their stools to look up at him. They didn't even think to stand. Giorgio had not removed his cap.

"We didn't know you were here," said Klara.

"I'm here even when I'm not here," Allward laughed. "I've been eating and sleeping stone for so long that it has become an obsession with me. And, incidentally, a nightmare. But no nightmares this morning. Have you ever seen such light?"

"I want her to carve the name," said Giorgio.

Allward was silent for a moment, considering. Klara's hands remained enclosed in Giorgio's. The chisel rested against the perfect stone.

Allward came up beside Klara and put his hand on her arm. "This is him then?"

"It's him," said Klara, not looking up. Giorgio did not take his hand away from hers, his forearm resting on her thigh, the chisel emerging from their joined fists.

Allward took all of this in, the two damaged people, the now distant pain of bereavement and lost youth, the warmth of the affection that surrounded the pair, a warmth that in some ways was engendered both by the bloody, endless tragedy of the war and this huge white structure meant to be a memorial to grief, on the one hand, and a prayer for peace, on the other. He took it all in. Soon the project would be completed, after fifteen years of accidents, postponements, labour problems, the harassment of several levels of government in a number of different countries. He thought of the clouds, the shapes he had spent hours learning all those years ago, even before he had found the marble, made the plasters, hired the carvers, thought of how reliably the vapour sculptures floated back to the site, how they so genuinely provided the perfect accompaniment, the perfect balance. Balance. For just one moment, and in the presence of Giorgio and Klara, the artist in Allward believed that he had achieved balance.

The weight of the sorrow he had carried for fifteen years was leaving him. The emotion was moving through the arms of these people who worked for him — no, these friends who worked with him — and he knew that passion was entering the monument itself, the huge urn he had designed to hold grief.

"Carve it with your heart then," he said, speaking to them, to himself. "Let it go out of your heart and into the stone."

The larger, the more impressive the monument, the more miraculous its construction, the more it seems to predict its own fall from grace. Exposed and shining on elevated ground, insisting on prodigious feats of memory from all who come to gaze at it, it appears to be as vulnerable as a flower, and its season seems to be as brief. And who among us does not imagine the stone crushed, the altars taken away to museums, the receding past vandalized. The day arrives when there is no one left to climb the tower, pull the rope, ring the bell of the magnificent, improbable church. Names carved in stone become soft and unrecognizable under the assault of acid rain. No one knows any more what the allegorical figures represent.

No one cares.

In 1936, the completion of the Vimy Memorial was announced to the world with great fanfare, the ribbon cut by a king whose own reign was but a brief season, while tens of thousands of pilgrims, veterans and their relatives, widows and orphans, French and Canadian officials filled the now altered, manicured battlefield. Speeches were made, cannons were fired, trumpets played, and aeroplanes buzzed overhead. The bereaved searched the white wall for the names of loved ones now almost two decades vanished from the earth. Whole oceans of grief were revisited, especially by women. Stories concerning the brief lives of young soldiers were told, absent fathers were explained to grown children, brothers were described to men who were so young when they died they could barely remember them.

Allward returned to a country he hardly recognized. The war had been over for twenty years; few people wanted to discuss the monument. Each day he walked through the bright rooms of his Toronto house, the memorial a fact in his brain, its white stone echoed by snow in winter, a cumulus cloud with a flat base in summer. He could not disengage.

Designs for further monuments were attempted by him — he wanted to move forward, wanted to re-enter his life. But like a long love affair that had ended in sorrow, the Vimy Memorial would not relinquish the large space it had occupied in his heart. He wouldn't let it go, and traces of its brooding presence entered every drawing he made. In the end the government was uninterested in his proposals, his efforts to document the past. And his reputation preceded him; his memorials took too long, cost too much money. The military bureaucracy wanted nothing more to do with him. Besides, it was too busy preparing for a violent future to wallow in nostalgia for a violent past.

When the Second World War broke out in 1939, less than three years after he had returned to Canada, Allward reacted with panic and rage. He deluged the Department of National Defence with telegrams begging for reports and demanding that the memorial be sandbagged against aerial bombardment. As the weeks passed and he received no replies, he retreated into an inner landscape of great bleakness, pacing the house in the middle of the night, imagining the worst. He accepted no invitations, withdrew emotionally from his family, sat for hours by windows staring at falling snow or at a winter moon the colour of white stone. Sometimes he wept silently, tears falling over the now creased and folded skin of his large face.

With sharp coloured pencils he began a series of small, secretive drawings, each one more violent, more angry than the last. Tangled bodies littered torn landscapes, burning clots of brimstone rained down from a savage sky. And, in the background, tiny, almost insignificant in the drama, the wreckage of the monument. He shared these works with no one, carried them around in his pockets or sometimes crumpled and twisted under his hat. He knew he would never exhibit these records of anguish, wanted to keep his despair private, close to his head, his heart.

The drawings seemed to feed his belief in catastrophe, his certainty that there was absolutely nothing on earth not subject to vicious attack. In his imagination, and on the rice paper he used, the allegorical figures of his sculptures stepped away from their fixed positions to engage in appalling dramas. Always with the ruins of the memorial smoking in the distance, he drew embracing lovers impaled by a single sword, cairns composed of lifeless bodies, a naked man straddling the torn, prone torso of a woman from whose chest he had snatched her bleeding heart. Allward knew, even before he had completed this particular drawing, that it was his own heart the man held aloft, a trophy steaming in his desperate hands.

He had spent fifteen years of his life obsessed by perfection and permanence, had used verbal descriptions such as "the impregnable wall of defence on the clean slice of the ridge" to describe the base of his memorial. He had believed that he was making memory solid, indestructible, that its perfect stone would stand against the sky forever. With this certainty threatened, his world collapsed.

Ironically, although the memorial survived the Second World War, the psyche of its creator did not. Allward remained a kind, courteous man who walked slowly through the city streets in a grey coat. Sometimes, especially in winter, when he was more likely to be alone, he visited the bronze sculptures he had created so many years ago for the park in front of the provincial legislature. He liked the way the gestures of dark statues that had first established his reputation were made explicit by the whiteness of the surrounding snow. But in this land so famous for winter, the knowledge of Allward's genius was quickly forgotten by the very nation that had commissioned the memorial where he was most able to demonstrate this genius. Even those Canadians who would later make the trip to France and who would admire the monument would rarely take the trouble to ask the sculptor's name.

Klara returned to Shoneval, walking up the lane toward the house with Giorgio at her side. For several days she insisted that he stand in various rooms while she leaned in doorways and smiled with pleasure at the physical fact of him filling up the empty hallways of her life. Years later she would still sometimes make him enact this ritual. Suddenly, she would think that she couldn't call to mind the way he looked in the woodshed, for example, or the pantry, and she would pull him by the sleeve to the place in question and make him stand in its light or its shadow until she had taken the sight of him there permanently into her memory.

In her sunroom, a few days after their arrival, she took his hand and showed him the incised marks Eamon's pattern had left on the floor.

"For a while," she said, "it was the only memorial I had."

"It's like an inscription," Giorgio said, "an inscription without words." And Klara agreed with the beloved man who had carved thousands of names that that was exactly what it was like.

Later, she took him outside and unlocked the door of the old workshop.

Once again, the folds of the abbess's clothing were edged with fine dust, and she was covered with the webs of the spiders that Klara's grandfather had insisted should stay alive. "I hate removing the webs," Klara told Giorgio. "I know what it's like to work with thread. Anything woven is so fragile, its chances for survival so limited." She was thinking of the first red waistcoat, now twenty years old, and wondered what had become of it. Had it been engulfed by mud, stolen by a German soldier, or was it covered with dust in the attic of Eamon's family, who had left the village years before? She had never known . . . there had been no one to tell her . . . that Eamon had worn it the day he departed for the wars.

Giorgio was circling the carved woman. "She's wonderful," he said.

"Maybe but not quite finished, though I worked on her for years and years."

"You should finish her now."

Klara rubbed the dust from a webless part of a window pane to let more light into the shop. "I will," she said.

A month later, when the sculpture was

completed, Klara presented her female saint to Father Gstir's church on the hill. She wanted it dedicated to the memory of her grandfather, whose own carvings graced the main altar and several side chapels. The week after, Klara and Giorgio were quietly married at the side chapel in front of one of Joseph Becker's altars, an altar where small European towns, not unlike those left smouldering by the war, remained intact, and a runaway boy stood, furtive, in the midst of crowds attending a crucifixion, a birth in a stable, a martyrdom, an entry into a city.

As they had decided against a four-day Italian wedding they had not yet told the elder Vigamonti and his tribe about their marriage. But some of the surprised nuns attended, as did Tilman and his dear friend Recouvrir, who had hitchhiked from Montreal for the small ceremony. On the way there, Tilman taught his companion some tricks of the road: how to sing Presbyterian hymns, for example, or the correct approach to a fellow hobo's campfire. But this was done for pleasure, not as a result of necessity, for when the work on the monument was completed, Tilman had convinced his friend to immigrate to Montreal, where they had opened a restaurant called Monument de l'Archange, which was soon prospering. "I always liked the idea of that priest insisting on the big church," Tilman said when Klara asked him about the name of the establishment, "even though it was much too large for the size of the town."

They had all returned from the modest wedding and were sitting on the sagging porch of the old farmhouse. Giorgio had just explained that he was going to be a market gardener as well as a gravestone maker, and that Klara, who would also do some carving, was anxious to get the Charolais cattle back in the field.

Tilman reached into his pocket and pulled out a small parcel wrapped in brown butcher paper and tied with string. "I have a wedding gift for you," he said, turning first to his sister, then to Giorgio. He hesitated. "I don't know which one of you should open it."

Recouvrir, who had been studying English, interjected. "Giorgio must make the strings," he said, "and then Klara makes the papers."

After Giorgio had removed the twine, Klara pulled a bright silver whistle out of its nest of brown paper, then smiled quizzically at her brother. "Thank you, Tilman,"

519

she said, then, after looking closely at the small object, she laughed. "It says, 'Royal Thunderer.' "

Tilman smiled at his sister. "When I was a boy, a woman gave the whistle to me . . . the same woman who helped me get free of the chain. For years it was my only possession. Sometimes, when things were bad on the road, I would take it out of my pocket and blow it. At first the sound reminded me of my freedom, but, after a while, I began to use it as a kind of summons, began to hope that someone would come." He paused, cleared his throat. "No one ever came," he said.

There was silence on the porch. Then Recouvrir said quietly, "Someone answered when it was a long time. It is impossible, I know, but someone answered."

"We've all been involved in some way with the impossible," said Giorgio as the warm white of the monument where he had found Klara slid into his mind. When he closed his eyes he could see the thousands of names he had chiselled into the stone, the way they looked in raking light.

"True," said Tilman, leaning forward to touch Recouvrir's arm.

Klara turned the shining whistle in her hands and thought of the fragile plaster angels lifted by ropes toward a sky chosen by Walter Allward after much consideration. Their shadows gliding up the pylons. About how the difficult, amazing man had altered the angle of the ridge to accommodate the clouds, had not destroyed what she had created in stone, had given her a voice.

She thought of Eamon's face, and his name, carved by her own hand with tools Giorgio had shown her how to use. And how several times in recent weeks, when she had made her new love stand utterly still in one room or another of her house so that she could believe in the fact of him, the blessing of him being there had connected with the honeyed voice of Father Archangel Gstir's miraculous bell floating on the hour through the partly opened window.

It was said that King Ludwig twice sent his equerry to Capri to memorize the precise shade of turquoise in its famous Blue Grotto, a model of which had been built at the king's palace at Linderhof. This was in a time before colour photography was invented, a time when the memory of the realistic hues and tints of the natural world were still carried in the mind. Painters rarely strove to imitate real colour, more interested — even then — in the transformation demanded by their art. The emerging craft of photography reduced all scenes to various shades of black and grey, making the images, oddly, more like printed descriptions of themselves.

How does one describe in words the colour turquoise? Even before the dust of travel was shaken from his clothing, the returning equerry would have been summoned to the false grotto where Ludwig, anxious to have his carefully constructed, imaginary world confirmed by one man's description of the colour of reality, would be drifting in a golden boat. But colour is something best shown, not told. Or if it must be told it demands comparison. "It is like the neck of that peacock strutting in your gardens," the equerry might have said. "It is like the summer sky one minute after the sun has set."

None of this could possibly have put the king at ease, of course, and the equerry would have known this. Constantly alternating between the desire to be enclosed by stage-set fantasy, on the one hand, and a need to be exposed to the sublime scenery of the Alpsee, on the other, the king was like a man with two mistresses of whose beauty he must be assured in order to keep the flame lit. "It is like this, Your Majesty," the equerry would have been forced to say, opening his hands expressively in the papier mâché environment with its rainbow machines and its ugly hidden plumbing. "The picture I have carried to you in my mind is just like this."

In the late 1860s, the prince, who was now the king, had continued to send funds to the little Bavarian settlement in the Canadian wilderness, the money arriving in instalments over the period of the next several years. Father Gstir, correctly intuiting the monarch's state of mind in relation to remote, fantastic landscapes, had sent more and more highly creative letters to the Ludwig Missions at Munich, hoping that his descriptions of massive trees silvered by ice and beasts whose antler systems resembled the wonderful tracery of the hanging wooden sculptures of Veit Stoss would be in some form or another related to Ludwig and in a manner that would excite the king's imagination and cause him to desire that architecture should be added to the scene. He was met with several inquiries from the mission, inquiries that could only have originated with the king. Would the surroundings lend themselves to opera, for example? Opera, Father Gstir had mused, of course, why not? Especially in winter when the mud and squalor were covered with a helpful coating of snow. *Wagner would love these forests,* Father Gstir wrote back to the Central Direction of the Ludwig Missions-Verig in Munich. *Arctic swans flourish here.*

There followed deep inland, on both sides of the Atlantic, a period of great architectural activity. While Ludwig bent over the first plans for the bright, small fantasy known as Neuschwanstein, changing his mind over and over about its exact position in relation to Pollat Falls, the parishioners in Father Gstir's log chapel cheered as the cornerstone for the great church was laid just steps beyond the door. While seventeen carvers worked for four and a half years on the boiseries for the king's bed chamber, Joseph Becker worked on the great altar for the church in the old barn of a nearby farm that he had managed to purchase with his wages from the gristmill. While dozens of humming-birds were released to fly freely in perpetuity through the Winter Garden Room at Neuschwanstein, Father Gstir and his parishioners were assembling the same sad collection of decorated animals for yet another Corpus Christi procession in Shoneval, the result of which was that the men of the congregation were moved to contribute another year of free labour high on the granite walls. And while the magnificent chandeliers were hung in the palace of Linderhof from ceilings whose Gods and Goddesses, Rhine Maidens, and Swan Kings were barely dry, Father Gstir lit forty candles in the log chapel to replace the light that had been blocked out by the increasingly high stone walls that now completely enclosed the little structure. And, finally, several years later, while Ludwig floated in a boat on a pool designed as part of a stage set for one of his *separatvorstellungen,* or private performances of Wagner's *Lohengrin,* a different kind of theatre was being enacted in Shoneval, Canada, where a few dozen young farmers, who had been working all day to dismantle it, took the wooden chapel, log by log, out of the wonderful tall oak doors of their large and splendid new stone church.

And so the impossible happens as a result of whims that turn into obsessions. A priest is struck by the light in an unexpected valley, a king requires rainbow machines, on the one hand, and a belief in the magic of distant landscapes, on the other. A Canadian man dreams the stone that will be assembled and carved to expiate the sorrow of one country on the soil of another. The men in the counting houses of government rage against the expense, preferring to hoard their coins for the machinery of war. And still the beautiful stone walls rise in barely accessible, elevated places. Heartbreaking operas are written and performed in various private and public rooms. Mass is celebrated. And the windows and statues and towers are maintained longer than you might think, in the face of autumn's bitter winds and winter's frantic storms. If you stand in certain parts of the valley you can see them shine. A clear flash of silver or alabaster in daytime, lit by a rich inner fire, or reflected moonlight at night, they disperse light and strength and consolation long after the noise of the battle has ended, and all of the warriors have gone home.

ACKNOWLEDGEMENTS

Walter Allward was an enormously gifted sculptor who worked in Canada in the first half of the twentieth century. His most major and best-known achievement is the imposing Vimy Memorial, the Canadian First World War Monument built near Arras in France. Allward is a character in this book and, as so, is used in the text in a purely fictitious manner. I leave it to others to write the factual biography his life and accomplishments so richly deserve.

A great number of scholarly works inspired and informed parts of this book. Of these, the most important to me were *The Rites of Spring* by Modris Eksteins, *Vimy* by Pierre Berton, and two theses: *The Idea of Vimy Ridge* by John Pierce and *A Catalogue Raisonee of the Work of Walter Allward* by Lane Borstadt. I would also like to bring attention to the fine work done on the art of Walter Allward by Christine Boyanoski while she was at the Art Gallery of Ontario. I owe her an enormous debt of gratitude.

Many other people have encouraged me and assisted me with my research while I was working on this book. My particular thanks goes to Peter Allward, Mieke Bevelander, Laura Brandon, Pat Bremner, Natalie Bull, Virgil Burnett, Jane Buyers, Terry Copp, Joan Coutu, Dennis Duffy, Sandra Gwyn, Ellen Levine, Stuart Mackinnon, Manfred Meurer, Anne Newlands, Louise Quayle, Roseanne (Buttons) Quinn, Peter (Tom) Sawyer, Sebastian Siebel-Achenbach, and Rosemary Tovell.

Thanks also to Veterans Affairs Canada, the Heritage Conservation Program of Public Works and Government Services Canada, Queen's University Archives, the Archives of the National Gallery of Canada and the Art Gallery of Ontario, as well as the Drawing Cabinets of the latter two organizations. At the Vimy Memorial, I would like to thank the enthusiastic student guides who were working there in the spring of 2000.

I shall always be grateful to my long-term Canadian publisher, McClelland & Stewart, to Avie Bennett, and to all those employees with whom I have had the privilege of working while Mr. Bennett was at the helm. My thanks in particular to the director of publicity, Kelly Hechler, for her tact, grace, and friendship, and to copy editor Heather Sangster for her painstaking efforts with the manuscript and for bringing my attention back to "the whistle."

As always, a special thank you to my dear friend and best adviser, Ellen Seligman.

Jane Urquhart is the author of *The Underpainter*, winner of the Governor General's Award for Fiction; *Away*, winner of the Trillium Award; *Changing Heaven*; and *The Whirlpool*, winner of Le Prix du Meilleur Livre Étranger in France. She lives in Ontario, Canada.

The employees of Thorndike Press hope you have enjoyed this Large Print book. All our Thorndike and Wheeler Large Print titles are designed for easy reading, and all our books are made to last. Other Thorndike Press Large Print books are available at your library, through selected bookstores, or directly from us.

For information about titles, please call:

(800) 223-1244

or visit our Web site at:

www.gale.com/thorndike
www.gale.com/wheeler

To share your comments, please write:

Publisher
Thorndike Press
295 Kennedy Memorial Drive
Waterville, ME   04901